# A Peculiar Grace

# A Peculiar Grace

Jeffrey Lent

Atlantic Monthly Press
*New York*

*Published simultaneously in Canada*
*Printed in the United States of America*

FIRST EDITION

Library of Congress Cataloging-in-Publication Data
Lent, Jeffrey.
    A peculiar grace : a novel / by Jeffrey Lent.
        p. cm.
    1. Artist-blacksmiths—Fiction.    2. Domestic fiction.    I. Title.
  ISBN-10: 0-87113-965-0
  ISBN-13: 978-0-87113-965-8
  PS3562.E4934P43 2007
  813'.54—dc22    2006049722

Atlantic Monthly Press
an imprint of Grove/Atlantic, Inc.
841 Broadway
New York, NY 10003

Distributed by Publishers Group West

www.groveatlantic.com

07 08 09 10 11 12   10 9 8 7 6 5 4 3 2 1

For Marion


And

Patricia Haynes Adams Lent

&

Henry Bolles Lent Jr.

# A Peculiar Grace

# One

When the vehicle passed through his yard in the middle of the night and continued up the hill and into the woods along the rutted ancient road Hewitt Pearce barely registered it. Kids out jeeping on an early summer night, a signal start to summer. What he had no way of knowing were the events unfolding that same night three hundred miles away that once revealed would alter forever his life of solitude. A second chance.

Now with dew on the new June grass heavy as frost Hewitt was standing in jeans soaked to his calves with his second coffee, just beyond the barns among the apple trees, an even dozen ancients with low-slung heavy branches, trunks twisted and thick and dense below the canopy of pink-hearted white blossoms. The sun was up over the eastern ridge and striking the top of the western ridge, the young leaves of the treeline illuminated more golden than green, glowing. Two weeks to the solstice, five twenty-seven when he'd left the kitchen. Shivering with his wet pants and the morning air, a flannel shirt open over the T-shirt which would be all he'd want once the sun rose higher. The old barn cat had met him at the porch and followed him across the gravel yard but stopped at the deep grass to avoid the wet, too old to care if there were mice among the apples. A sack of cat food was ripped open in the carriage barn, leaning against haybales yellow and moldering, gone to waste except for the warm winter bed they provided the cat.

A freestanding brick building was set in the bank that dropped off from the old orchard—his smithy, his hearth, his forge. The drop of the bank sharp enough so the door opened onto stairs that led down eight feet, deep enough so the building had windows and large double doors opening out the north side. He considered walking over and cleaning the clinkers from the cold forge and lighting a fire to bank and hold while he went back to the house for breakfast. There was work enough to be done. He swiped the mug out before him, spewing a mist of cold coffee. He just hadn't decided if it was a day for iron. He had no work week or month or pension or retirement plans. All he had was the work he chose. This approach created problems but not for him. For a time he'd considered having the telephone disconnected but hadn't, knowing this would lead only to more unwanted visits from people who thought the fact they wanted a thing made meant he'd agree to the job. Walter Boynton had provided Hewitt with an answering machine, relieving if not solving most problems of communication.

Considering the possibilities of his day, he paused.

From the ridgetop rose a pale thin stream of woodsmoke. And because he knew that ridge as precisely as each of the gnarled trees he stood amongst he knew the location of the campfire. And only then remembered the passage the night before. He stood a bit more and then said, "Shit." He was not interested in rescue but whoever was up there was obviously stuck. It was a nice place to camp but it's the rare camper who sets off at midnight. He could go on with his day and wait until whoever it was appeared to ask for help or get it over with now. So far he'd committed to nothing. But once he did he'd want no disturbance. He'd more than once resorted to hiding in the old stack of hay to avoid incoming interruption. His friends knew where to find him and he suffered no embarrassment in coming blinking back into the daylight with hay in his hair but it worked well on those who would bring only irritation.

He went to the shed and sat on the drawbar of the tractor to lace his boots. It was a sharp uncomfortable perch but it did the job. No need to check the fuel—he knew the old red Farmall had at least five or six gallons in her. He wrapped a log chain with a hook on one end and clevis and pin on the other around the drawbar and climbed into the seat, thrust the throttle up halfway and pressed the ignition button. The tractor coughed and choked and came alive and the shed filled with black then gray exhaust but Hewitt sat patient until the engine was running smooth before backing from the shed and turning uphill. He took his time, putting along in second gear. He was in no hurry and it was a pleasant morning, the sun now warming through the flannel on his back and his speed would allow whoever was up there plenty of time to hear him coming.

The road was rutted with spring melt and the frost come out of the ground but easy going—a farm lane between the hayfields that Bill Potwin cut and baled each summer and limed and spread manure upon each fall, the latter conditions imposed by Hewitt and held to with an unspoken grudging grump by Bill, an irritation manifested by his penchant for holding off doing the job until the last weeks of passable fall weather. Hewitt didn't mind, in fact rather enjoyed Potwin's small protest against being made to do what ought to be done anyway. Too many summer homes carved out of old farms where the hay was free had spoiled the farmers just a little bit—Hewitt had sympathy since free hay was free hay and welcome in an otherwise ungrateful business but then again he knew how things should be done as opposed to those who just wanted things to look pretty and placed no value on the hay. Hewitt knew of a couple of farmers who actually got paid to hay some of those summer home fields.

Into the woods now and he could smell the woodsmoke. The road got rougher and he idled down. These were big woods here, mostly rock maple, ash, beech and hemlocks. He crested the ridge, cool again under the filtering trees and gradually the road swung northeast as it followed the crest. Back in the woods were stone walls lining what had been the old road and time to time there would be an opening in the wall, often flanked with upright stone posts and back behind were the cellar holes and jumbled foundation stones of old farms.

He dropped into first as the little tractor worked along. Now he could see fresh tire treads, slick bare slipping patches. A nasty fresh scrape on a blunt pointed rock anybody who ever drove this road knew to swing wide of even in the dark.

When he came round the bend where he knew from the smoke he would find it, it was shock enough that he braked hard as he killed the ignition and the tractor choked a popping backfire and died.

Damnedest thing he'd ever seen. Even counting the mystery hunched like a huge stone turtle twenty feet back in the woods—the drystone chamber with a vaulted low entrance also of stone—one of five such structures ancient and unexplained in the area. But directly before him this morning was a Volkswagen Beetle handpainted in swirls and dots and symbols of unlikely origin in a mixture alarming even to his own unblinkable eye. Graffiti. Or Aboriginal rock art. Some far distant cousin to the handpainted rainbow ex-schoolbuses and micro-buses of his younger years.

The Bug sat in the road. No list from a flat tire or reek to suggest a split oil pan and blown engine. Just stopped. Off to the side was a small fire and a woman sitting on a rock. She looked at him and then back to the fire. She was not trying to cook anything. She sat on the rock with her knees pulled together and her feet apart, her hands open to the paltry warmth. In black jeans and a white T-shirt with black hair cropped badly down her nape and pushed behind her ears. She was studying the fire as if he wasn't there. So Hewitt folded his arms on the cracked rubber of the steering wheel and studied the car.

Under the paint it was a nice old Bug—early '60s with the wind-shield split down the middle and the oval rear window. The license plate was unfamiliar so he squinted and sat full upright. Mississippi. He looked at the girl, the young woman. Sometime in his late thirties he'd lost the ability to ascribe age to most women between seventeen and thirty or so.

He stood down from the tractor and went halfway the distance to both girl and car. Here he could see that the rear of the VW was stuffed with belongings. Clothing and such it looked like. She was watching him now and he was close enough so he had her pegged mid to late twenties. Her eyes dark as her hair and wide upon him but within that width there was a brilliant shining distance—something untouchable regardless of what he was to do or say. He felt something like a shiver not from cold but from her eyes as if understanding he could kill her and her gaze would not change. Her hands still open to the now dying twig fire.

He thought This is someone who can't even build a decent fire. He considered carefully and in an offhand gentle voice said, "I saw the smoke. It looks to me like you're not where you planned to end up."

She did not hesitate but said, "That car's useless. Can you give me a ride?"

Ignoring his tractor as much as she seemed to be he said, "Could be. Where you headed?"

"Austin."

He pondered a moment. "Austin?"

She nodded.

He said. "Austin, Texas?"

"Oh never mind." His stupidity too great to bear.

Something way off here. But she sure had a pretty voice. Deep but dragging sweet over the syllables as if words others took for granted were savored and valued throughout their possible peaks and valleys. He said, "What's wrong with the car?" And took a cautious pair of steps closer to her.

She said, "Not one thing in the world. Except where it is and quit." And he could smell her now, the long unwashed body so far past sour as to be nearly sweet, sweet that is if the earth made humans its own. A smell he associated with old men in winter-layered clothes.

"You said it was worthless."

"What's worthless?"

"Your car."

"Do you have a can of gasoline on that tractor? Or in your pocket?"

He smiled. "Nope. But it's your lucky day. This old tractor runs on regular gas, not diesel like the new jobs. So there's a tank down to the house. We can fix you up."

"No you can't," she said and stood and stepped away from him, not toward the car but toward the stone chamber tucked back in the woods. As if she had already determined it was a defensive position. "Who sent you here anyway?"

He took a breath and let it out slowly. "Well, my name's Hewitt Pearce and nobody sent me except myself when I walked out the house this morning and looked up and saw smoke. I'm happy to gas that Bug and you can be on your way to Texas. Although I have to say you're taking a peculiar strange route."

"Don't try that line on me."

"Listen," he said, his palms stretched open before him as if this would prove him harmless. "Pretty much everything you've said to me I don't understand. But you seem to be in a rough patch and I'm not talking about being out of gas."

She had her arms not crossed but wrapped around her chest hugging herself. She looked at him. A piece of her hair fell onto her forehead just above her eyes. Then looked away and walked to the car with her back to him, paused and walked back to the fire, her head down now studying the ground. She did this again. Several more times after that. Hewitt did not move, watching her.

Damaged and no telling how far or deep that ran beyond what he already could see. Get the goddamn gas and get her moving. Maybe even tow the car down the hill if she'd let him so he could keep his eye on her until the car was running and on its way. But he said, "What's your name?"

She continued her walking that had become nearly passive or restful someway he could not put his finger on and with her face turned earthward said a word he could not understand.

6

"I'm sorry," he said. "I pound iron and my hearing's not what it could be. I didn't hear you."

She stopped on her way toward the VW so her back was to him. He could see her shoulder blades through the T-shirt. And he was swept with a sense of her fragility even as she lifted her head still turned away and said, "Jessica. My name's Jessica." He thought she was trembling but could not be sure. It was possible—the fire was meager and her clothing not right for a night in the woods. But he had the sudden notion that it was not cold but the speaking of her name. As if entrusting something she doubted to trust. And he thought of the ancients who feared revealing their true names. Some power lost or perhaps an uncertain vulnerability revealed that the bearer might not know but the hearer certainly might.

Hewitt said, "Jessica, are you hungry?"

She turned then and looked at him without releasing her grip on herself. "I'm just fine," she said.

"Well," he said. "I'm not. I want some breakfast. What I was thinking was why don't we tow your car down to the house so you don't have to worry about it and we can fill it up with gas so you're all set to go and then maybe you could sit down with me and eat some eggs and toast. How's that sound?"

For a moment she looked like any other girl and was maybe a bit more than pretty and then the shade passed over her face again and she said, "That's kind of you. But I think I truly need to get traveling on. I think I got all turned around. But you should be careful what you eat. They put whatever they want in just about anything."

Hewitt was fascinated. "The eggs come from an old fart of a neighbor who most likely would agree with you. And the bread's baked fresh every day in the village by a couple women I've known all my life. The loaf in the breadbox may be a little stale but it'd make good toast. Jessica? I went through an awful hard terrible time in my life some years back and much of it's still with me but every now and then you have to trust somebody. Trust me if you want or not. But

I'd hate to see you drive off hungry. The truth is I'd be happy to have some company for breakfast. Let's get your car off this mountain and figure it out from there."

"Do you have a cell phone?"

"I'm sorry I don't. But there's a rotary phone at the house. You're welcome to use it, you don't run up a bill the length of my arm."

"Don't you be getting a cell phone. I'm serious as death, you hear me?"

"I never gave a thought to one. Anyways, what I hear is they don't work around here."

"Is that right?"

He shrugged. "What I hear." Hewitt was a little stunned with all this. He'd come up expecting a quick rescue and being sworn to silence by the children of someone he most likely knew. And her nipples were clear and dark through the thin shirt even as the morning was warming through the trees.

She said, "Can I ask two questions?"

"Only two?" He grinned.

She did not smile back. Just waited.

"All right. Shoot."

She said, "I got rid of that gun a long time ago."

He digested this and then said, "I meant go on and ask your questions."

"What happened to you?"

Well fuckhead he'd opened that door. "It's a bit of a long tale."

She nodded as if this was enough. She said, "Why on earth do you try to hurt iron? Does that stop you from hurting something else?"

He wanted to ask if that was one question or two but simply said, "I'm a blacksmith. I think I told you I pound iron. After it's heated the iron reacts in surprising ways. When it's right, beauty comes from it." And thought Shut up now.

She said, "But we all have iron inside us."

"Yes," he said. "We are stardust." Thinking if she doesn't want breakfast that's probably a good thing.

She said, "Hewitt? Tell me again I can trust you."

"You can trust me."

She turned again and resumed her pacing between car and now dead fire and he stood waiting wanting to speak but with no idea what to say. She was so intent it seemed she was reading the ground. Messages for her to decipher. Or perhaps easily read. He could not say but knew both possibilities were congruent with this wild wild life. He'd done the same. More times than he could count. He'd stood in a snowstorm with bitter wind out of the northwest and screamed a name into the night. Or on his knees forehead striking the ground over and over wanting to push his head down into the very earth. Both small events of an endless mosaic that was not so much behind him as one he now rode as a silent steady river he'd bled into and merged with.

There came now the image of a jam jar dropped to explode on the bare plank pantry floor. So he did what he could. He fired up the tractor and backed it around, then got down on his knees to wrap the chain around the rear axle and snug it tight. She stopped pacing and was watching. He went the closest he'd been to her and said, "Because we're going downhill you've got to keep the tension. Just keep pumping the brake and make sure you watch only out the back. It's better to have the chain get tight and jerk you than have the car run into the back of the tractor. Do you understand?"

"I'm lost," she said. "Not stupid."

"Well, sit over breakfast with me and maybe we can figure out where you got turned around."

Her mouth tightened, lips pressed. As if trying to learn if she was being led or not. Then she said, "I'll watch you eat. But Hewitt . . ."

"What is it?"

"Stop staring at my boobs. Okay?"

"Why don't you get in your car?" he said.

\*   \*   \*

WHATEVER SHE WAS or whatever she lacked she knew how to handle her car being towed through the woods backward and downhill. Hewitt appreciated this but the slow trip down gave him time to ponder this peculiar woman and he'd determined to give her the gas and send her on her way. He had too much to cope with as it was, although he refused to attempt numeration. He was not the man to take on someone else's problems. Not beyond a fifteen-minute solution anyway and that only applied if the problem was practical, tactile, something he could lay hands on and repair. So they came to a slow moderate halt in the farmyard, with a nice slack in the chain.

What he'd failed to consider was a change in her. She was out of the car down on her knees working the chain free before he even had the tractor shut down and so he removed the clevis and pin from the drawbar as she raised up and they walked toward each other looping up the heavy chain. She said, "I was raised with better manners than I've shown and I've been living off Coca-Cola and candy bars since I don't know when. I surely could eat a plate of eggs and toast." Then as if his hesitancy had transmitted itself she backpedaled and said, "Although I wouldn't put you out. You've been so kind and I bet you've got better things to do than put up with me so I'd be just tickled with the gas and go."

WITH THE EXCEPTION of a few conveniences added, the house was essentially unchanged from when his father returned in 1951 with his new wife. Beth was born a year later and Hewitt six years after her. The house was late Victorian with the large rooms, tall windows and rich woodwork and detailed trim of the time. Hewitt had only vague memories of his grandmother Pearce. He never had known his grandfather, any more than his father had known that man—a secret of history, an intrigue deepened by the fact that his great-grandparents, who'd built the house and prospered with a bobbin shop factory as well as the sheds and sawmills for the raw timber and ownership in the railroad spur line, were Pearces as well. Thomas Pearce then, a man seemingly shorn of paternity. Confounding the mystery, grandmother Lydia Pearce had died not at home but in Holland, in Amsterdam, a city where after she'd raised her son Thomas and seen him off to the Pratt Institute to study art, she'd spent months at a time annually until her death. She was buried up the road in the Pearce Cemetery where also rested an assortment of Snows, Duttons and Peeks.

The kitchen held a giant wood-burning range in soft charcoal black rimmed with heavy chrome aprons and trim and had double ovens and two cooktops, one meant for kerosene but now connected to a propane tank outside. Cabinets formed a dividing wall to the dining room—built not against but within the walls, two sets with glass fronts for fancy display. The kitchen table was drop-leaf bird's-eye maple that almost certainly had made the trip by oxcart north toward the end of the eighteenth century, the construction pegged and dovetailed, free of nails altogether and without a wobble. The dining room table could seat twelve and had not been used in years.

Jessica wandered the room while he worked at the range after putting new grounds and running fresh water into the coffeemaker. He'd done this without asking, her confession of her diet enough to tell him she would need coffee. The eggs were big with blood spots in the yolks, the gas turned low to cook them soft and slow.

They sat across from each other and ate. There was thick toast and tall glasses of orange juice. He broke a piece of toast into quarters and used them to mop the yolk and bits of white and cleaned his plate. Eating but watching her across from him. And doing his best to smile with his eyes. She was only halfway done eating, using her fork to cut small pieces of the whites of the eggs and dip them into the carefully broken but intact liquid yolks and bring them to her mouth. Not nibbling but savoring, making it last. Christ—Coke and candy bars. He stood and took his plate to the sink and poured two mugs of black coffee. He didn't need or want more coffee. But it was a prop and life wants props. He blew the surface for the updraft scroll of steam and pretended to take a small sip. He was in deep debate he'd already lost.

He said, "Jessica? Do you have clean clothes in your car?"

Her face tightened as he knew it would. "Why?"

He sighed, a sound he meant her to hear. "Because I think you don't. When's the last time you had a bath or shower?"

"I don't believe I care for the way this is going."

He sighed again. Then shook his head, nothing more than that. "What I was thinking. Is that you could do some laundry here. Maybe even wash yourself up. Because you need it. I can tell you that from over here. Again, and you listen to me—I've been closer to where you are then you can imagine."

"There's nothing wrong with me," she interrupted.

"I know that. Except both you and your clothes are wicked dirty. You wanted, you could take a couple hours and leave here good to go for quite a while." He paused and then said, "The way things are right now all that needs to happen is for some cop to pull you over and you'd have an awful tough time talking your way clear. You understand that?"

She was silent.

He did not wait but stood and said, "Come on. I'll get you a laundry basket and show you the machines and the big bathroom. I was you I'd take a bath. Soak it out of you. But you can shower if you want. I won't bother you. I've got work to do."

She did not move but looked close upon him. That shadow was back on her face but underneath he now saw something else. Then she stood and said, "Those were good eggs. I thank you." He was afraid he'd lost her. Then she went on. "If you're serious I could use to do some laundry. And a bath would be sweet."

"All right. Let me show you where the basket is."

"Wait," she said. "Let me show you something first." And very fast dipped a hand into her shirt and came out with a straight razor on a shoelace. As the razor came free of her shirt she snapped the blade open and it was the brightest thing in the room except her eyes. "You see this?"

He nodded. "I've seen them before. Come on, I've got work to do."

AFTER HELPING CARRY the reeking mounds of clothing to the house and showing her everything he could possibly think of he left her alone. He had no energy for the forge. So he took the wheelbarrow and a fork and rake and went into the flower beds and cleaned out what he should've a month ago. Everything was sprouting so most of the work was done on hands and knees and slow going. Which fit his mood. Restless, mildly rankled. And then found himself whistling as he pulled dead Siberian iris stems free from the slender bright new shoots pointed as if determined to learn the sky. After this he just worked. He cleared all the beds and wheeled loads of composted ancient manure from the barn pit to spread on the beds and then walked down past the forge to the small spring seep and stepping carefully used his pocketknife to cut the first dozen stalks of asparagus.

And stood holding the tender green spears in one hand and the clasp knife in the other and abruptly turned and ran to the house. In the kitchen he paused to compose himself. Laid the asparagus on the sink and listened to the house. The washer had stopped and there was no sound.

He went up the stairs to the big bathroom. He tapped lightly on the door but it was silent within. He could picture the water flooded and diluted rose. Or perhaps not so diluted. How much blood would a body offer against a few gallons of water? He took a breath and opened the door.

The tub was empty but for a gray grimed ring three quarters up. With a foamy residue of bubbles. There hadn't been bubble bath in the house for years and he knew it for a fact because when Amber Potwin left she'd cleaned the bathroom of all trace of her. But on the floor leaning against a clawfoot was the bottle of dishsoap from the kitchen drainboard. He almost smiled.

He went out past his own open bedroom door and to the next room down, the door there open as well. She was sprawled under a sheet with her hands beneath the pillow, elbows extended flat, one knee drawn up so the rise of her hip rounded up the sheet. Her hair was flying off her head in wet spikes from the toweling. Her mouth was open and she was breathing deeply. The cracked yellowed shade was pulled down on the bedside window but for the last couple of inches—fresh air. He looked but the wet balled towel was all there was on the floor. She was clearly naked under the sheet. Gently he pulled up the white cotton spread, thin and ancient even when he was a child, covering her only to her hips. Then he took the balled towel and went downstairs.

There was a load of wet washed clothes sitting in the washer. And a heap of stinking dirty clothes before it. The dryer was empty. He thought about it all for a minute and went back upstairs to his own room and dug free the pair of sweatpants shrunk too small for him. And an old soft T-shirt. He carried them down the hall and left them folded on the bedside table. He stood beside the bed and watched her sleep. Finally he leaned and kissed the crown of her head and left the room.

He didn't have any idea how to spend the day.

THAT SUMMER OF the Bicentennial.

The granddaughter of immigrant Danes, Emily Soren with snapping blue eyes that at times seemed green and oatstraw hair in a braid near to her waist or pulled back peasant-style under a kerchief, whose first words to Hewitt Pearce were "I know who you are" and last ones a year and a half later were "Keep the tears for yourself, Hewitt, I don't want them anymore" was by any reckoning from the moment she uttered those first five words or even the moments before as she approached him that early summer day carrying to his car the tray with his cheeseburger and strawberry milkshake just in the way she walked toward him seeing something he'd never seen before or the near-invisible hairs along her forearms that struck and entered him with a force both stunning and long-expected like brushing against an electric fence jolts, the one person on earth he was born to meet although it would be years of pondering that would allow him to see the multiple strands that led up to that time for both of them and those same long years pondering the events and likewise strands that led to her final statement. At first he couldn't, absolutely in his deepest core could not accept the idea that his wild-hearted passion of impossible range would not in the end slice through and be recognized for the inevitability that it was; that the sheer velocity of this passion had initially set their mutual course like twin blazing comets across the eons of the universe; and then later could not believe she had seen this, reciprocated, and then ultimately denied it. How could he not hold that as the simple most basic touchstone of his life? How could she flee?

Of course in the end he'd behaved badly. Not from intention and certainly not from malice but from stark utter disbelief as those comets either collided too hard and broke to fragments or simply slid by each other after a long grazing spark-laden interval.

Over time he realized almost everyone gets their heart broken and is expected to rise out of that, to learn and go along. But Hewitt's heart was not broken but split by a chisel and some part, something greater he came to realize than half was irrevocably gone. Finally he knew it didn't matter if this was a failure of a version of maturity on his part or not; it was how it was. It was what he got and every single day of his life he ached with the only real prayer he'd ever known— that Emily Scren was healthy and happy with where life had taken her. It was, this minor religious penance, the least he could do.

They were both seventeen, the summer before their final year of high school and she was right where she'd spent her entire life although Hewitt was three hundred miles west of home working with the smith Timothy Farrell and had finished his half-day Saturday and so was free until Monday dawn. He'd showered in the outside stall beside Timothy's forge and tossed his hiking boots into the backseat of the old Volvo, his hair released from its braid clean and flowing down his back and over his shoulders, dressed in cutoff jeans and a pearl-snap button western denim shirt with the sleeves rolled up, his bare feet glorious on the pedals as he drove down off the hill above the lake and toward Bluffport with no idea what he'd find but certain he'd find something and slowly cruised through town until he saw the drive-in burger joint and thought food was a good place to start and Emily Soren walked out with the order he'd repeated twice through the shaky tilted metal speaker. And even then watching her come and seeing everything like that first tingle of acid kicking in, would not have guessed it would be dawn Sunday before he'd sleep again. But at the time and forever after knew he was ready for whatever she brought.

"I know who you are," she said, hooking the tray on the doorframe, leaning in close to do it and holding there, waiting.

"Not yet, you don't," he said. "But you should." She had a pair of hammered silver bangles on her left wrist and a nice piece of almost green turquoise wrapped in a net of fine silver wire from a leather choker around her neck. Hewitt had a similar turquoise and silver stud in his left ear. She squinted a caution not reflected in her laughing eyes and said, "What makes you think so?"

"I don't know," he admitted. "It just sounds like a good idea."

Fifteen hours later they were sitting back to back on the long dock of her family's summer cottage not truly opened for the summer watching the sky lighten and stars wink out, a planet high and streaks of clouds turning from low dull blueblack to a slow simmering burn of sunrise approaching, the still lake with its small wavelets a somewhat denser mirror of color, Emily with her legs crossed before her and Hewitt with his knees up, their spines aligned side to side, sitting in the long silence of the end of a long night and the sublime beginning of the day and it had been her hand that crept easily back and found his. As he gently held her hand he knew he'd recall the feel of her hand, of her life flowing through it and against his, for all the days that remained to him. And so the night went down and they sat within the nether light of predawn.

He'd picked her up when she got off work at the Keuka Farms drive-in and as agreed driven her home to meet her parents Ellen and Gregor and an assortment of younger and older siblings he couldn't keep straight, being sent to the barn to chat with her father as he finished the evening milking. In the barn he made no attempt to help but instead followed her father from cow to cow as he milked and they talked about farming which Hewitt knew from helping his own father tend the homestead in Lympus and work he'd pitched in with among neighbors during the spring sugaring, the summer haying and fall getting up firewood and such, knew enough to know the farm he was upon was a vastly richer, more demanding and rewarding enterprise than those he knew and so was able to ask the right questions, offer comparisons based on experience and also checked but appropriate praise and honest appreciation. Gregor had a white paintbrush mustache and the same eyes as his daughter and wore a striped railroad engineer's cap tilted back to allow him not only to bring his face close to the side of the cow but look up at Hewitt without craning his neck. Several male children worked along, the older ones milking ahead or behind their father, the younger ones feeding calves or forking out stalls and one young girl perhaps eight or ten kept appearing and disappearing, bringing Hewitt one after another young or older barn cats for his admiration. About this child Gregor said as if in passing, "She's a pistol, that one," and then spoke shortly and to the point of his esteem for Timothy Farrell—a commentary Hewitt understood he was not expected to respond to beyond mild affirmations and was Soren's blessing and warning at once. Then all into the house for a mighty supper.

Driving out into the bright early evening Emily turned to Hewitt and said, "Dad's not made his mind up about you. Far from it. But he and I came to terms a couple years ago and while he doesn't always pretend he likes it he knows he's got no choice but to trust me." She had changed out of the bad shamrock green Keuka Farms T-shirt and still in her jeans was wearing a Danskin sleeveless top and carried along a flannel shirt. Then she dug down into her jeans and pulled up a bottle cap sealed tight with twisted plastic wrap. She said, "I've got this red Lebanese hash oil but nothing to smoke it with."

Hewitt was again barefoot. "There's a little bag of Colombian gold in the glove compartment, along with papers and a pipe. You can dab some of the oil on the screen and then pack it or if you know how the best thing is to spread a smear of the oil on top of the weed just before you twist up the joint."

"I can roll just fine. You got a matchstick to spread the oil?"

He reached up on the dash and from the accumulation there plucked out a matchbook and handed it over. He was quiet while she quickly rolled up what he already knew was a killer joint and then while she was blowing on it, turning it in her fingertips to dry it he said, "So is there a plan?"

"You need a plan, Hewitt?"

"Nope. You going to light that or you want me to?"

"It's not quite ready. Almost. The oil needs to soak in."

"I know that."

"Then why'd you ask? Oh fuck it, I'm ready to get high. There's always more where that came from. And there's a party. Are you up for a party, Hewitt?"

"Fire that up. I'm always ready for a party."

"You sure you don't want to get high first and drive around and then decide?"

"That party hasn't even started yet, has it?"

"Of course it has. And someone's always got to be the first to show up."

"Hey Emily?"

"Yup?"

"You going to talk or you going to light that joint?"

She was quiet until he looked over at her. He was already lost, up on the high country between the lakes where it was farm after farm spreading out all around and all he knew was where west was. When he looked at her she was waiting. "Hewitt?" she said. Then stuck the joint in her mouth and fired a match and hit it hard and held it as the dense sweet smell of the oil filled the car. Then she passed it over to him and slowly exhaled. "Hewitt," she said again as he toked. "Let's get ripped."

He didn't say anything but smoked and passed it back to her and they went along like that until he reached up to the rearview mirror and pulled down the alligator clip and smoked right down to the nub, until the last hard toke sucked fire into his mouth and he choked and coughed and then he said, "Hey Emily?"

She twisted sideways in the seat to look at him. The evening sun in full accordance with her luminescence. She said, "You all right?"

"I caught a buzz."

"Good," she said. "Me too."

"Only thing. Is I don't have any idea where I am."

She was fiddling with the buttons on the radio, then gave that up for the dial. She said, "You lost, Hewitt?"

"I guess you could say that."

She waited and then said, "Me too. But keep driving and we'll always find our way back home."

"You think?"

"Don't you?"

Now he waited. Then said, "I believe so. I do believe so."

She pushed her sneakers off and slid way down in the seat and propped her bare feet up out the window and said, "That's good. Why don't you just drive a while."

They sat high on the end of the bluff that broke the northern half of the lake into two branches and gave the village its name and watched the sunset and drank a four-pack of St. Pauli Girl and then at dusk retreated halfway back the length of the bluff past vineyards and wood-lots and scrub pastures before dropping down a side road to the east lake shore and then almost immediately up again, this time a narrow gravel rutted track that passed through two stone entrance columns heavy with moss and tangled poison ivy and up some more, then opening before a long three-story Italianate house with peeling white paint and some obvious dark places where windows had been either boarded over or covered inside with cardboard. At least a dozen cars were parked there as well as an old school bus painted blue and off to one side on what had once been lawn was the incandescent large cone of a teepee. Hewitt's first thought was I'm home and he would re-member this a year and a half later after he'd grown to know some of the people he met that night and the house itself well, far too well. But at the moment it was as if Emily were leading him toward what he'd somehow expected, as if she were part of all of it. Several people clumped on the long porch fronting the house and from within a wave of bass and drums and guitar far too dense and loud to come from any stereo system and he paused, rocking back on his heels, still barefoot and she paused with him, cupped her hand inside his elbow and leaned her upper body against his side. He gestured toward the teepee and she tilted her face up and spoke in his ear, "That's Max's. He's full-blood Iroquois—a Seneca. Very heavy vibe but a sweetheart, claims to be a direct descendant of Cornplanter. You can't miss him, bald as an old man. I think he shaves his head. And check it out."

"What?"

"He's the drummer, flat-out rock and roll. Come on, let's go in."

Emily knew everyone which didn't surprise Hewitt and at least half of them seemed to know who he was—guys running long eyes over him and some of the women as well but the air was thick with weed and the band was cranking and for a time he stood watching and listening as Emily made slow rounds, Hewitt thinking Well she brought me here she's not going to abandon me and then something else clicked in and he thought She's showing me off, and immediately pulled back, not willing to make such assumption. Even if he knew he was the exotic stranger he also knew that wouldn't last and then someone handed him a paper cup half filled with cranberry juice and told him Down the rabbit hole and he stood holding the cup until Emily glanced at him and he raised the cup and tipped his head in question and she nodded yes and he drank it down.

Sometime later Emily was back, glowing iridescence herself and they went outside and sat in his old Volvo while he quickly twisted up some hash joints and while she held the pipe for herself and Hewitt as he worked, both open naked souls looking upon each other and laughing, laughing and as they got out of the car to return inside he bent quickly to kiss her and she not only kissed him back soft and sweet as a peach but moaned as he pulled his lips away—Hewitt all liquid neon sparking and feeling those ten thousand trailing enraptured threads between them, and then inside again where they made their way to the front of the living room where the band was set up and people were dancing and the music was hot and clean and punchy with dirty drawdowns spiraling with singing lead guitar bringing it back up— Stones and Feat and Dead and Clapton and just about anything else he could hope for and the night opened like a pod splitting as he and Emily began to dance.

Hewitt liked to dance, liked the music filling his body and carry- ing it in such a way that he was a part of the music as the music was of him—but dancing with Emily was a revelation. They began slow as those around them, thumping and pumping legs and elbows and tor- sos and shaking heads with the beat and rumble, arms shimmying and fingers trailing with the vocals and lead lines and then although he could never recall how it changed the space around them opened up and they were flying within each other, passing and touching, hands meeting and sliding as they passed and turned and worked lowdown toward each other before one or the other would flare out spiraling away and they were off again, sometimes working backward without once looking and coming butt to butt with hair flying as heads bent low and once Hewitt heard her growl as they did this and the band seemed to have hit its own head as there were no more breaks between songs but long slippery sequences that would suddenly bounce home into what Hewitt already had heard coming and it seemed Emily did too as she was right there with him on every turn and now both of them with soaked hair and shirts and on they went going down the road and Hewitt had one inspired moment of clarity when he realized that they were making love for the first time and they were not fading away, not at all or ever because love for real won't fade away and then back outside in the cool night leaning against each other and silent, down off the porch on the ruined lawn by a copse of twisted cedars, Emily plucking out the front of her Danskin and blowing down toward her breasts and then looking at Hewitt, that face he felt he already knew sober and somber and laughing all at once and said, "Can you dance like that when you're not tripping?"

He reached a finger and slid it through the cooling sheen of sweat on her nose and said, "Can you?"

She smiled and said, "How about some peace and quiet?"

Two hours later they were seated back to back on the cottage dock watching the day peel back the night. They'd come through the village where Hewitt counted three dogs and a parked sheriff's cruiser and stopped at the all-night gas station where they bought eggs and bread and orange juice and drove around the eastern side of the lake to her family's cottage where she stretched up tiptoe to take a key down from the hook hidden by the upper door jamb and sat in the chill dormant house with the low background scent of mothballs while she fried eggs and made toast as they listened to crinkly crackly big band swing on the AM radio and then went out to the dock.

Hewitt was thinking he should be feeling ground down but he wasn't—all he wanted was to sit there holding her hand and feeling the length of his back against hers when she said, "You still have one of those mighty joints?" Wearing not only the flannel shirt she'd brought with her but an old Hot Tuna sweatshirt he'd had in the trunk of the car. Hewitt still in his cutoffs and denim shirt and watching the gooseflesh on his legs but not at all cold. He said, "I've got the makings."

"Look out at the water."

He did. The sun was striking down against the far shore.

"What do you see?"

"The sun coming up."

She said, "I really do believe if you reach down in the front pocket of your shirt you'll find a joint waiting."

He did and there was and they scooted around to face each other as they smoked and she ran her hands over his now cold thighs and pulled off his sweatshirt and placed it over him and tugged tight her flannel shirt and when the joint was done she said, "Look back at the water now."

"Do you want to swim?"

"Hewitt."

He studied the lake and then said, "The surface isn't flat anymore. It's broken up."

She nodded. "There's a chop."

"What's that mean?"

"Feel the air, turn your head or wet a finger and feel the air."

After a moment he said, "There's wind. Not much but there's air moving. Is that it?"

"I think," she said, "we should go sailing. Do you sail, Hewitt?"

"I'm sailing right now. But if you're talking about boats—"

She was up on her feet. "You wait right here."

A few minutes later the boathouse door next to the dock cranked slowly up and from the invisible depths she used a single paddle to bring out a small sailboat, an exquisite wooden craft he would learn was a catboat with not only a mainsail but a small flying jib and brought it alongside the dock and he climbed carefully down in. Emily paddled out and then was up all darting motion as she dropped the centerboard and raised the mainsail and hauled in the sheets and settled back beside him as the wind took the sail and away they went. She didn't ask him to do a thing and he knew enough to sit still and be happy watching her. She fled back and forth over the boat as they got on into the full morning breeze, adjusting ropes and slipping knots and for one beautiful moment stretched up on tiptoe facing into the wind, one hand raised to steady herself against the mast, her body as alive and separate from him as it could ever be and yet she was there showing him this of her. Then she came back and settled into the cockpit, one hand on the tiller and the other holding the sheet as air and water and girl all ran together and she looked at him and grinned and called out, "So, Hewitt Pearce. What are we doing? You and me?"

"Flying. We're flying, Emily."

She grinned and called back, "You betchum, bub."

When they finally quit the morning was well along and other boats were out, sailboats and speedboats with big rooster-tail wakes trailing water-skiers. As they drifted toward the boathouse with the sail flopping and Emily paddling, pushing a straight course, Hewitt jumped out as he saw the bottom coming up beneath the water and guided the boat into its berth. He waited while Emily stowed everything and furled the sail and wrapped it all up and last thing cranked down the boathouse door. Then she said, "I think it's time to go to bed for a while."

He only nodded which was a good thing because although she stripped down to her underwear and made no objection as he shucked off all his clothes once he slid in beside her she kissed him once, then kissed his forehead and said, "Good morning, Hewitt. I'll see you in a bit," and turned away from him and within minutes was asleep.

It took him a bit longer but not as much as he expected. And when he woke she was propped up on one elbow, with the sheet pushed off for the heat of midday and studying him serious as a science project. He reached for her and they tangled together sweet mouths and tongues until he slid one hand along her thigh and she pulled back and with delicate resolve stopped his hand, holding it in hers and drawing it up to her mouth to kiss and said, "No. Not yet."

He couldn't help the groan. "Why?"

She smiled. "Because we've got other things to do right now."

"Like what? Emily, I—"

She put a finger to his lips. "Don't think I don't want to. But not yet. Not here." She paused and when he was silent, absorbing, she went on. "Right now we're going to get dressed and I'm going to make this bed up not quite right but almost and you're going to go down the hall to the next room and pull apart the bed and then make it up again but not quite right. Then we're going to drive up to Farrell's and you're going to get some jeans instead of those shorts. Although bring the shorts with you."

"I understand the beds. You want to explain the rest? You're not trying to get rid of me, are you?"

She was smiling. "Even if I wanted to you wouldn't be easy to get rid of."

"I'm glad you know that."

"Listen—it's Sunday so my mother is at church with my grandparents but because it's warm and dry with that good breeze my brother Einer's out tedding the first cut we've got down and Dad's following him with the siderake and right after lunch they're going to bale that hay. And you and I are going to get you into some work clothes and eat some lunch and then you're going to help the boys put that hay up. Which will be good for you—"

"I've done my share of haying."

"It'll be good for you in more ways than one. I might be pretty much free to call my own shots but I was out all night with you. So you can sweat some of last night out and gain a point, because you're maybe two or three points down now if you understand. And since it's Sunday, once that hay's on the wagons, or in the barn if there's time, Dad'll milk a little early and then we all come down here to swim and wash off the hay dust and chaff and cook burgers or whatever

25

Dad decides out on the grill. And then maybe, just maybe, if it feels right we could slip off for a bit. Even if it's just to sail again."

He was quiet for a bit, thinking.

"Hewitt," she said.

"Emily."

She spoke carefully. "It's your choice. It's just I think it would be a really good idea."

"And?"

"And what?"

"You know what."

She stood from the bed in her underwear and pulled on the leotard and worked it up over her torso. She said, "And I'd really like it if you did. There. Is that what you wanted?"

He lay on his back with his hands laced behind his head. She was stepping into her jeans and there was a moment when they were half on and she raised her other leg and inserted her foot and went a little off balance and his heart lurched—that inelegant instant penetrated more deeply than any single moment since the afternoon before and he said, "I'll do anything you want." His voice thickened beyond all expectation.

She looked at him. He grinned and stood and reached for his clothes and said, "So the bed down the hall. Is your mother really going to look that close? We could've been anywhere."

"Oh, Hewitt," she said, and he knew she heard and understood all of him once again. "Bear with me. Okay?"

He went to her and kissed her and she wrapped up against him hot and hungry and then he pulled back himself this time and said, "I'm a little crispy. It'd be good to sweat. And food. Food would be good. What were you thinking about?"

"I get a discount at the drive-in."

"That's perfect. Any problem if I smoke a joint along the way?"

"Not as long as you share."

★  ★  ★

THE SUN WAS at its afternoon best and the heavy apple limbs were cool with the shade of new leaves and blossoms but his mood was off. It was no mystery that those long days of young adulthood would stand in vivid contrast to the otherwise downpouring of the years—not only moments but entire days etched forever vivid as if that very morning. He was a man alone and statistically at least growing closer to death than when those years fashioned and formed his life, but he was free of bitterness and knew this to be an odd blessing. He understood too well how bitterness seeps and poisons as if life itself was a liquid moving through old lead pipes. Yet the one passion most remote and untouchable was not static but grew and changed within him. He still had dreams where she was young as he remembered her daytimes. But the woman who increasingly replaced her girl-self for those night visits was more than his dreamworld keeping pace with age.

This was not merely some inner maturity of his brain. He cheated.

Although he didn't think of it that way. His method was he thought not only exemplary but clever and clean. No drunken phone calls late at night. No letters to be returned unopened or not. No surreptitious visits even in the years when he was still legally empowered to drive an automobile. None of that for him. Behaviors all perhaps equal to his passion and devotion but smacking clearly of violation. Passion has no degrees. It's either the wildfire raging in your heart or it's nothing. All else is simply control and respect. You have to respect the one you love. You have to drop to your knees daily at the silent invisible altar of your passion. And that's all that's allowed. His own code of honor.

He subscribed to the Bluffport weekly paper.

It had been four years between when he last saw her and that moment of staggering brilliance. So he'd missed her return to Bluffport. Thus mercifully both the engagement announcements and wedding pictures. And he'd had to take the chance to renew his subscription after a fruitless first year but had been rewarded halfway through that

second year with a photograph and story of the opening of the new
Bluffport clinic under the direction of Dr. Martin Nussbaum and read
the article which noted the doctor's wife Emily and their two young
children. Hewitt did some quick calculations and realized the children would've been born while Martin and Emily were in medical
school. So he'd knocked her up and knocked her out of her dream.
That had been a hard strange day that sent him briefly back into his
old dark dreaded self.

Several years later a short paragraph with a photograph detailed
how Emily Nussbaum was now a therapist and would be working in
her husband's clinic. The newsprint photo seemed to Hewitt somewhat grim and set, as if her achievement were only partial. He knew
this could be his own simple reduction.

The most recent photograph was three years old and of her alone.
In shorts and a polo shirt. This time her smile was as it ever had been.
She'd won the single-hand sailing regatta on the lake. She held no
trophy but the water was visible behind her and she was standing on
a dock of considerable size, speaking of a club or other such organiza-
tion. She had cut her hair.

He followed the scholastic and athletic achievements of the Nussbaum children. The perfect boy and perfect younger sister. John and
Nora. He did not clip these pieces but read carefully through. Not
admitting he was searching for some glimmer of discord, some registered childhood unhappiness. The boy looked like his mother while
the girl—poor child!—resembled her father with dark hair and a round
moon face. He wouldn't admit that running across her picture and
not knowing her parents he would have thought her pretty and likely
to be one of those girls who comes into her own significant beauty
later than her school companions. Sometime in her twenties.

And no way to know that even as he sat while the day sank toward evening, in the Bluffport pressroom an obituary and news story
of a tragedy were being composed. All he knew was he was hungry
and ready for a beer and only then remembered the girl left sleeping

in a guest bedroom. He stood and stretched while he surveyed the yard below. Then headed down to see what he would see.

THE VW SAT where they'd left it that morning but she was now walking on a stretch of the hardtop road beyond his driveway up and down similar to her walking in the woods earlier; a to and fro that had something of the mnemonic in it. Wearing his sweatpants which as he came close he saw bagged and dragged so her bare feet were covered in coiled bunches and his T-shirt so big the neckline almost revealed her left breast—the shirt twisted as she had made some attempt to tuck it in but only in front so it was badly skewed and flapped down behind her butt. Her hair was pressed flat on one side and high over her crown from sleep. A red pickup with work racks went by her, slowing and crossing the solid line to give her space—Roger Bolton would be talking about her next morning with his coffee at the store but if not Roger then someone soon.

Going down the drive he noted where it emptied into the road marked a rough halfway point of her march so he simply walked out on the blacktop and waited for her. At the moment she was still walking away from him. Her head down and her arms not flailing but describing patterns balletesque in the air before her. She turned and saw him, dropped her arms and stopped.

He knew she was not going to move. It was warmer here, out of the breeze and the blacktop radiated the day's sun warmth back upward. The road curved beyond her. If not for that he would've waited her out but all it would take was one person to come too fast around that curve. So he walked, slow as he could make himself down to her. Three feet away he stopped. Hoping not so close to threaten but close enough to grab and drag her tumbling into the roadside ditch if he had to. She'd locked her fingers together over her lower belly and was digging them gently into the folds of his shirt. He guessed this was for comfort not for hurt. Someway to keep her sense of where she was. He had no idea.

"Hey, Jessica," he said easy as if they were on the porch. "I set out those old clothes of mine because I didn't feel comfortable putting yours in the dryer. You get some sleep?"

"You gave me a blanket too." She went right on. "That room downstairs scared me. And my feet were cold so I came out to walk."

Already knowing he said, "What room downstairs?"

Now the bright fire of earlier came back into her eyes. "The red room. It's strange in there."

Steadfast externally he recoiled inward, not wanting to know her assessment. He said, "I sort of know what you mean. But my father did that work and we all doubt our father's wisdom. What do you say, why don't we walk back to the house and I'll get some supper cooking? If you want we can walk together through that room and maybe I can explain it a little bit." He reached out and feather boxed her shoulder. "Come on Jessica. Unless you helped yourself to something you haven't eaten since early this morning and truth told I haven't either."

She said, "What is it you want of me?"

"Not a thing in the world. Nothing more than maybe sitting together and eating and maybe talking a little bit. If you want to."

Swiftly, "Who've you been talking with about me?"

"Not a soul. If there's some reason I should I one don't know it and two wouldn't know where to start. But I do have a question for you."

"What would that be?"

"I've got part of a freezer of local meat but it's getting slim pickings since I ate out of it all winter. And I didn't even think to take anything out to thaw. So we're going to have to make dinner out of cans—baked beans maybe with some bacon and new asparagus I cut this morning."

"I don't eat meat. And I've had to eat plenty of food from cans. As long as I see it opened."

Only a half beat below the skittery paranoia he was inclined to agree. So he reached and took one of her hands and said, "Come on, let's get off the road. Now, would you drink a beer with me? I like a beer sometimes the end of the day."

She looked at his hand wrapped around her own and said, "You let me pop the top."

That was enough. Her hand was a small tremor within his and he let go and turned back to the drive without waiting to see if she was following. But as if it was the most natural thing in the world he answered over his shoulder, "Of course you can."

Suddenly with his own tremor. Remembering the days when he would crouch in the aisle of the liquor store testing the seals on the bottles. Trusting nothing.

OPEN BOTTLES OF beer in hand in the red room. So called because the plaster walls had been painted with numerous coats of simple barn paint. As well as the wide pine floorboards. The ceiling had been left pale oystershell plaster and the only light as if opposing the intent of the room was a slender old single-bulb unit with a knob-twist switch on the wall. Once accustomed to the room there was no other viable option—a measure of his father's vision. But until that moment came it seemed there was not enough light to see those stranded wonders spread along the wall. A pair of deep leather armchairs sat almost back to back—the leather old and supple and constructed so whoever sat was within the rising folds of the arms with head tilted back so the walls were the only thing to see. Incongruous within the room for the standing observer, perfect once settled into. In the same way the light fixture diffused at perfect angles to the four walls.

Four pieces each side by side on three of the walls. The fourth held smaller works that ran in an ascending random ladder from close to the baseboard to within inches of the ceiling in the opposite corner of that wall. All that was left. From time to time a letter from a curator would arrive, even these long years after his father's death. Hewitt had a letter of response so often used it took him no more than five minutes when he did deign to respond—all the finished work had been sold in his father's lifetime. And, with regrets but obeying his father's demand upon his death all studies and sketches had been destroyed if you have further questions please contact and here Hewitt inserted the name and address of the family attorney who mercifully had died ten years ago. This arrangement pretty much took care of things. The red room was a secret from the world. As were the metal map cabinets his father had installed in the basement room with temperature and humidity controls that held several thousand sketches and studies ranging over his entire career. Even the one drawer that held his childhood charcoal sketches of Lympus and a handful of Amsterdam. All this according to Thomas Pearce's disaffection with the art world in the decades preceding his death—no matter that his work consistently sold. His dictum was upon his death what work was not out in the world should remain that way. "The vultures," he proclaimed, "may swoop but not land. If they dismiss or categorize me now, offer them nothing toward their careerist reflections."

He'd been compared to Wyeth without that artist's draftsmanship; a colorist of the pastoral; a bold relic of social realism; an artist whose range and temperament could not comprehend the postwar explosion of bounds. "I'm not Pollock," he'd said. "And have no interest in attempting to be."

For Hewitt of most importance was knowing however bad things got he had his own refuge to go into. No longer a midnight black thicket but the place of controlled fire and heat. Where things could be reshaped. Or find the shape they sought. Or his shape found within them. And knew it had been the same for his father. A studio; a forge.

BUT SHE DIDN'T know or understand the forge yet. It was enough to be sipping beer together and following her through the room.

She would peer at some things and then step away without speaking and others she'd lean close and study. She said, "This is so strange."

He offered no help. He spent only a few evenings a year here now, mostly in winter. His friends knew better than to ask admittance although the door, always shut, was never locked. Some likely considered it a shrine best not mentioned. The only exceptions being his old girlfriend Amber Potwin who'd grown up knowing his father, and his friend Walter who had literally saved his life.

After her first comment she said nothing more but wandered slowly around the room, stopping, studying, moving away and then back. Sometimes abruptly stopping her circuit to cross back to view again one painting or another. After a while he became aware she was traveling between three paintings, two full size and one of the small ones on what he called the ladder wall. At this point he decided to leave her—this was a person whose relation to time was as skewed as her sense of direction and place. He still didn't know why she was up a back road in Vermont trying to get to Texas.

In the kitchen he popped another beer and went into the pantry and considered the shelves. All he had to go on were the stalks of asparagus and she did not eat meat. He stood blank. Then realized he wanted to give her comfort, some food simple and pleasant that would give her a sense of well-being, so quickly settled on a can of cream of asparagus soup with the asparagus steamed quickly and cut bite-size to float on top. Cheese toast—a light spread of butter and mustard on the bread under the cheese and paprika on top. That should do it.

Out the kitchen windows the long twilight settled so the sky in the west mirrored faintly the deep green sudden and new over the land. He glanced at the old radio on the shelf over the sink but left it off. The Trading Post call-in was not wanted this evening. He was not alone in the house. He couldn't hear her, her bare feet on the floorboards but this didn't matter. She was there.

Instead of the ease of the propane burners he walked through the pantry and down five steps into the woodshed and split stovewood and gathered kindling and returned to build a fire in the range. He opened the soup into a saucepan and pushed it to the rear of the stove which would warm soon enough but without the sudden surge of heat that would require his attention. He prepared the bread and cheese and laid them on a cookie sheet to wait for the oven and very nearly the moment to eat. The fire was popping now. He opened the firebox door and added three splits of firewood and then lifted the cast-iron plate from the rangetop closest to the firebox and set a pot with a half cup of water directly over the fire. He cut the asparagus and dropped the pieces in to boil, watched them turn bright green and drained the water off, running cold water over the stalks to hold them until the soup was ready.

EMPTY SOUP BOWLS with a membrane of pale greenish white dried on the inner edges, small plates with darkened crumbs of toast. Hewitt had considered the small candelabra of white porcelain decorated with tea roses and fragile petals but rejected it for fear of appearing romantic and settled on the frosted fixture above the sink with its forty-watt bulb that threw a soft slantwise light over the room. She declined another beer but of her own accord had taken a mason jar and filled it with the bitter-cold spring water and standing at the sink drank it down and filled it again before coming to the table. She thanked him for the food before they sat down and she opened her paper napkin and spread it over her lap, a subconscious gesture, oddly touching given the filthy condition she appeared unaware of when found this morning and he saw a younger different version of herself. Again the contrast as she leaned over her bowl in intense concentration suggesting that if she looked away the soup and toast might disappear even as she swept her spoon gently through the soup away from her before lifting it easily to her mouth. Table manners. Carried with her through times and places he could only guess at.

She looked up from the empty bowl.

"Was he terrible?"

Hewitt wasn't sure how to take this. "How do you mean?"

"For somebody to see things that way. It bunches my brain just looking at those pictures. I can't imagine what it would be like to make things like that. Was he terrible to be around?"

"Well," Hewitt said, treading carefully. "When he was working we knew better than to bother him. And if things weren't going well, if he was having a hard time with a piece he could be quiet and sort of lost from us for however long it took to work things out. But no, he was not terrible. Of course you never know what a person hides from their children."

Very fast. "Oh yes you do. You most certainly do. Children always know. Didn't you? Nothing's ever hidden."

He said, "First of all they're paintings not pictures. And maybe you're right about things not being hidden. Or being able to be. He had his moments, his sorrows."

She squinted at Hewitt. Then said, "Do you care what I think about those paintings?"

"Sure. I'm always curious." The truth being he had long since stopped caring about theories and opinions. But not hers. Whatever she saw might be different, surely was.

"I think part of his soul was burned. And the paintings were the only way he could find through to the other side of that and then they came forth and he . . ." She paused and he waited. She said, "Rested. They allowed him some peace."

Hewitt paused. Her idea was simplistic, near absurdly typical. What was arresting was her choice of words. That long-ago fire. By random synaptic collision of her own experience she'd struck upon something he was not about to reveal.

So he nodded and said, "I guess you're right. He never would talk about why he made what he did. But then, not many people do."

"You think?"

"I do. Mostly."

"Because it took the power away from him?"

"I couldn't say."

She was quiet and then said, "So those paintings. Are they the only ones he made?"

"They're the only ones I still have."

"So there were others. What happened to those?"

"Well. He sold a few."

She cocked her head as if this was somehow a new idea. "Did he make a living from them?"

Casual as could be Hewitt said, "I guess it helped some when he sold one. I wouldn't call it a living though." A small fortune was more like it and none of her business. He reminded himself to turn the key in the red room door that night. If she stayed. Which was seeming more likely. And then decided when she did leave, that night or the next day or whenever, he'd lock things up for a few days. Because if nothing else he'd learned over the years that the more fractures in a person the greater chance some were hidden for good reasons.

Her voice was sudden, abrupt, that deep sweet voice scraping with frustration. "I would give anything to be able to do something like that, some way I could take even the smallest portion of what's inside and get it out in a way I could see. I'd think, every time you could do that, it's got to cut back some of what pours round and round. I wish I could. But I wouldn't know where to start." Then she laughed. "But it wouldn't be painting. I had an art teacher in eighth grade tell me I had no sense of perspective. Now that I think about it, that was probably the sum of my education. No perspective. You know what I mean?"

He said, "I always thought real perspective depended on where you're standing. Move ten feet and it changes. Half a mile and it changes again." He paused and took a chance. "A thousand miles and who can say?"

She smiled and this time it was just a smile and she was a pretty girl. "That's good," she said. "I like that."

They sat silent. Hewitt liked that she had relaxed. There was no reason to think she would stay that way but he didn't want to be the one to break it, to take it away. Both needed this moment of grace and both, wordless, knew it. Burning wood popped in the range.

"So Jessica," Hewitt finally said. "How did you end up here? It's not on any route to Texas or much of anywhere else, as far as I can figure."

"I got turned around." Her eyes wide, bright.

Well yes turned around. Hewitt understood that well enough. But wouldn't quite leave it there. "So." Drawing the word out. "Did you think it was a shortcut somehow when you went up my hillside into the woods last night?"

"I saw the track went on and there weren't any cars around and anyway I had to quit. I was done in. That's the truth."

No arguing with that. The firebox was dying down but the bulk of the stove was warm and the room was gaining that soft glow. If it radiated from him that was fine—it was enough that it came at all. Balanced against these soft evenings were the years when whisky was only so good it allowed him to weep. That he now looked back upon not with embarrassment but something more akin to wonder. The melancholy of loss when that terrible raging subsided—the loss yet one more small deprivation from what he regarded as his rightful essential self. From that sprig of time his life thus far was laid out. As if planned. Except that he was patient. Things had changed more than once and this, reasonably speaking, meant the odds were they might turn yet again. A foolish heart perhaps but better than no heart at all.

He nodded and said, "I know how that feels."

"Don't you be taking those medications."

"I don't. But it sounds like maybe you have." Casual as could be but still he watched her and saw movement of some sort. A tightening. Constriction. Her face had closed.

She stood and walked to the sink and stood facing the dark version of her face in the window over the sink and then she turned and said, "I can't ever have babies."

Hewitt rolled with this. "I'm sorry to hear that, Jessica. That's got to be a tough thing to know."

She laughed but there was no color, no humor to her laugh—a choked grunt.

"Oh Hewitt it's so simple. I can't stop taking the pills long enough to have a baby or I'll fall to pieces but if I tried to have a baby while taking those pills there would most certainly be defects. In the child." She paused and snarled laughter again and went on. "A monster. That would be the risk. Or worse. An idiot or even one of those little weensy things born too early with its brain open for all the world to see and dead before I could ever even hold it in my arms. I'm sure of it."

Now she paused. Hewitt watching her, trying to determine how to respond. But before he could she said, "Those fuckers. But the joke's on them. I quit those pills. My glove box is stuffed right full of pill bottles almost all of them expired. It's shit, Hewitt. You listening to me? You hear me?"

The weasel of experience made him wonder how many other people she'd told this story to. He slowly said, "Sounds to me like you've worked your way right around that problem. Sounds like you can go right ahead and have babies when you want to."

"Oh Hewitt. Don't be fucking stupid."

"Well that was a nice thing to say."

"Look, I'm going to ride this out whichever way it goes. But I'm fucking nuts. What if the baby turned out like me? That would be the cruelest thing I could think of. To even take that chance. So you see those fuckers got me—I can't go back and I can't stand still and I can't go up. Down is all that's left for me."

Quiet a bit. Then he said, "You know, Jessica, nobody, doctors or anybody else can predict how it might happen. But things change."

"I heard and seen too much of that bullshit to buy even the smallest sack of it. Although I do believe you meant it kindly."

Hewitt sighed. Then he said, "So, Jessica, you hardcase, tell me this. Are you dangerous? Is there any reason why you shouldn't spend the night in my guest bed?"

She was backed up against the sink. She said, "I'm not dangerous to anyone except myself."

"You tried to kill yourself?"

"No. There was what you'd call a real strong pull for a while there. I'd lie in my room sometimes and play with my razor—that straight razor belonged to my grandfather. But there was never what I'd call a persuasive argument. Maybe I was just chickenshit. But that was a good while ago and I came up with a better solution."

"Which was?"

"I left town. Hell I left Mississippi."

"That took care of things?"

She laughed, again the easy laugh. He was beginning to enjoy hearing that from her. She said, "It helped. Along the way I met a few people that helped with others." She darkened again. "Along with some assholes that fucked me up other ways. The road doesn't solve anything except it keeps going. Shit." She paused and laughed again. "Hey Hewitt?"

He was beginning to sense the rhythm of her cycle. At least this evening. "What is it, Jessica?"

"I bet you never dreamed you'd find anything like me when you chugged up the hill on your tractor this morning, did you?"

"I've had worse company."

She came toward him and he stood. "That says a world," she said. "But thank you. I'd stay the night."

She hugged him. Free of seduction or even sensuality, a hug delivered between friends in the easy way of the young. He held her, the first time in a while he'd felt a woman against him and the intense warmth of another human body against his was shocking and soothing. How easy to forget how cold we are alone, he thought.

Her acceptance was exactly what he wanted. But now out, come from her, he was suddenly unsure. All wisdom shrieked feed her breakfast, wish her on her way and hope that whatever inner map had let her find him would be erased from her skittering brain within days if not hours. But there was something greater lurking and simple—be kind. Offer kindness in a world that was largely shorn of kindness.

He spoke quickly with his voice low, stepping back from her as he did but holding her shoulders so he touched her at arm's length. "Jessica," he said. "You go on if you need to. But if you want a quiet place to rest another day or two, you've found one here."

He didn't wait for her response. "Although, you feel like doing your pacing thing, stay off the road. Okay? You can march around the yard or up and down the hill or wherever out in the fields but stay out of the road."

She cocked her head. "I had you pegged as someone who didn't care what your neighbors think."

"I just don't want you dead or hurt. All right?"

Now she was quiet, studying him. Then she nodded.

IT WAS A hard night. He slept three hours and then woke from a dream he could not remember. If the dream was the prompt it did not matter but with the acute single-mindedness that only comes daytime in work or restless nights his father was with him. No ghost or shadowy filmy presence but fully occupying his mind.

As if the true paternal legacy was an acid trickle of misfortune, of weight carried inevitable as guilt, as if those hands had struck the match itself.

The fire Hewitt learned of only after his father was dead and so deprived of ever discussing. The secret not only Hewitt but his sister Beth also lived within without knowing—that surrounded them as players upon a vast stage they knew nothing of, a world behind the world they walked through and thought they lived and knew but would be revealed as a veil and shroud. An illusion of necessity and love.

MARY MARGARET DUFFY was a recent immigrant who worked by day in the kitchen of a hotel and lived just off Second Avenue south of Murray Hill in a two-bedroom coldwater flat she shared with four other girls. She had a nursing degree from Dublin but in 1948 there were ample well-trained American nurses to fill the hospitals and private clinics, a frustration she never forgot, that colored and embittered her life in ways hidden or explosively misdirected although at the time she believed she was happy enough, rising early to take the subway to midtown where she entered into a labyrinth of steam and heat and spent the first half of her shift preparing huge pans of soft scrambled eggs and the second assembling a stream of endless club sandwiches in every variation anyone might dream up. Mary Margaret was a quick study and so with the exception of her Tuesdays off she ate at work and held tight to her cash and allowed herself the pleasures of the great city rapturous with postwar elation although she did most of this as pedestrian and observer. Not for her the museums and grand concert halls or the wonders of Fifth Avenue where afternoons ladies with hats and white gloves were shopping, but as the nimble slip she was, quick on her feet and fleet with her eyes, her strawberry blond hair curled to her shoulders in the style of the day and her three good off-the-rack dresses, her skirt and sweater set, she spent her afternoons along the avenues and cross streets and found refuge in the reading room of the public library or further uptown in the smaller more comfortable rooms of the American Irish Historical Society. Evenings she would stay in and read magazines or listen to the radio or often as not slip out with one or more of her roommates down to the music hall which was nothing more than a bar with pool tables in the back and a jukebox with Sinatra and Goodman and the Dorsey Brothers but also Bing Crosby and Ruthie Morrissey and Christopher Droney, the mighty John

McCormack and others all set to get the lads singing together and dancing with the girls on the ten square parquet feet of dance floor, and very quickly abandoning her glass of ale for a gimlet, ordered after overhearing the name and then sticking with the drink for the lightness it brought her head and body.

She'd noticed him from one of her first evenings but hadn't given him much thought, the tall fair-haired older man sitting hunched and quiet over his whisky always at the far end of the bar in the small corner with only room for a stool or two, a man large enough and silent enough so more often than not regardless of how full the bar was, the corner was his own. What she did notice was what he was not—no devilry or merriment to his eyes, no effort to speak or even watch the girls as the other men did, no apparent motion at all beyond lifting his glass always half-full and furthermore he was of an age she couldn't quite place but seemed lacking all vitality. But she kept noticing him, noting his rough sweater or denim working man's shirt, his heavy overcoat that once had been quite fine and his raincoat of the same sort. Most notably, she never saw evidence at all of a hat, surely a mark of eccentricity that seemed to her carelessness as much as negligence.

Until finally Nancy the roommate she was most fond of one evening elbowed her ribs and near shouted into her ear, "If you won't at least ask Frank as regards that one's caught your eye I'll do it myself. But it's each to her own from there."

Motioned close Frank leaned and told her, "I can't tell you much, love. But he's a timepiece of sorts for me. Two years now it's the rare day he's not in right at the spot of four and sits until half past ten and then is gone. All I can say is his money's always on the bar and he drinks enough for most of the younger men but never so much as wobbles on his way out. He's the sad man, that's what he is." Frank glanced down at the man and back to Mary Margaret. "There's plenty men from the war with the long stare but that one, that one's eyes are empty. Whatever's brought him to that place is not, I'd swear, a thing I'd want knowledge of."

So Mary Margaret Duffy slowly finished her drink and glanced at her little Woolworth's wristwatch and ordered another and at ten minutes after ten stood off her stool. Nancy was twisted about, talking to two men at once and never saw Mary Margaret lift her purse and drink and walk down to the corner where there was no vacant stool but a space beside the sad man. If he saw her approach he made no sign. She placed her drink on the bar, leaned her hip against the wood and lifted her foot to the rail and gone suddenly all skittish and boggy brogue said, "I'm thinking if there was ever a man looked to need a kind human ear I'd wager you're the one. If I was the betting sort of girl but I'm no gambler or grabber or whore. An there's more to me than ear. I can set an brood as well as the next. I've seen it done champion. My da was first place and me mam not a full step behind. Listen to me run. Tell me to be off and I be a vapor to ya."

His elbows heavy on the roll of the bar, his head down with his hair dull and she thought, The man needs a haircut. Then without looking at her his voice came, a near steady rumble. "Leave me alone. Please."

His voice so unexpected and her own speech leaving her tilted she was sipping her drink when his words came and so she set her glass down and laid a hand on his arm and said, "I will. But ya have to look at me an tell me to my face," only adding the last because as she was swearing to leave him she also felt the convulsive tremor jump his muscles when she touched him. She took her hand away and gathered her purse and looked long at her drink and decided she'd proven she'd had enough of that and turned and made her way shifting and dodging and short of breath out toward the avenue, out toward the air. Out to where she did not know but away from her fool self. A cool September evening with her purse hugged tight and the pooling yellow light of New York night shot through with other lights bright and dim as she walked, the lights of passing automobiles and taxis, storefronts both closed and open, the gray of the sidewalk almost soft to look at but hard under her short heels and for a striding moment she wondered how long it had been since she'd walked on bare earth and then her lip curled as she walked toward her empty night when she heard the voice behind her, the voice which had been there for at least a block but penetrated finally as meant for her, directed toward her. Coming not only after her but already surrounding her.

"Wait," he called. "Please."

She stopped under a streetlight and stood, huddled tight to herself. She wouldn't look up when he came upon her.

Tender and tentative as spring rain he said, "I want to drown you."

The sidewalk had bits of quartz the size of an eyelash embedded in it. She faced about to him, her arms folded tight over her chest and said, "I'm sure I heard ya wrong. Speak clear or I'll scream Police."

He stepped back, his hands extended slightly, open, harmless but halting, fumbling. His eyes in a panic. She almost believed he was a madman when he said, "I'm sorry. I wasn't thinking. I'm out of practice with formalities I suppose you could say."

"I could say most anything." She ventured a cautious frown. "But it's not a great line to try on a girl. Telling her you want to drown her."

She watched roiling emotion scudding fast over his face. Fear and something close to revulsion and he worked his lips, wet them with his tongue and said, "Draw. You misunderstood. I'm an artist. I'd like to draw you." The words now thickly encumbered as if his tongue was loathe to let them out.

"Sure ya would. Without a stitch, is that it?"

He blinked and then a smile came and went. "No, no. I'd like to draw your face. Just trying to catch your face with a pencil. That would be enough."

She studied him, her frown deepening. She said, "You're frightening me. I think you should leave me alone." The bog gone all out of her now, stiff and clear.

He made another attempt to smile, this less successful and she knew it was because he was trying. "I will if you want. But would you give

44

me another chance? I could introduce myself and we could walk back to Frank's where your friends are and we could talk there. I'd make an attempt at explaining myself."

Mary Margaret looked hard upon the man before her. He wasn't as old as she'd thought, perhaps in his early or middle thirties. His face was creased with weather and cares and his eyes freighted as he blinked under her scrutiny. She said, "If you're a true artist you'd be a madman to want to draw the likes of me. And I've had enough of the bar tonight. If you had it in mind to walk and talk I'd be willing to do the same. If nothing else, you're a story needs out."

THE LONG HOURS of night following the afternoon when Hewitt's father died and he sat with his mother in the basement room next to the wine cellar, the locked room with its old rolltop desk and the wall of wide shallow steel map files, his sister Beth waiting in the Charlotte airport for a flight to New York and the train up from there, Mary Margaret told him all she learned that long-gone night but also of how little; how the stories that came out did so over the next year; of how Thomas Pearce would come into her life for days at a time, then weeks gone, and how she knew even from that first night that it would be this way until one way or another it would not. And she was prepared to await that answer.

SHE SAT FOR him and he tried to draw. His studio was a cheap gutted apartment far down on the East Side, work tables of planks on sawhorses with cans and thick tubes of unopened paint, stacks of blank stretched canvases leaned against the wall, a pair of spotless easels. An old worn velvet daybed with a heavy mahogany scroll at one end, a mattress on the floor behind a curtain strung on a wire, a small gas cookstove and a sink. None of it quite new but nothing like she'd expected; the only color, the only pigment, the only paint was not the speckles and smears she'd expected the first time she went there but a broad oval on the plaster wall that even her untrained eye could see was nothing more than deep blue paint squeezed straight from the tube into a palm and then the hand working in furious swirls streaks and daubs upon the wall. She contemplated it as she sat for him and slowly the obvious rage began to make sense to her; a man had been forsaken by old and trusted tools. Or as he sat perched on a tall stool with a pad on his knees and a handful of sharpened pencils in his shirt pocket and after fifteen minutes or three or an hour and a half would rip the sheet from the pad and hurl it crumpled onto the floor all this wordless unless she moved when he spoke his frequent command "As before, as before."

He saw her as what might save him long before she understood this. By the time of that comprehension on her part she knew it was true. And believed she would.

In the end it didn't happen in New York although those years were as necessary as the two visits over two years when they took the train to Vermont to spend unholy weeks of manic infused vacation with his mother where Mary Margaret understood it was the place as much as the woman he wanted her to learn but also knew his mother saw her very differently than Thomas Pearce did and both women knew nothing was to be done about that although Lydia Pearce did outright ask if Mary Margaret was sleeping with her son and why bother with the charade and extra work of separate bedrooms. This over tea and cookies with thimbles of sherry on a summer afternoon when Thomas was wandering the woods above the majestic house.

The summer after that they went to Nova Scotia and the vast pile of the rest of their lives together that she'd seen from the start and held to finally tumbled and came to rest about their feet. Around them as sure as the frothing tide-rise.

But before this, long before this, she learned what had to be learned and then a lid clamped forever, nothing more. There came the dawn they'd been up all night when suddenly the wave of high energy she'd almost gotten used to came over him and he ordered that they dress and go out into the fog-drift of morning and hiked up to the bridge to Brooklyn and walked across it as the sun began to burn through and he led her up toward Clinton Hill and then down a small side street where they stood looking at a three-story brick building and as they had walked there he told her not only where they were going and what to expect but also where they were going in the past. To that evening distant and immediate as this spring morning. Which did not stop her from sitting on the curb across the street when his account trailed to nothing and he stood gazing upon what was not there, would never be there again, and she left him and sat facedown into the fabric of her gay spring dress and wept.

As if describing events happened to another, he told her. How he'd rented the third floor apartment while still a student at the nearby Pratt Institute and how it was not long after that he met his wife not in Brooklyn but Manhattan, a student of ballet, of galvanic personality and ambition but when the two met both knew their destinies with each other and he knew he was the perfect foil for her acerbic stringent wit and laced fury, believed she was as necessary as oxygen, and it was in these early days when he began to be noticed, to be taken a bit apart from his own crowd—a place he admitted he'd always thought himself to be. And still she danced and he loved that she danced, was happy to see her off mornings to classes and wait expectantly and braced late afternoons when she returned from auditions and what he did not say but the young Irish woman knew was that this woman was lovely and lithe, athletic and demanding and very likely angry also as his recognition grew as hers did not for then there came the baby, the little girl. And it was here and only here that his account faltered before he gathered and went on. How his love for Celeste and hers for him was instantaneous and ferocious but the morning Susan was born and he held the newborn looking down at her he was then and there flooded with a love he'd never dreamed existed, never expected from himself or thought possible in any human being. And how that never changed, as Celeste resumed her now more daunting efforts at the barre, and he took much care of Susan so very quickly a toddler and then a little

47

girl who was he said in a voice as if recounting the previous day's weather the only thing, human or otherwise and especially human, who was never ever an interruption to his work, who he'd hold on one hip as he worked on the canvas before him, learning to rethink his actions and speed as a one-handed man. How she knew the names of the colors and could find the right tube by the time she was three. How she'd go with him down to the naval yard or the piers or further south to the leather tanning yards, the boatyards, the ironworks and manufacturing blocks, the warehouses of goods bound for the ships or across the river to Manhattan, or setting up on the rocky shoreline of the East River within view of the magnificent bridge as he sketched boats and barges and tugs and freighters of all manner and size. The little girl leaning against his side so she could watch the pencil work on the paper. How Celeste slowly and without apparent bitterness retreated from auditions but never the classes and how the phonograph was in constant play ranging from the great ballets, primarily the Russians, to swing records but also music Celeste found and brought home and introduced him to—the older Negro jazz and race records of music she called the blues and also hillbilly music or the wild peculiar mixture of western swing and also the food, the food gained and gathered from all edges of the city as if for Celeste learning food was learning languages. And Susan grew and on her fourth birthday they held a party for her that was all adults, all people she knew and how he stood watching these formally attired guests and the poised little hostess and knew those people were here not only because of him but honestly for her as well and how she would lead, was already leading an extraordinary life. Now fully away from Pratt and almost all other formal ties except for the midtown gallery that handled his work as well as the Philadelphia and Chicago collectors, the wooly-haired duke or earl or whatever he was—an Englishman—who sent monthly telegrams and appeared two or three times a year and at the moment was bent at the waist in his tails as he led Susan in a delicate and not altogether disastrous attempt at a waltz. The upswell of cheers in the dark-

ened room as she blew the candles and opened the pile of brightly
ribboned boxes and someone handed her a half-filled flute of champagne and she sipped it as if it were the only reasonable complement
to the occasion.

How he worked. From noon until three in the morning and back
up two hours later to work again until sunset. Then dinner and a
short exhausted sleep on the sofa trickling in and out as Celeste read
to Susan and bathed her and put her to bed and then came to him
and slowly woke him and they would sit talking quiet, or loving,
and then she'd go to bed as he brewed a pot of coffee and went back
to work. How this would go on for days at a time, weeks even, and
then he'd fall apart and sleep three or four days around the clock
waking only to eat once or twice, then always beefsteak and nothing more with a tumbler of whisky and back to sleep. And how sometime during this wonderful catastrophic haze he lost sense of things,
lost track of himself and of his two girls, as he thought of them.

That night two years ago. The second autumn after the war. A
soft evening when he'd finished a marathon of three linked paintings,
of days and days he couldn't count and so kissed his daughter and spat
a No at his wife with her offered dinner and walked out and down
the block around the corner to a bar because his head was blistered
and reeling and he needed not quiet so much as nothing demanded
or wanted or hoped of him for a few hours and how he sat there into
the dark hours and even heard the sirens and saw the window-speckle
of racing fire engine lights and pushed his glass across the bar for another drink. And was sipping that down when a man, a neighbor he
knew only by face, was pummeling his shoulders and shouting at him
and Thomas Pearce knocked over his stool and ran out and up the
street already seeing the fire rising above the buildings, already knowing what he was heading toward.

And stood at the inner edge of the great circle of watchers, the
inner circle a snake nest of canvas hoses and huge puffing pumper trucks
and the useless ladder extended toward an empty flame-licked blackness

of night, held back by men sanctioned to be within that circle from which he was excluded, the firefighters and the nervous less well-protected police as the top half of the building spewed upward and as he knew he would Thomas Pearce heard the popping explosions of jars of turpentine and thinners within the abhorrent tornado of fire and standing there, held there, restrained, he saw clear as if he was within the leaping orange fluid structure, the pile of rags soaked with spirits and gum and turpentine that had accumulated to the side of his big easel, into the corner to rest and ferment and foment.

To be picked up and discarded another day.

Last thing he said to Mary Margaret Duffy before she sank backward to the curb and cried as he stood silent before the rebuilt building, arms strapped across his chest was, "Once it sank in there was no hope I pulled away from those men. Of course they needed to talk to me, wanted to talk to me. But I got free and walked away. I walked for days. Days and nights. It was both of them, I want you to understand that. It was all of it. But what comes back over me again and again, what I do not understand and never will was Susan. She was not just another person. She was her very own self all ways but she was part of me. She came from part of me. Where did she go? Where did my Susan go?"

HEWITT COULD LEARN nothing more. There were no photographs, no letters, no papers left behind. His mother would not or could not recall his father's first wife's family name or where she came from. She did not know where they were buried. His father, if he ever visited those graves, did so alone on one of his occasional trips to New York. Or wherever they might be. So he had two names and the enormity of what his father silently lived with. All those winter evenings with a big fire popping in the old fireplace in the living room how often had his father stared deep into those flames and considered those other greater malignant flames? Twice a year birthdays came and went unnoted. And two anniversaries. The one in stark counterpoint to the other but both annual bookends of a sort.

And now, at three in the morning, older than his father not only when he lost his first family but gained the strength and courage to try again, Hewitt Pearce stood at his night window and looked out on the summer starlit land and was most amazed by the love that pierced the brooding man. He wondered at the struggles held silent in his love for his family. For the love between his parents had been a visible thing, a vivid living presence that enveloped them all. A strong man, Hewitt thought. Trying to determine the difference between the passion of one's life and the love of one's life. And could not. Yes, a strong man. Stronger than himself.

# Two

Despite his restless night he was up early. He was always up early. Winter mornings he slept in, sometimes until six o'clock. When summer days were longest he might lie in bed past four listening to the birds rioting over the pleasure of a new day for as much as half an hour before rising. The house this morning was cooled down but the kitchen held a touch of warmth from the range. A thick fog from the branch of the river ran along the valley but by ten it would be gone and the day would be warm, dry and clear. A slight breeze perhaps. Well up into the sixties, perhaps low seventies.

He'd heard nothing from upstairs and wouldn't be surprised if Jessica slept most of the day. He still wasn't clear where she'd come from or how long she'd been on the road. He didn't even know her last name.

He went into the fog already backlit with the faintest of yellow glows and down to the Volkswagen and made a slow trip around the car. The inspection sticker was current, with seven months left. The tires were in bad shape but he already knew that from observing the tracks on the woods road the morning before. At the rear he eased down to kneel. The plates were current as well. He popped open the back, feeling this was not invasive but mechanical and his intent helpful. The little engine seemed in good enough shape, reasonably clean with cables and even the dinky heater tube was solid. Finally he lifted the dipstick but even that was better than it could be—the oil was perhaps half a quart

low and thick and black as a skillet. So it wanted an oil change. Everything else looked good to go. He rocked back on his heels and quietly
shut the compartment door and pressed until he heard it latch. Somebody had watched over this car and Jessica was the obvious caretaker.

Hewitt's own driving life ended a couple years after his breakup with
Emily—those nigh mythic years of slow but determined destruction and
absolute inability to see anything beyond his own flopping bruised heart.
The final incident had been a winter afternoon when he'd been drinking since well before dawn the day before and without the least idea
how he got there watched in bemused detachment as the old Volvo
spun three accelerating circles on black ice up above Emmett Kirby's,
then at sharply defined greater speed went down the embankment to
crash through the ice of Pearce Brook, shivering to a crunching grinding stop in the thick ice, boulders and frigid water, which while only
two feet deep left Hewitt stranded with a broken femur, clavicle and
cracked ribs. He sat placidly in the car and exchanged pleasantries with
old Emmett who'd hitched down on his double canes to see what the
Pearce boy was up to now, awaiting the official arrivals when the humor
pretty much ended.

For most of a year after the accident he'd taken a sliding member-
ship of painkillers but quit them all at once when he was astonished to
realize he was a junkie. During the bad first month he'd thought his
body couldn't function without the pills but he set a deadline to go
clean for six months even if the pain was so acute as to throw him off
everything else. He could take the time. Three months along he still
gimped and ached but owned his brain again. He'd been stoned as a
loon during the final DUI hearing when he was still on crutches.
Halfway through these proceedings he knew which way it was going
to go and dug his license from his old wallet and so when the judge
asked if he had anything to say on his own behalf, he'd tugged down
by the coatsleeve the old family attorney who would reiterate all the
arguments from the past which Hewitt knew held no water and hobbled
up to the bench and said to the judge, "You've been more than fair

with me in the past. I expect you want this." And laid the license down before the judge and turned and went back to his seat.

Everything after that was a formality. Except the conversation with Walter right after that final accident, which had been shock enough to take seriously. Of course it'd been easy to quit the death-by-whisky drinking when he'd been flying on unlimited Percocet. Walter was no fool and suggested Hewitt allow himself a couple of beers or wine if the occasion fit. Walter had said, "We all have something eats our ass. And nobody can tell another person when the time's come to stop dancing in the dragon's jaws. But you've gone past tragic to pathetic, Hewitt. I'm probably the only person who can tell you that. And I'm kinda sick of you just now."

HE WENT ALONG to the forge. He had no definite plan to work but didn't discount the possibility either. He had to sit there a while to see if it was a day for iron or not. This was the essence of what his customers perceived as a great problem—the fact he refused to state a deadline however vague. The customer could bring the most precise drawings of what he wanted and the finished product would often not resemble the drawing at all. Until installation Hewitt would visit the job site only once—to make his own measurements regardless of the precision of those already handed to him. This was now his reputation and he grumpily knew it added rather than subtracted from the value of his work. On the door to the forge was a sign, hand painted in black block letters against a plain piece of plank. The legend ran:

IF YOU WANT IT DONE YOUR WAY LEARN HOW TO DO IT

& MAKE IT YOURSELF.

YOUR COMMISSION IS NOT MY VISION.

Beneath that in slightly larger letters:

NO ENTRY WITHOUT PERMISSION.

Gordy Peeks had built the rough shell of bricks and the hearth and chimney but Hewitt had finished the rest himself. The brick reached to shoulder height and above that were wooden walls and an open-raftered tin roof. The only windows were on the north side so sunlight never altered the precise reading of heat through color and therefore malleability of the metal. The floor was hardpack. A pair of anvils fastened with giant forged staples deep into chunks of upright log stood in the center of the floor along with a wooden tub of water for annealing. On the brick front of the forge pegs studded into the mortar held several dozen pairs of tongs. Behind him close to the anvils a workbench kept all the small tools within easy reach—the hardies and fullers and swages, holdfasts, chisels, punches, bicks and forks, rivet headers and nail headers and bolt headers, various plates and taps, clippers and shears, also somewhere close to twenty hammers each different in weight and size and function, files and rasps, calipers in diverse sizes and metal rules of varying length. The tools with wooden handles were a special joy, the wood so old and used the handles were smooth, almost soft in the hand, sweat-polished like wood butter.

Along the wall was a second workbench of heavy two-inch hemlock planks on hardwood foundation posts cut from abandoned beams. On this bench was the long post vise with its leg that reached clear to the floor, beside that a smaller bench vise for lesser work, a hand-cranked post drill he preferred because he didn't burn up bits that way, a bench grinder with a foot-powered treadle; wads of steel wool in a wooden lard box stained through now with linseed oil, a dozen or so metal brushes of various shapes and widths, some with brass bristles for finish work and others with steel for rougher work. A good-sized vat filled with motor oil he could soak heavily rusted iron in. Above the bench on the wall hung a calendar from Sanborn & Sons Harness Shop, two months out of date.

In the far corner covered with a piece of canvas was the set of tanks and oxyacetylene torches, his welding helmet resting on top like a discarded fencing mask. The beauty of the acetylene weld was undeniable. And many of the finer steels he was forced to work with required it. It was almost impossible to find high-grade wrought iron anymore—now mostly steel or steel alloys. But Hewitt was known to junkdealers from Machiasport to Troy, from lower Quebec to the Berkshires. Almost all who would call him when they came across true iron stock, so he had an ample supply resting on chocks in the barn. He saved this for special projects, although he could never predict when a project would became special, requiring that fine metallurgy. And the variety and consistency of the modern steels were not without their own merit. He knew much of what he did, seen through other eyes, was an unnecessary pain in his ass. But he did what he had to do to live with the work.

Resting against the double doors was his current project, a set of driveway gates for a summer home up in the Pomfret hills. When he took the job he told the owner not to construct the brick columns that were meant to hold the gates and meld them with the white board fencing. Because the gates would be too heavy to simply drill into mortar and he'd have to sink iron posts for anchors. Hewitt had leaned back against his own fencepost at this point and gone on to explain the gates he was building could not possibly be ready that fall. He advised the man to leave his driveway open for the winter—it would make it easier for the plow truck. Otherwise he could go to Agway and buy a cheap tube gate that should do the job.

The more they came prepared to deal with his difficult approach to the work, the more difficult he became. Some days he thought he should just quit. But there wasn't enough money to do that. And there was the huge question of filling his time. He'd boxed himself into a corner by making a sincere effort to do the opposite. His work was good but he wasn't so proud to not realize that it was the focus he brought to it more than some special gift. Nobody paid attention anymore, was what he thought. Mostly he stayed to himself. He belonged to no association or guild and disliked nothing more than being cornered by another smith eager to talk technique. Because too many people confuse technique with vision. You get to a certain point and then you can do it or should quit. Although, as with all rules there was the exception—his long strange luscious friendship with a smith from northern Vermont, Julie Korplanski.

He studied the gates resting against the north wall. Heavy rect-angles outlined with great straps of four-inch stock were the frames of the gates. The rest interweaving hammered straps that left perfect ten-inch squares throughout the gate, the straps both horizontal and ver-tical not single but paired with one slightly wider than the other, the pairings reversed every other time, the way patterns reverse in a tar-tan. The ten-inch squares framed delicate inner circles of round stock. Inside these circles he planned something that so far eluded him. So the work waited as did the man in Pomfret, who probably wouldn't arrive for the summer until Independence Day weekend. Hewitt would hear from him.

For a moment he contemplated the possibility that the gates were done. Except for the mounting hardware they could go up and be beautiful. Wire brush them down and work them with steel wool and then warm the forge for a week running and apply coats of linseed oil as often as possible. He studied them, even intentionally blurring his vision to see them as if in passing. They were beautiful, but not done— he knew when a project was complete. So he would leave them a bit longer. The other option was to fire the forge and do small-job work, not the sort of things he sold but latches and hinges and such that he'd give to friends. Or use himself. There was a barn latch of forged iron that had broken that past winter.

Timothy Farrell had said, "Take a chain now. Which link is the strongest?"

The summer Hewitt was sixteen he'd been at a craft fair, tagging along with his mother, hoping to connect up with one of the freaks there and score some weed but found himself watching a fellow with a long ponytail over bib overalls with a portable forge and anvil pound-ing out the simplest of wall hooks. Hewitt stood watching until his mother had had enough of crocheted pot hangers and heavy pottery and dragged him away. But not until he'd seen the alchemy of the forge and the red-hot iron and also realized the work he was seeing was badly done.

He asked around and found Albert Farrell. Albert was in his late eighties but happy to take Hewitt out to the forge behind his house and sit and talk with the boy. Albert had shod his share of horses and oxen in his day. But Albert was not a farrier. He was a smith. They worked together and by the end of three days Hewitt had beaten out a serviceable roasting fork, proud of the graceful curve of the handle down to the tines. Over the following weeks Albert taught by words as much as action and Hewitt learned the basics of the craft. How to evenly draw out a rod or bar, how to use the pritchel hole on the anvil to make a square right angle. How to put an even twist in a poker handle. How to mend his own tools.

Finally Albert said, "You're welcome to putter around out here all you like, long's you don't set fire to nothing. Tell you what though. I got a nephew. My brother's boy. Well by Jesus I guess he's more a man than you be now. Anyway he got the good blood. It came down through Pop who worked the fireboats in New York City and that was a long time ago but ain't it all? Anyway Pop was a true man, an ironworker before anything else. Hell's fire he'd use the boiler in the boats to heat iron to fix whatever needed fixing. I tell you what. You write Timothy a letter. Tell him I said to work the bejesus right outa you and you'll learn the trade. Work with him a year or two and then if you come back here and pound out something other than a oven fork or door hook, why, I'll give you all this. The tools and such. Otherwise it'll all end up in a scrap yard. There's tools here not another man owns. You know why? I made em myself."

The following spring he'd driven with his father to the Finger Lakes in western New York State, spent an afternoon and a long day talking and working with Timothy Farrell and arrangements were made. There was a sleeping loft in the forge. No money would change hands. Hewitt would earn his board by assisting Timothy with the simple work and in the process learn the details and techniques for the complicated work. There would be a two-week trial during which either one could call it quits. But Hewitt knew that wouldn't happen. They were already easy with each other. Timothy was wiry and lean with tightly curled black hair cropped close to his head and a slow smile that seemed to live in the corners of his mouth.

He said, "I'll work you hard. If what you're looking for's here, you'll find it."

Hewitt nodded. "I think it's going to be a good summer."

Timothy said, "It's a good life."

HE STOOD AND stretched, looked again at the gates. And still had no answer for those circles. Then in ten steps he ran up out of the forge where he heard her calling his name. Jessica was in the dirt of the drive, not far from her car and not far from the entrance to the forge. She wore sneakers, long nylon shorts and a sweatshirt two sizes too large, her hair wet from a bath, her eyes serious, stunned upon him.

"I got scared. I didn't know where you were."

"What," he asked. "You think maybe I hitchhiked out of here?"

She studied him, as if parsing his words. She said, "What do you want Hewitt? Me to hightail it out of here? You said you got gas."

"There's a tank in the shed. It's my tractor gas. But you know, that little Bug needs an oil change bad."

That darkling face. "You went through my car?"

"I popped the back and took a look at things She's in pretty good shape except you'll want to change your plugs sometime not too far off. And the oil. The oil's bad."

"I know it is," she said. "But I've kept it topped off. I been waiting to find a place to change it."

"That so?"

"Hey," she brightened. "Maybe I got the gas I could drive out and buy four quarts of oil and likely you got a place where I could back her up and drain the old sludge. A little wash or ravine or some-place like that. They make you pay to take used oil now."

Hewitt was thinking. "Well, that oil soaks on down until it finds a brook or river or into your spring water. It doesn't just go away you know."

"Save the whales," she said.

"I keep old oil. I use a fair bit of it. So it's no problem at all."

"What were you up to? You sure came running."

He said, "I was in my workshop." An awkward word.

And she heard it. "Your forge, right?" She went on. "Did you make that bed in your room?"

He looked at her. The bed was simple with traditional arches for the head and foot boards but run through with leaves of ivy and brass snakes up the four corner posts and each post topped with a copper bunch of grapes. No apples there! The first truly beautiful thing he'd made, all in the haze of hangovers and small snorts.

She said, "That's right. I snooped. I can't help it." Then she said, "Who's that pretty blond on your bedside table?"

Hewitt breathed deep even as he nearly laughed at her choice of words. As if Emily herself was draped over that little nightstand instead of the framed photograph she was speaking of.

He said, "I made the bed. And that girl's an old girlfriend long gone. But that's my business." Before this could be pursued he said, "Well Jessica, this is what I was thinking. You've either got a lousy sense of direction or were just ambling your way to where you were going. Would it throw you too far off track to spend another day here? What I was thinking was we could fuel this Bug up and maybe you and I could take a little trip. No big thing. Just where I can't get to on my tractor. There's stuff I need and I could show you the sights. People spend fortunes to come up and ride around in the country and they never do see what they should see although of course they don't know the difference. Because nobody but the local folks get off the main roads."

She spat into the dirt. "Goddamn. It's cold up here." There was gooseflesh on her thighs and arms.

"Wait till midday. You'll sing another song then. So what do you say, Jessica? Shall we drive around a little bit?"

She looked all around the yard, her head moving as if taking it all in for the first time. She said, "You don't have a car."

"I used to."

"Did you wreck it?"

"There was a time I couldn't have more than a couple drinks and had to get out and roam around. I was lucky I never hurt anybody except myself. And yup, the last one did in the car."

"You never got another one?"

"Can't drive. The state took my license. I use the tractor to get back and forth to the village and mostly get what I need there. But every now and then it's nice to get out. That's pretty much what I was thinking of."

"It's not like there's a soul waiting for me to arrive anywheres." As if she had revealed herself she shook her head and turned partway from him so all he could see was the tip of her nose and cheekbone and the hair over her ear on that side.

A plume of tenderness washed over him.

It was as if each pebble and the grains of dirt between those pebbles kept her in some acute study or potential rapture or both. Her eyes snaked slow across the ground between them, finally striking his boots to work their way up his pantlegs and shirt where they rested or perhaps even sank deeply into the skin of his lower throat exposed behind the open collar of his shirt.

He waited.

Finally her eyes came to meet his. Her dark eyes seemed wet to him but with no evidence of tears. Looking into her eyes he felt his mouth twist one end up and the other down, his own hidden sorrow unleashed beyond command.

She said, "How far are you talking about?"

"Not so far. Over the river to New Hampshire. Twenty-five, thirty miles."

She nodded. "Let's do it. Although I'm not sure I can pay you just now for the gas. But I'll get you the money. I will."

Hewitt considered this. She wasn't strictly saying she didn't have any money but the implication couldn't be avoided. Of course she might be fine for what she needed but saw no reason to pay for his joy ride. And it might even be possible she worked this angle, the poor stricken girl every chance she got. He shrugged and said, "It's a small spit of gas. I'm happy to spare that if we could get out and let me shop a little. You don't have to worry about paying me back. We'd be even is how I see it."

She paused. A moment of consideration. Then smiled and said, "That bed is sure beautiful. Can I see your forge?"

He smiled back. "Nope."

ONCE ON THE narrow dirt roads she drove as if she'd been on them all her life, easing along at thirty-five or forty miles an hour. They were climbing up through woodlands that opened here and there for a house lot or a somber wornout century-old sheep pasture or down in the low spots small bits of bog. Coming onto any sort of turnoff or intersection he'd silently point the way, giving her plenty of time to note his choice and the ride was smooth and unhurried. She was quiet and that was fine. Her legs and arms were pale white, causing him to wonder where exactly she'd come from most recently.

His boots rested on a cushion of trash and a quick glance down told him her comments about her diet were understated. She seemed to have an affinity for Coca-Cola in cans and Snickers candy bars. And even with the backseat emptied there remained the reek of the unwashed. He glanced over at her. She was intent on her driving but also active, her eyes and sometimes her face moving to take in all around her, as much of what was passing as she could.

He finally spoke. "So'd you paint this car yourself or'd it come that way?"

She flipped her head at him, eyes hooded and hair bouncing his way. She said, "I told you I plain don't have any perspective."

They drove on. For the next mile or so he felt as if he was taking the temperature inside the little car. Things felt alright. He put his right foot over his left knee which was a considerable job and twisted the least bit sideways toward her in his seat and as if commenting on what a fine day it was said, "So what happened to you, Jessica?"

If she was upset or perturbed by his question she did not show it but drove on in silence long enough so he had to point another road juncture. He wondered if she was taking this time to prepare her answer or simply to have rote words appear that way. And immediately decided that he could not do that: even if he was wrong in the end he had to trust her. Or there was no point to any of this.

She said, "You don't smoke, do you? I mean cigarettes. I could use a cigarette just now."

"I never liked it. Made food taste funny and I couldn't smell a thing."

"Well there's other things do worse than that. But it's not like I need to smoke, you understand?" She glanced at him.

A hen partridge dusting in the side of the road blew off. Hewitt said, "But sometimes it comes in handy."

"This was my grandma's car she gave to me when I turned sixteen so I could get back and forth to work and school. I was trying pretty hard about then. And my grandmother was the only one who really ever understood me. The Bug was twenty years old with thirty thousand miles on it and Grandma's eyes were failing her so it was a good thing all around, school all day and then drive up to Oxford to waitress at the Holiday Inn and then home to do my schoolwork, at least what wasn't done in study hall already which was most of it—I hated getting home at ten thirty eleven o'clock at night wasted from smoking pot with the guys worked the kitchen and try to do home-work. But even then things had gone downhill and I knew I was danc-ing not walking like everybody else. You know what, Hewitt, it's a pure shithole trying to figure out what was really going on with me and what others said was. It was a fuck all the way round. A bad one. You know what I mean."

"I believe I do."

"I was a happy little girl, at least I thought I was. Sure there was weird shit going down in my family but I never seen a family didn't have that. I thought I was normal. I had my moments but I thought it was just part of life, of growing up. Like when the thoughts in my head got racing far ahead of what I could keep up with. Or times when I would get so lonesome for no reason I could name that I'd lay on my bed and cry. But it all seemed okay. Course my mama and daddy weren't talking much to each other but I never saw any fights either."

Hewitt heard the pause and said, "That doesn't sound so strange to me. I think most growing up is like that. One way or another."

She drove on a while. Hewitt was a little lost but knew where east west north south were and so he just waited for the roads to pro-claim themselves. At some point they would start downhill and all would be clear from there.

Jessica said, "All the sudden not a thing made sense. It was so fucking weird, Hewitt. I was going along and doing fine I thought and all the time my mama and plenty others were talking about me behind my back. It was about this time my daddy run off to Mem-phis with that girl Tina which I don't much blame him for. It was more show than he was getting in Water Valley. Or being a diddly country lawyer. And I shit you not, Hewitt. I think in my heart that's where things really went wrong. You can't be sixteen years old and have your daddy run off with a woman just barely out of college herself and not expect some effect. Kids have that shit happen all the time. But me, I rolled up like a caterpillar touched with a stick. But the thing, the funny thing is everybody had to believe it was bigger than it was. While all it was was just me. For a good while I was out of school more than in. Dragged here and there to see different doctors who expected me to explain myself to them which was like asking dirt to explain itself and they would get angry or frustrated and decide I needed some kind of pills. Except they wouldn't work. Off we'd go to another one. And more pills to try. I felt like I was the itsy-bitsy spider there for a while. And the drugs were like a long dragged-out dreary day with nothing to do. Then came the afternoon I overheard the doctor talking to my mother about maybe having me hospitalized. For my own good, he said. For the first time I was really scared. I realized those fuckers could do anything they wanted to, so I stopped fighting them. I took the pills and went to my sessions and did my best to look like I was trying to do my best, which is what they want. They don't want more than that I can tell you. That lasted six months and I counted every minute of every hour of those days. I kept taking the pills because there was too many people keeping track. But I still had my waitress job and there was this guy Daryl working the kitchen I trusted. So I saved up a couple hundred dollars and one night I went to work and never did go home again. I'd smuggled clothes out a piece or two at a time until the front of that Bug was stuffed full. That night after work I went over to Daryl's house and we pulled the Bug into his garage and shut the doors and he had all these cans of spray paint and we smoked reefer and did a few lines and stayed up and painted this fucker ever which way we could think to. About four in the morning I drove the fuck out of there. Summertime and that red sun coming up like the eyeball of the world turned upon me so I went until I hit the interstate and turned west. Not because I had a plan. I just had to get rid of that sun."

Hewitt remained silent. They were dropping down through the last hillside and while she couldn't see it, he knew those flashes low in the trees were sunlight on the big river. After a time he said, "When was that?"

She didn't look at him. "I guess close to ten years."

"You ever been back?"

Now, one hand on the wheel she glanced over at him, the other hand pushing her hair clear of her face. "I float in and out," she said. "I go close enough long enough to keep the car up to date paper-wise. Basically," she looked hard at him, "I'm doing the best I can."

TOO MANY HOLES, was what Hewitt was thinking as he went about his errands. She turned herself loose in Hanover, agreeing to meet back at the car in an hour.

So he paused after delivering the mixed case of wine to the backseat of the VW that at least here in Hanover wouldn't attract the sort of scrutiny it might in other towns around. Even the story of that paint job. What was that about? She was smart enough to know you can repaint a car but with the same plates they can find you if they want to. The multiples of they that might apply. Yet her telling had been so matter of fact, nearly off the cuff as if the story related what happened to someone else instead of an ongoing present.

This all told him nothing he hadn't known yesterday when he found her at her spindly campfire up in his woods. The details provided since were nothing more than a half-dozen nails in the walls of an otherwise empty room that he might hang her fragments of story upon.

He knew the smart thing was to send her ass down the road.

He also knew he wasn't about to do that. At least not yet. His curiosity was piqued. Beneath this was a genuine desire to know more.

He whistled softly, almost a whisper of a whistle as he hiked down the street to the Co-op where he could buy the couple of sacks of grocery items he couldn't purchase closer to home.

THREE HOURS LATER he was pacing about the general area where the Bug sat well laden but with no sign of its owner. He'd walked both sides of the street a couple blocks either direction from the car. She'd taken the keys and he could see her driving off without him, without even noticing or paying attention to the bags and boxes in the backseat. It was so late past their meeting time he knew there was trouble of some kind. There was money enough in his wallet to call a taxi for the trip home. But the more he paced the more he was inclined to stay. He felt he couldn't abandon her—a part of him even wondering if this was some test of hers—a notion that rankled yet he understood. That, he decided, was his big problem.

Compounding his reel of judgment was that he was in the last place good for him to be stranded with this sort of sticky mind-fucking. All those children out in their summer clothes, skin and hearts and minds taut and flushed and tracking as they never would again and their walking around not knowing and he watched in fear of encountering some version of his younger self or selves because she was always with him. Although he had not once been fooled—there never was a girl with hair like hers or the radiant presence that shone just walking. There were a handful of pale imitations but certainly no Emily. He could see each movement of her mouth, lips and eyes saying this to him—those rare occasions when doodling along on some project or sitting gazing blank in the evenings some near forgotten fragment would come back and her voice would be fresh in his head as if she were in the room. Time to time he caught her smell also. For years until they quit making it he used the brand of shampoo that had been hers. Then, suddenly he could no longer find it; replaced or discontinued in the vast shuffling of corporations. Although every once in a while he'd be in a grocery store and a woman would pass him and he would smell that scent. For all he knew it was something else altogether, the whiff of memory false.

It was really time to go. He was beginning to sweat. The package of haddock, bought on chance, was slowly softening in the heat. He unrolled all the windows to let air in, which was not a bad idea. Stuck another quarter in the meter. If he called the emergency room a peculiar void would leave him fruitless—he did not know her last name, could not claim to be a relative or tell anything about her that would be of help. To her or him. The same with the police. He knew he could learn more if he opened the glovebox to dig through for the paper registration. And gain exactly what? A last name. Perhaps an address in Mississippi that despite whatever half-truths or omissions was not a place she wanted the dogs set loose.

All this a combination that was grumbling up darkly upon him. He saw and felt and smelt it coming. It was the batwing beating of his heart, the river of youth pouring around him as if he was an old rock stuck midstream.

"Cool car dude." A kid passing spoke to him. Hewitt was up on the hood sitting crosslegged. He tried to pick out the body the voice had come from but couldn't. It was enough to get him down off the hood though. Quickly he peered a last time up and down the block and then dropped down three concrete steps from the sidewalk into a bar. The small tables were filled with hamburger-eaters and salad-grazers and the bar was mostly empty although the bartender was busy with the soda gun. Hewitt sank onto a stool, craning to see if he could spot the Bug through the one small window of eight panes in a single row. The bartender looked at him and Hewitt raised a finger. The bartender nodded, that old wait a minute nod.

Hewitt said, louder than he meant to, "Please." And was ignored.

Then the face struck the air close to him. "Get you man?"

Hewitt had a draft and drank it down, left a one hundred percent tip and went back out. Christ, beer in the middle of the day. Nothing was working, a nice morning soured, all things changed.

And there she was. In the driver seat with the door open and her legs lifted to prop through the window. Her feet were bare, the red sneakers gone. She stuck an arm out and waved.

"I got us some weed," she said as he got in.

"Good for you. Can you drive us home now?"

She looked at him. "Are you alright?"

"No. I am very much not alright."

She was quiet. They sat in the warm car, the smell of fish clean and distinct. Then she said, "Can you show me the way?"

He sighed and said, "Why don't you back this buggy out and start to drive."

"I didn't mean to be gone so long."

"What you should do," he said. "Is shut up and drive."

"You don't have to be nasty." She backed slowly out and started down the street.

"I'll make a deal," Hewitt said. "I'll point the turns and you take them and we don't talk."

"I was having kind of a nice day."

Hewitt pointed right for a cross street and she made the turn. They went along a block of big houses and came to a stop sign. He was already pointing again, his finger a bullet. She put on her turn signal and came to a stop, peering up and down for a break in the traffic, found one and pressed hard on the gas and the Bug jumped forward across traffic and down out of town toward the river.

HEWITT TOOK A long afternoon nap and left her on her own. When he woke and washed his face and looked out the bathroom window at a scurry of red-winged blackbirds up within the orchard he felt cleared and if not new at least ready to tackle things again. So he went down to find her.

It was late afternoon, the light softening and the air still. First thing he did was glance out to the road but of course she was not there. If this girl had a pattern it was not going to be simple to discern. He strolled around the flower gardens beyond and above the house, somehow already knowing he was wasting his time.

No premonition or inspiration but a swollen burst pip of knowing what he would do in her place. His stride smacked home this insight. Across the hard-packed yard passing the VW as if it was not even there. To the forge.

The door was shut tight but as he pulled it open he smelled the sweet almost evergreen scent of the weed. He went down the steps into the cool of the smithy. She wasn't there but he was violated. He stood for a minute looking around, then put his hands behind him and leaned back against the big workbench. On top of the brine in the annealing tub was a scattering of sodden ash. And lined up on the edge of the big anvil were five small roaches. Otherwise nothing was out of place.

He took a little time, studying those roaches. They represented more grass than he smoked in an average couple of months. He could not bring himself to consider what it would be like to smoke five joints in a row and yet there they were. He'd slept only maybe two hours. It was an awful lot of dope. He turned to the far end of the bench where his fine tools were, found a pair of featherweight needlenose pliers and took up the longest of the roaches. Clamped in the end of the pliers and touched with a match he was able to pull three good tokes. Then swiped the four remaining roaches off the anvil and stirred them into the dead coals in the middle of his fire. Before leaving he took up the old pitted poker and stirred the tub of brine so the ashes broke apart and floated downward. He was leaning over the tub watching the small gray motes break apart further and disappear when he realized the dope was kicking in and was pretty good. So he went up the steps already stoned and thinking Good God five of those fuckers.

Once outside he stopped and drew a breath. It was an elegant evening coming on. A niggle of urgency came over him to find her before it was dark. Then out loud he said,

"It wasn't me smoked all that."

PERHAPS IT WAS being stoned but he tapped into himself and went directly to where she was. Far back in the collapsed yellowed haybales in the carriage barn—his own hiding place. Knotholes in the barn sheathing let in long slender glides of light. He climbed on all fours over the treacherous stack of bales and hovered on top and then

A Peculiar Grace

let himself down into the chamber of broken bales where she was flat on her stomach, the barn tomcat above on the bales watching Hewitt as if standing guard over the girl.

He was too high to touch her. Her face was buried in the hay but one eye tracked him. Hay tangled in her hair and stuck to her clothes and welts reddened her legs bare below her shorts where she had hit the hay. He guessed she had gotten to the top of the stack and tumbled down into the nest. He lay beside her, not speaking. The cat above churned forth an engine of contented sound. As if he'd been waiting for Hewitt to show up and take charge.

Hewitt rolled onto his back away from her and propped one ankle atop the other on one of the sagging bales. Gazing up at the roof rafters dotted with the clay nests of last year's barn swallows. Who would be returning soon. Way back before the first jet aircraft were invented some farm boy had gazed at swallows and imagined aeroplanes as swift and sleek in swoop and dive as these small birds.

After a while he said, "Catch one?"

She said, "When I walked in here the hay looked soft, a dream of a bed. But it's itchy as shit against my bare skin."

"What every farm boy ever spent a summer afternoon on the back of a hay wagon learned long ago."

"My trouble is, I smoke one joint and don't feel a thing so I fire up another and about then things are kicking in sweet so I go for a third and it starts to get weird and I think what you need to do is get a little higher, get beyond this. So I keep going. Usually four joints gets me way past the point where I'm looking back at myself hating what I'm seeing."

"Five," he said. "It was five roaches I found on my anvil."

"If you're going to get mad could you please wait until later?"

He paused and said, "That's reasonable."

"Five," she said. "Hah." She rolled over on her side to face him and pulled her knees up toward her chest, her hands wrapped together to cushion the side of her head. The whites of her eyes seemed

71

ready to seep blood. She said again, "Five. Oh Christ, look at my knees."

They were scraped and roughened, red with long scratches where blood was drying brown. Not something the hay had done. He said, "What the fuck happened to you?"

"I went up the stairs of your workshop on hands and knees. But when I got outside it was so bright I kept trying to pick a point and walk but my brain couldn't connect with my legs. Then I thought of the barn—I saw this stack of hay earlier while you were getting the gas. That cat showed up and rubbed against me and walked ahead and turned and looked back like he was waiting for me. I fucked up my knees. Hey Hewitt, you ever notice, how on even the most beautiful women their knees are kind of ugly? I mean when they're standing. Like little bunched up faces?"

"I don't know," he said. "I always had more of a thing for that soft hollow on the backs of knees." And told himself Shut up.

She was quiet also.

Finally he said, "Can you walk now?"

"I expect so."

He had to help her up over the stack of hay and down the other side but he did so in the way you'd help a less able hiker over a steep series of ledges and she seemed to understand this. Just in the way she accepted that help. He knew the difference even if it had been a long time.

Out in the yard he was easy enough to take her hand and perhaps she understood the human touch, harmless but not without meaning. And just when he was thinking somewhat the same she said, "I'm growing comfortable with you."

There was no reason in the world to reply.

The sunlight was breaking apart against the lengthening shadows of evening although the air was still warm. He led her around the house, into the midst of the flower gardens. Where a long foot-thick slab of granite lay across two chunks of the same stone, all three

pieces marked every eight or ten inches with drill holes that two
hundred years ago had been bored into the stone. They sat on the
bench, the sun falling against their backs and spreading the paling
light down before them and their seat was soft in the curious way of
warm stone where they could spy down over the gardens his mother
and father built together; had started with the base of the lilacs and
peony beds and clump almost a thicket now of ancient Siberian iris
and the deep beds of regenerating hollyhocks and tulips and daffo-
dils but then had gone on to build stone walls and terraces and, without tearing out any of the old, had added to what was there, pruning
back the old tea and cabbage roses and transplanting some so there
was a rose garden and adding new varieties as they went. And bringing
in clumps of the more passive wildflowers to dot along the walls,
the field daisies and black-eyed Susans, and where the ground ran
moist along a seep the beds of ferns and wild columbines and even
a careful placing of red trillium. As well as another thirty or forty
flowers that Hewitt either remembered the names of when they
bloomed or failing that could bend low and still make out his mother's
cursive script of black paint on white placards the size of playing cards.
It was a fine garden. From earliest snowdrops and crocus and on
through the summer until the frosts of fall had killed all but the asters and butterfly plants a full beauty of flowers surrounded the house
—the sort of beauty that demanded to be walked through and observed each day for the changes and to note the short-blooming
plants, the rippling rises and falls of color. For Hewitt the gardens
were equal parts beauty and fond melancholy; while he tended them
best he could it was more in the sense of memorial than as an active
partner—the couple who had worked together shaping this struc-
tured land and stone and growing ever-changing beauty owned it
always. For it took two working in disagreement and glory and frustration and everlasting love to accomplish that.

Far above to the east the first tendril clouds were turning as the
westering sun struck that ridge.

Jessica said. "Oh my. This is so beautiful."

"Well," Hewitt said. "We don't have much of a growing season compared I guess with Mississippi but when summer does come it's a veritable explosion. It's a weird place to live in a way because you spend so much of the year in cold either coming, staying or going. And then there's three four months where the earth bursts to generate. Like every growing thing knows its time is short."

She turned on the bench, one lock of dark hair a thick just-curl down her forehead, and said, "Did you do all this Hewitt?"

He didn't laugh. The garden around and below was rising and falling in waves of color that brightened and dipped as the sun rode across the flowers and shrubbery. "My mother and father made this. I do my best to keep it up."

She sat quiet. The sun was on its slow June track as the earth turned. Where the shadows fell cool air was beginning to rise. "My oh my," she said. "They certainly loved each other, didn't they?"

When he spoke it was no simple statement but a full intractable testimony. "They adored each other."

She put a hand on his knee and said, "What happened?" Her voice near tender as his own.

He looked off. The little clouds over the far ridge were gone to blue and black. He did not look at her but in the last of the golden light seeping over them said, "My father died. Mother held out here a couple years and then finally found a reason to leave. Which I think now she had to do once he was dead. She was just waiting for that reason."

"What was it?"

"Me. I was what happened."

He thought she was going to ask what had happened to him. The details of what happened to him. Instead she said, "He was truly a good painter, wasn't he? Maybe even a great painter."

Hewitt looked off. The shadows were denser, lengthening, but light remained over the land. He said, "There's people with opinions all over the map. I never knew how he felt about it himself. He didn't talk about it. But it was a thing he had to do. I knew that much as a child and know it even better now."

"Because you do it too."

He faced her and his voice near shredded said, "I do what I do because it's all I can."

She blinked, looked away and looked back. Her voice changed, a tremble. She said, "It sure is peaceful here. Doesn't that help?"

Without knowing it he'd tiptoed right up to the edge of his own emotional fault line on all fronts and her tone more than her words snapped inside him and he said, "I don't know. Sometimes." As he spoke a fragment of doubt or worry or pain came over her face and again without any idea beforehand he said, "No, you're right. I lose sight of it. And I don't know anything about where you came from or where you're going but it seems a few more days here wouldn't do you any harm. Unless there's some reason I shouldn't offer it."

She took her hand away from his knee. "What do you want, Hewitt? A list of where I've been the last ten years? Shit Hewitt, you want it, I can tell you what it's like. Some things are always the same—there's always the others. They all live off in the edges, the bits of woods or the underpass or sometimes in shelters but you try to avoid those. And there's always a big dog guy who's fucked-up but has a rap about this is the only true right way to live. Like he chose it or something. Nobody ever chooses. It's easy to get in and hard to get out. And there is always cops and if you've really picked a bad place people from social services out tracking you down to give you help which is not the kind of help you want. Night is better than day. Even if at night it's all drugs and boosting, all crack and heroin and big-ass boys who will work you over even quicker than the cops to try and get you to do what they want which is the only time you get crazy and that stops em fast. Even those boys know that shit's no good for their needs. Women strung out on whatever gets them through the night because getting through the night is what it's all about. But there are also the ones who walk up and talk five seconds and are gone and they're the ones you can trust—they tell you where to go and where not, they tell you which fast-food dives will tolerate you for hours on the price of a cup of coffee or where it's best to try to sleep. It's fucked up because there is almost no one you can trust but you got to trust someone so you pick and take a chance. The sad thing is mostly you can't trust the women. Because most are already sucked down and terrified of some man. The worst time is the couple hours before dawn. It's when you're the most cold and tired and all the sudden the traffic picks up with men on their way to work and they roll those trucks alongside you and say 'Hey girl' and I know what they want and I've been up all night trying to make sure nobody steals my car and trying to figure out a new place to park it the next night and then there's twenty bucks all yours to suck a dick and I'm already days dead on my feet and I think Leave me alone shithead and if I'm lucky enough to be working I get a meal later that day or night at work so I skip lunch. If I eat some breakfast I can move my car to all-day parking and cover up in the backseat so no one knows I'm there and sleep until it's time for work and then go to the Y for a shower. And maybe if I'm lucky there's a convenience store clerk who'll like me enough and knows I'm not a crackhead hooker and they'll maybe give me a hot dog. And a packet of mustard to spread on the bun and I'll walk out of there at four in the morning feeling like I'm doing alright. All the while patting my jeans pocket to make sure the keys are still there and back behind to check my license and feeling every step the three twenties folded tight under the lining of my shoe and hoping I didn't fuck up and park where they'd tow my car and the hot dog has slicked enough grease into that bread so I can eat it walking along thinking I just have to last a couple more hours but at least I'm eating a hot dog and swearing I'll never eat that kind of shit again, someday, and then some guy in a truck rolls slow alongside and says 'Hey girl' and I'm faced with that all over again. And all the time knowing this is not what I should be doing but it's all I can do. It's all I can do."

She hadn't moved although her body was arched tight and her eyes electric and furious. She said, "You know what I mean? Hewitt? You ever been down *that* road?"

He was silent.

After a bit of time she said, "What other questions do you have?"

When he was quiet she said, "You can change your mind you know."

He finally said, "I've seen a few mornings where a hot dog would've been mighty welcome."

He rose from the cooling stone. She had to be cold. She stood also and they were standing close. Twilight draining around them. Less than a foot apart. Her eyes were clear again and she reached up and touched his cheek with one finger and said, "I'm freezing my butt here. Could we go inside now?"

Then they were holding on to each other, hands on elbows, eyes wide. Hewitt said, "Close your eyes."

"What?"

"Close your eyes tight. Don't open them until I tell you."

"Where're you leading me?"

"Nowhere. Will you close your fucking eyes?"

She did. He waited. The western low sky was pale bright blue and the sky above that was a void. And as he gazed at the void one and then another star appeared. But look down around and there was plenty of light still pooled around the ground. Caught in the flower beds and blooms.

He said, "Open now."

She did.

He waited and then said, "Can you see more than before?"

"I be damned." She still held his arm. "The flowers are glowing."

"Good," he said. "Let's get to the house."

# Three

They entered into days of a slender domesticity. Hewitt continued to cook suppers but the rest of their meals each took when they wanted. Jessica was a sleeper, often not rising until midmorning. At first Hewitt thought this was a womanly thing—his greatest experience with women had been in those years when it seemed all women could hardly be roused from bed. After a couple of days he realized that she was depleted to full exhaustion. All she had told him seemed worth weeks of rest.

Meanwhile he was caught in a splurge of energy, demanding that he set things right about the place. Every June he went through the same ritual. It might after all prove to be the summer his mother or sister and her family or, God bless them, all, might decide to visit. It had been half a dozen years since any had come north for a spot of New England summer. The last visit with Beth and her husband and daughter had been more or less a disaster. And his fault although he'd chosen not to acknowledge this but continued with the yearly round of birthday cards and Christmas gifts, all of which Beth herself, regardless of the recipients, chose to answer. Beth had manners. Beth was a proper citizen. Beth was a colossal pain in the ass. He suspected he was at least partly responsible for her deliberate decision to have only one child. As if her younger brother was an outstanding example of the risk involved. At least his mother had a sense of humor. Although she too tended to stay away but in this case Hewitt had sympathy; it was not himself she wished to avoid as much as the place itself.

The work he'd done on the flower beds was just a beginning and so he worked with wheelbarrow and trowel and hand cultivator to clear the weeds and loosen the soil and transplant a few things that would bear the strain. And sometimes just sit somewhere in the garden and watch around him. In a small nook with a circle of slates perhaps ten feet in diameter with a two-foot opening in the center sprang the most magnificent bleeding heart he'd ever seen, the circle hidden by other plantings on the terrace above and the one below, the pods of white and crimson flowers a treasure available only to those who searched. In the same hidden glade but out where the sun struck fully was another discovery: a stub of granite post buried with an old grindstone resting atop. The granite worked up to a point as if his father had possessed a swage expressly built for stone, so the granite post fit through the grindstone opening as tight and smooth as if they came out of the ground that way. Atop this was an old sundial his father had found somewhere. The bronze base was warped and the crescent wobbly so the dial was never close to accurate time. Which Hewitt was sure had been his father's intent.

One of those afternoons she changed the oil on her Bug, backing onto a pair of hemlock planks up on concrete blocks. Hewitt showed her where the tools and oil were. Then he sat back and watched. They'd been eating his lunch and her breakfast of peanut butter sandwiches when he suggested it might be a good time to get the work done. Not mentioning he'd like the car out of the driveway and maybe tucked under the ell shed extending out from the side of the barn. Jessica had strawberry jam on her cheek and she wiped it with the back of her hand and told him she'd like to do that if he'd show her his tools. But she wanted to do it herself.

He thought at first it was that taint of mistrust going on, so told her that was fine. But perched on the old milk can where the used oil would be saved, he watched her. Once she went to work he felt like the usual asshole guy who thinks a woman can't do a thing with a machine, a notion his female friends and neighbors had long since disabused him of. She put tools back where she'd found them. She drained the oil from car to trough to can with slow patience so those last drips came. When she was done she kicked dirt to cover the few spots dripped.

He thought perhaps she was lighter, her smiles easier come by. But couldn't say for sure. It wasn't his job to track her. But still it was a strange pleasure to go to sleep at night knowing someone was down the hall in their own room thinking their own thoughts or dreaming their own dreams.

And Hewitt Pearce felt something he could only guess was what a father would feel. One night late stood at his window and looked out at the star and moon lit hillside and wondered if this was his daughter. Not one bred and born but the closest he would get. Some remote undefined rough compensation for that child never born.

Jessica was a substitute for no one.

THREE DAYS ALONG, Bill Potwin showed up middle of the day to cut hay. Hewitt met him in the dooryard and Potwin killed the big John Deere, reared back in his seat and propped one foot atop the fender.

"Bill." Hewitt nodded a greeting.

Potwin said, "You doing, Hewitt?"

"A bit like always."

Potwin nodded. "Well now," he said. "June's come off nice so far, ain't she?"

Hewitt nodded. Bill's eyes traveled the yard even as he pretended to look at Hewitt. He said, "Thought with the weather I'd get to your hay this year fore it gets all stemmy. Got a lady, horse lady up to Corinth, wants some. Told me she wanted rowen and I sat looking at her till she piped up she'd heard I was the feller to call. Shoot, I ain't gonna sell her my milk hay. The hay's bright and leafy she'll be happy. Won't know the difference. And hear this. She wants six hundred bales."

Hewitt said, "That right?"

Bill shook his head. "She idn't got but two horses. And real good summer pasture. It's them great big Dutch or German horses and I imagine they'll take a bit of fuel. But Christ. She feeds that all out they'll look like they got foals to drop come May. But I didn't tell her that."

Hewitt shook his head. "Not your job."

Bill leaned now and spat a line of tobacco juice. "She only asked at the end how much a bale. I said, In the barn? And she looked at me like she was wondering did I expect her to do it. So I told her three and a half. Didn't bat a eye. Got her checkbook out and I said Now hold on. Wait until the bales is at least in the barn. I think I'd of passed out she handed me a check for over two thousand dollars right then."

Hewitt said, "You might of took it. She could be asking around."

"Naw," said Bill. "She's got more important things to do. Ride them big friggin buggers every day. All she wants is to see the hay in the barn. Makes me think. I likely could've said four."

"Well Bill, you're close enough to a price she'll tolerate, she thinks it's special quality. So you're getting rich off my hay now."

"Do it yourself, Hewitt."

"Hell no. I'm glad for you."

Now Potwin turned his head away to look directly at the Volkswagen parked next to the Farmall. Taking his time registering the car but also the paint job. A minor theatrical that Hewitt waited through.

Potwin locked back. "Got yourself a new car?"

"Nope."

"They still got your license?"

"For good I guess. I gave up keeping track. I still got my hunting license."

"Don't be out jacking deer or they'll take that too."

Another stream of juice shot from Bill's mouth. This one landing an inch closer to Hewitt than the first, still feet away, a gesture too small for most to notice. Potwin said, "Saw Rog Bolton down to the store the other evening. He's working that job up to Tripp Hill, fancy cabinets in the kitchen and such. Said he saw a girl out along here that afternoon. He was just picking up his beer."

"That so? He hadn't already had a couple riding down?"

"Come on now, Hewitt. It idn't gonna stay a secret for long. You finally got a new lady friend."

Hewitt made a small frown, his brain an insane chipmunk. The truth of her, at least what he knew, was too odd for general circulation, especially the way truth as it circulates becomes both less and more than how it started. And he knew Bill Potwin had, in studying the car, noted the exotic plates.

He said, "Bill. I'd appreciate if this stayed between us." Knowing this would get the story spread as fast as possible and perhaps with that speed kill the worst of the speculation. He went on. "You remember the Kimballs?"

Bill squinted. "Those the people summered at the Dodge place when we were kids?"

"Middle of the sixties, Bill. But yup. And the girl, the youngest one, Dana, she and I were friends."

Bill was still turned back, thinking. "Those Dodges, they was partners with your great-grandfather and them, wasn't they?"

Hewitt said, "That's right. The lumberyards and the sawmill and such."

"They're all gone now. Cept for the cemetery."

"When the bobbin business petered out I think what was left of them took their money and went west somewhere. Indiana, Iowa, somewhere like that. But—"

"I recollect those Kimballs now. He wore sneakers without any socks. She was an eyeful of a woman. From Rhode Island, wasn't they?"

"He was some sort of machine tool manufacturer. But anyway—"

"So their daughter was your little girlfriend, that what you're telling me?"

"I'd say she was the first girl I kissed but your niece Amber got me first."

"We all know that. What's it got to do with a Mississippi Beetle painted like a merry-go-round?"

"Well, some years ago that girl Dana Kimball and her husband came through to see the leaves and stopped and we all hit it off. And kept in touch. Nothing much, Christmas cards and such." Hewitt paused but was too deeply into what was unrolling to let it stop. "He's a professor at some university down there. Near Jackson, I think."

"Got married in a fever. Hotter'n a pepper sprout."

Hewitt blinked, thought Johnny Cash and laughed. Then was quickly sober. "So this girl, Jessica. She's their daughter. Been going through a pretty rough patch in her life and her family knows I've had some tough times myself. So they called and asked could she stay with me a bit. She needed to get out of where she was. Maybe she got left at the altar, as they say. And so she's here for a week or so. She's young. Young take those things hard sometimes. You know what I mean, Bill?"

Bill looked thoughtful. For quite a time. Hewitt was sweating and thinking Bill wasn't buying any of it. About the time Hewitt registered that Bill was looking beyond, toward the house, Bill said, "I guess here she comes now."

Hewitt turned and Jesus Christ here she came. In soft tan leather boots to just below her knees and a sleeveless dress of thin copper-colored material that ended just inches above her knees. The dress was thin and so flowed and worked itself against her forward motion. With the boots and the color of the dress against her white skin and her black hair brushed out if not otherwise arranged she was still, for the time and place, something stepped out of the television or the pages of a magazine.

She walked right past Hewitt to the tractor where she leaned up tiptoe, extending her arm and it seemed to Hewitt her whole body projected slightly toward Bill Potwin. Hewitt was without words.

Jessica said, "Hey." It seemed at the moment that the gravel and accent of her voice intensified. "I'm Jessica Kress from Water Valley, Mississippi. I never once thought the North could be as pretty as this. I always thought it wasn't a thing but cities. But this certainly is beautiful country. So cool and lovely for June."

Bill Potwin sat on his tractor looking down at her. He rubbed the several days' stubble on his chin. Then dropped his hand long enough to touch hers and took it away again. And said, "Jessica. That's a pretty name."

She shrugged. "My mama had so much imagination she named me after a song."

Potwin seemed to roll this information around his mouth. Hewitt guessed he needed to spit from his chew but wasn't about to. Bill said, "And Hewitt, now he's an old friend of your mother."

She'd taken her arm back to her side but shifted a hip which the boot accentuated. "Oh my yes. I can't ever remember not hearing about Hewitt."

Hewitt thought That was good—she didn't flinch.

Potwin said, "I guess this hot we got here idn't anything you're not used too." Getting comfortable looking at her.

And Jessica said, "Oh Lord no. This time of year where I come from hot is like being naked and rolled up in a boiled blanket." She waited for Bill Potwin to absorb that image and added, "And that's nighttime."

Bill leaned back harder against his seat and looked up the hillside to the fields of waiting hay, flowing in patterns as the breeze moved through. He hawked his juice off the far side of the tractor and looked back at her. He said, "Well missy. I got to go cut some hay. But this weather holds a couple days from now I'll be baling. I like to bale onto a wagon. I need someone who can make a load. If you got long pants and want to work I'd be happy to hire you. I'd show you how it's done."

She looked off, appearing to study the haybine although from where Hewitt stood he could see her eyes darting. Then in a brave disdainful voice she said to Bill, "I've worked plenty."

"Well now." Potwin briefly scrutinized Hewitt. "It depends on what the weather does. You might not get much warning."

Jessica said, "Right now mostly I'm not hard to find."

Bill looked at Hewitt. Who did not move. Nor let his face change at all. Bill nodded then and threw high the throttle and fired the Deere and puffs of diesel smoke spouted from the stack and lifted skyward. Bill shouted something down to Jessica. Then put the tractor in gear and it and the haybine went up the hill.

Jessica turned to Hewitt and said, "What did he say?"

He now was free to study her up and down. He said, "Why did you do that?"

She was quick. "I can't hide, Hewitt. So I figured the least I can do is distract them a little."

"I'd say you did that just fine."

She looked at him a disconcerting while. Then said, "Old men are the saddest thing."

He wasn't going to let her off so easy. He said, "For a girl trying to stay hidden you can sure put it out there."

"It's sex and dreams, Hewitt. Young girls and old men. Me, I'm just waiting for that happy day when I'll be a ugly old woman."

He was having enough difficulty with her transformation, as well as his own unrolling spewed story. He hoped it wouldn't come back to bite him in the ass. And it was useless to try and explain to her certain women as well as men grew more desirable with age.

She was no longer looking at him. But up the hill where out of sight they could hear the rhythm of the tractor and the chunk chunk chunk of the mower spitting swathes of hay behind it.

Then she turned back to Hewitt and said, "What was it he said? As he was revving up and leaving?"

Hewitt looked at her. She shot her eyebrows and held his gaze.

Hewitt said, "He said if you want to stack hay, you need to get some gloves." Leaving off "for those pretty little hands."

She shook her head and said, "They always want to make you spend money on something, don't they?"

Hewitt ignored this. He said, "I've got some you could use. But I think he was tossing out a little test to see how you'd take it. Bill always uses a kicker on his baler and bales into high-sided wagons. Not the sort of deal where you stack the load but let it just pile up." Wondering if he was right, wondering if Potwin was thinking about a nice tightly stacked load. Kicker loads always had a fair number of bent and broken bales. Not the kind you'd get three and a half dollars apiece for. It wasn't his worry. If Bill Potwin could talk Jessica into doing the job the work might be good for her.

"I'm going into town," she said. "Anything I can pick up?"

"Town?" he repeated, nerved up high just like that.

"Lympus?" she said. "I drove through there the night I ended up on your hillside. Isn't that the name?"

He said, "Not much to Lympus anymore. The post office. A store of sorts, a gas station with some groceries and junk food and beer. You could get your fishing license there, buy nightcrawlers too. That's about it."

"Sound's fine," she said. "It's just a couple miles down the road isn't it?"

"Jessica, and I'm not being nosy, but I can't imagine what you'd need there I probably don't already have." He still didn't know her well enough to guess when or what might set her off as she'd been three days ago. And within this was a confusion, of wanting to keep her as much to himself as he could, at least for the time being.

"You are too being nosy. I want to buy one of those phone cards."

"Oh hell," he said. "Unless you're going to call Spain and talk a couple hours you can use the phone in the house."

"What do you think? Am I overdressed for downtown Lympus?"

He smiled despite himself. "They'll notice you."

"That's alright. They'd notice me anyway. And thanks but I'd as soon make my calls in private."

"I wasn't planning on listening in." Guessing she didn't want the record of her calls on his phone bill.

She nodded and said, "Well then, do you have any tampons?" A slow smirk of pleasure twitching the corners of her mouth. She went on, "And I'm the crazy daughter of an old friend of yours, is that the story?"

He shook his head. "Going through a bit of hard time. Your fictional mother came up here a couple summers a long time ago. Dana Kimball. But there's hardly anybody who remembers her. Nothing anybody's going to grill you about." Then because he couldn't help himself he added, "You can buy lightweight leather work gloves at the store that would fit you. Mine would be too big and you'd end up with worse blisters than no gloves at all."

"What are you talking about?"

"I thought you were going to help Bill Potwin put up hay."

She studied him a bit. She had the Volkswagen key out and was jingling it in one palm. She said, "Like I told you Hewitt. My boobs are not my eyes. I got no time for a fool thinks otherwise. Old Bill's going to have to get along without me." And she walked over and smacked an almost cartoon kiss on his cheek and walked on toward the shed. He watched her go. Her shoulders dropped into the length of her back and the dress drew against her hips and tightened over her ass as she walked. Abruptly she spun and dropped into a movie gunfighter crouch and pointed a finger pistol at him and said, "You are so busted."

Hewitt grinned at her. He said, "It's biology is all it is Jessica."

"No," she said. "Biology is a dissected frog." She opened the door of the Bug and then said, "Lust is not a dissected frog. It's a much uglier thing."

"I do believe," Hewitt said, "there's a strong distinction between the appreciation of beauty and lust." As she stepped down into the little car. She started it and drove it out into the yard and pulled along-side him. Her window already cranked down. She had the trace of a grin again. She said, "I'm a frog, Hewitt. And don't you forget it. Or I'll tell my mama you're a dirty old man."

And she pressed hard the gas and dropped into second and spun a plume of dust down the drive and he could see the brake lights flash through the dust as she came to the road and then she was out onto the blacktop and gone.

So Jessica was down to Lympus. A good thing Hewitt decided. Even if she were to stay only a few more days, better to let his neigh-bors meet and learn something of her. The phone card nagged. He didn't care really who she was calling. But had a glimmer of fear a handful of people met in her wayward trek might be alerted to a good place to come to. He didn't think she'd do such a thing. But admitted he could not say for sure. He was disposed toward her but didn't know the first thing about her.

So he went strident with purpose down into the forge. To keep himself busy and not worry. He stirred the dead fire and pulled out a handful of clinkers and arranged the old coal with some new in a well and crumpled a single sheet of newspaper and struck a match to it. Burned that off and ignored the edges of coal showing lines of orange—the first sheet was to warm the chimney—and then wadded paper again and pulled the coal closer and fired it. This time waiting and watch-ing for the right moment for a light puff from the hand-cranked bel-lows and watched and cranked again. There were jets of smoke and the chimney caught them and they rode up out of sight and the fire was lit. Now a matter of waiting for a hot working fire. Coal trans-formed to coke. Unsure what he'd do this day. He hadn't yet looked at the huge gates.

Sometime later that afternoon he heard Bill come down the hill and idle briefly in the farmyard but Hewitt did not come forth from the forge. By then he was working. He'd rifled through the stack of sketches for the gate and didn't like any of the original ideas for how to fill the slender circles within the heavier woven straps. The main structure, the interwoven flattened and hammer-worked straps had been a design stolen from an accident. The autumn before he'd been in the carriage barn and his work boot came down hard upon an egg basket, a beauty at least a century old. Woven from inch-wide strips of ash split thin and soaked for pliability, it crushed and flattened under the heavy boot. And even while he was mourning the loss he was struck by the way the splintered basket did not fall apart but spread, the ash splits warped from the long tight weaving but opening as if a fan, a latticework holding a vestige of its old texture suggesting a new form—the geometry contained in the weaving, now set free but indelibly marked.

So he returned to that original notion. Staring and squinting at the gates he saw immediately that the quarter-inch round stock he'd made circles from was the beginning of where he'd gone wrong. Those circles were not meant to hold anything and so broke the symmetry of the design. He spent the afternoon with a welding torch and a cold chisel and fine double-faced hammer, heating through the welds and tapping them free, swiftly using the cold chisel to remove traces of the weld from the flat bars as the circles fell away. He felt no remorse in undoing what had taken weeks of work—if you didn't have the patience to undo what was not right you shouldn't try to make anything. Not even a plank stand to nail a mailbox on a post.

It was dusk when he finished. Thirty-two iron rings were neatly stacked and the gates were upright again, side by side, all beads and needles of the welding gone, filed off with a half round. He'd switched on the pair of adjustable floodlights overhead but could still see the pale twilit sky out the northern window lights. It was warm in the forge but not hot—he'd not ended up using the hearth so the fire had burned itself down, warmed the bricks and died away. For a time he sat on the bigger of the anvils. Not trying to figure a thing out. Just being there.

He looked again at the gates and again the pile of circles.

Tucked under the main workbench was a series of small deep drawers. Not something he had made but had come with the hemlock bench from Albert Farrell all those years ago. He pulled open the drawer under the bench vise. From the back he pulled out a carton of horseshoe nails, the cardboard softened with age and the blue lettering all but illegible. He removed a small stone pipe and an old metal screw top can that once held an assortment of cotter pins. He unscrewed the top and lifted out a tightly packed flowerbud half the size of his thumbnail and crushed it slightly as he placed it in the pipe. And sat on the anvil and smoked the pipe down. It was a year old but Jesus give a farmer a seed and within a couple of years he'd know what he was doing. Especially if he was motivated.

He shut off the lights and stood a moment. There was more light now in those northern windows. He went up the stairs and out into the evening. The softening glow gone from the sun but not the land. And within this came floating down the crisp sweet smell of the new-cut hay.

The house was dark. And he looked but already knew that Jessica was not back, the Volkswagen nowhere in sight.

Twenty feet on toward the house he stopped. He paused and tipped back his head and studied the big elm behind the house, a risen thin-leafed crown. One of the last elms. So isolated as to almost be safe. He could draw a metaphor from that but decided against it. Thrust his hands deep into his jeans and rocked foot to foot. Trying to discern if it was true insight or simply an easy solution. Finally there was only one way to find out.

He went back to the smithy and nursed the hand crank until orange appeared deep in the coals and pumped the foot bellows twice and sat back to wait. The fire came up fast, deep and hot. Good bituminous coal holds a fire. He did not need to measure a thing but took up one of the circles and placed it into the fire and pumped again the bellows and waited. When the metal was past orange but not quite cherry he lifted it quickly with tongs and held it upright on the anvil and beat the circle into an oval. He turned and tapped and reheated and tapped again and then cooled it in the brine. Lifted it and laid it atop the fire long enough to only warm and rubbed it down with a cloth crimped and dried with linseed oil and the oil went onto the warm surface and the cloth softened under his hand as he stood polishing. Then left the oval on top of the bench without even trying it against the gate.

He shut things down again and went out into full dark. He'd walked this so many times it didn't matter there was no light in the house. But in the dark he looked once again, already knowing the answer. Her car was not in the yard anywhere and was not in the cavern of the shed. So he went on. He was hungry.

Jessica would have to take care of herself. Which she'd done before. Without thinking too much about it, he hoped she was doing that now.

And on the bench in the smithy behind him was an oval. Which would not fit, he knew, but was the right idea. Two rows of ovals across the gates. Tips up, bellies down. The round stock would be flattened slightly, smoothly, all the way round. So the eggs would blend with the whole but retain the essential quality of an egg. Which was an unblemished thing.

The rows of eggs would make the gate complete.

The best things were always a mystery. But a mystery only worked if there was a grand design behind it. He and God understood each other. It had happened too many times for him to doubt. And, he reminded both himself and God, if he was wrong, who would know?

He drank a beer while chopped bacon slowly cooked and then broke three eggs into the pan, sprinkled them with diced scallions and a handful of grated hunter's cheddar, eight doses of Tabasco, salt and pepper. Stirred this slowly over low heat so the cheese melted into the eggs and the eggs gathered in light curds and he tipped this out onto a plate, rinsed out the iron skillet, set it back on the warm rangetop to dry and sat to eat. He had another beer with supper. As he ate the scheme and design for the gates fell fully into place. Along with the open ovals he'd hot-forge four solid iron eggs from heavier round stock—no mean trick but the job of crafting solid eggs from raw bar, the eggs perfect and unblemished, all by hammerwork stirred that edge of challenge. Two for the top of each gate, one on the inner and the other on the outer of the highest upright rods. So the iron eggs would appear to balance atop the points.

He sat in the low glow of light from the kitchen for a time. The house was very quiet and familiar but there was also the sudden and strange sense of it being empty. He wondered where Jessica was, if he'd see her again. He wouldn't let himself worry about her—there was no indication whatsoever that anyone in the world worrying about another person had ever once had any effect. Not to confuse worry with action but then for action you have to have direction and Hewitt was without direction as far as Jessica was concerned.

SOMETIME AROUND THE end of the day that his father died and the beginning of the next Hewitt sat with his mother at the small table in the locked room in the basement. It was no accident Mary Margaret had pressed Hewitt to read the will before Beth arrived. All was straightforward enough, with assets and insurance policies intact.

Then there was the codicil on a separate sheet of paper, the two short lines addressed only to Hewitt and his mother.

He'd looked up from the will and said, "Why's he leave Beth out of this part? It doesn't seem right."

Mary Margaret Pearce poured out a great sigh, one that moved her entire upper body. She said, "There's no earthly need for her to know any of this. We must trust your father's wisdom, Hewitt. By the time he wrote this out, he knew her well, and knew what she might make of it. There's damage enough as it is. It's going to be hard enough to convince her why he chose to leave the paintings to you. Although she'll be well pleased with the money, I suspect."

"Mother."

She held up her hand. "As I said, I love her as a mother loves a daughter. With clear eyes."

"Alright. But the sugarhouse?"

Now Mary Margaret looked down where her hands were turning in her lap. Hewitt waited. When she finally looked up she was wet-faced and tears ran silent from both eyes. "Oh," she said and caught her breath "Oh isn't it just like him Hewitt. You know it's no accident it's raining this night."

He was silent. Taking in this suggestion of how great she believed his father's powers not only had been but remained. It was the grief of deep love.

He stood and went behind her and held her shoulders, kneading gently, feeling those strong small shoulders suddenly gone weak and knobby. As her son he'd not until this night had to comfort his mother. Quietly he said, "You want to burn it now? Tonight?"

She rocked against the pressure of his hands, just the right amount of love in touch she could tolerate from another human, son or not. After a bit she said, "No, no. I'll call Robert Dutton and tell him what we plan for first light and see if, barring a true emergency, he could have a truck and small crew on hand. He wants the sugarhouse burned, we'll burn it. But I won't be looked on as a crazed widow." And she craned her head up to look at her son. "Or perhaps a crazed widow but one had enough sense to have the fire department boys on hand."

She stood from under his hands and said, "Now lock this place tight and upstairs we go. There's a story about your father you need to know."

"There's more?"

She looked at him and said, "There's always more."

Upstairs they sat with glasses of wine as the steady autumn rain watered their reflections in the windows.

"You remember your grandmother?" Mary Margaret asked.

Hewitt was thinking about Emily, now driving through the night to be with him. After a moment he said, "I think I do. I know she

93

was here some when I was little but, Mother, I can't recall her face. I remember *something* of her. A sense of her being in a room or eating dinner with us. I felt uncomfortable around her. I guess just the fear of a little boy around someone I was supposed to know but didn't really. I don't think I was ever comfortable with her."

His mother studied him briefly and said, "You'd not be the first to feel that way around Lydia Pearce."

Then she said, "Although it's a curious thing about mothers; any disaster that befalls their children could've been averted if only they'd been present. And so there she was, first stuck in Holland and then evacuated to England but unable to get home for the duration of the war. And finally home just long enough to get to know her son's wife and young daughter when they were lost. It was several years before I was to meet her and she was far too fine and grand to be hostile toward me but there was a caginess about her that never went away. I think by then she'd grown wary of all the workings of the world and perhaps she had better reasons for that than some. But I'm meandering."

THOMAS PEARCE SKETCHED and sketched but threw everything away. Sometimes she'd not see him for days at a time, even after without great discussion one Sunday afternoon he moved her belongings into his studio, Thomas going out the next day while she was at work to purchase a sturdy chest of drawers and comfortable chair for her. He worked little in the studio but would always turn up, middle of the night or any time of day with his sketchpad and box of hard and soft pencils, the case with the pens and small compartments for nibs and tucked-tight bottles of ink. But if there was ever anything completed and brought home she never saw it.

The easel and paints and stretched canvases remained untouched. And he didn't talk about it or complain or voice his frustration in any way. Except the deeply brutal brooding. Her girlfriends told her she was crazy living this life lacking all signals of permanency and she

laughed and agreed with them and went on her way. The kitchen
manager of her hotel learned she was living with a man and fired her
and she told Thomas nothing of this but simply walked a dozen blocks
and found a job in another hotel with the same hours and in the interview all she said was that her husband was disabled from the war
and that was enough. And she felt less guilt over living with him without the sanction of the church than she did from this lie; not because
of the lie but the terrible truth that lay behind it. As far as she was
concerned she was married to Thomas Pearce. She was as bound to
him as any life she could imagine and in ways she couldn't articulate
even to herself lying silent in bed beside him at three o'clock in the
morning but she knew it was true.

Time to time someone from his old life would appear. She had
no idea if he saw any of these people outside the studio but doubted
it. Some were painters, obvious by the dark pigment crescents packed
snug against their cuticles, while others were harder to characterize
—well-dressed men and occasional women who made her nervous;
the conspicuous air of the solicitous about them, an attitude she disliked but Thomas seemed to meet with a suspended fatigue, as if he
understood more the people who sought him out then he did himself. During those visits she'd retreat behind the curtains into the living
quarters to wait their departure, although sometimes with the other
painters this was a long wait, with the voice of the visitor often grown
loud enough so if she could not clearly hear the words she understood the terror. And when they did depart almost always an unopened gift bottle of wine or gin or whisky was left behind, which
would disappear within days. Thomas Pearce was not drinking and
so Mary Margaret wasn't either. Only time to time as he sat looking
out the window onto the adjoining rooftops and the sliver of East
River as the light turned to night did she feel the least twinge of
something passing her by. But she'd never dream of exchanging what
she had for anything she might imagine. Even if what she had she
owned no words for.

Then in the spring of 1950 she arrived home from work one early afternoon to find a pair of serviceable used steamer trunks on the floor of the studio.

"What's this?"

"Would you take a trip with me?"

"Where to?"

"Nova Scotia. A little town on the northwest coast. For the summer."

She'd thought a long moment and then said, "Perhaps it's time we have a talk."

And he'd come to her and taken her hands and said, "That was one of the things I intended for this summer."

"And the others?" she asked.

He was pensive a moment and then said, "It's a risk. But I think if I'll ever paint again it might begin there."

She said, "And if it shouldn't happen that way? Will that change what you and I talk over?"

He looked at her a long beat of time. She heard a boat's whistle out on the river. That she would always recall as the sound of arriving and departing, never known. Then he said, "Not for me."

"Why Nova Scotia? Have you been there before?"

"No. Although it's where my father came from."

"Are you looking for family then?"

"No." He was adamant. "They'd know nothing of me and no reason to." And that was all he'd say of the matter. A few months later when they were married she learned his middle name from their marriage certificate and recalled not only the people they rented their cottage from bore that same name but the large fish processing plant and one of the mercantiles did as well.

He took only his sketchbooks and pencils and pens. She didn't question how this squared with his desire to paint again.

The village lay at the end of a long spit of land and pair of islands parallel to the northwest coast with the great Bay of Fundy just over the spine of land. The wind- and sea-stunted trees and low bushes reminded her of Ireland but other than that it was like no place she'd ever been  Their cottage was on a rise above tidal flats that the village and fishing works and docks surrounded in a horseshoe shape while at the end of the land the waters churned through the passage separating this tip from the final island. The first few days she hiked with Thomas but his concentrated silence was too great for her and she retreated to the cottage, grateful for the crate of books she'd packed. Daily she walked to market and bought fresh foodstuffs and fish and made their meals. The people were friendly and curious in their reserved way and she held herself likewise, knowing it was enough to say her husband was an artist from New York.

The first week they made small talk over meals and sat high on the ridge watching the long slow sunset and deep northern twilight and once he arrived home midafternoon in a great hurry to take her down to the bluff overlooking the passage to watch a pod of whales moving through. Each morning he set out with his rucksack of pencils and pads, a thermos of coffee and a sandwich and each afternoon he returned and said nothing of his day but she saw the color from the sun and wind coming up into his face and saw too something gaining, a newness about him and she hoped things were going well.

Evenings he'd sit at the kitchen table and work at odd-shaped pieces of driftwood he'd found, using the jackknife he sharpened pencils with and not so much carving the wood as bringing out a bit more the form already seen there. Her favorite was a rounded knobbly wide V-shaped thing bleached to a whorl of silvered wood colors and already resembling a nesting bird that he would study long before taking a small curling slice from one place or another. They'd play cards or word games and listen to the come-and-go Philco radio in its immense cabinet before going to bed.

Sometime late in the second week he began to leave much earlier in the morning and often not return until dusk and there was a curious controlled animation about him, as if he were flying a kite at the limit of its string, taut and near breaking any second. If they talked less during this time she was patient as he would sit in the evenings with a tipped distance in his eyes new or different to her.

Then Wednesday of their fourth week, as she was getting to the bottom of the crate of books and wondering if she should cautiously respond to the handful of women who'd made overtures of if not friendship than at least social niceties and realizing it had indeed been a long time since she'd had a cup of tea and biscuits afternoons and by that time confident she'd no reason to reveal or give the least tip of her nonhusband's connection to this place, that afternoon he came in early. He placed his rucksack on the table instead of setting it carefully away on the shelf over the icebox.

He said, "There's a ring belonged to my great-grandmother I'd like to see you wearing."

"Is there?" she asked. "And why would you want me to do that?"

"I'm asking you to marry me."

"Is that what it is? I'm thinking it's something more than that."

He considered her carefully and said, "We wouldn't be living in New York any longer."

"And so where would we be living? Here? Has it been that good for you?"

"Not here. But yes, it has been."

"Will you show me then?"

"In a moment. In a moment I will. But there's something else you need to know. And if you say no I understand."

She stood and walked to the window over the small sink and gazed up the hillside afire with wild blueberries and flowers she did not know. She watched a cloud dip into the spruce atop the ridge. She waited until half of it was gone and turned and said, "I've as much as lost my church for you. I'm willing to go wherever you want, although I suspect I already know that answer. But you don't want to have any more children, with me or anyone else. I already know that, Thomas Pearce.

Do you think I'm thick-skulled? Now then. That's a great promise you're asking of me, a great sacrifice and one I'll not swear to—"

He interrupted, "It's not reasonable to ask, I know that. You'd make a fine mother—"

She said, "For the moment, you're work enough. Now, what do you have to show me?"

He stood and paced about the room not looking at her. Then he stopped and studied her and his face sagged and it was the only time she came close to seeing him cry. She remained against the sink, hands laced before her.

He leaned over the table and pulled open the rucksack and drew out a sheaf of paper and spread it over the table. He looked at her backed against the sink and said, "You know I didn't bring any paint. All hope was to draw well. But last week I went down to Dorn Brothers and found a tablet of typing paper and a child's set of watercolors. Come over and see what I've done. It's awful and better than anything I've ever done. But come look."

LATER, WHEN SHE counted back she realized Beth had not been conceived there but a month later in Vermont just about the time they were married by a justice of the peace—a term she found strangely consoling, as if a more than adequate stand-in for a priest. No one from New York was present or even aware and so they stood with Lydia Pearce behind them and the town clerk as witness on a hot September day, repairing to the grand house afterward for a quiet dinner and champagne, as she twisted the gold band with its three demure and perfect diamonds, wondering briefly what ring he'd presented to Celeste in New York with Lydia in England and thought it likely had been something inexpensive, the sort of thing a very young man and woman would find all to be necessary and then Lydia made a blessing toast and Mary Margaret Pearce watched her fine husband reenter life.

★   ★   ★

99

THE TELEPHONE RANG as it had incessantly and largely ignored all evening and Mary Margaret rose to answer it, leaving Hewitt alone with the boulder of his father's death and unknown history in his lap. He was eighteen years old and his father was dead and his mother had enlisted him in her thorough undertaking of managing this death, and he knew this was wrong but believed he must trust his mother was correct in her judgment. That once more they would all step into familiar roles in the days ahead and the alternative was unimaginable. And so first glimpsed the difference between truth and compassionate deceit. Beth would be wild with her grief and his mother would be the public face of the family and Hewitt would be the rock of his father's seed and so the only place his sister might turn to hurl her grief and he would be silent.

Then headlights swept the side of the house and it could've been most anyone, any of a number of people including some who'd certainly been trying to telephone since dusk but because he was eighteen and because throughout all of this long night into morning he'd been tracking the time and miles he knew exactly who it was.

He went down the hall and past the kitchen where his mother was on the telephone and stepped into a soft raining October dark on the porch with the yard light and the dun-colored Plymouth sedan came to a stop and he went down the steps into the circle of rain-streaked light and she stood from the car, her hair falling loose and white in the light down onto her flannel shirt, her new jeans tucked into Frye boots and he went down to her and held her tightly as she tugged him even closer and she was now more than ever all of his life and he snuffled his nose through her hair down into her neck and he was alive and they stood in the rain until she breathed his name and tilted her head back. His life was in his arms, come to him and surrounding him, completing him. And the rain came down.

THERE HAD NEVER been a studio inside the house but one built into the old sugarhouse up the hill. Thomas took breakfast with them and then up the hill to work and back for lunch, then back up to work. But rare days, in all seasons he would of a whim it seemed, declare he was taking the day or the afternoon and this might be as ordinary as father and mother and children working in the gardens together or hiking up through the woods with the satchel of field guides and binoculars and small jeweler's magnifying glass. Summer afternoons they might picnic high in the old fragrant pastures already growing over with black raspberry and young cherry and alder or in winter they'd strap on snowshoes and head up into the woods, hiking high while the twilight built in the valley below and slowly rose to meet them as they descended in the pale amber light that threw shadows of blue and gold and purple in the woods around them. Beth usually needed coaxing to go along. But for Hewitt it was as if the love of his parents caused the black-eyed Susans to bloom or the crows and indigo buntings and bobolinks and drumming partridge back in the woods, the unfurling ferns beside and swarms of tadpoles within the small pools of the downhill brook—as if these things and all more came as a gift, a sideways glimpse of beauty and peace.

There were rules. The only one inviolate never ever to bother or even approach the old sugarhouse studio while their father was working. He made it easy for them. A sap bucket, rusted evenly as if made that way and with holes broken through the bottom would hang from a nail on the shut door when his father was working. Crude letters in white paint on the side of the bucket facing out declared NO.

Most other infractions were detailed at the end of the day, explanations demanded and offered, and that was that. Their father understood they already knew they had done wrong and only expected them to comprehend and verbalize their transgressions. And in this way the brother and sister learned that right and wrong were not merely a caprice of adults. But an innate understanding they held within themselves.

Which they not only might but should tap. That they should consider actions and consequences. And if Thomas Pearce was harder on

Beth it seemed to Hewitt as a child that his sister deserved it, even was responsible and seemed to know it. As he grew older he thought each had the same temper and brought it out in the other. It took much longer for him to realize how one-sided from the beginning that contest of wills had been. Hewitt in the pale June starlight with that quarter moon hiding in the trees as he sat on the Farmall before the ruins of the sugarhouse was not sure he had truly absorbed this lesson. But like all generations he'd taken the wisdom of the elders and smote it to his own needs. And produced therefore his own code. He felt quite sure if his father were alive they would quibble over fine points but not waste time on the larger outlooks. Yes he was quite sure of that. As much as you can know a man twenty and more years dead.

All that remained of the sugarhouse was the chimney and the brick arch. His father had left the structure intact as a working place, build-ing a table over the evaporator pans atop the firebox and against the solid north wall a pair of drafting tables but opening up the woodshed so he had a space for stretched canvases and shelves and tables and paints and solvents and an odd assortment of items that struck his fancy. The only windows were a single pair of six over sixes and these in the south wall which was not ideal but had never seemed to bother his father. And for many years, with not a one of his family knowing, once he began work on a canvas he brought all his sketches and studies down to the house to store in the map files. Not for any sense of the future but because once the paint began to go onto the canvas he no longer had interest or desire to view the studies. Because the painting was always a new thing, regardless of how much thought or rough ideas came first. And once that first line of paint, thick or thin or outlining went upon the canvas, the canvas owned the end result. There was no turning back. This method was not so much a secret as something he simply did not speak of. Throughout the years in Vermont he re-fused all interviews. Because he would not, most likely could not, speak of how he arrived at those layers of paint and how they built toward the closest he could come to his original, never-realized idea. It was the mystery and he was smart enough by trial if nothing else to attempt to explain.

Because there was always the risk of losing it. Not necessarily through attempted explanation but that couldn't be discounted. His father held it tight.

Hewitt sat on the tractor. It was late and he was cold and the chimney reared up straight and true among the giant sugar maples. That little moon was hidden in the hilltop, lost in the leaves, the stars and the breath he sent out as smoke toward them and whatever deeper mystery they held. Remembering the fine thoughtless almost gleeful blaze the sugarhouse threw up as it burned. He was very tired and it was late. There was work to do. There was a fucked-up girl gone missing. Or just gone. He cranked the tractor, swallowed the last stale beer from the bottle and went down the hill toward the one faint window-light of home.

FOR THREE DAYS he worked first light till dark on the gates. The first day was slow going as always but as they took their new form he could not stop. He was on fire and breathless. Jessica was receding. He missed her company, then decided he didn't. The rows of hammered ovals slowly marched across one gate, then the second. He was only another stop on her road, perhaps a bit of kindness that would linger, that might go out into the world with her. Even beaten flat the round stock was finer than the heavy woven strapping and even heavier framework. And the effect was exactly what he'd envisioned—one of physical and visual balances. Well, shit, he still missed her. The ovals set within the squares appeared delicate, almost as if they could be lifted free. His sleep was broken. The gates were in everything he thought or felt or saw. To the point that he balanced an actual egg in the pritchel hole of the smaller anvil. To look at as he worked. Not a guide so much as a counterpoint.

On the fourth morning he was done but for the four iron eggs to top the gates when he heard the car come off the road and into the

Hewitt said, "I'm going now."

No response.

He waited and then called her name.

After a bit he called again.

She took what time she needed. Then said, "Just. Leave. Me. Be." A voice filled with sorrow loaded with tears.

He paused and almost quit and then knew he could not. He said, "All right. I will. But Jessica? Is there anyone after you?"

This time there was no hesitation. He heard something striking the wall within the chamber. It could've been a stone. It could've been her head. But over it all came her cries. "No No No No No."

HE DIDN'T EVEN bother with Mississippi, guessing there was no one there he'd want to talk to. So he sat at the tiny telephone table and dialed information for Memphis. Trying to think if Memphis was one or two time zones behind. It was near six o'clock. Then informed the computerized voice that he needed to speak with an operator. A clicking and a buzz and for a moment he thought he'd been discon- nected. A woman responded.

"Help you."

This was going to take some work. Hewitt said, "Good evening, ma'am. I'm trying to find the number for a Mr. Kress."

"First name."

"I'm sorry. I don't have one."

Her sigh was audible. She said, "In the greater Memphis metro- politan area I show thirty-six listings for that name sir. Do you have an initial or street address?"

"No I don't but—"

"I can only provide two numbers per service call. I'm sorry sir."

She was going.

"Wait. Please. I know he's a lawyer. An attorney."

"I don't show yellow page listings, sir."

"Yes, ma'am," he said. "I understand that. But this is a matter of some urgency concerning his daughter."

"You should call the po-lice then."

"Ma'am? It's truly not an issue for the police."

Silence. She was guarded now. She didn't respond but didn't hang up either.

Hewitt spoke gently. "This girl, this man Kress's daughter. She's not in the sort of trouble the law could help with. In fact they could make it worse for her. She's just a disturbed young woman who sort of washed up on my door and needs more help than I can give her and I'm trying to contact her father is all. What she's told me, he's the only one might be able to help."

"If you can hold please sir." And the line went into static. But she came back quickly with the name of a law firm. Malcolm & Kress, the phone number and even the street address.

Hewitt thanked her. All she said was, "Have a nice day, sir."

The law firm of Malcolm & Kress was closed but the machine informed him he'd reached the offices of Winston Malcolm and Joseph Kress. He was gaining on his man.

Another round with information. This time the pauses and clicks of automation and then the number was read to him not once but twice at a rate an alert seven-year-old could grasp.

The man himself answered the phone. Hewitt introduced himself and began to explain where he was calling from when Joseph Kress interrupted him.

"Is this about Jessica?"

"It is."

"Are you a social worker? Or from a shelter?"

I guess so Hewitt thought. "No," he said. "She just sort of appeared about a week ago and—"

"And you want her off your hands?"

"You've been through this before, haven't you?"

"Too many times."

Hewitt turned that phrase over in his mind, wondering how a parent arrived at too many. And what that meant. Was it great fatigue or resignation or just calling it quits? He said, "I'm not try-ing to get rid of her. But what she tells me is circuitous and often contradictory."

"We all pretty much feel that way."

"Mr. Kress. I'm not a father. So I can't imagine what it must be like. But what I see, when she's fine, is a bright young woman with a quick mind and a sense of humor. I'm not trying to save her. But I don't want to do anything that would make things worse."

There came now a sigh over the line. Hewitt had an image of a man still in his suit, perhaps his coat off and tie loosened. Somewhere in the house his wife was likely preparing dinner.

"You said your name is . . . ?"

"Hewitt. Hewitt Pearce."

There was a pause, then Kress said, "Listen, Hugh." There was a pause and the distinctive crinkle of ice cubes striking the sides of a glass. Kress said, "She's got a sheet as long as your arm. Shoplifting. Vagrancy. Public nuisance. Never any drugs or violence or prostitu-tion or anything like that. A handful of dismissed things like public menace which were only brief stops on the way to the hospital. Some-times they called me and sometimes not. Four times she's been com-mitted. The first two by her mother and myself. The other two also involuntarily but by the authorities. You following me?"

"Pretty much." Maybe it was the drink. Something had changed in the man.

"She can be normal as you or me one minute and then she's gone again. I believe she can turn it on or off. Stuck in a room with a shrink she can come out an hour later with the guy swearing there's nothing wrong with her. She's been diagnosed so many times it almost seems like she's the one pulling the strings there. Don't get me wrong—I know she's around a curve from where the rest of us live. And every couple years the medical boys and girls change their minds about what's what and so she glides through one thing to another. I'm an attorney. I've seen every scam in the book. But whatever else she is, Jessica's no grifter. That doesn't mean she won't take what she can get if it's offered. Hell, we all do that."

"Maybe so." Hewitt paused. He already knew this was a dead end but was determined to ride it out. He'd learn something one way or the other. So he said, "So, what prompted me to call was we'd been getting along pretty well and I thought maybe this was a good place for her to rest. She seemed more worn out than anything else when she first showed up. But this afternoon she went up the mountain behind my place here and when I went to check on her she kind of took a potshot at me. That sorta spooked me."

"Damn. That's my fault. When it became clear she was going to stay out on the road for some amount of time nobody could guess at I gave her that goddamn gun. For self-protection. I thought I was doing the right thing. She sure as hell hasn't shot anybody, though."

"Well, she missed me."

Joseph Kress sighed. In a flat voice he said, ' I last saw her two years ago for two days. I drove to west Texas to try to help her because she asked me to. The second day we went out for lunch and she went to the bathroom and didn't come back—out the damn window and gone. Fucking disappeared on me and I wasted another day driving around cheap motel parking lots looking for that fucking car. Other times I sent her money to come home and that was that. And I've had more conversations over the phone with people trying to help her than I can count. You listening to me, Hugh?"

"I am."

There was a long pause. Then Joseph Kress said, "Look, call me. If I can help. Whatever comes up."

Hewitt held the phone hard against the side of his head. His ear was hot. He thought At least he didn't offer to send money. He said, "I will."

★　★　★

111

AFTER HE HUNG up he went out to the screened summer porch. There was still no trace, no faint smoke rise to announce her presence. There wasn't anything he could do about her; he certainly wasn't going back up the hill this evening. The phone call had offered illumination, but of all the wrong kind. It put him too dearly in mind of his own plummet and the years of despair when even his mother had finally told him, over the phone, her voice thick with tears that he had to stop calling her like this. Among the least amusing aspects of her confession was Hewitt had no memory of late-night telephone calls to her. No wonder his sister had largely bowed from his life. In fact she had declared as much. But she had called him one morning to tell him his most recent telephone call had left their mother in wild despair. And Beth would not tolerate this. Nor would she be part of it in any way. He had to gather himself. Then finished by swiping hard: How would their father look upon Hewitt's self-indulgence? "Think about it Hewitt," she said before the line went dead.

A night in the woods might do Jessica good. Whatever chased her up there didn't seem to have anything to do with him. He'd check on her in the morning.

There was a cob-smoked ham steak in the fridge and he thought half of that would be just the ticket after his day of work. He should walk out to the asparagus bed and cut the fresh stalks certainly up since his first supper with Jessica.

His hand swiped down along his front pocket to feel the weight and length of his jackknife. He walked to the screen door opening off the porch down into the yard, recalling Joseph Kress admitting he'd provided his unstable daughter with a handgun. For protection. Standing on the soft evening grass, now with the barn in sight and the swallows in their furious end-of-day feeding on insects. It was a frightening thing. Not that a man would feel he should take that step, knowing there was a deep unholy gamble involved. But more a profound sadness a girl so far off kilter lived in a world where such a choice had to be made.

He went down to the patch and worked slowly through, cutting the thicker stalks and tucking them into his shirt pocket.

He was halfway back to the house when he realized it had been days since he'd picked up his mail. Nothing would be there except bills and catalogues and other rubbish. But while the box on its post was large there was only so much the rural route carrier could stuff in. A single mother with three kids. No reason to make her life more difficult. Or his—at least a dozen times Stuart at the post office had called to remind him to empty his box. So he went out the drive on to the hardtop and lifted out the armful of mail, hugging it to the right side of his chest to not break the asparagus as he walked to the house.

Inside he spilled it all down on the kitchen table and then laid the tender spears in the clean sink. He'd noted the Bluffport, New York, paper wrapped around the mail and thought he'd page through as he ate. He took the ham wrapped in white butcher paper from the fridge and laid it on the counter, about to pull the tape free to unwrap it when he stopped and stepped slowly away, as if backing from coiled danger. After a moment he returned to the table and pulled free the paper and unfolded it so the entire front section lay flat below him. He placed his knuckles either side of the newspaper and leaned down to the lead story.

Sweet Mary Mother of God.

NUSSBAUM WAS DEAD. Emily's Dr. Martin Nussbaum was dead. According to the account near midnight his Lexus struck a cow that wandered through a broken fence on to a county road. Died of massive head and chest injuries. The article gave little more information. So little in fact Hewitt had no choice but to conclude there was more story but not to put in the paper. The blessing of the small town weekly which still, near alone in these days, regarded privacy as an essential quality of integrity. No mention of why the good doctor had been out driving at such an hour of the night, nor where he'd been traveling to or from. If he'd been at the hospital or a medical crisis this would've been mentioned. The piece largely focused on the loss to the community. His survivors. There was no comment from his wife but then why should there be?

Nussbaum was dead. Hewitt wandered back and forth across the kitchen. Dead and buried. He bent and leafed through to the obituary but this provided no information Hewitt did not already know.

He wandered. Was it possible he'd somehow wanted this? Hoped for it? No. A divorce yes. But not this. Dead and buried. Hewitt could not have precisely stated the day of the week so he got down the feed-store calendar and placed it next to the paper. Son of a bitch. Emily's husband died the night, not far from the hour, that Jessica had first driven into his life. Was buried three days later, the morning service and committal would have been the day after he and Jessica had driven into Hanover.

All things someway are connected. Jessica was disturbed and disturbing but she was no dark angel. And, however he looked at it, neither was she an impediment to any plans that might result from this tragedy dropped from the sky.

What plans?

A sudden image of himself arriving in Bluffport by bus, if such service even existed anymore, and then what? Stroll over to the home of the recent widow and present himself? As if Emily would be waiting for him?

He could send a cautious condolence note. And wait each day for the return letter in the mail. Which might or might not come. And saw clearly this could take him down again. He wasn't sure he could endure a version in his forties of what he went through in his twenties. He should be wiser. In fact he thought if anything the expansion of the years would render him less capable of surviving another episode, another hurling into the morass of self that might very well prove endless this time.

He had no idea. But his agitation was severe and growing more so as the evening ticked along. A literal ticking since the only audible sound was the steady drone of the old electric clock on the shelf over the sink, next to the AM radio of similar vintage. For farm and weather reports and the daily noontime call-in Trading Post.

He was shaking. Walking the room and shaking. Each thought that ran through his mind seemed to reach out and snag some arcane or nonsensical tag that played along as if mocking him. He felt himself suddenly dangerous. Serious slippage. The fucking clock was driving him nuts. He walked to the sink and reached a hand down under the shelf and was about to pull the plug when he thought The clock is driving me nuts?

He went to the cabinet over the sink and took down the bottle of whisky and rolled it in his hands. The seal unbroken. What better time than now? Or worse. He put the bottle back on the shelf and went to the telephone, lifted the receiver and dialed.

Eight long rings. Hewitt knew to wait. On the twelfth a voice broke into his ear.

"What."

"I need you," Hewitt said. His voice a radio wave.

The shortest of waits. Then, "Ten minutes."

Hewitt started to say Thanks but the line was dead.

WALTER BOYNTON WAS eight years older than Hewitt and so was the remote teenager with the motorcycle when Hewitt was a boy. When Walter returned from Vietnam, Hewitt looked with silent fear upon the long-haired man with his wornout fatigues and permanent sunglasses who was home only six months when his wife of five years moved out, taking their three-year-old daughter with her, moved back to Pennsylvania and then, last Hewitt had heard from Walter, on to Oregon. Hewitt stayed away from him and Walter seemed oblivious to his existence. For Hewitt then the war was not complicated but simply wrong and thus, sophomorically, fighting in it was also. At the time he'd already made up his mind to go to Canada if it ran on that long. They only became friends after the three-year disaster that began with Thomas Pearce's death, the bad next year with Emily and then the final winter after which Mary Margaret decamped for warmer climes. It was then Walter came into Hewitt's life, just showing up one afternoon and letting himself down into the forge and making small talk. He was the only person Hewitt had never thrown out for entering without an invitation. Walter lived with his grandmother who took him in after his wife and daughter left, Walter later telling Hewitt, "She was deaf so she slept right through my bad nights. My father was nervous about it, afraid I'd prowl around the house and strangle the old woman in my dreams. But I'd a never hurt anyone and my grandmother piped up and told them to mind their own business, she'd been through it with my grandfather after World War One and could do it again. That shut em up." Hewitt went a few times to have dinner with them, the old woman with her massive hearing aids seated at the end of the cherry dining room table set with the good china and lighted candles and at Walter's probing told stories of her life, wonderful tales of humor and tragedy and without being too greatly aware of it, herself at center stage and always trudging through, head high. Walter said, "I've heard em all at least a dozen times but it does her good to tell em and truth is, long after she's gone I'll hear that voice and those tales and if anything except my own cussedness saved me it was her. And not just putting a roof over my head."

When the old woman died Hewitt was, excluding great-grandchildren, the youngest person at her funeral. Hewitt remembered well the autumn weekend Walter summoned his brother and three sisters and they arrived to find all but the most simple furniture arrayed on the front lawn. Take what you want, was Walter's command. He allowed none inside the house to see what he'd reserved for himself but this didn't matter because the pile of lovely ancient pieces on the front lawn produced a near comic effect amongst his siblings. Hewitt was there. By two in the afternoon the yard was bare except for an old chair with a burst rush seat. Walter had walked over and lifted it and said, "Brian Cranmore will recane the seat for eight dollars. The chair was made around 1790." He'd looked then at Hewitt and said, "The world is full of fools." And led him inside.

He withheld enough so the house was furnished but just. And already had begun to transform the place, painting over the white plaster walls in each room according to his fancy or Hewitt suspected, some unspeakable plan. The dining room was still white—Walter had not yet coated those walls with the aluminum paper. What few people saw was the empty room off the kitchen that had once been a living room and was now heavy plank bookshelves, with a single upholstered wingchair and stacks of more books in random spirals on the floor. There was also a writing desk—a secretary jammed against one wall with an old three-legged milking stool before it as a seat. What Walter was up to in that room not even Hewitt knew.

Everyone assumed Walter had inherited enough money, along with his benefits, to live this quiet life. Perhaps he had, but the old cape village home had an extensive and complex garden in the basement. On certain days if the weather was right, despite the ventilating system that entered the furnace chimney in that same basement you could sit upstairs and smell the plants below. This was not a worry for Walter. No one came to his house uninvited. His customers were all far from the area. He wouldn't even sell to Hewitt. Although once a year he'd appear and chat and leave a small gift behind.

Walter walked in without knocking because he was already invited, with a fat spliff just lighted clamped in the side of his mouth like a comic hoodlum and without removing it let loose a burst of rich smoke into the room and said, "S'up, bro?"

Then took the bomber from his mouth and handed it to Hewitt. The small end as dry as if it had never known a mouth. Hewitt held it, looked at it, considered where it might take him which this evening was anywhere at all and handed it back.

Walter said, "Oh it's bad, huh?"

Walter laid it fire end out on the counter. Hewitt said, "I'm in a world of shit."

Walter nodded, pulled out a chair from the table and turned it around so the back was facing Hewitt, swung a leg over it and settled down, his arms folded gently over the rounded back of the chair, his chin resting on the arms. He said, "You want to tell me?"

The old part he didn't need to go into. Just the news and the absolute benumbing confusion of what to do next. If anything.

Walter listened through it all. Without moving. And sat a time after Hewitt stopped, still silent. Then he stood and retrieved the joint and fired it and in a floated cloud said, "So what's the plan?"

"I don't have a plan. Why do you think I called you?"

"To tell you what to do? I hope not."

"Fuck you. You're the only person who really understood the whole deal with Emily."

"And?"

Hewitt paused. Then said, "And you kicked my sorry ass out of the ditch. And I've got no idea what to do."

Walter squinted and said, "Not necessarily the sort of situation that will do you much good."

"I can't ignore it."

"I imagine not. So?"

"I don't know Walter. I really don't."

"Of course you do." Walter shrugged. "You held it for twenty-some years. Suddenly things have changed. What makes you think you should know tonight?" He smiled and said, "You'll have it sorted out by tomorrow afternoon."

There came a crash on the back porch and both men turned toward the door. Beyond which there was dim cursing and futile struggles with the door that opened out trying to be pushed in before it popped back—the sharp sound of wood against flesh. Jessica came into the kitchen. Across her forehead was a bright red slashmark. She was a mess, clothes wet with dew and smeared with dirt and mud and grass stains but she was upright in the kitchen and was waving the handgun back and forth, but holding it by the barrel and then stopped and drew tight to herself upon seeing Walter, the gun loose down at her side.

Who said, "Hello there." To Hewitt, "What's this?"

Hewitt walked right across to her and put one arm around her shoulders and with his other hand took the gun away like waltzing, set it on the sink drainboard, kissed Jessica on the cheek and said, "Walter. This is my friend Jessica."

To Jessica, "And this is Walter. He's an old old friend of mine."

Jessica said, "Are you alright Hewitt? I didn't hit you, did I? Damn I didn't know what I was doing—"

Hewitt said, "No, honey. I'm glad you missed. Now be polite and say hello to Walter."

Jessica looked at Walter. "I don't know you."

Walter glanced at Hewitt. Back to Jessica and said, "Did somebody throw you down a mountain?"

"It's dark out. I was in a hurry. I had a little misunderstanding with Hewitt earlier and wanted to clear it up."

"I guess that explains the gun."

She looked at Walter. "I don't mean to be rude but I really need to talk to Hewitt."

Walter said, "That's funny. Because Hewitt really needed to talk to me. I guess this is the night everybody's in a tear to talk." At the same time walking to the sink.

Walter looked at Hewitt. As he did he lifted the gun from the drainboard of the sink.

"Hey," said Jessica. "What're you doing? Put that back." She turned to Hewitt. "I got something to tell you and got all clear about it this afternoon and then was driving back and my shit fell all apart . . . I said put my gun back."

Walter ignored her, turning it over in his hands. He said, "A nasty little piece. Thirty-two caliber, cheap." He slid out the clip. "Good for sticking up a convenience store except the clerk is likely to have a better weapon. But it's your gun." And replaced it on the drainboard. Hewitt saw him pocket the clip, the deft motion of a man used to such things.

Walter turned to Hewitt and said, "I've got to get going. Walk out with me?"

"Sure." He turned to Jessica. "Settle down, Jess. It's okay, whatever it is. I'll be right back."

She picked up the fat joint. "Hewitt. I gotta talk to you. Okay if I finish this?"

"No. Can you just sit tight a moment? Have a beer or something."

"Can I take a bath? I'm wound like an eight-day clock."

"You're too young to know what an eight-day clock is. Go ahead, have a bath."

The crescent moon of a week ago was gone but the night sky was awash. Hewitt and Walter stood in the dooryard next to the 1958 Thunderbird, black with red leather seats—his only noticeable display but even this was disguised by knowledge; the car had been his grandfather's and then his grandmother's and he'd simply kept it. No local cast a second eye. Even the sheriff deputies and state troopers knew the history of the car. Walter was golden.

"What the fuck is she all about?"

Hewitt was gazing up at the night. He said, "She showed up about ten days ago. Out of the blue. She's one fucked-up girl, although sometimes she's normal as you or me."

"Not saying much."

"All I'm trying to do is help her along."

"Along to where?"

Hewitt looked at his friend and said, "I couldn't say. I got a kind hand a couple times myself."

"Don't blame me for that."

Hewitt grinned in the dark. It was quiet.

Then Walter said, "You're going to go see her." Even in the faint light his eyes were bright. He said, "You can take the Bird." And reached down and ran a hand over the rear taillight.

"Walter you know I can't drive."

"Of course you can."

"Not legally."

Walter sighed. He said, "You know, sometimes you're a real pain in the ass. I mean what, twenty-some years ago your license was suspended, right?"

"I don t know what my legal status is but let's just say I haven't gotten any letters from the state inviting me to retake the exams, and most likely be on some sort of probation with the whole deal."

"Well, it's your business. Although you risk becoming a colorful character."

"An ornery cuss."

"That would be it. But you're going to roll in out there, and when you go, you're going in style."

"Jesus, Walter."

"I trust you. If you get out there and things go to hell and you smash up the Bird I'll be pissed. But it's the right thing to do. Maybe not for Emily but certainly for you."

Quiet again for a time. Then Hewitt said, "I'm already pretty fucking nervous."

Walter reached out and took Hewitt's shoulder in a firm grip, the touch of love between men. He said, "Of course."

Hewitt said, "Then there's this other deal. The girl inside."

"Fucking her?"

"Not even close."

"The necessary friend."

"I hope. I'm trying."

Walter said, "Well don't let her stop you. Ten days is not twenty years."

"Christ there is a world of assumption in what you just said."

"That's why I'm here, buddy. Listen, I'm serious about the Bird. If you call in two hours or two days or two weeks the deal stands. And if you need someone to watch over your little orphan of the mind I can do that too."

"Walter."

"Don't even go there Hewitt. Remember who you're talking to. The one with a single ex-wife and child, my dear heart Kimberly. She'll be thirty in August. I've been kind of hoping the last ten years or so, you know? But she's going to do what she's going to do. I can't imagine she thinks much of me. But I have to hope. Hope she has some curiosity. So if you need I'll poke my head in time to time and see if I can't at least be a friend to your little roomie. She seems to like to smoke—maybe we can make peace over that. There's nothing stopping you. All right?"

Hewitt was quiet. After a bit he said, "You're an ace Walter. I'll let you know, okay?"

Walter paused too. Looked up at the night-smeared sky. Then he looked back to Hewitt and said, "So are you. So are you buddy. Just don't think too hard. Go with the gut."

"The gut," Hewitt said, "is all I have left." And turned to the house.

"Wait," Walter called. When Hewitt turned back Walter was holding out the clip from the .32. He said, "Whatever happens, I don't want her to think I stole this from her. The rest is up to you. But I'm clean."

Hewitt held the clip in his hand. It was heavier than he'd expected. He slid it into his pocket and said, "Yup. You certainly are."

Back in the house the gun was gone and he took the clip and placed it on a high shelf over the sink. The remains of the monster joint were also gone and ash was scattered over the front page of the Bluffport newspaper. So she'd read it, perhaps put together some of what his night held.

He went into the living room. From the upstairs came the fine mixed smell of steam and soap and the lavender bath soap she'd bought. All floating down the stairs. Jessica, whoever she was, invited his trust. Wanted his trust.

He sat on the couch and gazed into the darkened living room. His brain for long painful moments so full it stopped altogether, some chemical shutdown against overload or the swamping emotion and fear. He was close to weeping but would not.

With the smell of a woman bathing over him as a lovely thoughtless caul.

SHE CAME DOWN barefoot in clean black jeans and a black T-shirt and her hair wet and black-shining. "Could I drink one of your beers?"

"Sure. Hold on. I could drink one myself."

He went to the kitchen and popped the tops off two bottles and carried them back. They sat in silence for a time, both taking small sips like ladies drinking tea.

After a bit he said, "Let's get this out of the way. What was that all about this afternoon? I don't mean just the gun but disappearing for three days and then roaring in and hiding the car and all that shit."

She said, "I was over in Hanover and realized I needed to tell you something and started back here and halfway back chickened out.

"What happens is everything becomes twisted and weird. I get in the car and drive and the only thing I believe in is my bottle of water until it's half gone and then I wonder what's in the rest of it and I'm too scared to throw the fucking thing out the window. Or I'm on an interstate and the road is empty for miles and I don't know why even if it's snowing and raining all at the same time but the only thing I know is that way back in my rearview mirror is a trucker drifting along after me, thinking he's far enough back so I don't notice him. And then I'll drive really fast until I get to an exit and get off and go in and there'll be thirty or forty rigs out in the parking lot idling against the snow and cold and I walk in and every one in the place turns to look at me and each and every one smiles at me but there is no joy in their smiles, the welcome is the same as the truck that was behind me that maybe does or doesn't stop but I just go to the bathroom and pee and get a cup of coffee even while the waitress is telling me the highway's been closed down but the cash register is barking hard at me to Go go go.

"When I took off the other day it was because all the sudden I was crowded. Way crowded. You remember when we sat and the flowers were dancing? I knew then I had to go. A good man was what I thought. Who doesn't need this shit in his life. So I got out."

Hewitt took this in. Then he said, "Why'd you come back?"

"Because I had something to tell you."

Gently he said, "And what's that?"

She lifted her beer and looked at him with one eye over the top. Then she blinked and lowered the bottle and said, "Do you trust me, Hewitt?"

"Pretty much, I guess."

"Maybe this afternoon was the right time. But tonight is not." She said, "That girl Emily? That's her husband, right? The guy in the paper?"

He rolled that one around a moment and had to agree. Whatever it was, whatever trouble or secret or danger less or more, he'd had enough for the day. He said, "That's correct."

She said, "You've got enough on your mind just now. Without my little drama."

Some period of quiet. Then he said, "Hey Jessica? Promise me?"

She waited.

"No more crap with the gun. Period."

"It's as good as gone."

"Okay, then."

They sat quietly. Hewitt finished his beer and set the bottle on the floor.

Then she said, "So what're you going to do?"

He said, "I don't know. Go see her, I guess. Walter says go soon."

She nodded. "Two days," she said. "No more. You have to get used to the idea. Then just fly. Don't think it to death." She flinched. "Not quite what I meant."

"I know what you meant."

She nodded. "I mean, just fly with it, Hewitt."

"You think so?"

She shrugged. "You really won't know shit until you get there."

He took a break and went upstairs and peed. The bathroom still moist and redolent of lavender soap and damp towels and her dirty clothes on the floor. He found the formidable end of Walter's joint and lit it and carried it downstairs.

Jessica was hunched over the long rows of vinyl recordings, her head tilted down trying to read titles. "So did you bogart that joint or bring it down with you?"

He walked over and handed it to her. Her T-shirt billowed out and he saw a nipple dark as love. He said, "You find something you want to hear, put it on. I'm going to get us some water. The truth, I'd be happy with silence."

"There's no silence. It's either music or me. What do you want?" She reached up for the remains of the joint.

"I want Eric Clapton sitting in that chair over there playing acoustic blues and not saying a word. Why don't we sit quiet and light candles and mellow out. It's been a terrible hard day."

And did not wait but went for mason jars of water. And heard it before he believed it but came back into the room with three candles and a girl back up on the corner of the couch and Charlie Haden soft and low somewhere deep within the speakers. And smoke furling and curling and inviting it all out around the room. He sat on the other end of the couch and they finished the joint and Hewitt said, "After I came down the hill this afternoon I talked to your father."

Her voice extraordinarily simple she said, "You what?"

Solid but easy he repeated, "I talked to your father."

She looked down and picked at the fabric of her jeans. Hewitt waited. She finally looked back, her face gone now blank as Greek tragedy and said, "So what did Daddy have to say? Did you learn anything helpful? Do you know me better now?"

Hewitt studied her. The girl at the end of the couch. He walked all the way out the plank and jumped. "He said to let me know if there's anything he can do."

Now she looked at him. "That's what he said?"

"That's what he said."

She chewed her lip.

He was quiet. There was nothing to say.

She came down the couch like a wounded creature and wrapped herself around him and cried. This not some woeful weep but a deep racking from far within her. Hewitt held her, stroked her back. One side of her face was pressed into his shoulder, the other up against his cheek and he stroked her back and held her as she wept. He wasn't sitting in for anyone, least of all her father. He was just there and sometimes just there is as good as it gets.

# Four

In the morning he left a message for the man in Pomfret—there had been a death in the family, but the gates would be completed and installed no later than mid-July.

Jessica hiked up the hill and cleared away the branches from the VW and they drove to Hanover where he left his one summer sport coat with the two-day dry cleaners, along with a pair of slacks and two dress shirts to be pressed. He bought new socks. With the feeling he was overpreparing. He suspected he'd wear only his usual Levi or Carhartt jeans and T-shirts. But there was the faint sense, not fantasy so much as image, of Emily consenting to be taken to dinner. He also took Jessica to the Co-op and bought a sack of groceries, things she picked out.

Driving back Jessica broke his contemplation, his building apprehension. "Can I tell you a story? You've got several days to scare the shit out of yourself. Let me tell you about this man I met."

He glanced at her. She was watching him and did not take her eyes away. She'd done this before and it was impressive but disconcerting. As much to get her eyes back on the road as for any illumination she might offer, he said, "Is this somebody I might know?"

But she was peering ahead again and didn't pause for him. She said, "It was last winter. I try to stay pretty far south in winter but somehow I'd landed in Norfolk, Virginia. I was down along the waterfront, away from the harbor but where the river there, the James, comes down. I found a little patch of woods behind some kind of factory, a

127

strip of woods where nobody had bothered to put up a fence. And the building hid the woods from the main road. So you could camp out and risk a fire. I'd been there about a week and was trying to figure out how to trade food stamps I'd gotten hold of for some cash. The stores are hip to you. You can't get any real money back, not to speak of. Some coins. The rest of your change is always food stamps. Which is good if you're hungry but useless to buy gas. Which was what I wanted. To get the fuck south from there. I mean it was cold. Rain and wind off the ocean and ice over everything. And sailors everywhere. Tell you the truth it was the only time ever I thought about selling my ass. A couple tricks would have taken me all the way to Florida.

"So one night I'd found a safe place to park and was slipping around that building and getting close to the woods. I had my sleeping bag under my arm and all the sudden I saw a campfire down there. The woods were puny and I was halfway across the parking lot and I knew whoever was there was watching out too and so it seemed best to just march right in. So I did. And there was a man, an old man with about twenty layers of clothes on and a rabbit or a squirrel or maybe even a cat roasting over the fire. With thick gray waves of hair down on to his shoulders and a beard the same color stained and stuck together but even in that pale light he had the most lovely yellow cat's eyes I ever saw on a person. And he called out for me to come on next to the fire.

"I kind of stomped in and threw my sleeping bag down and told him this was my spot and he'd better scram before I kicked his ass. But he just smiled at me and told me there was room for both of us. Then goddamn he pulled a switch knife from his pocket but didn't open it and tossed it over. All the time looking at me. I didn't move. That thing was right up against my foot. My old razor, no matter how fast I was, was no match for that. Then he stretched out his right leg and dug into his trousers and came out with a regular old barlow jack-knife and held it up. Told me he'd need that back when the meat was cooked but that was the end of what he had. He laughed and said, 'Go on and kill me now girl.' I told him I expected he'd showed me maybe half of what he had and he nodded and said, 'Ain't half enough?' So I tossed his mess back to him. At that point it was clear if he was going to kill me he could do it. He kept grinning at me and those yellow eyes was lit up like candles. The sort of crinkled eyes and smile that you flat have no choice but to trust."

She went on. "He ate that meat, whatever it was. Then we shared some Southern Comfort. And he told me his story. Damn, I can still see his face. It's all stories, isn't it Hewitt?"

He nodded, watching her, intent on driving and her telling now, and said, "Go on."

"He was in the war, you know the Second World War. And married to the woman he loved. He spent three years of that war living because of her. I guess he was also lucky but the way he told it, it was waiting to get home to her that kept him alive. And you know what? The war ended and he came home. He said he was in the big parade in New York City. The next day he took the train home. Chicago. And he walked in and she was still the most beautiful woman he'd ever seen, just like he remembered her. But she had a baby. A little boy. Not even a year old. And he freaked. She tried to explain about how it happened. But nothing mattered. Because what he'd thought was keeping him alive hadn't been enough somehow for her.

"So he left. He told me some of how he spent the years since. None of it pretty. But you know what Hewitt? You know how he ended it?"

Hewitt was feeling sick to his stomach. He just waited.

"He said he couldn't forgive her but he couldn't let her go either. He said he'd have done as well to die in the war but for one thing. That best he knew she was still out there somewhere. And it didn't matter if she knew it or not. What mattered was that he did. And he believed because he did there had to be someway she knew it too. That he'd never betrayed her. That until his dying day he'd be true to her. He said he knew he should've gone back and let things be as they were. He understood all she'd needed or wanted was solace, someone to quiet her fearful heart and the boy wasn't the fault of anything. Except life itself. But by the time he learned that it was too late. He sat across that fire from me and drank the liquor and his eyes burnt into mine and he said that until he was cold she would live inside him always. He told me he knew he was a fool but had no choice. Because fool is just what's in the eyes of other people. And he laughed and poured a little of the booze on the fire so blue flames jumped and then he was serious and handed me back the bottle and thanked me for listening to him. And began to roll up in his blankets. I asked him his name. He said it didn't matter. All that mattered was he prayed he would be dead soon and released. 'She's an old woman now,' he said. 'Probably with grandchildren doting on her or ignoring her as the world works. But I'm just a crummy old bum and the last thing she'd even want to know about. So let me die,' he said. He lifted his head from the blankets and looked at me and said, 'It's an awful way to live.' Then he settled back down and within five minutes he was sleeping peaceful as if he was beside her.

"Once he was good and asleep I got my sleeping bag and went back to the Bug. The needle showed there was no gas but I drove maybe ten miles and then stopped at an all–night gas station and went in with my handful of food stamps. It was late. There was a kid behind the counter. I gathered up maybe ten dollars' worth of food and while he was ringing it up I told him a story how I had to get somewhere that night and needed gas for the car and spread out what was near a hundred bucks of food stamps. And he came out and filled the Bug and checked the oil and shit and as I was thanking him he handed me back the food stamps but as I was getting into the car he ran his hand real slow down over my ass between my legs. I gently pushed away down into the car and started it although the driver side window was open and he had both hands on the doorframe so I looked up at him and asked him to kiss me. I already had the car in gear. So he leaned in like I knew he would and I slammed my foot on the gas and was gone."

They'd come all the way back and were idling in the farmyard. It was dripping hot in the car and neither of them could look at the other.

Finally Jessica said, "I always overdo it, don't I?"

Now Hewitt looked at her. He did that for a long moment. Then said, "I wouldn't say that. No. I would not say that at all."

"Kiss my ass," she said and got out of the car and walked toward the house. He watched her go.

THREE DAYS LATER the Thunderbird was washed and waxed, the whitewalls scrubbed and the chrome polished like so much fun-house mirror.

"Jesus, Walter. Why didn't you just paint *Notice Me* on the trunk?"

Walter shook his head. "I fear for you, man. I truly do. This baby is creamy. You're going to get a lot of looks but only a citizen maintains a car like this, only a citizen takes it out on the road. Unless you do something really stupid the cops'll leave you be. Except maybe to cruise up and pass slow as they take it in, maybe give you a wave. But remember, it's a friendly wave. Smile and wave back. It comes with the territory. All you really have to worry about is the random accident that's completely beyond your control. Even there, the odds are low. People pay attention to a car like this. Nobody wants to get too close."

"That's supposed to be reassuring, right?"

"Sure. Look at me. Just pretend you've got five pounds shrink-wrapped in the trunk and drive carefully. But not too carefully. I generally run about four miles over the speed limit. Never had a problem."

"Okay. But say I do."

Walter laughed. "I'll just tell em you stole it."

"Thanks, man."

"No, seriously. Don't sweat it. I loaned you the car. I have no idea you don't have a driver's license. I just thought you were one of those green weenies who go everywhere by bike."

Hewitt was quiet a moment. Looking at the car. "You know, I appreciate this."

"What're you doing with your little urchin while off on this quest?"

"Leaving her in your care."

"Ah . . ."

"I'm serious. The official story is she's the daughter of an old friend of mine who's going through a rough patch. Beyond that she's house-sitting for me while I'm out of town on business. That's the story. And I think she'll be okay but I can't say for sure. I don't think she'd hurt herself and I think, without her exactly telling me, that she's sort of looking forward to some time alone. She's stocked with food. She should be okay."

"But."

"I'd appreciate it if you could check on her a couple times. Your jeep still running?"

Walter looked at him as if the enormous stupidity of the question was too much to bear.

Hewitt said, "So if you could swing by. And if you see any strange cars here I'd appreciate it if you came in like gas on a fire. She knows people all over the place and I'd bet a fair amount of em aren't exactly who I'd want hanging around. There's also the fact she really doesn't have a clue about my dad. She's seen the paintings but that's about it. I haven't talked about him to her. But I could see her thinking she was doing me a favor if some slick fuck showed up with a wad of cash."

"All I'm doing these days is tending my tomato plants. I'll drop by. She seems like a good shit."

Hewitt nodded. Then he said, "Walter?"

"What is it, worried man?"

"It's just, well, try to leave her be. I mean there's times when she's pretty fragile and is scared of people but wants to be comforted. I guess—"

"Hewitt, what're you trying to say to me?" Walter's eyes bright and hard.

Hewitt paused. "Nothing, man."

Walter nodded. "Go say your goodbyes. You're wasting a pretty day."

"Already done. She's settled in, cooking up some kind of lentil gruel. I was to go back in she'd think I was hovering."

"Good. Then go. And I'll walk up to the house and see if she'll give me a lift home."

"I could do that."

"Hewitt."

"Alright. Thanks Walter."

"Is nothing. Oh, one thing. On the highway keep the top up. That's what the serious boys do. Keeps the sun from fading the leather. But if you get that woman to go for a ride put it down. There's nothing like it."

TWO HOURS LATER he had gone over the spine of the Greens and was out on the four-lanes. Down I-87 to Albany and the thruway west. Then off into the Finger Lakes. Six hours total. It was great to be driving and his stomach was roiling. He had the windows down and the air rushed through the car. His hands slick on the steering wheel. Walter had been right—other drivers were polite, almost deferential, certainly in good humor just at the sight of the car. It was a juicy little machine. Even with his long absence from driving he could appreciate how it handled, how it felt. Some cars went from place to place—others were always moving and always exactly where they were and the T-Bird was one of the latter. He really had to watch his foot, watch the speedometer.

He couldn't think about Emily. He had no plan. Except to get to Bluffport and find a place to stay and maybe drive around a little. There were some places he wanted to see. He certainly was not prepared to see her this afternoon. He wanted to get his feet under him. Or at least on the ground.

He was also aware plans were fruitless when it came to other people. Things worked according to a pattern or rhythm unknowable.

He was prepared for that.

What he thought he might do, unless a wild hare got into him, would be to spend that first afternoon and evening alone. First thing, once checked in and washed up, would be to locate and visit Timothy Farrell's grave.

In his pocket was a single hand-hewn nail—a heavy one pulled from a beam in the barn and no less than two hundred years old. Not a cut nail, not a stamped nail. But a big spike with centuries-old hammer marks visible on the crown and down along the taper. Which he planned to not set on Timothy's gravestone but with the heel of his hand drive deep into the soil before the stone. Deep enough so the cemetery caretaker would mow right over it. He knew Timothy would like having this piece of simple handwork close by, even if many years late. And the other part for Hewitt was also a gift. This one to himself. Driving a mild stake into the master to assuage as much as he might his guilt.

For while he'd learned of Timothy's death he had made no effort to come. He'd wept but in those days weeping for Hewitt was near as thoughtless as another man's blowing his nose. And his reasons for his absence were good—good at the time and still good now. Except for one small fact: he'd failed. His courage had failed. And Timothy's entire life had been made from courage. Hewitt had no doubt his death had been the same.

Hewitt was near tears and screaming along the thruway beside the remains of the Erie Canal merged with the Mohawk River, with barges and tugs moving slowly and across the river a freight train running the opposite direction when he looked in his rearview and saw the New York state trooper almost tailgating but with no lights or siren and Hewitt breathed deeply, took one hand from the wheel and stroked the nail through his khaki pants and ever so slowly allowed his right foot to lessen the flow of gas to the thrumming engine. And within a mile was down to that reasonable four miles over the limit Walter advised and they continued that way, the trooper pulled back now a bit but Hewitt didn't know if this was response to his own slowing or to make room once the blue lights came on. And then he thought What the fuck, if he's going to pull me he's going to. So he lifted his right hand from the wheel and palm flat up near the rearview he waved at the man behind him. As if to thank him for drawing Hewitt's attention to the speed.

Then the trooper pulled out in the passing lane and went by as if the Bird was already parked on the roadside. Going by the cop turned and by Jesus smiled and let loose one full round of his siren.

Welcome to New York. And Hewitt had the presence of mind to smack one sharp hoot from the Bird's horn. Both thanks and a shared chuckle. Citizens.

His shirt was soaked through.

OFF THE THRUWAY, he headed south leaving the state highways almost immediately and following the grids of back roads that in this rolling land would have been near impossible to get lost on even if he didn't already know most of them by heart. This allowed him the dubious pleasure of passing by the farm where Emily had grown up and which he guessed was being run by her older brother. Or her father in partnership with that brother. The place looked much the same. Other farms had clearly changed, neater, tighter, all available land in cultivation, often the barns in better shape than the houses and each with the telltale signals of iron-wheeled tractors and implements and horse-drawn buggies of a plain gray or black boxlike design. When Hewitt had been here only the first half dozen or so Mennonite families from southern Pennsylvania had arrived in the area but the community had obviously flourished and grown. Several times he slowed behind a buggy with the incongruous bright orange triangle on the back. Although it seemed to Hewitt the striding trots of the retired standardbred horses drawing those buggies was a lovely and ample speed. Perhaps, however things fell out, when he was settled back in Vermont he should consider a horse and buggy. He wouldn't need a license for that he guessed. Not to mention the figure he'd cut.

His spirits were high. Perhaps it was his goofy sense of freedom, perhaps it was some jog of memory brought on by what lay about him or perhaps even mild humor underlying the bizarre nature, the uncertainty of this journey.

He bypassed the village, heading into the late afternoon sun toward the western shore of the eastern branch of the lake. And here on the hill overlooking the lake, standing out like a thick mat between the neat rows of vineyards, both wine grapes and the Concord of jelly and juice fame, high above the water was a large orchard, mostly apples but with a number of peach and apricot trees. These long lakes, aided by the great lakes of Erie and Ontario to the north and west, had their own temperate zone. Those horizontal blizzards that blew in during the winter could freeze a vine but by March the air was soft and mild and the snow gone and it was the rare frost that nipped buds or blossoms.

He went up past the orchard and above that was the old Farrell place. A small holding of sixty acres, the house and barns surrounded by pasture always let to a neighbor for heifers in the summer. The house a simple two-story farmhouse where Timothy had lived with his parents. Both of the old people were short, not heavy but low to the earth and Timothy had been a tall lanky man with ropy strong arms and body. Hewitt could barely understand the old woman at first, as if she came right off the boat and directly to this place and never left it. She'd fed him well.

The house and barns were still standing. Slightly downhill was the forge, a large two-story structure built from round lake and river stones. With the loft where Hewitt had stayed those two summers. All was still there and none of it as it had been. Strings of hand-washed laundry beside the house, a gaggle of children in simple dresses or shirts and trousers, all barefoot. And the buggy in the yard, the shafts dropped to the ground. Hewitt went to the top of the hill and turned around and sat a moment. From here he could see the pale blue drift of smoke rising from the forge fire. And he thought Of course, someone has to fashion the hardware the Mennonites would need. It was a strange moment: an upwelling of grief that Timothy was truly gone and great relief the place had not been simply dismantled and turned into a lovely home. The site was astonishingly beautiful. He thought of the children in the yard. What a wonderful place to grow up. Although he'd only met a couple of those early Mennonites years ago it was enough so he knew he could easily drop by one day and talk to the smith, relay his history and perhaps learn a bit more of Timothy. Or not. Perhaps he would be the educator.

Far out the deep dark water of the lake was disturbed by a breeze he could not feel, even here hilltop. Small white flares of sails marked boats and other places the water was split by ever-widening vees as speedboats raced heedless and lovely through the endless summer day.

A pickup truck with rust-ridden fenders sailed around him and down the hill. So he put the Bird in gear and drifted on down as well. Past the forge, past the family. Small children, three to ten or so. The smith was a young man.

He went into town. Little had changed. A new fire station had been built and on the way in a short strip with the usual fast-food outlets. There were still no parking meters. He made a quick stop at the chamber of commerce and plucked a handful of brochures from the rack and sat in the car as one after the other he discarded lodgings. In the past quarter century up and down the hillsides above the lake wineries had appeared, a rather too obvious attempt to mimic California with tasting rooms and offering bed and breakfast. He settled upon the Towne Motel despite the critical addition of that suspicious letter— the place was right in the center of the village. He had a vague recall of the place and found it easily and checked in, carrying in his bag. At least he had a room upstairs on the back which might be somewhat quieter. He ran his hand over the pillowcase. As suspected, the linens could use a shave. But no matter; for the moment it would do. He turned up the air conditioner and left.

The next quest was a bit more complicated. He knew it was here, in the village, knew he recalled passing it. But still he worked his way up and down the main and side streets of the downtown before he found Our Lady of Compassion. He went first into the open church and made no prayer but left a twenty in the donation jar in the vestibule. Then went around back into the modest neat burying ground and walked slowly up and down the rows of stones and humble monuments. Until he found them. It was no surprise that Maude and William Farrell shared a double headstone. It was also not so much of a surprise that she had outlived her husband by five years, dying in the spring of 1983. And it shouldn't have been but was shock enough that Hewitt fell to his knees before Timothy's stone when he learned the man had died within the year after his mother. He wasn't sure how long after the death he'd learned of it. Until this moment could not have placed a date to the event. But he sat now with the chiseled letters and numbers stark against doubt or monstrous self-pity.

Fuck all. Timothy had only three more years of life than Hewitt could claim now.

In the late afternoon the trees woven through the iron fence of the burying ground blocked direct light although the sky overhead retained the high blue of daylight and the back of the church was lit soft flaxen. But kneeling there, time shuddered down upon Hewitt Pearce. And he did not know what he was doing. Too far from home.

Seeking a woman who had rejected him when both were little more than bright hormonal children.

He bent forward from his knees and rested his head on the cool grass. And doing so felt the big barn spike dig through his jeans pocket into his thigh. He stayed like that, thinking that the pain was somehow good for him. Then reared up and lifted his head to watch the pigeons circle the spire of the church. And finally pulled out the nail and kissed the pitted head and pressed it deep into the ground before the headstone. And sat a moment reading again the legend in the stone which was already losing its potency then stood and bent and kissed the rounded crown of the stone and without looking back walked past the church to the street where the Bird was parked.

If it was a last lesson from Timothy it was a good one. When the voice calls, you have to go. When you go, expect nothing.

Anything else is grace.

He went back to the motel and showered the road grime away. He was hungry but more than that restless. At loose ends—a term he disliked not only from his long experience within an elaborate version of that condition but for what it had implied ever since. He sat on the edge of the bed. He thought of calling home to check on Jessica but dismissed the notion. If she didn't answer he'd have more to worry about but if she picked up the first question she'd ask was the last he wanted to answer. He looked at his watch. Quarter after seven. He was winging it now, trying to determine a schedule of, he had to admit, a person unknown. And one whose circumstances were drastically altered from routine. Still he might make some guesses. Casting away the variables, the evening events, the presence of her children.

Chase yourself in a circle. The one thing he would not allow was ruse of any sort, even the mildest kind. Not even calling the clinic where she'd finally worked with her late husband.

Simplicity is not always what's desired. He could indeed go out to eat and have a couple beers and come back for an unpredictable night's sleep and start the next day already feeling one step behind. Or he could quit fucking around.

He dressed in clean jeans and a French blue dress shirt and rolled the sleeves up over his elbows. Considered his shoes and settled on his plain black sneakers. The old-style Converse with not a fancy trick about them. Knowing if somehow he did manage to pull off an audience with her and was wearing more formal shoes she would at some point notice and know he was nervous.

Deep sudden resolve. What he'd been waiting for. Into the bathroom to brush his teeth until his gums hurt and a last swipe of a damp hand through his hair. Then the motel ritual—wallet, room key, car keys. Last moment he grabbed his charcoal soft-draped sport coat and folded it over his arm and went out into the much warmer air of early evening. Down the steps and to the car. He paused a moment and then said Fuck it and laid the coat over the passenger seatback. If he should need it, it would be there.

He put the top down on the Bird. And went through the small blocks of downtown, heading south, toward the road that ran along the east side of the branch of the lake. Toward the East Lake Road. Driving to where he knew South Avenue ended so he could backtrack the avenue from there. His best bet.

Driving by the Keuka Farms drive-in he saw the outside tables were gone, the parking lot larger and the storefront also. And a drive-through window. Trying to meet the expectations created by the national chains. Hewitt could smell the burgers and fry grease as he went by. They should've kept it the way it was. As if he could pull in and that girl would come out again, over and over forever with his cheeseburger and fries and milkshake and hook it on to the rolled-down window frame and lean a little to peer in so he saw the opening at her throat toward her breastbone and she'd say, "I know who you are."

He drove on and slipped a back-angled turn on to South Avenue. The street signs here still white with black letters. He was seeking 804. Almost all the houses were old and almost all set back from the road but there were giveaways. Every now and then a small metal oval on a post showed the house number. He was in the 200s. He went along, over cross streets where the numbers jumped higher. Settled low into the seat, his elbow out the window, he steered with his right hand. He could always backtrack. Although he wanted, really wanted, to find the house first try. It felt important.

And there it was.

An elegant late Victorian with a wraparound porch extending from the lower floor, a smaller porch framed on the second floor and a round tower running up one side. And all of it, from the porch railings to the gingerbread trim along the eaves and highlighting each window frame and dormer and door, all of it in a multitude of colors. Unlike similar homes that at most boasted a single color for the house and another for all the trim, this house was painted in the fashion it had been built for. It was beautiful. And Hewitt thought he could've driven the street with no attention to numbers and known this was hers.

The yard sloped down to the street. A simple lawn. Surmounted by a pair of big oaks and a string of shagbark hickories and a hedge of spotty evergreen along the street. Some sort of juniper or cedar. Untended. A line of old dying Lombardy poplars waving in the lake breeze above. Of course, he thought. Just keeping the lawn mowed summers was enough. Nobody who lived here, nobody who had lived here, had time for flower gardens.

He was feeling a little foolish in the Thunderbird as he went up the white peastone drive. His jeans were stuck to his butt and thighs and loops wet his shirt under his arms. Even with the top down he felt a flush on his forehead. As if he'd run here. And maybe he had. But once again it was too late to turn back now.

He parked and got out and turned all the way around as if admiring the view, swinging his arms to stretch them. All the sudden he felt the day's journey. Nothing, he reminded himself, compared to Emily's recent journey. He sincerely hoped he wasn't about to be an idiot. Then lifted up the charcoal blazer and slid into it. It was a best guess. He had no idea how he should appear before her. His hands were shaking and his legs didn't feel much stronger. He went up the steps to the front porch and was about to knock when he saw the bell button. He pressed it and could hear the echo from far within the house. He moved foot to foot and then, refusing to try to see in the bubbled leaded glass of the door, turned a quarter away so he had a view of the lake.

The door opened and a boy about sixteen stood there in the opening. Looking much too small for the space he was trying to fill. In new jeans and a white polo shirt he was clearly not happy. With this job or any other.

Hewitt was stunned. Although he'd guessed it from the newspaper photos he was unprepared for this beautiful scowling boy. Who except for gender was what Hewitt had very nearly glimpsed in memory when he passed the ice cream and burger joint moments before. Hewitt pushed back the front of his jacket and stuffed his hands in his pockets. Wordless. Fuck he was wordless already. And his face piping pearls of sweat.

The boy saved him. "You're the insurance asshole right?"

"Well." Hewitt had a minor coughing fit, wiping his eyes. "Actually—"

"Actually." The boy drew the word out to farce. Hewitt trying hard to remember his name but it was gone as an ice cube in his armpit. The boy said, "Actually, you hate coming late in the day like this but it was the best you could do."

Hewitt said, "Truth is, I'm not. What you think. But I'd speak to your mother. If she's home."

The boy looked at him.

Hewitt reached out and took hold of the door. Which was floating free halfway open and halfway closed. He said, "Why don't you do us both a favor. Go tell your mother there's a man at the door wants to speak to her. That way, at least you're cut loose."

"Who the fuck are you?"

Hewitt moved so one foot was just in the hall and the boy stepped back. Hewitt said, "Nobody you know. I'm sorry about your father. I truly am. But at the moment I need to speak with your mother. Now. You're a good guard dog but all I have to do is call her name down this hall and she'll at least come to find out what's up. Which is not what I want but I'll do it if I have to. That's it—you're John, aren't you? I just remembered. So, John. Do you want to get your mother or should I?"

John studied Hewitt. Hewitt did the same. The boy was so goddamn beautiful and so tender and so tough Hewitt wanted to touch him, shake his hand, something. He waited.

John turned and left the door open and walked down the hall as he called out, "Mom? I think it's the insurance asshole."

Hewitt watched the boy disappear. Glanced over his shoulder and saw plenty of daylight and the car sat right there, waiting. He stepped back on to the porch, tripping on the sill.

He heard footsteps coming up the hall. And tried to recall the last time he'd heard her feet hitting square on the ground. But could not. Then she was standing before him in a plain white sleeveless dress, her hair cut above her shoulders as the last photograph he'd seen of her and her head tipped to one side trying to place him.

He said, "Emily. I never was worth a shit at timing but I want to tell you I hate this has happened to you. I just wanted to tell you I'm sorry."

She stood in the door. As if this run of words meant nothing to her. As if her grief was intact and untouchable. As if she'd heard countless versions of the same in the past two weeks.

Her lips opened in a crooked oval over pressed-tight teeth. She said, "Hewitt? Is that you?"

He said, "I'm afraid it is." And in the golden late light of day he tried to bring a small grin to his face.

He never knew if she saw it. "Oh, God no," she said. And the door swung shut in a decisive thump. Then he heard the lock turn.

LIKE A BERSERK siren the telephone chattered staccato bursts. Hewitt groaned and rolled over. The bedside clock revealed it was quarter after seven. Only one person might have been able to track him down, and he was as far from ready to speak with her as one of those howling winter nights lost up in the woods under an oystershell moon twenty years ago. He lay on his side with the pillow wrapped around his head. Somehow the room had grown not just warm but hot overnight. After four rings the telephone quit and the red message button began to blink. He could swear to God he could hear the faint electric pulse within the button. He was in horrible pain. Then he was out of bed where he finished vomiting into the sink just in time to sit on the toilet. Christ he was too old for this. For all of it. Hewitt had made his share of hangover promises but never in such depth of humiliation.

He drank tepid water from the sink and threw up again. He went naked into the bedroom and plugged in the two-cup coffeemaker. Then back for a long scalding shower, heavily soaping and rinsing his genitals several times. At the end he turned the hot off and stood enduring the cold pouring over him until his scalp ached. Little tricks that were nothing but cheap stand-ins for time. The quick single shot remedy had been abandoned years ago. Toweling off he told himself he'd find some breakfast and then gas up the preposterous Thunderbird and go home. He was a fool, had always been a fool and probably always would be.

★   ★   ★

WHEN HE'D LEFT her porch and driven slowly down toward the lake and the layered beauty of sunset reflected on the water, he was not feeling so much a fool as the recipient of a gut response and he had no idea what came next. Except the obvious which was to return to the last place, the scene of the scene so to speak, the scene of the crime although to this very day he was not certain what that crime was beyond the inevitable still incomprehensible divergence he hadn't seen coming, or had denied the signals she did float like small paper boats in the bloodstream of their lives that second fall. So he drove along the Bluff following those familiar roads until he came upon the driveway to the Ark and saw the new white brick columns and the fancy-looking cheap gates, the grounds cleared as far as he could see up the drive and he knew whatever lay up that drive, whether the old house restored or something newly built, wouldn't resemble the place of his memory. He drove on and up the backroads through the scrub and vineyards until he came to the high end of the Bluff where he watched the last of the sunset, as the first night she'd brought him here.

That second summer Hewitt had arrived in time for her high school graduation which followed a week after his own, the spring when as soon as the frost was out of the ground he'd had the bank excavated and Gordy Peeks began the brickwork of the forge but once he walked across the stage and gathered his diploma he kissed his mother and went to where the Volvo sat parked, packed and waiting and drove west. And because this summer was different he was more determined than ever to learn, to wring every bit of knowledge he could from Timothy who was glad to see him in his undemonstrative way and Timothy seemed also to comprehend the difference, partly no doubt from the inclusion beginning late the summer before of Emily who dropped in one afternoon about an hour before they were done work for the day, Emily in denim cutoffs and a tank top, her long braid swinging over her butt. Hewitt had long ago learned the hard way to tuck his own braid into the front not back of his shirt since the bending and straightening over the anvil would work it free if tucked in behind and the brittle whiff of burnt hair would cause Timothy to shake his head and chuckle. And Hewitt had visited Timothy on more than a few of his weekend trips to see Emily during the year. So without it being spoken of all three knew this summer was different, that in the words of more than one commencement speaker one world was being left behind as a new world was being entered.

Hewitt knew Emily had written letters late that spring deferring her entrance into Cornell as well as polite rejections to Alfred, Colgate and SUNY New Paltz, and Hewitt, with no plans at all to attend college had lightly joked it was the year of living by one's wits; this the afternoon he helped two of Emily's high school girlfriends pack their Karmann Ghia with camping gear to head south toward the coast of North Carolina and the Outer Banks, where they intended to travel as much as possible the barrier islands south until Florida where they'd make a beeline for the Keys and a winter on the Gulf of Mexico— Hewitt silently grateful for those girls and their choice as it seemed to lessen the moody hesitation that had overtaken Emily during the time between her writing the letter to Cornell and actually mailing it. But as he'd nervously hoped once he arrived and summer was underway they had a fine high old time, Hewitt working long hours with Timothy but now with the weekends completely his own, more than compensated for by not only what he'd learned the summer before but the time he'd spent in Albert Farrell's forge over the winter and even as he carried his accomplishment and ability well he was always quick to step back and watch Timothy take over something new, something complicated, work to be witnessed before attempted. Emily had kept her old job nights and weekends over the winter but three days after her graduation was fired when she didn't show up one morning for work, the result of an unanticipated large quantity of mushrooms consumed with Hewitt and the folks out at the Ark—Max the solitary drummer, Ken the bass player and his lady Barb, Willie the Wonder Boy lead guitar player and whichever girl was around that night, Dave the keyboard player and his lady Stacey, and Drew the rhythm guitar. The residents. As well as a handful of other usual suspects. And while within days she was working at another restaurant and making real tips instead of a crummy check, in the course of that long night the Ark began to be their second home, or rather the place where they could always go. Willie held the lease, or it belonged to some member of his family but in any event he gathered rent and also decided largely who could and couldn't live there. Mostly it was the band. There were empty bedrooms and they all liked it that way—plenty of room for wayfarers but none that could take up permanent residency. With the exception of Drew who was only a couple of years older than Hewitt and Emily, the band had been in the house for ten years, enough time as Willie said for the sixties to finally fade into whatever the seventies was all about and Willie had greater authority beyond proprietary; it was he after all who'd gone AWOL in 1968 and holed up in the house until the day the sheriff and state trooper cruisers pulled in along with an unmarked black sedan and he crawled out of his elaborate hideout in the attic after spying them through his peephole and covered with dust and bat shit had walked right out and offered no resistance even when one of the MPs grabbed his hair in a knot and slammed his face on to the roof of the car, sending roses of blood down his shirtfront before they loaded him in and drove off and this was not a sense of patriotic duty or inevitability Willie felt but rather the fact his housemates had three keys of Mexican grass and five hundred hits of windowpane along with a baggie of assorted reds and yellowjackets and white-crosses and a month later when he had his pre-court-martial hearing he was stoked on smuggled MDA and talked nonstop for two meetings in the morning with officers and army shrinks and right through a solitary lunch and then through the more formal hearing in the afternoon which concluded with an exasperated offer of a less-than-honorable discharge whereupon he became highly agitated at this affront to his honor and after another harangue he was declared unfit for service at which, famously, Willie finally paused and fully serious said, "I most certainly am." It was Max who drove through a sleet storm to pick him up, Max then not yet shaved but with black hair under a rolled red bandana and his face painted red black and green and when the pissed off guards finally brought Willie out one of them said to Max, "We'll get your ass, Tonto," and Max smiled and said, "Sorry man. Sovereign nation status. Check it out." Twenty hours later the sleet had turned to ice and at three in the morning the whole crew had made their way to downtown Bluffport tripping their asses off and when the deputy sheriff finally managed to bring his cruiser to a sliding stop nose-in against an iced-over parked car and demanded what the hell they thought they were up to it was Max again who grinned and said, "Sliding. We're sliding, man. Want to try?" Local legend. From the beginning there'd been an unnamed tension, mild dislike, between Hewitt and Willie but nevertheless Hewitt respected him, knowing the courage and outrage needed for his life.

The summer before, they'd gotten to know Hewitt and accepted him although at first he knew it was because of Emily but by the second summer he felt he was holding his own and so the Ark became their occasional second home, where without it ever being discussed they had their own room which Emily painted and decorated with Indian printed fabrics and a pair of splintery wicker lawn chairs and a new mattress on the floor, the mattress Hewitt insisted on buying rather than going to the used furniture store in town and when they hauled it in and wrestled it up the stairs there was a round of applause, no offers to help but a flurry of lewd suggestions. Still mostly they slept apart, Hewitt in the loft of Timothy's forge and Emily at her parents'. Where at the beginning of summer there was a decidedly notable tension which Hewitt ignored as much as he could and Emily handled mostly silently but after a couple of times trying to talk to her about it he realized he more than she was the central target although never to his face. But it was the pitchfork in his ass that in early July prompted him to suggest to Timothy if he was to share the cost and buy the stock outright he be allowed to produce some of his own work to try and sell. It had taken Timothy two long silent days to agree to this and so Hewitt assembled a pair of display boards of kitchen utensils and various hooks, hinges, latches and decorative hardware that even then he knew was only a beginning but also was equal to similar work coming out of the forge and so one weekend he and Emily loaded the goods into the car and drove back to Vermont for a few days where with little effort he placed one of the displays in the gift shop of the Woodstock Inn and the other at the Equinox in Manchester, all on a commission basis but as high-end as he could hope for. And the work sold and orders came in and it was good to be making money from his effort and, he knew certainly now, skill, artisanship.

It was a grand summer. They spent time with her family, both at the farm and at the lake cottage and many long nights at the Ark rock and rolling or just sliding in the groove and sometimes late on those nights with a candle stuck in a bottle for light they'd lie in bed and Hewitt would talk about his own forge and what he hoped for it and sometimes his grander ambitions which were already forming, although outside of books he'd seen little of the work he envisioned. His mother was home and planned to stay there until as she said, "You marry that girl and come back here and set up shop and then I'll get out of your hair. Your grandmother was smart enough to do that for your father and myself and you deserve the same. You're an artist, you know Hewitt. Take it seriously as your father did and my life will be happy again."

The week after Labor Day one morning Timothy was sitting in the forge waiting when Hewitt climbed down the ladder from the loft.

He said, "The summer's over."

Hewitt said, "It's getting that way, isn't it."

Timothy looked down and scraped some cinders into the dirt floor with his boot. Then he looked back up and said, "I've taught you most all I know and the rest you have to learn on your own or it won't mean a thing to you. And it's time I'm getting back to my own solitary ways. You need to go home and finish building the grand smithy you've told me of and get to work on your own."

Hewitt laced his boots. "I thought there'd be no harm in working together through the fall."

149

Timothy looked long upon him and then shook his head.

Hewitt said, "Are you kicking me out?"

Timothy said, "It's time for you to go."

EMILY AND HEWITT moved into the Ark. It was the roller-coaster autumn, the fall of cocaine.

Early on, as the resorts in Vermont were gearing up for their fall foliage season he'd been forced to make a lightning trip back to retrieve the near empty display boards and offer poor excuses why he'd be unable to fill orders for the time being. They'd stopped for an overnight with his mother and Emily spent most of an afternoon hiking the land and then studying Hewitt's half-finished forge, the hearth and brick walls built in his absence but otherwise a shell. He'd found her there, sitting on a round of rock maple intended one day for an anvil and squatted beside her, one hand on her knee and waited like that until she'd looked at him and said, "Why don't you come back and finish this, Hewitt? You could have it ready before winter," and he'd met her eyes and asked if she'd come with him and she'd looked away, not yet ready to answer and he wasn't about to push. Although they had one of their first furious fights on the drive back to Bluffport the next day over his intention to press on to the next service area on the thruway despite her flatly expressed need to pee. The last hour of the trip in silence until they carried their backpacks up to their room in the Ark, turned and looked at each other and she began to laugh.

They picked grapes, cold in the morning dew and sweating in the afternoon sun, working fast as they could down the rows to get ahead of their coworkers so they could snort spoons which let them get even further ahead so they could smoke one of the joints Emily rolled each morning and brought in an old Bugler cigarette tin, then do another spoon to gain their lost ground. When the grapes slowed they picked apples and then went back to the vineyards for the last of the wine grapes, those left on the vine until the last possible handful of days. It was briefly a satisfying time—the weather high autumn, the sky filled with geese in a way he'd only seen flecks of in Vermont and rolling fleets of autumn clouds, scurrying shadows here and then gone over them and while the weather held it seemed they were within the vestige of a waking dream. Emily didn't really like coke which didn't stop her from taking it when offered and while it was wonderful in bed for both of them afterward it left her quiet and withdrawn. Hewitt would stretch on the bed under the covers of old quilts and sleeping bags and watch her curled in a blanket in one of the chairs, sometimes reading but often as not gazing at the blank black window and more than once he thought of the house in Lympus and how she'd fit there and wondering why he just didn't ask her to go there with him now—even with winter coming on he could roof and outfit the forge in a few short weeks and have it up and running by the first of the year. But he didn't, partly because he was having too much fun most of the time.

Partly because he feared she'd say No.

As the weather turned cold she returned to her waitress job and Hewitt went back to work in the vineyards, following the trimmers to pull the cut vines, the brush, the long new growth from their twisted lives on the wires stretched taut. On cold days the brush would come free with a whip-crack and snap against his cheek, hard enough to bring tears to his eyes. More than once he quit and walked off the job only to return to a near empty Ark where everyone now except Willie was out at day jobs and it was ever more clear Willie didn't really like Hewitt. At the time Hewitt thought this was jealousy over Emily; years later he figured out Willie already knew he was a short-timer. And now it was Emily who brought home the greater share of groceries and the big house was cold except for the kitchen and the band room that had a large gas heater. Old coal grates were in all the bedrooms but the chimneys were bad and they couldn't be used. Portable kerosene heaters were used although if one was left on during the day in a feeble attempt to maintain warmth in the room, the occupant would return to find it shut down. This Hewitt understood—Willie's fear of fire—but he kept out of those long-running disputes. Evenings they'd drink homemade wine and smoke dope and sometimes the band would play but as often sit huddled in the big room and listen to records or reel-to-reel bootlegs of Dylan or Janis or the Dead. All of which more or less depressed Hewitt—it was warmer somewhere else and he'd be slumped in the broken sofa, the heater flickering queer blue and orange reflections on the ceiling when he'd realize Emily was watching him. Often when he'd look, she'd be looking away.

It wasn't all bad. Days off they'd take long walks through the snow-skimmed woods hand in hand or chase each other, laughing until one or the other would fall to the ground and then be tackled gently. Evenings they'd drive into town and drink Irish coffees for the heat and flush it gave them and sit outside later in the running car kissing each other as if for the first time. Or out with the band when they gigged and those were wonderful nights because whatever else was working or not between them once dancing they were again as smoothly connected as if they'd been born that way. And always love, even after the fights over who ate the last Oreos or forgot to buy bread, even the argument when she threw a cheap aluminum pot at him and dented the pot and the old plaster where it hit and Willie had stood up, about to speak when Emily said, "Oh fuck off Willie," and chased Hewitt upstairs to grapple on the bed and leave the clamps of her toothmarks on his upper arms, that would throb the next day in the cold lowering sunlight, the marks of her love upon him, the idea that she would consume him, eat him if she could. This physical pain was nothing compared to how he felt looking at her, how he felt away from her only a few hours and how she felt also, he knew. So at Thanksgiving which proved to be a wonderful time, a warmish spell brought rain the night before and then a pale sun and warmth on the day itself, a turkey stuffed with mushrooms and hash brownies for dessert, the house filled with people. That evening in the kitchen after he'd happily volunteered himself and Emily to clean up while the band was setting up, leaning back against the sink and holding her, their hands running up and down each other, her eyes lit and tender and teasing, the love flowing from her suddenly overwhelmed him and he went to his knees, his arms around her and his head pressed to her stomach, almost crying, just holding on to what he knew was his very life and in those moments before he'd slid down saw she knew it too. Later that night as she slept beside him and the music had long died away except the unknown melodies running through his head he resolved that at Christmastime, that unspoken quiet anniversary of sorts, he'd tell her it was time to go, time for them to go back together to Vermont and by spring the forge would be running and she could do what she wanted; he was thinking UVM for premed and then wherever she needed or wanted for medical school. Dartmouth, for that matter, as much as he disliked it had gone coed a few years before and there was a good program there. Or Massachusetts. Far more—anything she wanted.

Five days later the weather turned and he'd come home early with two red welts across his cheeks from the snapping grape canes and saw her car inexplicably in the driveway and his first thought was if she'd quit her job they'd shower and change and go out for a night on the town, a good meal and Irish coffee and then cruise for the inevitable party. He walked into the kitchen peeling off his quilt-lined Carhartt overalls when he glanced up to see Ken, quiet Ken with his thick mustache and gentle drooping cornflower eyes looking at Hewitt as if Ken wanted nothing but to be anywhere, anywhere on the planet than where he was right then and the look explained nothing and everything and Hewitt said, "Where's Emily?"

Ken sat down at the table and began to roll a Drum cigarette. He could roll a joint fast as the thought but he labored over the cigarette. Finally he looked up at Hewitt and gently rumbled, "Talking to Max. I think you should leave her alone just now man."

Of all of them Ken was the one he was most comfortable with. Briefly it flashed that it was no accident Ken was alone in the house when Hewitt arrived. He said, "Hey, man. That's cool. That's cool."

Ken struck a farmer's match off his thumbnail and blew smoke and said, "Just hang loose, man."

And then Hewitt was very much not hanging loose. "What do you mean? What's she talking to Max about, Ken? What's going on?"

Ken nodded. "They're in a powwow of sorts."

"A powwow? You mean they're holed up in his teepee? Shit, man. Are they out there *fucking*?"

Ken looked at him. "No man. I would say they are not doing that."

"Then what?"

"Hewitt. Why don't you sit down and cool out? They're talking is all. She came in around noon and wanted to talk to him. That's all."

Hewitt was out the door in his socks and jeans and two layers of shirts. He walked through the crisp crusty snow and stood twenty feet from the teepee with its thin vent of smoke, silent, listening but hearing nothing. He tipped his head back and the first small dense flakes of new snow came out of the trees and on to his face, into his mouth as he opened it wide and cried her name.

Maybe an hour later he was tramping a tight circle around her where she stood with her arms wrapped around the brown and white Peruvian sweater he'd given her last Christmas, her hair wet from the snow and turning the gold of honey, Emily silent as she'd been for some time and Hewitt unable to slow or stop himself. "Why didn't you talk to me? What makes you think you couldn't talk to me? What have I done that you couldn't talk to me? Emily what the fuck do you mean? I don't care if that's what you really want. I mean I do care but why exclude me? If you want to go on to school that's fine. I mean that is just absolutely fucking fine with me but what about us what about you and me Emily I mean this decision clearly says something about you and me or am I just plain goddamn wrong? You're sick of this life? So am I. Can you do more than just tell me you're going to Cornell in January and that's all? How the fuck can that be all Emily? Don't do this to me I can't stand it, I'm falling apart here why the fuck won't you talk to me? Emily Christ I can do anything with you, I'll do anything with you, I'll let you do anything you want just don't goddamn Emily are you even listening to me? I love you, answer me damn it do you love me or not? Stop standing there like a fucking stone and talk to me Emily do you love me or has this been all a joke is that what it is, was I just someone to fill a little time, to kill a little time goddamn goddamn goddamn Emily fucking answer me!"

AND WITHOUT THE least idea he was about to do so or even doing it as he did he reached out and swatted her hard across the top of her head with the flat of his hand

"ASSHOLE!" SHE SCREAMED and broke and ran for the house

HEWITT STANDING STARING after her not believing what he'd done and knowing he'd done it stood watching the door shut behind her and seeing then what he'd known all along—the line of faces pressed against the lit kitchen windows that had seen and most certainly heard it all and the snow came down

ALL I WANTED he thought Was for her to say something, To let me know she was hearing and feeling some if not everything of what I was saying and feeling

ASSHOLE SHE'D SAID and he stood in the snow a long time as it grew dark and stared at the house asshole

WHEN HE FINALLY walked up to the house and into the kitchen Max and Willie and Ken waited. They were drinking dark Beck's and passing a joint. In the middle of the floor was all his stuff. Backpack packed. He noticed that.
He said, "Where's Emily?"
Ken said, "She doesn't want to talk to you."
"I'd like to talk to her."
Willie said, "You already did. Now get your shit and go."

"I want to talk to her."

Max stepped forward. He said, "I'll carry your stuff to your car. You can follow me or wait right here and then I'll carry you to your car."

Hewitt was shaking, cold, angry, frightened, misunderstood. He said, "Come, on guys. I just need to talk to her."

Ken said, "Hit a woman."

Willie said, "You got about a minute. Then Max and I are going to take you apart and you won't ever fit back together."

Hewitt said, "Come on and do it then."

There was a pause. Then Ken said, "Don't make it worse, Hewitt. Don't make it worse."

He sat in the Volvo in the yard with the backseat piled with his stuff. They left him be. From time to time he'd start the engine to warm it up, also to let whoever in the house might care know he was still there. It was getting very cold and the snow was coming down heavily, the powdery snow that could encase the car in a foot or more by morning. He'd stopped crying a while ago. He thought he could, probably would, die by dawn. But he was going nowhere. And then well after dark, the snow still tracking heavily by the lights from the house suddenly there she was, face against his window, wearing her green down vest over the sweater, a ski cap pulled low on her head so her hair pressed tight down over the vest, her eyes red from crying and her lips pouched full, chapped to blooming. He started to roll down his window and she backed up a step, slipped and went down on her rear in the snow. Then he was out of the car pulling her up and they stood holding each other pressed tight not caring about the cold and he was crying and saying her name and she was crying also but silent and she led him into the house, through the suddenly quiet and empty house and up to their room, her room, whatever it was, where in the meager warmth of the heater they held each other again and kissing, kissing feeding each other as they stripped all four hands seeming to belong to one being as so many times before and then scurrying under the quilts and bedding where he sank into her so moist and close as if they'd never done this before and he came almost immediately but remained erect and then the long hard sweaty love that was like all times and like no time ever known to him and he knew for her also, her eyes wide and bold upon him, his name released like sucking air each time he'd take his mouth from hers and then somewhere he realized this was the final time and he began to cry and slowed, his rhythm with her matched exactly and she watched him still no longer saying his name until she cried it out one final time as she arched under him. Then they curled together silent, his tears and sobbing gone now as he simply lay with her and held her and she held on to him and it was so quiet in the room they could hear the faint swish of snow against the windows.

He woke while it was still dark and lay beside her, composed and patient, certain that in this new dawn they would talk and repair themselves and each other and go forth someway together into the new life he also wanted, was amazed and awed and grateful she'd seen it first, had known the change needed to come and pressed him into this place of not simple acceptance but full cooperation, even if he wasn't sure what that meant beyond her going to Cornell and his going back to Vermont to finish his forge and go to work and wait for summer. And he saw also the folly, the sheer selfish stupidity that had not allowed him to see and understand that need before, how he'd wanted to hold on to something that was already gone and then she slipped out of bed and in the light of the heater pulled on socks and sweats, already wearing a T-shirt to sleep in, and left the room as quiet as a cutpurse and he let her go, knowing as so many other mornings she would bring back coffee and climb into bed as they sat with the heavy insulated mugs to talk and perhaps make love again.

She handed him his coffee but finished dressing and when he began to talk she asked him to please be quiet. He was rattling loose with all he'd thought about but she walked to the window and stood watching the gray dawn as his words fell off before she turned and said, "The driveway and road's been plowed. The snow's stopped. You should get going." And left the room.

When he was dressed he stood at the window and saw that not only was the driveway plowed but his car alone among the vehicles had been swept off. He turned and leaned against the sill and looked around the grimy falling apart room, the orange crate of her books, the old chairs, the Morrison Hotel poster and the Indian fabrics on the walls, the mattress on the floor, the rows of candles on the narrow mantel above the coal grate, the missing tiles from around the grate and knew he'd never see this again. He wanted something and for a moment considered the pale green underwear he'd pulled from her the night before but turned away and saw on the wire strung tight among her clothes two of his own shirts left, one of them the Black Watch flannel she wore in his favorite photograph of her and he rolled it up and stuck it in his pocket and went downstairs.

He didn't know and didn't care where the others were but Ken and Barb sat at the table in the kitchen with Emily and he stood in the doorway and announced he was on his way and Barb got up and left the room as Ken nodded, a thoughtful nod that encompassed all of Hewitt's sorrow and a kind farewell and Hewitt looked at Emily who sat in the corner spot as far from contact as possible and he started to speak and then looking at her was unable to and began to cry and she said, "Keep the tears for yourself, Hewitt, I don't want them anymore."

ALL THOSE YEARS later he drove the Thunderbird slowly around the length of the Bluff back to the village, those years collapsed upon him with the precision of his own ticking bomb. He parked in the motel lot and locked the Bird and walked jauntily down the three blocks to the lit windows and without the least hesitation threw open the door, shouldered his way to the bar and leaned over to wait the bartender, something even with the crowd he knew wouldn't take long, feeling bouncy and edgy and jacked right up in his dress shirt and soft coat, palmed a fifty on to the bar and ordered a double Jameson and a Genny Cream Ale—the ale nothing more than a gesture toward slowed intentions. As the first drink went down he felt raw and out of place, looking around at the working men and women, mostly younger but a few hard lined faces and old men with stubbled chins drawn close on their stools. There was a loud jukebox right where it always had been although this one played compact discs and toward the rear was the hanging light and clumped bodies that indicated a pool table, the occasional smack of balls making way through the noise and the second drink slid down and he felt the soft infusion creeping and hitched forward on to his stool to work his way out of his coat and draped it neatly over the stool back. The glass of ale was flat and the bartender understood his desire and kept careful eye on his whisky glass, ever ready with the bottle, a top-shelf item here and one Hewitt already regarded as belonging to him. Oh the whisky was fine and he thought What in the world was I thinking? Of course it was all different now, he'd have one more, perhaps two and then get something to eat and walk back to the motel and sleep a dreamless sleep and rise in the morning and head for home. It's all a question, as he slid the empty glass to trade for the full one waiting, of moderation. He was as far from drunk as possible, simply loosened a little, nothing the day didn't call for. The day. What a fucking joke. He held the glass up at eye level and watched the lights reflect in the whisky and wondered what he'd gained or lost by leaving it alone for so long. Nothing seemed the only answer. The last twenty-three years, the past quarter century, a considerable chunk of whatever time was his gone like that and here he was, doing nothing more than recognizing it. Leave those years right there with the change from the fifty.

Briefly he considered calling Emily to apologize and knew he couldn't but sat then lonely, wanting something, wanting some human touch or voice.

Sometime later he was in the wooden old-fashioned phone booth with a folding door punching in numbers he knew by heart and waiting as the phone on the other end rang three times and a machine picked up. He sat through the message and then, against all sense, begged Julie to pick up, talking on until the machine hit the end of its recording time and he was foolish enough to go through the entire process again only this time to get a busy signal. He sat in the booth with the dead phone in his hands. He pressed the greasy receiver to his forehead. He knew this wasn't damage that would last. Or maybe it would. At the moment he didn't care.

When he came out of the booth he lurched and caught himself, ran his hand through his hair, then shook his head like shaking off water and went to the men's room and peed in the trough and came back out needing the drink he'd left in the phone booth but simply went back to the bar and like magic a full glass was waiting for him, his stack of bills still high, or perhaps it had grown low and been replenished again. He leaned and waited and the bartender came down while Hewitt was studying the menu on the board behind the bar and told him the kitchen was closed and pointed to the big Rolling Rock clock where he saw it was almost twelve thirty. So much for supper.

A voice in his ear.

He turned. A pretty woman. He grinned. "Howdy."

She leaned in. "I'm Carol. And who are you?"

Hewitt was truly fucked-up so he skipped evasion. "A bunch of years ago I was in love with a woman here. So I came back to see what's happened to her. So far, it hasn't worked out too well."

Carol said, "God I hate that shit. Look at me. I got two kids already out of high school. You believe that?"

Hewitt looked closely at her face. He said, "No."

She said, "You a cop?"

"Fuck no."

She took his hand. They were turned to face each other, halfway away from the bar. The room was late.

She held his hand and slid it up under her blouse so that suddenly he was cupping her breast, the nipple a jolt into his palm. Just as he realized what she was doing she removed his hand from her blouse. She said, "If you're a cop you just fucked up. You want to smoke a joint?"

"In here?" he asked, already knowing the answer. This woman wanted to fuck him.

She grinned and leaned to run a hand from his knee up his thigh. "We take a walk," she said.

Hewitt stood, leaving the pile of bills on the bar. The big tipper. Then, with Carol watching and waiting, pulled his sport coat on. They stumbled side by side through the swarm toward the door.

They went up the street toward the fire station, toward his motel. He wanted to take her back to his room. Then she fired a joint and stepped off the sidewalk through a torn opening in a chain-link fence. They were behind an auto-body shop. A small lot filled with junkers, cars waiting for parts to be found and used.

Carol said, "Here." And passed the thin joint. Hewitt leaned back against some metallic shell and sucked in. Let the smoke drift out into the warm summer night air. And passed it back to Carol. She looked tired but he was tired also. She toked hard and passed the joint back and he held it down at his side and reached out and drew her in. It was not a lovely kiss. Hewitt knew this was his fault—too much, too much of a day. They pulled away, still holding the other and Hewitt brought the joint back up and was about to hand it to her when Carol dropped to her knees. He thought she was passing out. Then felt her hands opening his jeans. And he let her.

He stood with his head tilted up to the sky and smoked his way slowly through the joint as she worked her mouth upon him. Either he was too drunk to feel much or she lacked particular skill.

It was not anything he wanted.

He smoked until the roach was burning his fingers. He kept one hand on her head, loose in her hair. Making contact.

And then had to take a break from the slide of her head, the furious work she was not accomplishing and so began to look up to the few faint stars beating down through the streetlights and saw out there right in the open empty middle of the yard as if stranded an almost new Lexus with the hood and glass and top all collapsed in an accordion of disaster. And knew what he was looking at. Carol patted him back into his pants, rose and glanced where he was looking. "The doctor. Sonofabitch hit a cow loose on the road and rolled that fucker three four times. They say there wasn't even no skid marks. He musta been all fucked-up." She paused and then said, "Well, if he wasn't when he started he was by the time it was over."

"No shit," Hewitt nearly whispered.

"Say, you got a spare fifty?"

So IN THE morning he was horribly sick and knew he had to leave but after his hot and cold shower he sat on the edge of the bed and drank the bad coffee and finally lifted the telephone and pushed the message button.

"I've got an hour for lunch at noon. Come up to the house. Bye."

He had to smile. Since she'd shut the door to him the evening before if there was a thing he could've done to make himself feel less worthy of visiting her, of explaining himself, of offering what consolation he could, he was hard pressed to find it. At least he hadn't called her from the bar. Briefly he wondered if she knew the woman, what the hell was her name? If she was perhaps a client of Emily's and two weeks from now she'd be sitting in Emily's office telling the story of her own bad behavior. Fuck it, he thought. Not likely.

So, a plan. If ever there was a need for one. No winging it today.

Four hours. Breakfast, and reminding himself to keep it light, to let the hangover work itself out on its own and not try to pack it down with protein. Besides, he'd recalled clearly enough where he was bound when he packed and so had an old pair of swim trunks in the suitcase. A long hard swim would be the best curative of all.

He dressed and went out toward the East Lake Road and found a
bagel shop where he ordered two plain with butter no cream cheese,
two large orange juices and a coffee. Almost fifteen goddamn dollars
but the juice was freshly squeezed and drinking it he felt as if the poisons were already being expelled. The bagels also felt right, carbohy-
drates he imagined soaking up and nullifying the residual bile coating
his stomach.

The park was for children and families, with picnic tables and
permanent grills all locked into concrete footings. Then it sloped down
to meet the small waves of the lake, the pebbly shore. The swimming
area was defined by nylon ropes and buoy balls, alternating orange
and red. There was a small lifeguard tower. Hewitt walked down in
his trunks and talked to the girl perched there. His head was at the
level of her seat, her knees inches from his face. She wore a sunshade
hat and dark glasses and a neon green one-piece suit. It was not yet
July and she was brown as almond butter. He guessed she had a few
prework sessions at a local tanning salon.

"Morning," he said.

Her head turned an inch from her steady gaze out on to the water. Where only a small handful of children were in the water. It was
early. She was a beautiful girl too well aware of it and behind her
mirror-blue shades she was taking him in. He also knew her averted
gaze was as much as he was going to get for the moment.

He kept it short. "I'm traveling. And I need a long hard swim this
morning. So I guess you don't have a problem if I go around the kids
and swim across the lake and back." It was only about a quarter mile
over. Perhaps a third. Nothing he couldn't do.

She kept those blue metallic eyes upon him for a moment. Then
said, "Once you're outside the designated area I'm not responsible."

He smiled and nodded and said, "Of course not. Thanks."

As he went down the five feet to the edge of the lake she spoke
again, just loud enough for him to hear. "Watch out for the motor-
boats. They sure won't be watching for you."

He didn't look back but raised a hand and made a circle of thumb and first finger high over his shoulder. Then waded into the water which was colder than expected and rendered a slipping smooth dive and came up blowing, already in a deep pacing crawl. He slid under the buoys and went on. He reminded himself, not just his briefly exposed ears but all of him to be attuned to the deep vibratory thrash of inboard or outboard engines. And he did try to look around. But mostly he swam hard and strong. When he came up on the opposite shore he was in front of a cottage, near a dock with a pair of boats moored and a man standing watching him. Hewitt stood in the waist-deep water a moment, breathing in and out fully. Then he turned and began the return swim. This time stroking even harder as he felt his body coming together into the rhythm of muscle and move-ment. So much so that partway across he rolled on to his back and went a distance in a lazy backstroke, the sky dome cloudless, the hills either side visible and the water had replenished him and he felt the best he had in days. Far to the south but gaining under a steady breeze he saw a group of sailboats approaching. So he rolled and again began the hard precision of the crawl. Something returning of the best of his time here.

He slowed and stroked in among more children than before. Their shrieks of pleasure and mock terror somehow the perfect conclusion to his swim. When he stood and walked out of the water he passed the lifeguard and nodded to her. She said, "You've got power but your stroke's a little ragged."

He paused and looked up at her. Those insect sunglasses were pushed up on her forehead and she had pretty brown eyes. He said, "Tell you what. When you're forty-three come make the same swim and see how you do."

It was eleven thirty.

He drove back to the motel and hung the trunks on the shower curtain rod and changed again. Nothing fancy this time. Green frayed Carhartts and a short sleeved denim shirt and his old black sneakers.

*  *  *

AT FIVE MINUTES past noon he walked up the steps to her porch and found the door open and heard music. Still pumped from his swim he was cheered not so much because she'd put music on but from the choice. Bach's cello suites. Somber and elegant, comforting and uplifting.

He stuck his head in the door and called her name.

Her voice seemed to slip through the cello. "Down the hall to the end, Hewitt."

He went in and walked toward her, purposefully trying not to take in too much of the house. Except the lovely woodwork which had never been screwed with and so was gleaming and dense, the sort of wood impossible to build with today. A thick old runner on the hall floor. Doors opening into rooms registered as he passed—living room, dining room, a library with floor to ceiling built-in shelves. Along the hall framed photographs, which he walked past the way he swam through the small waves of the lake. Then he was in the kitchen and so was she.

Emily was moving back and forth between the stove, refrigerator and table. Pulling containers from the fridge and peeling back the lids to inspect and sometimes smell before she made a decision. Hewitt realized they were about to eat the food of the dead, not simply what had been brought at the time of the tragedy but much that had arrived since.

She wore a dark blue sleeveless dress with faint green and gold oblong outlines. A professional dress that could be seen as somber or lacking flamboyance. It fit her loosely. He stood in the doorway and saw all of her and realized the dress was brilliant as a stained glass window. Her hair, captured summer sunlight, was pulled back and held in place behind her ears.

She looked in one last container and said, "Yuck," and threw it back into the fridge and turned to face Hewitt. Who was motionless in the doorway with his hands cupped before him. His face he hoped a blank screen, a neutral thing free of intent.

The table had two plates on it and silverware haphazard on the plates. Four or five containers of food were open on the table.

She stood across the table, her face incredible with unknown animation and said, "My children aren't here. Which is the only thing that makes this possible. John's at sailing day camp and Nora has a little bay mare she keeps out at the farm and works summers to pay board. She bikes out mornings and often Dad brings her home with the bike in the back of the pickup after dark. She's fourteen so in the next year or so we're going to learn if this is only a phase. Jesus you had a bucket of balls just walking up and knocking on my door. If it was just me I could have handled it but the children—you don't have children, do you Hewitt?"

"No."

"Children by their nature are unable to comprehend any lives their parents may have had before they became parents. Because their parents are the one steady certain thing in their lives. In some way they don't even believe their parents existed before they were born. And you know what, Hewitt?"

He said, "They're right?"

She sat and motioned for him. She said, "I'm serious—I only have an hour. I don't know what's going to happen with the clinic. I'm just the resident therapist and can't imagine at this point trying to find a doctor to step in full-time. The fellow who filled in for vacations is helping out now but he's in a practice with his own partners in Rochester. So I can't just close things down for as long as I'd like. And to tell the truth, the work helps. Because there's nothing else I could be doing right now anyway. Except taking care of the children but they're both at ages where their hurt is so profound they're either walking stones or completely crumbled and boy do they hate to have me see them crumble. I tend to think Nora's having the hardest time because she's holding up the best. Tough Danes, you know. And I apologize for John's behavior last night but he's the most open with his anger and surges pretty much between being seven and thirty. So you see how it is here. How are you, Hewitt?"

She hadn't made the effort to move food from the containers to her plate and Hewitt hadn't either. He said, "I'm alright. I'm doing well, well enough." He paused and with kind but firm emphasis said, "And you?"

She reached and snagged a stalk of celery and crunched a bite. She said, "I'm fine. I'm holding up, doing the best I . . . Oh screw it. I'm all fucked-up and not sure whether to thank God for the kids and the practice or if I wish I could fall apart and lie around the house and try to sort out what this means. This. Jesus, Hewitt. This being my husband suddenly and without warning dead and in the ground. Martin was a good man. And more important than that, he tried hard to be a good man. He was a good father, a good doctor, a good husband . . ."

Hewitt noted the order but was determined not to attach importance to it. Emily went on. "—and we worked hard together, as colleagues and parents. Yes we'd been going through a hard time which I was sure we'd come out of. But Hewitt there's not a person in town doesn't know he was on his way home from his weekly Tuesday night poker game with the boys, as he called it, and was stinking drunk and everyone in town knows that because—"

"Because it's a small town and everyone knows everyone else's business."

And she picked up one of the containers of food and with a deadly overhand sent it wheeling through the air against the refrigerator and the contents and container stuck to the door a moment and slid down.

Emily said. "Because the only poker that was going on those Tuesday nights was him out in Guyanoga fucking my sister Elsa. And I don't have the first idea how many people know that. The sheriff. Some of his deputies. Certainly others. Elsa, of course. So I walk through this grief and feel surrounded by lies and eyes studying me to try and catch what I know and don't know. If it was anybody other than my sister it wouldn't be so bad. But that's bullshit, don't you think?"

Hewitt paused, taking his time. Absorbing this and also waiting to see if she was done or if this was an interlude before she began again. Because if there was one person she could tell any and all to, he wanted to be that person.

Finally he said, "Men are as complicated as women, Emily. Sometimes just different ways."

"I thought because it was my sister in the end it was less likely to be anything other than what it seemed to be. Don't forget, I work with people fucked up by life. The least likely men and women are the one's that'll surprise you. And the real bitch of it is I feel sorry for her. Not that I'm not ready to tear her head off. She came to the service but that was self-preservation as much as anything else. She burst out crying and held on to me. As if, what? I was supposed to console her? I tell you Hewitt, what a fucking mess."

Emily took up a handful of carrots shaved to resemble small kindling wood. She tilted her head as she chewed. Oh she was lovely. And a woman in the middle of her life who was turned inside out. She said, "I know you're not married. Ever been?"

"I came close." He paused. "A couple of times."

She didn't ask what happened—perhaps she didn't want to hear the answer. She said, "As terrible as the shock of Martin's death, what I fear most is the children will learn the truth behind it. If it was simply an Other Woman sort of thing I could probably get through it. I could help John and Nora understand it was a wretched thing, and wrong, but people make mistakes and I loved their father and he loved me. In other words, everything would have been fine. There were no divorce flags on the horizon. I would've made his life miserable for a while but he deserved that. And Martin would've been determined to set things right. But this is a different twist. It's not just their father's betrayal but their beloved aunt as well. Elsa is a strange woman, a genuine eccentric I guess would be the word. She has this little farm

168

in the valley and raises goats and makes cheese and has a huge herb garden and is famous for her garlic and lives on no money. You remember her, don't you?"

"Not that well. Emily, she was barely in her teens when we split up. But even then I could tell she was always going to be trying to catch up to you."

"And I guess she did," Emily said. "You're not eating."

He said, "I had a late breakfast and a swim."

She set down the carrots. She put both hands on the edge of the table and leaned toward him. "Right now," she said. "Right now I'm trying to figure out if I should sit down and unload the entire thing on them and just deal with the fallout. I'd lose a sister and they'd lose an aunt in the process and God knows what the ramifications would be within the family. Or, the other course is no action and just wait and see what happens. Simply wait and hope for the best."

"Look, Emily. At some point they'll find out. So their father and aunt will go way off their map, at least for a while. But you'll be the one to stand up and face them and while they might be angry with you at first, at least they'll have heard it from you. So that trust won't be violated."

She gazed across the table. "God. It's just not something I want to do."

He was silent, not needing to point out that life was full of things a person didn't want but still had to do.

She said, "Elsa has a deep survival instinct and believes she can get away with most anything. Or at least can get through it. But she's got to be aware how all this would impact if it came out. So I don't know."

"Not married?"

"Twice, for about a day. She lives by her own rules. Which does not make a marriage. People like Elsa, they have fences a mile wide and a mile deep between themselves and the world. On the other hand, this might be the point where she realizes she's gone too far."

Hewitt considered carefully and then said, "If you'd like, I'd go check on her."

"You will not."

They both sat silent. Hewitt serious as could be except far inside was a jittery disbelief this was actually occurring.

Then Emily said, "All I really care about right now are my babies. The truth is I am absolutely totally pissed off at Marty. For all of it. Everything. For fucking my sister, for drinking too much and driving, for being so drunk he didn't see a cow, a goddamn fucking big cow and getting himself killed. For being dead. Gone. Just like that. For doing that to himself and for doing it to the children and for doing it to me. I don't care it was an accident. What the fuck is an accident, Hewitt? Being in the wrong place at the wrong time. He drove off one evening and that was that. He had a choice. He was too smart not to know he was taking big chances. Shit, if he'd just been banged up and survived I don't know if I would've taken him back or not. I trusted him. I trusted him to do what he was supposed to do and now there's no trust, none at all. Dead and buried and what do I feel? That bastard violated me, tore something right out of me. Was he so sure of what I'd put up with that he could do that and think I'd forgive him? I would've pitched him out on his fucking ear and let him explain it to the children. I would've cleaned his clock every which way from Sunday. That son of a bitch took it away, took away every chance I should have had. I'd like to think he's burning in hell right now but all he is is a dead man in a hole in the ground. Maybe someday I'll be able to look back and think what a shame it was to lose him but right now I don't feel anything except rage, fucking rage he'd do this to me, leaving me with, . . . with . . ."

She put her elbows on the table and held her face in her hands and cried.

Hewitt sat until he realized he was holding his breath and slowly exhaling and drawing air he scraped back his chair and went around the table and stood behind her and ever so gently rested his hands on her shoulders, shivering once as he touched her and then pinched his eyes tight and focused on the top of her head as he tenderly rubbed the strung muscles of her lower neck and shoulders. They remained like that a long while, as her sobs slowed and subsided and she rested her head on her hands and sank slightly beneath but not away from his hands.

Gently he lifted his hands away and she stood and turned and came against him.

As he held her every fiber and filament and smallest cell of blood was dancing like winter starshine. And he told himself, This could be the last time. This could be it but it could be the last time. Don't expect. Don't ask. Try to be what she needs. And so held her and smelled her and absorbed her into him and then, before she could, he stepped back. His hands now touching her face her head stroking her cheeks her nose her hair her ears her chin one finger running over her lips almost as if to shush her instead of himself. Then she tucked her head to one side as she wiped her face.

She stepped to the sink and splashed water over her face and surprised him by coming back and holding his elbows with her hands. She said, "I'm sorry. I've been holding all that in."

"I kinda figured that out."

They were quiet a moment, although she hadn't let go of him. He reached and held her upper arms.

"Hewitt?"

"Emily."

"Why did you come?"

He paused. Then again simply said, "Emily."

"Oh, no. Hewitt."

He shrugged. "I didn't have a choice."

She leaned forward. "How'd you know? Did someone call you?"

And Hewitt knew she was talking about her mother, who had liked him, the two of them had liked each other. Enough so, on that terrible last morning, after he left Emily he'd still stopped by the farm to see Ellen Soren and say goodbye. Something Emily certainly knew.

"Nobody called me," he said. "But I've been getting the weekly paper from here for Oh quite a few years. Which was why I couldn't just send a condolence card or come to the service or something like that."

"The paper?" she said.

"Mostly what I've done is hope you were having a good life. The few things that popped up in the paper made me believe it was true." He let go of her and said, "I'm sorry. I shouldn't have come." And turned toward the hall.

When he was at the doorway into the hall he realized he wasn't sorry and was going nowhere. Even if it meant a melancholy week of silence in the motel. So he paused at the kitchen door at which moment something hard and wet struck his back and he turned slowly and looked down at a mess of food on the floor and felt the wet in the middle of his back.

"Don't you dare walk out on me right now."

He looked at her.

"What do you want, Hewitt? What do you expect? Should I take you to bed?"

"I don't think that's a good idea."

"Well, you're right. It's not even a possibility. There are no possibilities, Hewitt."

He said, "I think I should go now. Do you know it's half past one?"

"Oh fuck. Hewitt, why'd you come? Don't answer that. I can't handle you, Hewitt. Please go home."

"It's not that bad a motel."

She wrapped her arms around her breasts and for a moment looked nineteen again and with her mouth working cried out, "How much am I supposed to stand?"

And Hewitt, knowing he was doing the worst thing but knowing it was now finally beyond any control, stood in her house and years of words fell forth.

"You've never left me, Emily. I went truly crazy for several years. I drank so much that for no reason but plain old bald-ass luck I should be dead. Then it only became a smaller insanity I could manage. It means I'll do whatever you want, I'll wait as long as you need. I'm a middle-aged man who knows better but still believe you're my twin, my missing half. And I know once upon a time you felt the same about me. And here we are. I know I've come crashing in on you when you want it the least but I couldn't live with myself if I didn't come to you. All of which I promised myself I would not say. But it's how I am and how I expect I'll always be. I'm not a practical man. I don't believe I ever had a choice in the matter but if I did it was when I met you but I live by passion. And passion is cruel but the most true thing. Christ I'm really fucking up. My lovely Emily. Life is unbearably sweet and shorter every day and maybe I should've waited another month or a year or sent you a letter or maybe even just left you be. But I couldn't. I love you, Emily. God help me but I do. And always will."

There was a silence hanging in the room. Then, as if having waited to make sure he was finished, Emily stepped back a couple of paces. Watching this, he knew he'd said what had to be said and knew also it was impossible for Emily to see him as anything but totally mad, an insane unfeeling toad dropped from the sky.

She said, "Hewitt—"

"I know," he said. And turned and walked in long deep strides out of her kitchen and down her hall and out of her house on to her porch. He heard her speak his name again but the tone was low and he thought Don't stop now. He could not imagine worse behavior than what he'd just done. He could not imagine otherwise. Oh Emily. It had, in some ways, always been like this.

The boy was sitting on the hood of the Thunderbird. In long shorts and an armless T-shirt and his hair wind and water swept. A small backpack on the ground at his feet.

Hewitt walked down on to the peastone and said, "Get off my car. And take a walk around the block. Your mother needs a few minutes alone."

John remained where he was, looking at Hewitt. Then ever so slowly slid off the car and bent for his backpack. Hewitt went around the car and got in. The boy stood upright and stepped away from the front to the driver's side. Face to face with Hewitt. John said, "Who the fuck are you?"

Hewitt pumped the gas and turned the key and the Bird roared and shivered and Hewitt pumped the gas some more. And raised his voice so he could be heard and said, "Nobody. Nobody at all." And shoved the car into gear and, foot deep on the gas, screamed down the slippery drive toward the street. Hearing the small stones thrown up by the rear wheels striking and bouncing off the body. He came to a hard sliding brake at the end of the driveway and then aloud said, "Fuck it," and pressed on out into the avenue with no idea if there was traffic or not. The car hit the pavement with a surge as the tires purchased and he was going down the street toward the lake with the Bird out of control, sliding and whip-tailing back and forth down the suddenly narrow pavement.

Halfway down the next block he removed his foot from the gas and let the car drift to the side of the street. Came to a stop and he sat there for a moment. And then put the car in first and drove away, drifting up into second as the tears started silent from his eyes. The only thing he knew was he had to get home.

BACK AT THE motel he paced the room. He was desperately angry with himself. He'd intended to present himself as an old and balanced friend in a time of need but failed to realize Emily would never be able to see him as such. And he'd misbehaved accordingly. His need for truth was a clear violation. Even the thought that she might, if not now at some point, respect that honesty would not change a thing. Not content to be the proverbial bull, he'd driven a herd of cattle into the fragile porcelain of her mind and heart and stood back in the triumph of his own anguish. Fool, fool, bloody fool.

For all his prattle about passion he'd been selfish. That was the bottom line. An idiocy of supreme violations. Christ. He smacked his forehead with his hand and then turned and drove his fist into the painted cinderblock wall.

AN HOUR LATER, with a hand towel wrapped around his torn and bleeding knuckles he carried his suitcase down to the car and waited there until the delivery boy arrived with a small pizza and large coffee. He set them on the passenger seat and went back up the stairs for his last sweep of the room.

The message light was blinking. He stood a long time staring at it but finally decided against listening. He needed no one to tell him it was time to go, no one to beg him to be left alone. So he discarded the towel in the sink and studied his hand. The bleeding had stopped, his knuckles were crusting over. He went to the office to settle up and then drove the Thunderbird across the street and filled the tank. And bought a bottle of water for later and a roll of paper towels to keep pizza grease off the leather interior.

At the first thruway service area he calmly walked to the restroom and threw up the half-digested pizza. Rinsed his face and mouth at the sink. It was dusk and he was on his way home.

# Five

Along night drive with the windows down as his handful of ashes dribbled bit by bit out into the passing night and then were altogether swept away. By the time he crossed into Vermont it was past midnight and his jaw and head ached from the unending grinding of his teeth. Which even when he became aware of, he was unable to stop. As if he might chew through himself, chew himself down. So he'd have something to spit out.

His father had liked Emily but after her first visit told Hewitt she would break his heart. To which Hewitt replied, "She already has." Standing in the living room alone with his father on a September evening after Hewitt's first summer with Timothy Farrell—Hewitt just having returned from driving Emily home after her long Labor Day visit. Sharing cans of Narragansett beer. And Thomas Pearce looked at his son and in a voice so mild and emotionally complete it halted Hewitt altogether his father said, "I hope you're right. I truly do."

It would be almost three months before Hewitt got the first clue of what his father was saying. And another twenty-three years till, on that black drive in the floating car on the pitched-awry night, before he would fully comprehend his father had not been warning him but offering in succinct words, Thomas Pearce's tender concern for his son.

He stopped at the all-night diner in Rutland and ate a plate of corned beef hash and poached eggs. An hour to go and he wanted to slide into the house silent without waking anyone. Swipe a bottle and go sit in the forge with the exhausted furies working their peculiar energy upon him. The food had no taste because his mouth was smacking for whisky. But he cleaned his plate, mopping the last of the egg yolk and ketchup on to the soft white toast.

It was quarter past two and a very bad time for him to be out on the road. Sure enough a cruiser followed him all the way through Rutland up into Mendon and then up the mountain and only dropped back and disappeared when he turned off on to Route 100, a road that almost led to nowhere unless you were patient and then came out into the valleys of the White River and not so many miles past that the turnoff running north all the way to Canada but only a half-dozen miles to Lympus.

He glided in with the lights and engine off. There was a light in the kitchen window and the yard light was on which was a good thing because otherwise he would've coasted into the Volkswagen. Which was a heap of dead elephant. Only when he stepped out of the Thunderbird did he realize what he was looking at: the Bug coated in gray primer and all the chrome and windows wrapped and taped with newspaper. The car was being painted. He guessed Walter was behind this, if only in the efficiency of the preparations. There was mild assurance that the job was being done right out in the yard and not, say, tucked up in the haymow or behind the barn. Whatever was up he didn't have to waste time worrying over. He stood on the ground beside the clicking cooling Bird and looked toward the house. He ran a hand over his forehead still wet with sweat from the cruiser that now seemed a ghost of fears. And bent his head back and looked for the stars. But the warm night should've alerted him and none were visible. He drank air deep through his nose and knew by morning it would rain.

Fuck. He was shaky from the road.

But there was nothing for it and, silently cursing whoever hadn't paid attention to the weather, opened the driver's door and let down the parking brake, fiddled with the shift knob and as suspected easily slipped the car out of gear. The VW didn't care about the clutch and he reminded himself to tell Jessica or Walter they might want to crawl underneath and take a look at the linkage. He held the door open and put his shoulder against the roof and with a slow rocking start got the car moving and rolled it into the shed. Hearing newspaper rip free here and there. Better than the whole effort soaked with rain in the morning.

And stood outside the shed with his back to the shelter and almost laughed. Vitriolic clamor chugging in his chest. Goddamn but he'd finally done what was clearly a good deed for the day. Even if today was actually tomorrow.

Hewitt had never really been able to comprehend the notion of irony. Sarcasm, yes. The upheaval of circumstance also. But irony. Once accepted then all life was ironic. And he doubted that. Tremendously. Still, as he crept soundless as could be into his own house and lifted the bottle from the pantry and then back outside, he suspected the ironic. Stealing into and out of his own house.

In the dark he went down the steps of the forge. He found the box of farmer's matches and struck one and went through the drawer under the workbench for the handful of candle stubs. He pulled one free and lit it and stuck the cold end in the pritchel hole of the smaller anvil, knowing tomorrow he'd have to scrape the dripped wax free. The light flicked and quivered. And he broke the fifteen-year-old seal and tipped the bottle into the smeared dirty glass kept forever in the forge. He drank half the glass and took up the iron egg resting there and turned it around in his hand, feeling and seeing at the same time. It was close to done.

He laid the iron egg back down and took his glass and the bottle to the bench next to the vise and set them on the heavy planks and then hoisted himself up and sat. He was home.

IT WAS RAINING and the bottle was half-empty when he came out of the forge into the pale predawn light and his body ached as if he were an old man.

He stood in the yard, the light drizzle upon his upturned head, the muted birdsong, the yard, buildings, trees and gardens in the gray gloom of old known ghosts that were in fact his life. And once and forever swore that he wouldn't allow ever again the idea, come late that night, that Emily had grown up and he had not. He was not letting himself off the hook. But the ticket only allows so many revolutions upon the carousel and by God he was going to pay attention to his ride. Recalling how his father at so much younger an age than himself had to again step back on to the earth. How easy it would've been for that man to have locked himself away into his past, a literal fire of all he knew and loved. For many years Hewitt had thought his father a stronger man than himself. And perhaps he had been. Or perhaps Hewitt was just arriving. Each person has their own juncture. His face wet with the rain he realized it didn't matter one Goddamn when this becomes clear—the point was the clarity. Recognition.

He went to the house. Out of the lilac grove flushed the fifty or so mourning doves roosting there, the birds whipping away in flights of eight or ten at a time, their cries almost like owls, small whoops of sadness trailing after them and then gone in the streaking rain. Their cries how they'd gained their name. Hewitt was sorry to disturb them although he finally understood the contradiction between the lovely birds and their nomenclature. How much else, he wondered, his hand wiping his wet face, do we corrupt with our needs and failings?

HE WOKE CLOSE to noon. Outside now settled into steady rain, water that would seep deep into the soil but not so drenching it would swell brooks and rivers to muddy whirling chutes of limbs and washed-away riverbank trash. He rolled over to check the time and saw the framed photograph of that long-ago teenaged girl. A color photograph so time and sunlight had dimmed the brightness of her eyes and made even more white the blond of her hair. She was wearing the Black Watch flannel shirt. Her head tilted to one side, hair swept over her shoulders. Smiling into the camera as responding to a joke. He remembered the day he took that picture. He placed the photograph back on the nightstand.

He'd worn that shirt apart. Until the day he stretched up and it tore clear across the back, buttons already gone, the pocket also long ripped away. Late that night he'd placed the remains in an old shirt box and climbed on snowshoes up the hill to the stone chamber. Each fall he stacked dry cordwood along one side, covered with an ancient waxed tarp. So there was wood ready for a fire whenever he wanted. Which sometimes then was two or three times a week. With his mittens he brushed and scooped the snow from the outside fireplace and lit a fire and nursed it slowly as the wet from the snow residue died and the fire grew, feeble at first and then, Hewitt sitting back on a cold rock and the whisky running free as a mythic horse, stick by stick the fire turned to a hot steady blaze of leaping twisting flame. The night sky almost chirping.

He never could remember when exactly he placed the box and shirt on the fire.

Now, rain washing down, he lay in bed and remembered how for weeks after he'd raged within, having lost the central memory of a grand ceremonial.

And was close to laughing over this suddenly explicit nonevent when he caught himself. Remembering those long wonderful winter childhood evenings with his mother and Beth and his father gathered around the fireplace, both children assuming their father was absorbed in the beauty of the fire as they were. When certainly many nights that man was watching something else altogether.

He took up once more the photograph. He resolved at some vague point in the future he owed her at least a letter. It would be a long one. Or a simple paragraph. He'd know when the time was right.

IN THE KITCHEN was the most wonderful gift—a fresh pot of coffee all set up and ready to go. He peered out the window. The

Thunderbird was gone but Walter's old rust and red jeep was in its place. On the table a note—*Welcome home. We've gone to the auto parts store for paint and some other shit we need for the Bug. Thanks for pushing it under cover, neither one of us guessed it was going to rain. Be back early afternoon. Love Jessica. PS I think your friend Julie is pissed off at you.*

So he stood with a hot mug over the answering machine, the number 3 blinking steadily. He sipped and took a deep breath and pressed play.

"Mr. Pearce this is Jim Ralston returning your call—" Hewitt deleted this, having no desire to hear condolences for anyone, real or imagined.

"Hewitt, it's Julie. Don't ever call me from a bar late at night. There's nothing more pathetic than a drunk asking to get married and thanks to you I was up most of the night assuring my *dear loving partner* that you and I are only old friends who spend time talking shop every now and then. You sounded really fucked-up. I thought you were pretty much over that. When the time comes I'll give you a buzz or stop in when I get down that way. Bye."

The third call was a hang-up. But in his own way, Hewitt had learned how to patch the off-day and off-time announcements of the machine to the day and time he lived within. So he knew that long silence and the dead buzz of dial tone had been recorded the night before. Probably about the time he was vomiting pizza.

But what was working most foul was the message from Julie. Julie Korplarski. He didn't even want to recall the night in the bar and could not for his life recollect what his message had been. One more fuckup in a long fucked-up couple of days. Ah Julie. Ten years younger then Hewitt so when they first met he was cast in the role of teacher. She was cautious enough at first to keep their focus on pounding metal. Even as they rounded out very quickly to long evenings eating and drinking and sweaty sex that left the bed a mess and both of them curled tight together in delightful sleep. Driving down from Hardwick to spend an afternoon in the forge and then the evening with a good dinner before repairing to bed. Where mighty repair was made. He'd made the drive to Hardwick a few times and loved the pretty spot where she'd built a small passive solar house and a somewhat larger forge and workshop. She needed more work space than Hewitt because she'd settled into a never-ending exploration of the equine form. Which was where she eclipsed him. And he knew it and was proud of her. Her horses were crafted from any and all types of metal but despite the methods of assemblage one could walk around and around one of her horses and see nothing but horse.

Julie did not own a horse and was secretly terrified of them. Which would not stop her from spending hours and days at the neighboring farm in Hardwick studying the big Shire horses kept there. She could watch one for twenty minutes or four days and all the sudden know what she had to do at home. Once she spotted how her hands would translate what she saw she would not go back. Until the next time.

She laughed when her work was reviewed finally in *Artforum* and despite the praise the writer felt the need to point out that her horses seemed to emerge from some giant unknown breed. Even her curled foals loomed.

But came the winter day they spent in bed and her long hard thigh was pinning his legs to the bed as she rolled over to press against his chest and look into his face and inform him she had a new lover. One who was living with her and one she planned to spend the rest of her life with.

Hewitt lay silent beneath her, this lovely strong woman gazing into his eyes waiting for the first blink from him and he knew he had to lose her and knew it was perhaps the central error of his adult life. But it had to be. And he'd not moved except to reach a hand and take a handful of her thick brown hair and told her he was happy for her. At which she reared back and slapped him hard across the face.

She was out of bed dressing. He lay watching her and then said, "I do love you, you know. But that's not enough, is it?"

Buttoning her shirt over her firm brown breasts, she studied him an uncomfortable amount of time and then said, "We'll still get together now and then."

Then she was dressed and came swiftly to the bedside and kissed him lightly and he lay in the bed listening to her go down the stairs and out of the house. Heard her truck start and back around and then leave. And he lay in bed, thinking *That's the end of that.* An hour later he was wandering the house in his sweatpants and flannel robe, wondering what he'd missed. And relieved at the same time. Whatever unspoken thing she'd wanted from him had been resolved.

Three hours later he was outside in a drifting sweep of snow, dark now but the snow settled over him and flitted his face with cold gone kisses. His head tilted back to let that snow strike his face and mouth. Knowing he'd lost something once again.

It was three months before she called him. Two hours later they were in bed, a bottle of wine uncorked and glasses still filled on the bedside table. She talked briefly about her Charlie but fucked Hewitt slowly sweetly that afternoon. He was asleep when she woke him, dressed, leaning over the bed. She kissed him and told him she'd see him. He said, "This is really goodbye. Right?"

She'd said, "No baby. This is what you get from me. I happen to like it. Nobody owns me Hewitt. Except me. You should wish as much for yourself."

HEWITT WAS IN the forge with the rain overhead on the roof steady in soft counterpoint to the hammerwork. He was turning the second of the fist-size eggs that would top the gate, after deciding to fashion all four from the forge so he might compare the rough eggs to bring them to aligned size. And only then finish them. It made sense— if the four matched in rough form then the goal in finish work would be merely to bring them to indistinguishable dull-gleaming texture. Not an original idea but one articulated by Timothy Farrell and, much later Hewitt realized by his own father—build up the basic structure in however many forms it would end up taking on and then, therefore, the conclusion became not a matter of chance but of careful eye. So he heated and beat slowly the compression of the rod first to round, then onion head, the ball beginning to stretch and elongate as the ovoid took shape. Stopping to eyeball the iron egg in the pritchel hole of the smaller anvil and go back to work. Hewitt had time to consider the process. In fact his brain was a flooded stream that the work pulled by demand into one long braided rivulet.

He paused work and considered the bottle of whisky from the night before. Now holding what seemed a good deal more than it had when he'd gone to bed. The long abstinence was worthless against the events of the past three days even if the booze played roles in his screwup phone call to Julie and certainly hungover not on sharpest tacks with Emily but all that was done and so he walked over and unscrewed the cap and took the smallest sip. It was good and he took another and felt the soft flush up his arms and left the bottle open on the workbench and went back to work, thinking of the wonder of the egg.

EMILY WAS GOING to come for the Thanksgiving after his father died but canceled because of a bad bout of flu, leaving Hewitt and his mother alone to celebrate the holiday that was Thomas Pearce's least favorite, a day he described as one of too much brown food consumed to the point of a stupor, a vivid symbol of what he considered wrong with the country although he and Hewitt had argued over this the year before, Hewitt maintaining it was a matter of how much one put on one's plate compared to the rampant corporate rape of the world's natural resources, causing Thomas to respond acerbically that symbolism can be more potent than a sheaf of facts. That had also been Beth's final Thanksgiving, starting as she did the next year her not-so-slow climb in the resort industry, an ambition that was neatly and pointedly avoided during conversation. But a year later Hewitt and Mary Margaret ate a pair of Cornish game hens in near silence while a cold rain muffled the gunshots of deer hunters up and down the ridgelines. The meal was not a reflection upon the previous year but a bow to practicality and left them both quietly maudlin, a sadness within the house marked by Mary Margaret's taking an afternoon nap, something she almost never did and certainly not the result of over-eating. Leaving Hewitt to slump in the living room, missing his father and missing Emily and working himself into a full-chested knot of loneliness, sorrow and a touch of self-pity, waiting for the clock to edge toward five and the appointed time to call his love.

Who still did not sound well but had news that cheered Hewitt greatly: her parents had agreed that if Hewitt were to come for Christmas he might bring Emily home the day after for the week until the New Year—they didn't want her driving herself in winter, a notion she sniffed off but Hewitt was happy he'd be with her for Christmas. Emily passed along her mother's invitation for Hewitt to bring along Mary Margaret, which Hewitt knew would never happen but made clear to Emily how touched he was by the inclusion and then was off and running with his plans to show her Vermont in the winter—moonlight snow-shoeing and daytimes they'd go over the hills to Killington and he'd teach her to downhill ski, something she'd never done but he'd taken advantage of ski club in school as a way to get out of school Friday after-noons throughout the winters starting in second grade. She was hesi-tant but he was exuberant, insisting she'd be a natural at it, delighted at the idea of the two of them burning down the slopes when she inter-rupted and said, "Hewitt, I don't feel so hot, okay? I've got to go."

He drove out alone two days before Christmas, the backseat of the Volvo packed with modest gifts. A recurring erection due to the exultant expectation of having her in his eyes again, being able to touch her hand, hear her voice. To touch the skin, the soft invisible down along her arms, to feel the strong lock of the muscles of her back as she held him, the curve of her buttocks beneath his hands. Oh dark snow skies he wanted to slide into her as much as he wanted the rest of her but was prepared to wait, to be patient. To bring her back to Vermont.

Christmas Eve afternoon they rode together out to the Farrells'
where Hewitt was, as intended, a surprise, with his gifts of maple syrup
and cheddar cheese and cob-smoked bacon, feeling a little foolish over
the corny tourist gifts which however were met with a delight that
clearly extended beyond the gifts themselves and they spent a pleasant afternoon sipping wild foxgrape wine in tiny crystal glasses and
mostly talking shop and plans for the following summer. Emily in
rabbit-lined boots and high wool socks with a deep green velvet skirt,
white blouse and paler green vest rocking in her chair and with a keen
flush as she watched Hewitt with the old couple and Timothy.

Driving back to her house for what he already knew would be an
elaborate dinner he asked if she wanted to get stoned and she did, and
then he asked if perhaps later, after the dinner, there might be a party
out at the Ark or someplace and she'd turned and said, "I'm sure there
is but we stay home tonight."

He slept down the hall from her, sharing a bedroom with her next-
to-oldest brother Hal, although he'd had a brief moment of hope at
the end of the evening when she offered to do the last barn check but
Elsa insisted on going with them. Once in the warm barn with its muted
lights and rustle of cattle sleeping or chewing cud in their stanchions
they were finally able to kiss the way they wanted to and even with
Elsa playing with the barn cats and not missing a single move on their
parts also able to confirm, Hewitt knew for both of them, their desire
and intent for each other was intact and bold as ever. Her tongue in
his mouth a hot bolt to startle and enchant his heart.

Next morning he gave her the Peruvian alpaca sweater and admired the small jade elephant on a fine gold hoop to replace the turquoise and silver stud he'd worn for two years and she'd leaned close
and whispered Elephants never forget. The rest of the day was a blur
of food and longing, a feast of wild geese and pheasant the Soren men
had shot that fall and while Hewitt at the time was disdainful of hunters he kept quiet and was rewarded with Emily's hand on his thigh
beneath the drape of the tablecloth.

The next morning was bright and clear and there was no mistaking her meaning when Ellen Soren took Hewitt's arm as they were packing the car and, her eyes squinted tight, ordered him to drive carefully.

Heading east, the thruway clear of snow or ice, the traffic light, Hewitt with growing excitement was outlining his plans for skiing and snowshoeing, this time in greater detail and with some helpful preparatory information included when Emily said, "Hewitt, I'm not going to be doing much of that."

"Why?" He was thinking about rolling a joint, having Emily roll a joint, certain he could talk her out of her fears or uncertainties and also thinking ahead; his mother who slept alone in the big bedroom at the top of the stairs hadn't bothered to make up a guest bed, knowing better.

"Because ten days ago I got everything set up so no one would know and Barb drove me to Syracuse. Hewitt, I had an abortion."

"What?" He looked over at her and she looked back at him.

He pulled the Volvo off into the breakdown lane and stopped. He twisted in the seat so his back was against the door and he was facing her, his right boot flat over his left knee. She looked straight out the windshield. Again he said, "What?"

She said, "It happened when I came to your father's funeral. At Thanksgiving I was pretty sure but not certain although I'd already talked to Barb. I was just waiting for the test results. And the rabbit died. We already had everything all worked out. Although it was a lot harder than I'd expected. I felt really crummy for a few days. I don't know if Mom suspected or not—she seemed to buy the flu thing but still, she's no idiot."

"Wait a minute," said Hewitt. "Wait a minute."

She turned to face him. She was pale, blanched, her upper lip trembling but her eyes steady as the frozen wetlands around them. A raft of ducks lifted in the distance and circled, a low blot against the horizon. "What?" Her voice as dreadfully flat as the land spreading around them, as the road ahead and sky dome. Hewitt knew she was steps, miles ahead of him.

He said, "Why didn't you call me?"

She looked out her side window and, her hands wound together began to pick with fingernails at a cuticle, stripping slips of dried skin away.

He said, not a question, "It was my baby. Yours and mine."

Low she said, "Don't you think I know that?"

He sat a moment, his heart a clamor. Then he said, "You should've told me, Emily. Why didn't you tell me?"

She looked at him and said, "What would you have done, Hewitt? How would you have helped?"

"Well, you should have told me because it was my baby too. And then we would've figured out what to do and I would've helped you anyway I could. I mean, shit. I could've slipped over here and driven you to Syracuse and been with you afterwards. I could've done anything. But I would've been with you. You left me out, Emily."

She said, "I did the best I could."

"I don't think so."

"How's that, Hewitt?"

"I should've been a part of it. Of all of it."

She leaned back and said, "All right. How about this? All what I just said, all that was only a test. I'm pregnant, Hewitt. Knocked up. What should we do?"

"You're fucking with me."

"That's how it all started, that's for sure."

"Are you serious?"

She was silent, waiting for him, her face perched upon an undecipherable edge. Tilted, he thought, toward hope. He said, "If you're pregnant then you should have the baby. What a fucking trip! Did you think I'd say no, is that what this was all about? Emily. A baby. Oh God Em I can't believe it."

"So I drop out of school and we get married and have a baby?"

His chest hurt.

She opened the door and got out of the car and began to walk
down the edge of the breakdown lane, going away from him. There
was a strong wind and she leaned into it and her clothes seemed to
pull away from her body as she went. A semi went by and slowed,
brake lights lit as it passed her and then went on. And Hewitt was
angry she'd backed him into the corner of his own construction and
knew why she'd done it and so dropped the car into gear, popped the
clutch and went up the breakdown lane after her. When he pulled up
beside her she got back in as if she'd never been gone.

He said, "I want to pay for it."

Face dead ahead she said, "Don't worry about it."

He drove on. After a while they passed the Syracuse exits and still
neither spoke. If there was any exit in particular that mattered to her
she didn't so much as glance but kept her eyes on the road.

After a while he said, "I'm sorry."

"It wasn't anything I wanted to do you know."

His brain still screaming he calmly said, "Emily, I love you very
much. There's time to talk it out. We've got a week."

They rode silent several miles and then he said, "Em? Are you all
right?"

She slid over the seat and he lifted an arm and let her tuck in close
against him, holding her shoulders. She said, "I'm okay. Hewitt, I'm
okay."

Then she began to cry.

HE WAS ELONGATING the third egg, an exact swift striking as
he turned it on the anvil and now the rod and growing globe were
back in the fire when he heard the car come into the yard, Hewitt
standing patient waiting for the heat to come back into the metal, the
color to come Halloween orange again when the door above opened.
It was still raining, the windows steamed over; the forge homely
warmth. He knew it was Walter. He reached and took a small swallow

from the diminished bottle but left it right there on the bench. Then stood at the hearth, eyes on the heat of the coal, his right foot pumping slow thrusts of air into the fire from the big bellows below. Knowing Walter wouldn't speak until Hewitt paused his work. So he lifted the rod and moved the reddening bulb to the side of the fire, where it would remain warm. Then turned to his friend.

Walter had his hands shoved deep in his pockets. He said, "Quick trip."

"Yup."

"A dead fire?"

Hewitt considered this approach. "I suppose." He shrugged. "She's got a whole life, kids, job, a husband dead about three weeks. I would say I was most likely the last person she wanted to see."

Walter scuffed the toe of a boot against the hard-packed dirt. "It went that bad?"

"I'll tell you, brother. I would definitely not be looking for her to pull in here anytime in the next fifty or sixty years. It was stupid of me, that's what it comes down to."

"Holding on to something you believe in isn't necessarily stupid."

"No? I'll tell you what. I wasted a good chunk of my life holding on to her and man it might seem noble or something from the outside but from where I stand right now I'm pretty much an idiot."

"Ask you a question?"

"Shoot."

"Do you regret those years?"

"Regret? Regret losing my mind for several years and pretty much fucking up my life? Regret the plodding to patch back together what I could? Regret? Shit man I'm the guy they put a little picture of in the dictionary next to the definition of regret."

Walter ran a hand through his hair. He said, "That's not regret, that's feeling sorry for yourself. Let me tell you something."

"Sure. Tell me something."

"There's plenty men. And women too. Who've been together so long and been in holes so deep they've decided it's how life is. How it has to be, how one way or another the way it turns out to be. Who can't even begin to imagine the sort of freedom you've known."

"I think it's pretty sad and doesn't have much to do with me. Seeing her, talking to her, I learned I still am all fucked-up. That's not feeling sorry for myself. That's looking the big dragon eye to eye."

Walter had not changed position, hands still in pockets, upright. But now with his feet planted hard rocking back and forth. As if taking something in and plucking toward the truth through the feathers of camouflage. Finally he pulled his hands free, and Hewitt felt that gesture and knew he wasn't going to like what was coming. Walter said, "You waited twenty years and then you went and screwed it up. Isn't that right? Isn't that what happened? You poured yourself out to her. Probably the first time you saw her. The only big dragon around here is you."

Hewitt said, "Fuck you asshole. You know I couldn't go and play Mr. Cool. Then you stroll down in here and sum it all up. Well, listen. Thanks for the use of your car. Thanks for taking care of things while I was gone. And thank you for making clear that whichever way I twisted on this one I was bound to lose. Fuck you. And if you're screwing Jessica just take her back to your house and get both your shit out of my life because I don't need it right now. I'm sure she'd fit right in. I'd bet anything she'd approve of the idea of gluing aluminum foil to the walls to keep people from listening in or beaming thoughts into your head or whatever it is that makes you so fucking sane and me so fucking crazy. So why don't you just get out of here. You moron sonofabitch."

Walter glanced now at the bottle of Jameson on the bench. A slow sweep of his head, a gesture intentional and planned. He said, "My, my. I had no idea I was such a pain in the ass. And sorry, bro, but Jessica's your deal. I'm just helping her paint her car. No worries. We can move it to my place and do it there. If you recall, I've *never* lingered where I'm not wanted. And I see you've got your old buddy back. A much better fit, I'm sure. A load you can hump right along. Although of course it won't be that long and the load will be humping you but hey, I'm not telling you anything you haven't forgotten, right? You down with that bro? But what the fuck, why settle for that old shit? You can haul ass over to Rutland or White River and score top quality smack easy as pie now. Yup, all the high school kids are into that shit. So why not? Oh, that's right. You don't really want to pull down the veil. You just want heap big pain medicine. Hey, but who knows? Maybe this time'll be different. Maybe this time you can suck down the booze and let it all out and it'll be different because you'll have a full-time audience. Maybe you can work yourself right down into such a sad needy pathetic little mess of a man that Jessica will get her own power back. Taking care of you. It's what you need. Isn't it? Somebody to take care of you. While you and John Jameson there waltz around the room, falling over furniture and giving yourself psychic black eyes. Or how bout this? Maybe seeing you do all that shit will give her the boost—roust her right out of here. I mean, listen man—you never saw yourself sucked down into the bottle but I have and I can tell you it's ugly. And you can bet she's seen it too. Yup, I'd bet a dime she'll watch you maybe a week and decide there's sunny skies somewhere, hell most anywhere but right here. No, no, I'm going. But tell me one thing man? I'm just curious. Just one thing."

Hewitt was blazing, silent.

Walter leaned close without moving his feet. "How does it taste, man? As lovely as you remembered? Or better?"

Hewitt still had the tapered hammer in his hand although he'd forgotten it. But then it was there and he wanted to step forward and plant it in Walter's forehead. At the last moment he backhanded it against the far wall and heard the thud even as he stepped hard and fast toward Walter who was still rocking back and forth. Hewitt drew

back his fist and never even saw the mean uppercut that dropped him
to the floor.

WHEN HE WOKE it was near dusk and the rain had quit. Outside his bedroom window was a patchy sky where light bled through
so faint gold and blue colored the clouds, almost a winter sunset. His
jaw a thumping lump and his whole head hurt. But there was no confusion except for having no idea how he got to the bed. He was in
pain and humiliated, not for what had occurred but why. There was
a bad moment when he turned his bruised face into the pillow wanting it all just to go away. But the weight of his head against the pillow
was a red streak of pain and he rolled away, on to his back.

Goddamn, he thought. Walter clocked me.

He was some time getting upright from the bed. Still dressed,
thank those who had no desire or inclination to remove his clothes.
He held on to a bedpost with one hand as he sought balance against
the swimming of his head. As if his brain had come undone and was
sloshing side to side within his cranium. And then saw the tall glass
of water on the bedside table and three aspirin in a neat row. Enough
to make a better man weep but for this man at the moment just what
he needed. He went to the bathroom to, as old ladies liked to say,
freshen up.

Out in the hall it was very quiet. There was no inkling of anyone
else in the house. Perhaps he was alone. A prospect both earned and
dreaded but yet, if it came to that, so be it. He'd lived alone a long
time. As he inched his way down the stairs he thought Phantoms come
and phantoms go.

Jessica lay on the couch. On her back, eyes closed. In long loose
shorts that just covered her kneecaps, the shorts with military-style
pockets on the front and sides. Above the shorts she was layered. He
walked quietly close and saw a white T-shirt under a drooping V-neck
sweatshirt with an unbuttoned flannel shirt over that. She was barefoot but other than her dirty soles she was as hidden as a person could

be and still walk around. And he knew she'd worn this all day, perhaps the day before as well.

It was a strange moment. He leaned close enough so he could feel her breath against his cheek. He knew these were probably her preferred clothes, put on as soon as he left; what Walter saw. And standing over her his pain ebbed. It was illumination—this woman trusted him. For the moment he wasn't interested in any Whys. It was enough to know she did. And she slept. He straightened and looked at his reflection in the window above the couch. Somebody there wavered and pitched about in the glass.

In the kitchen he removed the jack from the phone. The number of new messages disappeared like a magic trick. He filled a quart jar with fresh water and went back to the living room. He sat in the old wingback chair across from the couch and slowly drank the water. The house was quiet enough so he heard the in and out of Jessica breathing as she slept. Twice the cistern pump in the basement kicked on and ran.

The dark was gaining and he went quietly through the house and turned on a few lights. Back in the living room the small lamp of the sort used to illuminate paintings he'd installed over the stereo rack and wall of shelved music—the perfect light to attend to an evening of music while the room itself spread soft from the slight overflow. He considered a drink but decided against it. He was feeling toxic and oddly at peace. Still he felt strange sitting in the barely lit room with Jessica sleeping on the couch—he didn't want her to wake and see him just sitting there. He was comforted by her presence and had a vivid fear of being mistakenly viewed as predatory, or any lesser degree of how she might consider his silent watching. The only thing for it was music but even the selection held enormous weight. Most simply not to wake her. He went down on his knees and quickly found his father's old vinyl recording of Borodin's String Quartet no. 2 in D major. Then went through the ritual of cleaning the turntable and cleaning both sides of the album, turning the volume low and placing the heavy disc on the table and slowly settling the needle down. There was only the faintest hiss and then the old near forgotten slow beautiful music tempered the room and softened it even further.

Hewitt thought it was the first good choice he'd made in a couple of days.

When it ended Hewitt rose and lifted the arm and placed it back in its cradle. He paused then, considering what came next.

Jessica spoke, just loud enough for him to hear. "That was nice. How you doing, Hewitt?"

He hesitated and flipped the album over and set the needle down in the outer groove. Still Borodin. String Quartet no. 1 in A major. Only when the music began did he turn.

She'd come up so she was sitting cross-legged on the couch, her arms loose, hands hidden in the fold of clothes in her lap. He didn't bother answering her, guessing she knew as much as she needed.

After a bit Jessica said, "Walter feels awful bad about slugging you."

"I know he does."

"He said it's the first time he hurt anybody in years and years."

"I believe that too."

They were quiet again. The flowing counterpoint of violins, violas, cellos and bass around them, as if emanating from the room itself, the walls and floor and ceiling.

Again Jessica broke the silence. "I'm sorry," she said.

And in her tone Hewitt knew she meant everything.

So he said, "Thanks." Then, not for pity but to clarify, he said, "I made a damn fool of myself."

She smiled, "I sorta figured that out. There's worse things a person can do."

"I guess. I'm not feeling so good about it right now."

She said, "All of feeble life recedes until there is but dust and air and the song of the morning bird."

"What the hell is that?"

"I don't know. Something I learned in school. Some old poet or something. But it's true."

"I guess. It's nice to think so." Then because he couldn't bear to go further this evening he said, "So you and Walter got along?"

She shrugged. "He's strange but nice. He hasn't hit on me."

Hewitt noted this and then realized it was none of his business. He said, "What's the deal with the Bug? You get tired of the old paint job?"

She was matter of fact. "He convinced me it was foolish driving a car that screams Look at me, especially the way I live. And when I balked, I mean nobody but nobody can say shit like that to me and not get flipped off, he went into this smooth little bit about the car itself and pointing out to me all the things about it that made it differ- ent from newer Beetles and man he had it down, he knew his shit and the next thing he was down on his back with a penknife and scraped away just enough paint so he could stand up and tell me things I didn't know. The car originally had been this creamy mint green but it was a rare color only used for a few years and then he went off about how there wasn't a speck of rust on the whole thing and we should repaint it that old color and he'd even go out and find the whitewall tires that would match it. He said he didn't want or expect anything in return except the chance to turn that car back into what it deserved to be. Hewitt, I got thinking about my grandmother and how she'd feel about the car, both how it looks right now and how it'd be when we were done and that was pretty much that. Truth is I thought we'd have it done by the time you got back."

Hewitt had to grin. Which hurt. So he said, "Well, I'm gonna have to threaten to shoot him next time he shows up, just for my pride. And he'll probably take my side-by-side out of my hands and crack me over the head. No, it won't bother me. You two go on and paint your car. I've got plenty of work to keep myself busy anyway. When he's done you won't believe your eyes. It'll look like the day your grandmother bought it off the lot. And now I'm going to bed be-

196

cause I couldn't even tell you what day of the week it is which is usually fine but I'm run over and used up and have offended more people than I care to think about. Including myself. So I'm going to bed."

And he stood and looked at her a long moment and she looked back at him and he dearly wanted to step to the couch and hug her but his reasons were selfish—he wanted to know that someone in this world cared for him. So he wavered a bit side to side and said, "I expect I'll be up early."

She pulled her shoulders a little tighter together, gathering herself. "Hewitt? You and Walter, you going to be okay?"

"I expect so. We go back a ways. He was just pissed because I'd done something stupid and compounded it by doing something else just as stupid."

She nodded, very serious. "It's not my business what you do. You do what you have to, you hear?"

"You know, Jessica? Sometimes you have to crawl back where you once were and get inside it all over again to make sure it's no place you want to be."

"I seen that myself."

"Walter's a good shit. He didn't change my mind so much as sharpen my focus. That's all."

"You read any of that book he's writing?"

Hewitt blinked and said, "Which book is that?"

She didn't miss the blink. "I thought you knew. Well, he didn't let me read any of it, either. But it's boxes and boxes of paper. He says it's every strange thing he knows about, every strange story he's ever heard. All the way back to some history that doesn't exist. Or maybe does, I don't know."

"Well, I'll be damned. You think he's going to try and get it published?"

"He says that'd be the last thing he wants."

Hewitt nodded. "Sounds right. All right, girl, I'm off to catch up on two three days of sleep."

"Good night, Hewitt."

"Good night, Jessica." He turned away toward the hall and the stairs. She called after him. "Sleep tight."

He glanced back, still walking, mere degrees from a stumbling shuffle of exhaustion. And said, "You too, sweetie. You too."

UP EARLY, THE sun streaming over the hills into a sky near startling for its clarity. Sometimes, he thought, a good clout to the jaw lets you be surprised by the world. While the coffee was making he walked out to the forge and pumped up the fire and took stock. The third egg was ready for its final hammerwork. Then the fourth and after that the finish work and, for this job, for the delicacy of touch he wanted and also the strength needed, the final spot-weld with the oxyacetylene torch. Hewitt preferred the challenge of forge welding but the size of the gates along with his determination that the eggs appear to be simply resting atop the gate ends, made the torch inevitable. Then what remained was gentle warming of the gates, section by section and applying coats of linseed oil. This would take days. Most smiths were content with three coats, perhaps for a fixture like this that would be outside, four. Hewitt worked with a minimum of six and these gates would likely get eight. The initial difference in appearance between three coats and eight would not be apparent to near anyone. But Hewitt knew however much he insisted on the importance of yearly tending with steel wool and on a hot summer day a new coat of the oil, the owner would almost certainly neglect this. Until the iron had lost the accretion of the oil and slowly began to gain the mottled patina of rust. Hewitt knew his clientele and so one day, four or five years down the road they would come to a stop and notice their extraordinarily expensive ironwork was rusted and like as not spend an afternoon with a half-dozen cans of flat black spray paint, or, if the work was lucky, they might instruct their caretaker to wire-brush it before painting it. The linseed oil would not be a distant memory but something forgotten altogether.

The fire was up enough in the forge so he could leave it while he had his coffee. Maybe a small breakfast of toast and juice. Last minute he grabbed up the bottle of whisky and carried it with him. Up the stairs back into the day. Glorious day. A day for symphonies.

Back in the silent house he poured a cup of coffee. He was starting to think about bacon and eggs. He felt hollow, as if he'd not eaten in days and started bacon over low heat and worked at his coffee, then without pause poured the rest of the whisky down the sink drain and tossed the bottle into the trash. As he moved back toward the stove he noticed the phone unplugged from the night before and smiled without humor. He crawled under the table to retrieve the dropped cord and plugged it into the back of the answering machine which lit up with a solemn blinking zero.

He went back to the stove and poured another cup of coffee, fussed with the bacon with a fork but the heat was so low the meat wasn't ready to turn. That was fine. He drank his coffee. He was feeling pretty good. Even the lump in his jaw was almost gone. He thought he'd have to tell Walter it wasn't much of a punch. And smiled, thinking this.

The phone rang. As far as Hewitt was concerned the day was well advanced. The coffee was working and he had a solid plan for the next few days and the sizzle of bacon starting to rise in the room. So he stepped over and picked up the phone. "Good morning," his voice rolling and thoughtless. His mind was on eggs. Fried or scrambled.

"You went home."

He drew a breath.

She said, "You showed up at my door without even the decency of a warning. And I told you everything. It wasn't a conscious choice. I couldn't stand holding it in anymore. And for the shortest of moments you felt safe. But you weren't safe, not at all. You bastard."

"Emily—"

"A stronger man could've allowed me that opening. And understood it. If I was religious I could've gone to the Lutheran minister but I'm not. My only other option is to travel to Rochester and see a therapist but to pull that off long enough to do any good would involve more lies. And I'm sick of lies right now. Then there you were and you felt safe. Are you listening, Hewitt? You felt safe. And I unloaded, the nasty story hidden behind the destruction of my life. And what did you do? Were you a stand-up guy? Did you realize I didn't want advice or somebody who knows nothing about children telling me how to deal with them? Did it occur to you I simply needed to get the words out from poisoning my brain? Not for an answer but just to get them out. Because maybe, just maybe, by doing that I could begin to begin to work forward through this?"

"Emily, I—"

"Can you even begin to imagine what it was like standing there in my house which feels one minute like it's smothering me and the next like it's the only place I can hide although every time I turn around an entire life that was vibrant and full and everything a life should be is gone and will never be again? Not just my life Hewitt. But the life of the man I expected to grow old with, watching our children grow up and go out and make their own lives and have them come home married with children of their own. Can you understand that? And then you, goddamn it, you stood in my kitchen and confessed your own sad little dreamworld. Your undying love for me? Who the fuck do you think you are? You bastard. And then, and then," she was gulping air, "on your way out you were nasty to my son who came in as soon as you left and found me sitting on the goddamn floor weeping. Do you know why I was crying, Hewitt? Do you really want to know?"

Now she was quiet. Waiting. Because he knew she was not done and she was exacting this from him. There was no choice.

Simply he said, "Yes."

"Because, because," and she was crying now. "Because until you showed up I was all fucked-up, my life pulled inside out, but I was either tromping onward or doing my best imitation of it. But then there you were. Spitting and sputtering about your life and I stood there and thought This is too fucking much, the universe or God are truly ganged up to break me. And I broke. I just collapsed. And there's my poor little boy kneeling beside me and stroking my back and telling me over and over that it would be okay. You bastard. What business did you have? What in the world made you think you had the right to come to me? And spill out your shit on top of me? We're all grown up now, Hewitt. Aren't we?"

Hewitt was pressing the phone so hard against his head that his ear hurt. His arm ached, his head ached. His heart was not pumping, best as he could tell. The room swimming around him. The silence, the faint electric crackle. And only then realized she was done. Waiting for him.

Finally he said, "I never intended to do that to you. It just came out. It's why I came home. To leave you be."

"I wish you'd done that to start with. I have to go now. I have to get dressed and go to work. Goodbye, Hewitt. And good luck."

The line went dead. After a time he slowly put the receiver back in the cradle, but stood looking down at the phone. He hated the telephone.


"YOU TRYING TO figure out how a telephone works or do you like your bacon burned up and filling the house with smoke? I mean, it's your house and all but I'm sure as hell not going to eat that pig meat so you want I should toss the pan out back to cool off or what?"

Jessica in the doorway, wearing his old sweatpants and a large denim shirt loose over the pants.

Hewitt scraped the crusted bacon into the trash, rinsed the pan and used a copper brush to clean the pan under cold water before setting it back on the stove to dry.

He turned back to her and said, "That coffee's fresh. I'm going to be gone most of the morning. Is Walter coming to work on the Bug with you?"

"Best I know. The car wasn't all wrapped up like a ugly Christmas present I could drive you."

"I appreciate it. But remember, I did just fine before you came along." And grinned against misinterpretation.

She said, "You know what Hewitt? Since I've been here that evidence is not so strong. Or maybe it's me." She seemed to brighten with this declaration. "Shitfire, it wouldn't be the first time I was the one blamed for things going wrong."

"You're fine. You're the most fun I've had in a long time. Don't you worry about that."

She paused, taking this in, her face showing slight doubt but he was used to that. Then she said, "So, you walking? Or hitchhiking?"

"Hell no. Some lunatic might pick me up. I'll take the tractor. Where I'm going, it'll get the job done."

She tipped her head to one side. She was waking. A grin straight from Puck popped over her face and she said, "You should get you a horse, Hewitt. You could sneak up on people and not stink up the air like that tractor exhaust."

"Thanks," he said. "But I've got an old barn cat to watch out for, and myself and other stray humans and I'd hate to think of an animal counting on me."

"Wouldn't that be terrible. To have some living thing count on you."

It was time to go. He walked over and kissed her forehead before she had a chance to pull her head away and said, "Walter shows up, tell him I said he can't hit worth shit. I'm all but healed."

He pulled the Farmall around to the five-hundred-gallon farm tank and filled it up. Technically he wasn't entitled to the agricultural gas but the fuel company didn't care or question and Hewitt felt no guilt over duping the state and feds from their taxes. Now, filling the tractor and fresh from Emily's succinct comment about his maturity or lack thereof, he wondered if this stubbornness was only another manifestation of that condition or, as he'd long believed,

an appropriate response to inappropriate action. What the fuck. He
liked driving the tractor.

He had the two miles to go to the village, a brief stop there and
then near another four miles. All told a round trip of a dozen miles,
perhaps a bit more. The old tractor clattered along, the spread narrow
front tires wobbling and the steering wheel shuddered and called for
a firm grip.

He rounded the bend in the road that followed Pearce Brook and
came into the cluster of homes, church, single store and post office
that was Lympus Village. His immediate destination the outside phone
booth attached to the store. This call he could not have made from
home—it had been too early and then there was Jessica. Not that she
should matter but he figured just because she was living at his house
didn't entitle her to more than she already knew about him, which
was plenty.

It took a moment to register the county cruiser parked nose out
by the store. Where the deputy could see traffic coming and going.
The speed limit in the village was thirty-five but only tourists and old
people observed this. Lympus was not a destination but a straight stretch
on the road to somewhere else. Hewitt atop the Farmall was well under
the limit but cursed silently, avoiding eye contact with the deputy,
Pete Snow.

Hewitt slowed and even remembered to use the small fender-
mounted light that indicated he was turning in. He passed the cruiser
and a sedan and pickup parked before the store and came to a stop
before the phone booth. A small dilemma; he had no desire for Pete
to stroll up while he was on the phone. So he went into the store and
bought a Coke and six donuts made fresh that morning. Then slapped
out the screen door and saw Pete walking slowly around the tractor,
as if admiring it. It wasn't candied up like some of the old rigs that
spent the year under a tarp in a barn and were brought out for parades
and the Tunbridge World's Fair each fall—just a well-maintained serviceable rig with everything original intact and pushing sixty years old.

Hewitt stood reading the various notices tacked to the outer wall of the store. Services offered included butchering, backhoe and bush-hog work, babysitting by a girl last he'd seen was being babysat herself, massage, rabbits for sale, a friendly male llama in need of a good home, Barred Rock pullets ready to go, yoga classes, contra dancing. A pair of snowmobiles (used one season!). And so on. Pete was still at the tractor, seated on one of the short narrow little front tires. His butt bloomed either side but then again, Hewitt told himself, if I had to pack myself into polyester each day and cruise the county roads I'd likely spread a bit too. And Pete, with the unspoken mandate to leave people be as much as possible, to overlook all but the accidents and overt violations of the law did a pretty good job at this. Unless he didn't like you. And Hewitt wasn't quite sure how Pete felt about him. An attitude likely intentional, to keep Hewitt off balance.

He jogged down the three steps and came to a stop before the deputy.

"Pete."

"Hewitt." A pause, then, "Nice weather idn't it?"

"Keeping us all busy."

Pete rubbed his chin. "Heard Bill got the first cut off your place. Nice hay he said."

"It was. He got the timing just right."

Pete patted the tractor tire. He said, "So. You out farming this morning, Hewitt?"

This was bait like a fat night crawler. But unless he was intoxicated, Hewitt had as much right as anyone to drive the tractor anywhere he wanted to. Eight-year-old boys routinely moved tractors, towing equipment, from place to place, using the roads as needed. And Hewitt knew Pete was likely just spending time. The problem was that the pending phone call, and hopefully the visit about to be made, was not one Pete would like. For purely personal reasons. So he played along.

"I'm heading up Duffy Hill. Heard Crosby Duffy had a trailer to sell might fit this rig. You know Crosby, he won't answer the phone much more than I will. So the only thing's to drive up, hope he's home and hope the trailer fits."

"What're you needing a trailer for, Hewitt?"

"Well, I thought I could haul my dreams around in it. Goddamn Pete, you looking to bust me or just give me a hard time?"

"Curious is all. Trying to keep the peace."

"I'm peaceful Pete. But my sugarbush is filled up with old trees and my firewood's low. I thought I might clean it up over the summer. That trailer would come in handy."

"There idn't nobody sugaring that anymore is there?"

"Well, I thought I got it cleaned up perhaps somebody would come in and tap. Hate to see those trees just standing there. Big buggers."

"I sugar a bit myself."

"I know it. Tell you what, come fall why don't you drive up and take a walk around. A man could run pipeline and set up a gathering tank and haul sap out of there would make a deaf man sing. Now, you'll excuse me, I'm gonna try Crosby one more time on the phone here and then get on up there. Even if he idn't there I guess I can find the trailer and make sure it'd work so I don't waste more time."

And Hewitt turned away from Pete Snow. Praying Pete would take the hint and at least go back to sit in the cruiser.

Pete said "Hewitt."

Hewitt turned. Pete said, "That trailer of Crosby's don't do you any good, call me. I got one might fit this old rig. Needs new tires but it's good to go otherwise."

Hewitt studied the deputy. "Thanks Pete. I'll let you know."

And turned then with clear purpose and strode to the public phone. Which was not a booth the way they used to be but a machine with a minimum of hood and siding. Privacy depended on who was standing around. He didn't look back as he fished for coins in his pocket but he could hear Pete moving away on the gravel of the parking lot. He slipped the quarter into the slot and dialed the number and turned a bit sideways, enough to see Pete settle into the cruiser.

Hewitt turned back and leaned in tight to the phone and waited through three rings and she picked up.

"Amber," he said. "Can you talk?"

"What do you want?"

He said. "I need to see you."

"I'm a mess."

"So am I."

Another pause. Then she said, "Where are you?"

"The store."

"You want me to pick you up?"

He didn't even look to see if the cruiser was still there. It didn't matter. "No. I'm on the tractor. It'll take me a bit."

"Oh frig it. Come on up. I guess you know the way." The line went dead.

He ate a donut and climbed back on the tractor, set the bag of donuts back behind him in the toolbox and cracked the Coke. Reversed the Farmall and headed south out of town. The only question was if Pete decided to follow him. But there were three miles to go before he had to fake left on to Duffy Hill Road or go another quarter mile for the long driveway that led up through the woods to the log house built by Pete's brother Norton and his wife after years of pursuit, Amber Potwin.

She had been Hewitt's first girlfriend, a designation that began when they were both eight and continued sporadically and with significant interruptions until finally eight years ago she married Norton. Two years before that she'd moved in with Hewitt and they'd settled into a domestic routine that for a time was sweet.

Amber was so well known to him—he could wake with frost flowers scrambled on the windowglass and watch her sleeping beside him and still see the girl in her shorts and sleeveless blouse wading with him in stagnant snowmelt pools near the brook, her auburn hair trickling past her nose and her bright eyes watching him, a mayonnaise jar filled with tadpoles, the girl more than delighted to help the boy move these creatures from a drying death to the wealth of life in the flowing brook pools. And later those first tentative grapplings at eleven or twelve, sitting on the hillside when he put his arm around her and she turned her face to him and they kissed and then the frightening surge in his own shorts of erection. A year later when she began to swell her blouse and their kissing had advanced considerably there was the day they rolled in the tall meadow grass and Hewitt was on top of her and he said, "I want you," and she'd responded, "Take me," and then both lay kissing, the words uttered not their own but from books or the movies, not only unsure how humans proceeded but also knowing they were in drama, their passion was play, those words were in some way practice and everything else they were doing was close enough. And then finally, after she had dated a boy two grades ahead for a school year they were released back into their summer dreams and one night with purloined cans of beer and a pack of Old Golds they'd been up in the meadow and Hewitt was determined then to break through to what seemed the only thing he did not know and Amber was sighing and groaning in his ear as they kissed and writhing below him in ways that made clear she expected more also and part of him was angry because she'd moved beyond him. So when he sat back on his knees and went to work on the button and zipper of her jeans he was not surprised but exulted that she raised her hips to help him slide down those jeans and when his own were off and he lay upon her probing, she was the one who reached down and introduced him to herself. A short and strange excursion that was not at all what he expected, both less and more and he could not say which or why but he was even then a kind boy and so sat quietly with her afterward as they drank the last warm beer and smoked cigarettes and he did not profess love nor did she. The rest of that summer they met as often as they could and almost always the first thing they did was have sex. There was the remarkable afternoon when his parents were away that Amber came to the house and for the first time they shared a bed, a wondrously grown-up thing to do. Hewitt knew nothing of the sexual workings of women but did know that between one and five that afternoon he came four times with her. Which would prove to be a lifetime achievement.

Hewitt liked to believe he was never quite sure what happened. That year they lived together he began to believe he was inching and sometimes even sliding well into a new life. With a woman known and strong to him. That perhaps Emily was if not forgotten then at least subdued to the past. Beginning to believe in some pure but intricate way he was coming into not a dream-version but an authentic life—one that was not only opening but would continue to do so, an endless rose.

Somewhere around Groundhog Day, when she was working an afternoon shift at the nursing home on a rise of land outside of Sharon, he went for the first time in months out to the forge. It was only later that he was able to backtrack to this moment. But he hadn't been in the forge since early November when he'd finished a traditional fireplace screen. With the February sun on his back he'd spent an hour shoveling out the bank of snow blocking the door to the forge and then went down and sat in the cold hearth. All the materials from the bricks of the massive forge to the tools to the heavy anvils and swage block and even the packed floor seemed the antithesis of what it should be. That evening he was quiet and remote as they ate the chili and cornbread he'd made for supper. The next day he went back again into the forge and began a marathon session of work that took him through apple-blossom time during which he created an entire stair railing, from newel post on up sixteen risers to the anchor post—the piece the fulcrum of what would become his standard—a delicate balance of precisely aligned elements of weight and air, a seemingly effortless meeting of heaviness and light that both rooted the piece and gave the impression of being built in another age for another undertaking altogether. Gone were the vines and tendrils and leaves and ornamentals. Instead the balance lay in the materials, the only concession to ornamentation hammered buttons that suggested flowers by the cut of chisel work and slight swelling that served to hide the few rivets used—the exception a pair of those same buttons twice the size of the others flat atop the newel and anchor posts. He constructed the entire thing in six sections, each weighing nearly five hundred pounds. In July he loaded the sections into a rented covered truck, the ironwork wrapped in the thick pads moving companies provide, and drove west to the Shelburne Farms museum and craft center. With Walter, Robbie Dutton and Nort Snow, he'd unloaded the pieces and arrayed them standing on the grass, turned to the curator and asked, "Is this something you'd be interested in?"

The man removed his cap and rubbed his bald head and said, "Can you trust me with it for a few days?"

"Why?"

"So I can show it to the people who'll decide."

Hewitt shook his hand. Three days later he returned with Amber and found a beautifully constructed staircase in the field before the entrance to the exhibition tent. The work had been done with care and thought equal to the railing—the staircase was freestanding and so was supported by a trusswork of six-by-six and eight-by-eight old beams. Beautiful wood but put together in such a way it seemed to be a portion of the guts of a house moved outside. In the same way the steps, the risers were of wide footworn butternut—truly stairs from someplace moved here for the moment. At the top was a sturdy platform of the same wide boards, large enough to hold three or four people. Not that anyone was allowed to climb these stairs—the effort had been solely to showcase the ironwork railing. Which Hewitt went to work assembling on these lovely stairs to nowhere.

These were the eight-thousand-dollar stair railings and the beginning of not only Hewitt's widespread reputation but also his ability to pick and choose and interpret commissions as he saw fit. Among his other unusual business practices was his refusal to photograph his finished work. He had no portfolio to show potential clients. They either knew his work and trusted him or they'd heard of his work and reputation and gave him a rendering of their best hope and left it to him. He wanted no smooth unblemished cuticle landing middle of a photograph of something made one or three or ten years ago declaring That was it. Because it most certainly was not.

The railings were sold within two weeks of the show's opening. When Hewitt met the buyer the first thing Hewitt said—disregarding the check in the man's hand and waiting with shifting feet through the praise that he would never welcome but would learn was part of the process, not wanted by him but needed by the new customer— "Did you measure your stairs to see if the railing will fit?"

Hewitt was not intentionally rude. But through his father he'd learned something of the world, and the power that flits throughout the world and how to not resist but ride that power and he was doing it now. The man's face said it all. He had a check already made out and this shaggy man in rough stained overalls and a denim work shirt was questioning if he knew what he was doing. The confusion blazed like sunburn across his face and he said nothing, stood holding the check which inexplicably was losing value as he stood.

Gently Hewitt explained the ironwork before them was complete, a finished thing that could not be altered.

He said, "Tell you what. Keep your check for now. Have a good contractor measure your stairs and I'll send you the plans, which have every dimension noted on them. Then you both look things over. The railing should fit if it's a standard set of stairs. But if you want them and alterations need to be done then that work has to be done in your house before we can install the railing. How's that sound?" And he grinned.

So it was and so it would be. The check sent in the mail the next week along with a note explaining that it would be fall before the railing could be installed. The man had the grace to add a note saying he fully expected to pay for the transportation and installation of the railing. Hewitt sent back a postcard with the single word message

"Fine" on the back. When the call finally came that the stairs were ready Hewitt again gathered a couple of helpers and made the trip to Putney and spent four days installing the railing, putting his crew and himself up in a motel. And at the end had again the satisfaction of announcing that his price covered all contingencies, including installation. It wasn't that the man couldn't part with another couple of thousand dollars. Christ knew what he'd paid to have his house altered, his stairs altered, to hold the beautiful railing. Hewitt knew the money out of his own pocket for the time and help of installation would come back to him many times over. And he also knew the stair railing was the last job he'd do on spec. Ever after he would have measurements of his own making before he even began a job.

It was a fine summer. While waiting, while the staircasing was still on view, he had at least a half-dozen job requests come in. He turned down all but two.

And all the while Amber seemed steady shoulder to shoulder with him. While he was working more than ever before during their time together there was still plenty of time for late summer picnic dinners high up on the hill in the dusk or in moonlight drinking wine and more than once chasing her down into the tall pasture grass and those summer clothes coming off as if they were made for that and nothing more. Or the long lazy mornings lying in bed on her days off talking over the small fortunes and misfortunes of those around them and even now and then nudging upon themselves but in a gentle laughing way, a way Hewitt took as loving. Because it was.

The long days he was working she went about her own business. She had a riding horse, a big legged, big chested Percheron Thoroughbred cross that she moved over from her parents and installed in the barn. She brought in a pair of geese Hewitt didn't care for because the gander ambushed him daily at dawn as he was making his way to the forge. And there was goose shit around the barns and in the yard but a hard scuffing of boots against gravel and dew-wet grass pretty much took care of that. It was a good time.

Then came the morning when he'd been up late and she'd gone to bed early because she had to work in the morning. Still in bed she roused him and was up on all fours over him as he fought to come awake. His eyes fighting the sleep tugging him back down but at that moment he thought he was still a good partner. Blinking hard, expecting some mild directive for the day.

She said, "Hewitt. I got to ask you a question."

"What?"

"Are you ever going to ask me to marry you? Or do you just plan to go along the way we been?"

And he rolled away, pulling a pillow to burrow his head. He said, "Christ, Amber, don't do this to me right now." When it was quiet too long above him, he said, "Amber, I don't want to fuck up my life. Give it a break, okay? Isn't this good? We'll talk tonight you want."

When he did get up at noon it was not a genius that saw her drawers rifled in the bedroom and the moderate destruction of crockery tossed into the woodshed. All of which he'd slept through. He had to respect that all she'd broken was junk anyway. It was the gesture she was after, not true affliction. First thing he checked the barn. The big horse Ben was in his stall. So she wasn't really gone.

He spent the afternoon sitting gazing into the forge fire. Trying to decide what to say when she came back that evening. But his brain was a loop. He wanted things just as they were. It was a long afternoon.

Which turned into a long night. He didn't eat or drink and sometime well after midnight went to bed. Thinking still he might wake in the morning and find her beside him. There was a long time of resolve to marry her. Which he knew would dissolve face to face. It was very much not clear if he was fucking up or being true to something. To Emily, he finally admitted.

When he woke midmorning there was no sign of her. His first thought was she just needed some time. Before his first coffee he went out to feed her horse. Who had been there the night before the last time he wandered around the yard and barns waiting for her to drive in. But Ben was gone. The stall door was shut tight and the saddle and pad and bridle were gone as well as the big horse's halter and lead rope. A sack of grain remained and the hay. He went out into the yard and stood and could see where the big horse had disturbed the early fall dew on the tall grass going up the hill.

He went down into the ground, down into the forge and built up heat and spent the day doing bad work. That got worse as the day went on. So bad that he quit before dark and repaired to the house to sit slumped in one of the chairs in the red room gazing without seeing his father's paintings. Wanting something to come through. A futile hopeless effort. Except that after a couple of hours of this he entered his father's work. Perhaps, except as a child which might or might not count, the first time entirely sober and fractured.

Not surprisingly this did not help. The work was frightening—the crude hewn figures of workers both urban and rural set against black or brown or dead green and with a piece, a shadow, or just an intimation of machinery all different but all of a scale, more an implication than concrete substance, the faces and bodies contorted not simply with effort but fatigue ingrained so deeply they drooped even in the sculptural muscle ever present and always mirthless below their grinding, the palette dull with rust or looming machinery, the workmen's faces and their clothes, but then would be the single thick bar of lime green or bright yellow that crept along one edge of the machines or fell diagonally across the men. These slashes of color almost more violent than the silent cry they cut across. And never, not once and it was here the brilliance of the work lay, were the slashes of color allegorical to any but the simplest eye, for in each usage, studied long enough, the organic origin of that color became clear. Thomas Pearce painted what he saw. The old family joke, which originated in one of the few interviews his father ever agreed to give, was he painted the way he did because he was nearsighted but too vain to wear glasses. Thomas Pearce loved to point this quote out as the best reason to never talk to the press.

Hewitt finally pushed up from the sunken leather chair and went to bed but his sleep was splintered and if he slept at all it was in spurts lasting no more than ten or fifteen minutes.

It was three months, the new year, before he saw Amber again.

Although she'd left the geese. Which he butchered and roasted for a decadent and dismal Christmas dinner with his mother and Walter.

HE CAME UP the drive at full throttle and with his foot holding the clutch down shut off the tractor and let it glide up the last of the incline and on to the flat before the immaculate house. A log cabin whose logs Hewitt noted were far too symmetrical to be merely cut and peeled trees. And took a last hit of the Coke and reminded himself to allow people to live other than he did. That he was here for advice not anything else.

Amber was on the deck to meet him. In shorts and a T-shirt, all exposed skin sporting an even dark tan. Something of a marvel this early in the year yet he routinely saw women with these tans well before the end of June, which was creeping up. They recognized the short summer season right from the beginning and embraced it, absorbed it, as if their bodies might store the short blast of summer heat and remember it through the long dark cold months. Her hair was pulled back and bound up on her nape. To allow the sun as much of her as it could have. Of course there was her work—coinciding with their breakup she'd left her job and mostly kept the books for her husband's well-drilling empire but worked summers part-time at a large organic vegetable farm over the hill toward Bethel.

Amber looked good, standing waiting as he walked up the steps to the deck. There were Adirondack chairs and a table with an umbrella over it and on the table was a pitcher of lemonade and a pair of glasses.

"Amber," he greeted her.

She came and touched his cheek with dry tight lips and said, "Pete called me from the store. To warn me he thought you might be headed up here. I said Yes indeed I believe he's on his way but I hadn't seen you since eighteen hundred and froze to death, or so it seemed, so it'd be good to talk to you. I figured there idn't a thing to keep from Nort anyhow and so best out with the truth. Nort's a good shit, you know that. And he's got no reason and never will have, not to trust me. But Pete's a trial. Jeezum, Norton's been gone three days up to the Northeast Kingdom and I've started talking to the plants. You look a little peaked, Hewitt. You want to set down and talk about it?"

"Goddamn," Hewitt said. "It's good to see you, Amber."

"Don't," she said. "Set and drink your lemonade and talk to me. You get a grace period, Hewitt. So what is it?"

They sat across the table. And he told her in nearly full detail what his last couple of weeks had been like, leaving out only the insertion of Jessica into his life. Which had no bearing on his bafflement and anger at himself.

Amber was quiet a time. Then said, "It's funny but I always sort of doubted she was real. I mean, I knew you'd met this girl when you were both pretty much kids. But I always wondered if you were using her as a way to give yourself some distance from other women. Sorry if that bothers you, but it's the sort of thing any woman would wonder."

"Yup," he said.

"Oh my God," she said. "You are such a moron. I mean for Christ sake Hewitt, her husband was dead a couple weeks and instead of handing her some flowers, saying how sorry you were, you backed right up to her front door and unloaded a pile of horseshit. Jesus, Hewitt."

He said, "You know, Amber? I'm kinda aware of that."

"Sorry," she said. "Look, the key thing is she called you. After you'd been a jerk and then tucked tail for home. She called you. A goodbye-forever-asshole sort of call, but think about it. She'd already told you off. And you left. End of story, right?"

"Right."

"But then she calls you to tell you what you already know. What she's already said."

"Yeah but she was pissed. I figure she wanted to make sure I understood that. I figure she doesn't want anything close to a repeat of my stupid self. I figure she was driving the nail home."

There was a long pause.

Then Amber said, "Hewitt, for a reasonably intelligent person you are dumb as shit about women."

"Lack of practice I guess."

She pointed an index finger at him. "Don't you fuck with me." Then she said, "Women don't drive nails—they let the man figure out he's already done that to himself." She paused again. "Go home and go to work. Keep busy. I know the part of you that's willing to coast. So go home and pound iron. And forget about everything else. Okay? You wanted advice, you took much of a day to bother me for it and that's what you get. That and a glass of lemonade."

"Hold on," he said.

"Oh for Christ sake Hewitt, buck up. Get strong."

Amber stood. Hewitt did too. He said, "I'm strong. I'm strong enough. Hell, I was strong enough not to marry you when it would've been the easy thing to do."

She shook her head. "There is nothing sadder than a man angry over what he doesn't understand. I'm telling you what you need to do. But you're missing the rest of it."

He was quiet a time. Then he said, "So you're telling me there's a chance, an outside chance, that sometime, I'll hear from her again."

Amber shook her head and said, "I know you, Hewitt. Don't sit by the phone. Just because she did one thing she didn't need to doesn't mean she doesn't regret it and will ever do it again. I remember your dad. I remember going in the sugarhouse one afternoon with you and watching him work. I remember those strange paintings he made.

He worked all the time, didn't he? Don't be so goddamn precious Hewitt."

"Precious. Right. That sums it up. You know, I appreciate the talk, Amber. And I have to say, best I can figure Norton's a saint." And he turned and walked off the deck which was an architectural device he hated and crunched gravel on his way to the tractor.

She was barefoot and he in boots and so he didn't hear her but felt her hand touch and slip off his shoulder as he climbed on to the Farmall. Where he stopped and looked down at her. Distress a contraction of her face. Hewitt pushed the clutch in and with the other foot clamped hard the brake. His finger against but not pressing the ignition button. He said, "Sorry, Amber. That wasn't called for."

She had a hand up on the rear tire of the tractor, tucked under the fender but he knew it was there. It was a strangely intimate thing to do. So he waited. Her face was turned up and she said, "She's a woman, Hewitt. Not a goddamn memory."

His finger relaxed against the button. And reached out and ran his hand over the top of her head, stroking her hair. She let him, both knowing this was new and harmless and long ago and never lost. Then she stepped out from his hand. She nodded her head as if the conversation was concluded. Which he thought it was. So he ratcheted up the gas and pressed the ignition. The tractor barked and spat oily clouds before it settled into a strong mile-eating tempo.

He looked back down at Amber. She was beside the tractor still, her mouth open and moving with unheard words. He backed off the gas and cried, "What?"

And she stepped up on the narrow running board and cupped a hand to his ear and said, "One thing Hewitt. You got to get rid of that little weird girlfriend everybody's talking about."

Hewitt blinked. Her deep brown and yellow eyes were inches from his. If he'd wanted he could've kissed her before she knew what he was doing. Instead he said, "She's not my girlfriend. And fuck what everybody's talking about." And he put the tractor in reverse and slowly let out the clutch and they were moving. For a moment Amber grasped his shoulders, to steady herself as she bent close and called above the noise, "Don't forget our party," and he grinned up at her before she jumped down.

"Wouldn't dream of it," he called, slid the tractor into second and lurched forward.

# Six

He finished the gates the week after the solstice, including latch and mounting hardware and the brute gateposts, fifteen-foot sections of railroad track to sink into the ground and hold the gates, each of which weighed several hundred pounds. Once up they would swing open as if floating and allow themselves to be pulled closed as if the motion were embedded in the gates.

During this same time Walter and Jessica worked together to paint her car. This involved not just the two coats of primer and the four of paint, but also vigorous buffing of chrome, even the strips along the vent windows, scrubbing the upholstery and roof fabric, then numerous coats of hard wax on the exterior and saddlesoaping and polishing the interior.

Hewitt and Jessica had been eating breakfast the morning after his visit with Amber when Walter pulled in, not in the Bird but with his red jeep, backing around to the front bumper of the Volkswagen. Hewitt asked Jessica to wait in the house. As he was going out the door she said, "He clobbers you again you want I should call the police or just come out and shoot him?"

Hewitt walked barefoot across the yard. Walter was unwinding the winch mounted on the rear of the jeep.

Hewitt said, "Seems it'd be easier to do it in the shed rather than have her walk back and forth to your place, or you running her each way."

"I can't imagine you've got much interest in having me in your line of vision all day long."

"A kicked dog'll shy off, unless he's been caught in the garbage."

Walter sat back on his haunches and tipped his sunglasses up on to his head. "What do you know about dogs?"

"Well, hell, I'm not ten."

Walter eased up on to his feet in a sinuous smooth motion and leaned against the jeep, his hands folded in front of him. "I'm god-awful pissed at myself. I made a promise a long time ago to never again hurt a living being."

Hewitt waited a moment and said, "Sometimes maybe a person has to break one of those promises to make sure they still count."

Walter studied him. Then he said, "That's a generous way of looking at it."

"Hey, bro. I was talking about myself."

"Is that so?"

"That's so."

Walter nodded a couple of times and then said, "I still want to apologize."

"I druther you not."

Walter looked off up the hill and said, "We're square, then?"

"I already forgot what we were talking about."

Walter nodded again and looked back at Hewitt. He stuck out his hand and they power-shook, locked thumbs with fingers over the backs of each other's hand.

Hewitt said, "Ask you something?"

"Sure, man."

"Jessica said you're writing a book of some sort. That right?"

"It's something."

Hewitt nodded. Then he said, "Is it about all those things you told me you can't talk about?"

Walter reared back his head. His sunglasses slipped and landed halfway down his nose. He reached up and adjusted them and said,

"No. Those are things can't be told. That was most of why Pam left. She wanted me to talk things out. She thought that's what I needed. But those are stories that are so strangely fucking true they become lies the moment you open your mouth." He paused and grinned and said, "She always thought that was bullshit. But it's not just me. You ride over to the VA with me someday, or down to the Legion. It's all the same. Not just the boys from the Nam either. The Korean and WW Two vets—they'd say the same thing. Oh they can tell you, so can I, where I was and when and all that shit that doesn't mean a thing. But the stories? What happened? Nobody can tell you that."

Hewitt said, "Because you can't understand it unless you've been through it."

"No," Walter said. "Because you can't understand it afterward. All it is, is what it was while it was going on, and no man can explain that. There idn't but one or two that've come close. Now, we going to stand around jabbering all day or is there work to be got done?"

Hewitt nodded. He said, "You going to tell me what your book's about?"

Walter said, "No."

THE LAST DAY Walter showed up late with a bucket of chicken and box of fried whole clams picked up at the Onion Flats take-out window and two bottles of wine. All three climbed into the orchard to sit and feast. For a person who did not eat meat, Jessica was wolf-ish. She preferred drumsticks and thighs, which would've been a prob-lem since they were Hewitt's favorite also but he convinced her to try a clam. After that it was a giddy free-for-all, hands and faces grease painted, shining in the slanting sunlight. The wine was good. Much better than what Walter usually would spend money on. But it was a celebration and Hewitt understood for far more than the two big jobs completed on the same day.

Jessica, a mouth full of clams and grimy wineglass in hand, said, "You two are corrupting me."

"You betcher ass," Walter said. "I never seen a person more in need of a little honest corruption than you. And you're doing fine. Like a duck to water."

"You know how these chickens are raised?" She waved a stripped drumstick like a baton, indicating the world beyond their view.

"A course I do. But you start ticking off all that's wrong with this day and age and so on and so forth and you'll die before your list is half done." He paused and then said, "Sometimes, a chicken leg is just a chicken leg. How many of those are left anyhow?"

"I don't know. I'm gonna concentrate on these clams."

"All filled up with pollution of all sorts. Bad shit. Clams are dug from the mudflats at low tide. Where all the chemicals and God knows what else have been piling up and settling for centuries."

"Will you shut up? I was having a good time."

"You still are, little sister. You still are."

"Pass me a fill-up of that wine," she said.

Hewitt already full, lying on his back listening. It was a fine evening. The sun was swelling into soft diffusion above them, those last long rays running down over them. The ground emitting the heat of the day. The apple trees over him.

MORE THAN ONCE Hewitt woke in the night to pee and from the top of the stairs saw the light on below and knew she was in with his father's paintings. He was curious which of those works she might like more than others but had not yet found the moment to talk with her about them. Part of this was his schedule and part was wanting to leave her privacy. It had taken Hewitt himself years and years to comprehend those paintings and while this was partly because of his particular link to them, he knew they exerted some version of that force upon others. So he waited. And in the waiting he found some new level of fondness for her—that his father's work would infect and compel her as it so clearly did.

\* \* \*

THE DAY AFTER the picnic in the orchard they moved the gates to Pomfret. It was a procession—the Volkswagen like a vision on the back roads over the hills, Walter with his jeep, the back filled with the rail-track posts and tools for digging the postholes, and leading them all the small U-Haul holding the wrapped gates and because it was a Sunday, Roger Bolton at the wheel and Hewitt in the passenger seat, his head out the window, straining to hear any disturbance in the back and flicking his head around to urge Roger to slow down. It could take most of the day to auger the postholes and set the posts and then mount the gates. At this point it came down less to mastery than luck. Measure and measure and measure again but still until the whole thing was in and up and working smooth as sleet on snow there was no way to control the process. A boulder two feet down could change the entire procedure. The owner, who lived most of the year in Katonah, a surgeon of obscure and expensive procedures, was not yet there. Hewitt loved the idea of the man arriving in ten days and finding the gates up and waiting. And it would happen. With either a morning or a long day of work ahead of them all.

First Hewitt measured the exact distance for the gatepost holes, using a chalkline to snap a triangle on the ground the bottom straight between the two holes and the two peak lines of the diagram going off at angles to meet precisely in the center of the driveway a dozen feet up the drive.

They got lucky. Roger had a four-foot gas powered fence post auger and with Hewitt hovering dropped the point exactly on the blue chalk cross and the auger sank into the ground, spewing soil dark and loamy. Then a hard hour with manual posthole diggers, one man on his belly to guide and another upright to work the handles. The steel track needed to be eight feet in the ground to support the gates, to hold steady through the deepest winter frost. It was hard work and nailbiting—the deeper they went the more likely to strike the buried boulder or glacial bedrock. But luck held and soon they were inserting the posts, Hewitt again dancing with a chalkline and a pair of five-foot construction levels as ever so slowly they filled and tamped the poles. It didn't matter to Hewitt that the sections of post above ground would be blocked in with columns of brick and mortar: he wasn't doing that part of the job so had only his own work to count on to keep those ties forever straight and upright. Then it was simply a matter of bolting the gate hinge hardware on to the ties and finally lifting each gate and aligning the three female ends of the hinge assembly above the male uprights and sliding them down into place.

With both gates on and wide open Hewitt stepped back a moment to take them in. The others were leaning against the U-Haul. After a long pause he gave the right-hand gate a light shove and it swung graceful and slow and paused just off the chalkline. Then the other and it responded the same way. The gates were within an inch of meeting freely on their own. Considering their weight and size this was more than acceptable—it was perfect. He stepped to where they met and aligned them, for the first time actually feeling the exquisite floating balance of them, paused again a moment with one hand on each gate before reaching and dropping the latch from the right side into the left.

He turned and said, "Thanks, guys. Let's get out of here."

Hewitt walked around the Volkswagen and got in the passenger side. The interior of the car was as staggering as the paint job. It could've been forty years ago. Even the sunlight cracks on the dashboard had been filled and smoothed and so were lost, gone now. For Hewitt it was a fine moment, the apex of two large jobs met and done.

Jessica got in and said, "They're fucking gorgeous Hewitt."

"Hush," he said, a voice too mild to take offense from. Then he said, "I'd like to show you something? You up for it?"

She paused and looked over at him. The pause went on, long enough so he knew she'd had some plan of her own.

At last she said, "Yeah, show me something, Hewitt."

It was fine to be driving the dirt roads out of Pomfret in the little car that seemed made for this prime summer day, traveling under the dappled canopies of roadside trees, both taking in while pretending not to notice the swiveling necks within other cars they passed. The first thing he did was direct her high into the hills and had her stop the car before the roadside marker, an ancient stone post driven deep and with faint letters still clear enough to be read that designated this almost lost road through the woods as the King's Highway, the date obliterated. Mounted lower on the flat face of the stone was a small brass disc clearly dated 1882 which simply read THE FIRST THOROUGHFARE IN CENTRAL VERMONT EST. 1764. The center of the disc had a profile of a man in a wig with smaller letters GEORGE III and at the bottom of the disc in larger letters the initials D.A.R.

Hewitt said, "Idn't that something?"

Jessica was quiet and then said, "Damn. This road. It's older than the country itself."

"That's right."

She was quiet a long moment and then said, "You got to wonder. Did those Vikings built that chamber at your place, and the others you spoke of—maybe they hiked through here too."

"Could be."

Again she was quiet and then said, "In Mississippi, there's speculation those old Spaniards wandered through. They found pieces of metal, swords and bits of armor and stuff like that. And there's the big Indian Mounds. Some really big ones in the Delta. People say it wasn't just little tribes stuck off in the woods here and there but a whole deal going on. Cities and all that. It makes you wonder how much what we think we know is true and how much just convenience. Know what I mean?"

Hewitt looked at her, her serious absorbed face. He said, "Well, for the moment at least we're the ones in charge. So we get to pick and choose. And we choose that history begins with us."

She punched the toe of her sneaker into the soft roadside dirt, where the grader had come through since the spring thaw. She said, "Is that what you wanted to show me? That nobody knows shit about how things ever really were?"

He said, "No. I just thought you should see it. We've got a ways to go to complete the Hewitt tour. Why don't we get back in the car."

They went slowly on down Cloudland Road, just driving and taking it in. They came out along the Ottauquechee River, turned on to hardtop and drove the two miles into Woodstock. Where they circled the Green three times before finding a place to park and then let themselves out into the waves of people on the sidewalks. It was summer and Woodstock was in high gear. Hewitt wasn't able to make the trip over often nor did he want to but when he did he always enjoyed himself. There was something about the place that reminded him of Fellini. Not the lovely village but the tumbling side by side improbable antique shops, art galleries, specialty stores, boutiques, but particularly the clutter of humanity. Men his own age with video cameras walking slowly backward, oblivious, trying to catch that elusive panoramic view. They walked two blocks from where they'd been forced to park and went down into a basement restaurant which was always filled for dinner but too expensive for the hordes wanting lunch. Or perhaps it wasn't the cost of the lunch but the reluctance of visitors to cut an hour and a half out of an already expensive day to sit over lunch the way lunch was served. Hewitt, who had never been to Europe but bet many of the people he passed on the street had, wondered how they dealt with the legendary French midday meal. Poorly, he guessed. The restaurant was half-full and Jessica and he took a table in the modest bar. And ate well and slowly. Jessica had wine with her food but Hewitt held off. He was all pumped up, coursing with vitality. Not just from the morning, although that was enough. But also for what he was doing now and what he planned.

Outside on the street she said, "I need to learn how to cook."

He laughed and said, "So do I."

Her face shadowed a bit and she said, "I'm serious. I can barely fry a egg."

He slowed. "The best food's not fancy just prepared with some thought. Anybody can learn that. And the rest, the fancy stuff, that's for special times."

She studied him. There was a small streak of dirt on her forehead she'd missed both times she'd gone to the bathroom. Hewitt liked it, wanted to touch it but did not. Jessica said, "What's that mean? Is this a treat because you got those gates done? Or what?"

He said, "It's a pile of things. Including getting the gates up. But there's one more thing I want to show you and then we'll go back to the house and I'll show you where the cookbooks are."

Her mouth pouched. Hewitt thought Is that serious or a pout? Then she said, "I'll cook some. But don't push or I'll bring home frozen pizza." They were stalled on the sidewalk and people flowed around them like water around a rock. And Jessica took a moment and looked around, not at the pretty village but the invaders. She said, "Shoot, Hewitt. Are these the beautiful people?"

"What?"

"Like the Beatles song."

He squinted, then laughed and took her hand, back toward where they were parked. She jostled against him as they went. After a bit he said, "I guess it's their Magical Mystery Tour."

At the car she sat behind the wheel, turned to Hewitt and said, "Now what."

He pointed around the Green and said, "That way."

She heard the change in his tone.

They went out the valley and began to climb toward Barnard, gaining ground until Hewitt pointed at a barn a quarter mile ahead.

"We're stopping there?"

"Nope. There's a road, just can't see it till you're pretty much past it."

She made the turn and they traveled along a lane between a pasture filled with Holsteins on one side and a sprouting cornfield on the other. Then began to rise and soon were in the woods, the lane smooth, well graded. They came out in a large clearing atop a broad ridge. The clearing was groomed like a lawn. Tucked against the edge of the trees was a two-story cedar shingled lodge with dark green trim and green shutters flanking the windows and across the front a screened porch. A big stone chimney stood at one end. The lane opened up into a neat circle for parking well away from the lodge. This afternoon there was only a single car parked there.

The other end of the clearing was a large pond, about eight acres. There was a modest dock with three green wooden rowboats moored —a fourth floated far out on the water. Except for where the grass was mown down to the dock the woods encroached upon the pond so huge shifting pools of shadow and shade moved along the shore and well out into the water. The whole thing cried trout.

They got out and walked down to the dock. The man in the distant boat peered at them and Hewitt waved and the man waved back. Hewitt was pretty sure at that distance Chip Howard didn't recognize him but most likely would close up. Which was fine. Hewitt just hoped for a little time before Chip decided to quit fishing and come investigate. The club was private but not well known and even the local rascals who sneaked on to posted property when the owners were downcountry to empty stocked trout from ponds, respected this place and left it alone.

There was a plain plank bench on the dock and Hewitt and Jessica sat side by side. He was quiet for a few minutes.

She said, "It's a pretty fishing hole. But we're not supposed to be here, are we?"

He looked out and said, "This place is called the Mic-Mac Club. It's been around since the late 1800s. Started by a handful of wealthy men from Woodstock, maybe Barnard and Pomfret too—I'm not too certain of the history because I never did care much. But it's a private club. You can't even apply to join. Some member nominates you and the rest vote and only then do they come and invite you to join. It's basically a fancy drinking and fishing club, although I guess they have some big family picnics and dinners and such—we never went to any. My great-grandfather was a member. So when my father moved back here, they liked the look of him and asked him to join. And be damned but he made them wait. Probably the first time ever that happened. Because on the one hand he was much happier killing a six-pack with the boys in Lympus. The fathers of the men you've met and a few more. These Mic-Mac men, they were another story. But my father loved to fish, loved to fly-fish. To come up here, where the lake was stocked and the fishing good and quiet and, hell, easy, he liked that. He'd fished up here as a boy with his grandfather, his mother's father—he never knew his own father. Or whatever he did know he never told. There's whole chunks of Dad's life I never heard much about.

"For instance, when he was a young man he went to study painting in New York and stayed on to live there. See, he was married. Not to my mother. This was before. They had a little girl and lived together in a big apartment he'd made a studio out of. I think he was still pretty poor but starting to get noticed. And there was a tragedy, a truly horrendous thing. He lost that wife and daughter, both of them. To a fire. In that apartment painting studio—he wasn't home when the fire broke out. He never once spoke to me about it. I didn't even know until after he died, when my mother told me.

"See, Jessica, the thing is, he actually was pretty well known. I kind of downplayed that on purpose because you wouldn't imagine the people that come out of the woodwork trying to find some piece of him. And those paintings in the red room are all that hadn't been sold, all he'd kept. And I've got no plan to sell them. Or even have people pestering me to see them or loan them for exhibitions or whatnot.

"Growing up, there was a sugarhouse he turned into a studio so he could be out of the house to paint. As a kid I thought because he needed the peace and quiet. It's only later looking back that I realize he wouldn't risk a studio in or even near the house. Shoot, he could've built one in the barn but he wanted it far enough away. I really believe he'd have been happy to stand out in the yard and watch it burn up on the hill, knowing his wife and children were safe in the house behind him."

He stopped and looked at her. All this time he'd been gazing out at the water. Old Chip Howard was working the far deep end of the pond. Where the shade was best. It was a warm afternoon to go after trout. But Jessica was wrapped tight, her arms around her chest and her feet jiggling up and down, knees together, her face screwed tight as if welded. He reached over and ran a hand over her hair and she nearly shied from his touch.

He said, "Are you all right?"

"Unh-unh," she said. "But finish your story." She didn't look at him.

He nudged her shoulder with his and said, "I'm coming up to the last part anyway."

She was silent.

Forty or fifty feet out a trout jumped, a twisting slippery vision that seemed more etch against eye than fish. The rings spread the water surface. Hewitt said, "What happened was one October afternoon of my senior year of high school I was out riding around with some guys, you know, farting around. Dad had come up here after lunch for what would be the last fishing of the year. Another week and the rowboats would be taken from the water and locked away in the boathouse for the winter. The afternoon went on and suddenly it was late, about five o'clock. My mother drove up here. But she didn't even get out of the car. Out there in the middle of the lake was a boat upside down. The sheriff took her home and sat with her until I got in. The first thing she told me was he died quick, doing something he loved. Then said, which I didn't understand then but did a few hours later, how fitting it was he died in water. Because his fear, his great fear was that he was destined to die by fire."

Hewitt raised an arm and said, "Right out there somewhere. A heart attack and fell out of the boat."

Jessica stood. She walked out to the end of the dock, looking into or across the water. She rocked back and forth, toes and heels rising and falling. Then swiveled on one heel and came to stand before Hewitt, her face grim, a hidden tremble. She said, "We need to go back to the house. I got something to show you."

Hewitt nodded, trying to sort this curt response when she stepped away, walking off the dock. She didn't look back and he quit watching her but heard the Volkswagen door shut.

Still he sat and waited and watched the old man pull at the oars, the dripping water slashes of light when the oars lifted. Hewitt had no interest in explaining himself, his presence there. So he rose and slowly walked to the car. A man not furtive but deliberate.

DRIVING THE TWENTY miles home she spoke only once. "Are you a member of that place?"

He slid his eyes and face in exaggerated slow motion toward her. "I haven't been asked."

At the house she went out of the car fast and he followed, her head-up, eyes-front march something not seen before—the opposite of her brooding absorbed pacing but also unlike her movements easy and natural on other days. Once inside the house she turned to him and took his hand and without a word led him into the red room, bright with sunlight that left some of the paintings vivid and others almost as if receding back into themselves. The tricks of light.

She pointed high to one painting, intentionally placed at the top of the descending series on that wall. Hewitt sharpened a bit. It was a piece rendered in ochres and deathly deep unlikely blues and almost stale muddy reds, a scene of dockworkers lounging in exhaustion on a wharf or pier, the suggestion of a building along one side as a depth of unfathomable endless endeavor. The men, three of them, were collapsed, two in shadow of the building with their legs sprawled before them, the third likewise but against a great coil of rope or cable, unclear because the blues of the coils were echoed in the man's face and naked torso. As if he were sinking into the coil or perhaps the coil was collecting him. It was a painting of the exhaustion of never-ending loading and unloading, of life repeating itself without hope or brightness day after day. It was, as far as Hewitt knew, untitled, but the bottom right corner, under the edge of the wharf plank where the color deepened into blue near black were the unmistakable initials and the date 1946.

She turned and said, "I like this one best. But why's it here? Why this and nothing else from his early life?"

Hewitt sat on the arm of one of the deep leather chairs and said, "That painting is the only one that survives from before he lost his first family. And all his other work up till then. The only reason it's here at all is the summer before the fire he came up with his family for a visit. And he brought this painting and left it here. That next spring was the fire. I only found that painting after he died. It was wrapped and boxed in the basement."

Jessica was standing over him, her head nodding as if taking it all in or maybe waiting for him to finish. She leaned toward him and said, "You wait right here."

He heard her sprint up the stairs and then there was quiet before a more measured descent. She came back into the room and without speaking handed him a manila envelope, maybe eight by ten and old-fashioned with rubber wafers on the flap and a string wrapped around them to keep it closed. He held it and said, "What's this?"

"Open it."

She stood watching as he unwrapped the string from the disk, pulled up the flap and reached inside. What he found were a pair of photographs. He took them out and shuffled back and forth between them and then let each settle, faceup in his hands. One was a photograph of a painting—a different view of the same dockworkers high on this wall. Even reduced to a photograph there was no mistake.

The other was a black and white formal photograph. Gazing up from the glossy paper were his father's eyes, his father's face. A young man in his early twenties. Hewitt had never seen this version of his father. It was a vision from the void. The young man in the picture was awkward with a thatch of blond hair falling over his broad tall forehead. He wore a jacket of tight small dark tweed. His mouth and eyes held a full smile. Pulled close against him, tall herself but straining up toward him, was a young woman with dark hair in bangs and pulled back behind her ears, the side of her face turned her lips open, her eyes glittering in the camera's flash. She had a lovely long neck, accentuated by the pose.

And tugged in tight between them was a serious wide-eyed dark-haired little girl, her head tilted just so, looking at her father as if the camera wasn't there.

"Jesus," Hewitt breathed. There they were. His father so young. The young woman exuding a graceful depth both physical and within her eyes, a long-limbed woman, willowish, self-aware. And the girl. He gazed at her. The never-known lost half sister. Back to his father. And knew he was not reading anything in but the tender wondrous pride and love fully living in his father's face.

He looked at the young woman living and breathing before him who was neither the woman nor the child in the photograph but some singular version of both.

His voice near languid with control he said, "What is this?"

She stepped back. "Hewitt—"

He stood. "Who are you? Where did you get these?"

She was breathing hard, running without moving. She said, "I tried to tell you before. That afternoon I came back and hid out on the hill and scared you off with my gun and Walter was here, you know the night—"

"Before I get mad. Who the fuck are you? I want you to answer my question—"

"I'm trying." She was shaking. "I knew I'd waited too long even then. I was driving back here all set to get these out and tell you and I freaked out. I'm sorry I didn't just—"

"I get that part," Hewitt said. "But I've got no idea who I'm talking to right now. Or for the last month. And you're going to tell me. Now."

"My name's Jessica Kress. Everything I've told you about me is true. I just had a hard time getting around to this part."

"You sure did. Jessica, what the fuck is going on?"

She made a small nervous smile. "Hey, Hewitt, as weird as this is for you, it's pretty fucking weird for me also."

"That could be," said Hewitt. "But I don't yet see how."

THEY WALKED OUT to the garden, Hewitt carrying the envelope with the two photographs gently, artifacts from a distant star, a bit of meteorite landed in his hand. They sat on the long stone bench amid the clumps and bunches of flower color. There was a foot between them and Hewitt placed the envelope there, then turned his face toward her and waited.

Jessica said, "That woman in the picture, that's my mother's older sister."

"Is that right."

"She was your father's first wife. The mother of that little girl, Susan. Her name was Celeste. Celeste Willoughby. Celeste Willoughby Pearce. From Water Valley, Mississippi."

"My father never talked about them."

She looked him bold in the eye and said, "Susan Lydia Pearce. She was named for your grandmother."

He paused. "You say."

He'd heard the names Celeste and Susan from his mother. No last name for Celeste, no middle name for Susan. But the stone for his grandmother two miles down the road held the legend: LYDIA SUSAN PEARCE.

Hewitt said, "After he died we went through all his papers but there was nothing about them. Most probably destroyed in the fire. I don't even know where they were buried, whatever remains there were. Stones put up somewhere maybe. I don't know. Maybe it was too awful and he had them cremated and spread the ashes somewhere. New York, in the harbor. Christ, maybe even up here."

"Or buried in the old cemetery in Water Valley."

"Is that right?"

"That's right."

He was quiet a time. Then said, "Be damned." He looked off away from her, out over the flower beds. Wondering how many times his father had brought that first family up here. Wondering if a little girl used to the confines of the city and a certain poverty of life had ever been set free here, had scampered among the flowers, climbed the low-slung apple branches, found the same hiding places Hewitt and his sister Beth with the innocence of children always assumed were theirs alone. Wondering what the young woman had thought of this place. And wanting to examine the photograph again. For a number of reasons but determined to wait.

Jessica said, "You all right?"

"I can't say. I guess. Why don't you tell me about them, what you know." He looked back to her.

She said, "It's sort of complicated."

"She was your aunt, right?"

"Within a broad stretch of time, yes. A course I never knew her."

"I'd guess not."

"Hewitt, you got to give me a chance here. Okay?"

"Go ahead," he said.

"The story was basically an example sort of deal—she was the lovely glamorous older sister who went off up North to set the world on fire and came to a bad end, which would not have happened if she'd stayed home and married well and all that."

"I get the picture."

"Celeste was the oldest of five and my mother was the baby. And then the other thing is my own parents were pretty much fucked-up when I came along. Matter of fact I overheard my father one evening telling my mother things seemed to be falling apart because of me, that I seemed like some sort of jinx on their marriage. Which when I'm on the street is the name I use. Because nobody uses their real names and Jinx seemed to fit. And there's enough souls out there who hear that word and decide to put a little distance between them and me. Which is always part of what I want. You know—just leave me be."

He laid his hand on the old brown envelope and said, "Hey Jessica?"

"Right," she said. "I don't know how they met, your father and Celeste. Her dream was to be a dancer. Ballet, not some sort of chorus girl. She went to New York because she wanted, and I'm quoting my mother here but without the mockery, to be a real ballerina. I admired her for that. I can't begin to imagine doing something in front of a bunch of people. Even inside a role. Although, shit Hewitt, I realize I've done my share of it myself. I just never got paid." And she laughed and Hewitt heard the nervous skitter behind the laugh and realized there was no breaking those two stories, of Celeste and of Jessica, apart. Because they were all twined together for her and with that insight came another—he too was entwined with both.

"And somehow she met my father," he said. "While she was trying to make her own career."

"You know Hewitt, I'd bet a nickel she was going to auditions and classes, trying to figure out how to live without begging money from home and one way or another, maybe she saw a sign, maybe they just ran into each other, maybe she heard about him from some other girl, but I bet it started with her modeling for him. I know one time my mother said something about the first they heard about him was a bundle of obscene drawings of her came in the mail. It just spat out of her mouth and when I pushed she clamped shut. They weren't obscene. She just didn't have any clothes on is all.

"The big deal at home was they got married up there in New York City by a justice of the peace or however they do it there outside a church. And she came down home with that tall gangly Yankee with her and her belly already stretched beyond the point of being able to hide it decent. My guess is Celeste didn't want to hide it. And she brought along this one painting of his, as if to dispel any doubt. I know she brought it because on the back of the canvas he'd written *To my love, my life, my Celeste, this and all else only for you.* It was hers. And I know this too: everybody thought it was strange, not anything like what anybody thought a painting should be. But still there was conflict in the judgment—after all he was from New York and an artist and what did anybody know about what that meant? I don't know how it is here in Vermont but I always found country people pretty firm in their ideas and scared to death they're wrong, all at once."

"Jesus," Hewitt said. "Good God I'd like a beer."

"You want to get one?"

"No," he said again. "Keep talking."

"There isn't a whole lot more. They went back to New York. She wouldn't come home again. My mother always said it was because of the war and how hard it was to travel. My grandmother laughed at that and said, 'Why would she want to come back after the way she was treated the first time?' It was a sad laugh, Hewitt. It's maybe why she and my mother didn't get along that well. Shoot, I don't know, maybe it even had something to do with why Grandma Willoughby was so kind to me. I don't know. But she was the goodness in my life."

"So," Hewitt said. "Next they heard of her was after the fire? When she died?"

"Oh no. She wouldn't come home but she sent letters about them. About the baby and how she, Celeste I mean, was still dancing. And always about your dad. How he was getting better and better, and people, important people were starting to pay attention."

Hewitt said, "There's more pictures? Photos of Susan?"

She was quiet a moment. Then said, "These are all I ever had. I figured you'd have some yourself."

Hewitt said, "It's all right. No, this is the first I've ever seen of her. Of either of them."

They both sat, an enormity of silence and void spreading around them, both within the curious spiral of life.

After a time Hewitt said, "So next thing the family, the family in Mississippi knew, was about the fire. And then they were brought back to be buried there."

"That's right."

"And my father was there for that? The service and the burying? Did they talk about that part? Anything about him?"

Jessica lifted a hand and placed it on her other forearm and began to scratch. She was raking her bitten nails harsh against her flesh, raising welts first white and then reddening. After a moment he reached over and lifted the damaging hand and said, "Jessica?"

Her eyes glaring anger, distress acute, she said, "Oh he came. You bet he came. What I heard my granddaddy met him at the station and told him to get right back on the train and go home. Threatened to thrash him or worse if he so much as stepped in the door of the church, the church not good enough for your father to marry in so why bother now, when it was all too late. And right then my grandmother showed up, driven down there to the station by the black man worked for them because she hadn't yet learned to drive. Fact is I think that VW was the only car she ever owned and drove herself. Now listen, Hewitt, cause she told me this story herself. How her husband came down off the platform and ordered the man, Tate was his name, to take her on home but she was already out and walked up to your father whom she said looked just wretched, not scared at all, as if he was walking and breathing because he had no choice. How she called for the porter to put his suitcase in the trunk of the car and led your father down and took him home. And Grandfather went uptown to the hotel and checked himself in. But Grandmother took your father home. And she said it was like everybody, not just the family but all the neighbors and the colored help was holding their breath to see what would happen. But nothing did. Grandfather stayed overnight at the hotel and next morning they all arrived at the church and Grandmother led your father right up front for the service and she and him sat on one side all alone in the pew and all the rest of the family sat on the other side. He rode out with her to the cemetery for the burying and then Tate, who was long dead when I came along, she had him drive your father not to the train for the local but all the way to Memphis so he could catch the express. She told me your father was polite as could be and would barely say two words, even that long evening they spent alone together. But yes, he was there. Oh my, he most certainly was there."

She grew silent and was gazing away, softened now as if finally out with something waiting. Then she said, "My grandparents never forgave each other over all that. And my mama was just a little girl herself. I think she sided with Granddaddy—he was most ferocious was how I heard it. Dead before I could remember him. And like I made clear, Grandma Willoughby was kind to me ever since I could recall. She was the one when I was about ten told me about Celeste which gave my mother fits. But Grandma, I don't know what she saw about me. But she wanted me to know that story. Which is how I ended up with the pictures. And somehow what started me thinking about your dad, trying to learn what'd become of him."

Hewitt sat with his elbows on his knees, chin in his hands, the garden a hazed diffusion as through the layers of years and words the particular vast sorrows of his father settled out before him, within and upon him.

After a time Jessica said, "Are you angry with me?"

"I'm not sure what to think. Not angry, though. Unsure what all this means." He stood. "But now I think I'm ready for a beer." He looked down at her, then reached and took up the envelope.

Her head tilted up, she said, "I'd have one too. Unless you want to be alone."

"You're welcome to it, you don't have to ask. Yeah, I'd like to be alone for a bit."

"Hewitt?"

"What?"

"I'm not up to any mischief."

"I know that."

"And I don't expect anything."

He looked off toward the house. Then he said, "Whatever you intended, it's too late for it to be nothing. Too late now."

And stepped away toward the house without looking back to see if she was following him.

HE GOT A beer from the fridge, slid the envelope into his shirt front and headed for the screen door off the back porch. Just going out Jessica came in. He said, "Have a beer, whatever you want. I'm going to walk up and sit on the hillside. I don't have the first idea what there might be for supper."

She said, "I'm not hungry. Hewitt, do you want me to leave?"

"No. I just need a drink and a think, as my mother used to say." Then, feeling he was being brusque, even though it was his mood, he saw the distress in her face and, not entirely sure he was speaking the truth, said, "I'm glad you're here, Jessica. But for the moment I need to let this settle. Then we'll talk some more. I don't want you going anywhere. In fact, I've sort of gotten used to having you around." And quit talking, turned and went out the screen door.

Up in the soft white and red clover, he settled in under the apple trees, his old friends. The leaves shading green swellings of hopeful fruit. He sat with his back against a thick trunk, his legs crossed, the beer tucked into his crotch and the envelope set out before him, resting lightly atop the orchard clover. He watched the glowing sheet of western sky and for the moment disregarded the envelope. The same way he refused to glance at the house below and all it held.

He drank half the beer. Then removed the photograph. Let it rest against the cushion of grass. The long-gone young faces beamed up toward him—so young, in their early twenties at most. His father attempting a deeply serious face—no doubt how he considered himself. No. How he wished to be viewed, a maturity he was striving toward. And the young woman in the first flush of life and wanting more of it. She was indeed lovely, not simply a beautiful girl but one who was radiant. Her face toward the camera, one arm extending around his father, the other hand lightly settled on the little girl's shoulder.

Hewitt picked up the photograph of the young family and drained his eyes down upon his father. And of a sudden was weeping for the young man caught in that moment not knowing what faced him but somehow certain of his destiny, and for the man who survived all that and dug deeply within and went on. And wept for the burden of sorrow his father had chosen to hold—such magnificent sacrifice—so his second round of marriage and children might be free of his guilt, or fear of failure or dishonor. And Hewitt wondered then, for the first time, how his father had really felt about his success.

How could he not, being the man he was, believe in the full cost of that success?

Throughout the meadows and hayfields and within the orchard birds flew in and out, their end-of-day songs urgent, exquisite, beyond comprehension.

Celeste. Celeste and Susan. However much he studied them, he could not help but see the girl down the hill wound into herself, clearly struck from a common mold. And studying the photograph more he could see the same shimmer of uncertainty in the young woman that her now older niece possessed. And knew his father had not only known but seen wealth in that shimmer. And the dark solemn eyes of the little girl—what sort of woman might she have grown to be? How far or close to her much younger cousin?

He refused to think some were chosen to suffer more than others.

Then he stood. The envelope filled again and tucked inside his shirt. The sky was thrilling down into slow red and blue upcast light against the western sky. He tipped up the beer and finished it and with a direct stride walked downhill toward the back of the house. A light burned in the kitchen and another window was lit upstairs. Which he realized he now considered her bedroom.

# Seven

There was a clumsy awkwardness for a few days, almost as if they had become lovers; admitting not only the attachment each felt for the other but in a way lovers never can, knowing that bond ran back decades with a full unknown generation between each other, as if some glint of the original passion between Thomas Pearce and Celeste Willoughby had lived on in the universe and come down finally between these two souls, to bring them together and allow them a small measure of grace. And each had no way to voice this until one morning Hewitt looked over a bowl of cereal across the table to where she sat.

As if talking of the weather he said, "It seems to me we're a great deal less at ease since we decided how much we mean to each other."

"Oh," she said. "I'm glad to hear you say that. I'm feeling kind of at loose ends, myself."

Hewitt finished his cornflakes. Something she'd nudged him to. He felt like a little boy with his bowl of cereal. He said, "What you need is something to fill your time."

Almost panicked she said, "I told you I'm a lousy employee. And I'm not broke Not yet."

He said, "I wasn't suggesting you get a job. I was thinking you need something to do that takes you outside yourself."

There was a pause and then she said, "And what would that be?"

"I don't know. Why don't you think about it. You come up with something, we'll figure out how to do it."

She seemed to chew on this, her jaw working. She was grinding her teeth, a habit he knew was old but had only noticed in these past days. Then she said, "What if it doesn't work out?"

As mild as September Hewitt said, "Then we'll try something else."

IT WAS BECOMING a purely hot summer. With the exception of a couple of furious and wasteful thunderstorms, the last good rain had come the day Hewitt returned from New York State. By Independence Day everyone except the farmers had lost track of the last day not nudged into the nineties. There was talk of springs going low or dry, wells failing. The rowen burning under the sun, the young corn too. People took to the ponds, the deep riverbend pools.

Perhaps the heat helped but the throb of tension between Hewitt and Jessica gently gave way. The days were slowed and long with twilight extending to near ten at night and even then it was warm. But Hewitt knew, and sensed she did too, that each was coming to a peace between them—that never again would either be alone in the way they had once been, in the way each had furtively come to believe was their lot.

Evening in the garden, waiting for dusk, praying for the stir of air that clearly would not come. Drinking bottles of beer dug from an old milking pail filled with ice. A serious effort was needed to get through a beer before it became warm and soapy.

Jessica said, "God, it's hot."

"It's summer," said Hewitt. "Southern girl."

"Hot is hot."

"I guess so. But not humid as what you're used to."

"There's no air, though."

"What do you mean?" He swept his arm through the small cloud of blackflies and mosquitoes toward the bleeding western sky. Bats were sweeping forth from the barn eaves and swallows were in their last feeding spree of the day. "What do you call this?"

"I mean air conditioning. Where a body can at least cool off at night enough to sleep."

"Oh that. Nope. But there's an old fan in the closet if you want it. And you can always take a cold bath to cool you down before bed. Or walk up the brook to the pool and soak in that bitter water until you walk down shivering and crawl into bed. There's ways to cope with it. But no, there's no air. Because while this heat might haul right along until September there's better odds it will break by early or mid-August so you might want a sweater or at least a long sleeve shirt this time of evening. What's the point of something makes you want to stay inside for the three four months of the year you can count on to want to be outside?"

"Damn Yankee."

"Damn right."

The next evening they hiked up the brook to what Hewitt had always known as the Pearce pool, which was a sturdy effort some lost years ago to dam the brook just below a bend where there was somewhat of a natural pool anyway. A dozen feet across and half that deep.

For soaking the heat out of a summer body it was a gift. That first evening Hewitt had cutoff jeans under his Carhartts and Jessica was in her long shorts and oversized loose T-shirt and when they came to the pool he turned his back and stepped out of his workpants and walked straight into the center of the pool where he sank down into the sweet breathless cold and turned to see her on the bank lifting one foot as she removed her underwear. Before she walked out toward him. He watched her come and heard her gasp as the cold hit her thighs and then belly and he slipped head backward and down away from her. So he was submerged but for his face staring up to the sky. The first star. She cupped water and threw it in his face and then she dropped under the water and came up gasping from the cold and he was ready for her and from behind took her shoulders and held her under the water, away from him, feeling the stir of her legs kicking. Then let her up and she bobbed choking and spouting at him and he stroked slowly around the edges of the small pool. When she got her breath back she moved close but not too close and said, "Shithead. What was that about?"

"You're buck-ass naked girl. What in the world made you think you should go skinny-dipping with me? I'm not a goddamn saint. Except in your particular case I intend to be. So get a bathing suit. Okay?"

She was in the deep part of the pool and he was already up against the grass and mud bank, about to get out and put on his pants. He was cool enough.

She said, "In Mississippi it never mattered. If it was two of us or twenty. We just ran out in the country drinking beer and went out to the lake and everybody stripped down and went swimming. Or if someone was out of town we'd have a midnight pool party. What's your problem with that?"

He was upright on firm land and had his workpants on and so he leaned toward where her white face above the water and her white form below were becoming both more clear and more vague as the evening gained. He said, "Well honey. It's simple as this. It's not just Mississippi. When I was your age a bunch of us would do the same thing. But you get older and it all gets more complicated. And you know it." He looked up at the summer stars. Without dropping his head he said, "I'm going back to the house. Can you find your way?"

A pause. Then she said, "Of course I can." Her voice sharpened up an edge.

He turned and walked away, uphill a little from the brook so he could walk across the steady bowl of pasture earth that led around to the house. He made about a hundred yards when she called his name and he heard her crashing through the grass after him. He stopped and turned and waited. She was dressed, dripping. She said, "I'm not trying to have sex with you, Hewitt."

He said, "That's reassuring to hear."

"Fuck you. All right?"

He stood looking at her. Both up to their knees in meadow grass. The warmth weeping back through their cooling skin. Finally he reached out and took her shoulders in his hands. Arms stretched. "How long," he said. "How long before you'll relax and just be here?"

She tipped back her head, her eyes dark and lost in the night, her stretched neck a white tendril in the starlight. "I don't know," she said. "I can't say."

Hewitt said, "That's all right, honey. You take as much time as you need." And turned but reached back and took her hand in his and together slowly they made their way through the rising grass though the warm summer night toward the house.

A CHECK ARRIVED in the mail from the gate owner in Pomfret, along with a brief to the point note of admiration for the execution of the job. The check contained a bonus of five hundred dollars, noted in the memo line, which Hewitt considered returning because his price always contained not so much a bonus as what Hewitt thought of as contingency fees. But in the end kept the money. For Hewitt the note would've been enough, that and the fact that the man comprehended this contact through the mail was appropriate instead of driving over to stand in the dooryard and praise the gate and hand over the payment.

JESSICA WORKED THREE days with Roger Bolton helping tear out lath and plaster from a house being remodeled up on Stinkbush Road. Coming home late grimed with dust, both white plaster and black centuries-old inner wall. She showered which halfway cleaned her up but did little to revive her otherwise. After half a beer she reeled with lost footing across the kitchen floor but sat down and ate the thick Angus tenderloin Hewitt had fixed for supper. The loin was near four pounds of marbled local beef and between them they ate it all. As she stood from the table she raised her beer bottle high and said, "I'm a meat eater. I'm a goddamn meat eater, Hewitt. And don't you forget it."

"Well, it's pretty good beef."

She said, "You should've seen us take down the ceilings. Between the downstairs plaster and the upstairs floorboards is maybe a four-inch gap. It was filled with two hundred years of mouse shit and corncobs and dust all stinking like pee. We couldn't take up the boards from upstairs because they want those to stay. We had to get up on ladders with hammers and pry bars and break it apart a foot at a time. And all that rancid crap pouring down on you, no way to get away from it. I never."

Then she laughed and fell down. From the floor she said, "Shit," and then pulled herself upright and said, "I'm busted, brother. Flat busted. I'm going to take another shower and go to bed. I got that fan working. And Roger'll be here half past six in the morning for me."

"That sounds like a good idea."

She was treading back and forth with her half-finished beer. She said, "Hey Hewitt?"

"Yup."

"There's all kinds of work. All kinds of life. You know?"

"I believe I do."

She said, "Favor?"

"You bet."

"Fifteen minutes could you make sure I'm in bed and not face-down swallowing water in my sleep in the shower?"

"You're fine."

"Promise?"

TWENTY MINUTES LATER she was sound asleep with wet hair and a sheet pulled up to her shoulderblades, the fan at full blast in the window. He guessed by morning she'd be chilled and so folded a light blanket over her feet with the lip stretched up along one side of the bed so she could reach it in her sleep. When he laid the blanket over her feet, one twitched. He stood over the bed looking down at her. Her face was smooth and no longer stark white, her skin infused with gained color. Her forehead free of fear or doubt or scorn. She was a beautiful young woman and Hewitt stood above her before leaning down to brush the least kiss on that transformed unworried brow.

He went silent as he could back downstairs. To sit in the near dark kitchen and drink a last glass of water before his own bedtime. He sat drinking the cold water and knew that one day Jessica would leave him. A part of his life was to try to help this occur. And he knew he couldn't predict time any more than time would allow him to predict himself. So all he had were moments.

He thought of his father and knew that man had known the same thing. As his mother still did. He wondered what was wrong with his sister, what was wrong with Beth that she didn't understand this essential fragility. And then knew it was not people like himself or his father or Jessica or Celeste Willoughby who propelled the world forward. It was, surely, his sister, the Beths of the world who had no use for the past. Who understood dead was dead and all you could do was go on from there. Who knew it was a bad deal from the first and were determined to suck as much for themselves as they could, who would not leave well enough be but insisted that well enough was simply the warm-up for what was to come, that held no sentiment but strident walking forward. It was the Beths who owned the present. Always.

Hewitt raised his glass of water and saluted his sister. Her persistence and certainty. And knew she was wrong and knew it didn't matter. He went up to bed.

JULIE DROPPED BY. Unannounced late in the afternoon with a boned leg of lamb for the grill, a sack of young beets, scallions, and tiny squash to wrap in foil to roast along with the lamb and two bottles of Lynch Bages. Hewitt could always gauge how things were with her depending on what wine she brought. She always brought the wine. This not a matter of miserliness on his part—just a ritual never discussed.

Hewitt was in the forge when he heard the truck come into the yard and waited to see who it was but some time passed and no one called out. So he finished the tightly wound scroll with the two inches of stock extending, cooled it in the brine and left it across the smaller anvil, then went up the stairs, pulling on a shirt as he went. Then out the open door and saw her truck.

Ah, he thought. The yard was quiet but faint music came from the house. Jessica had finished her job with Roger a few days before although it seemed likely he'd call her again when he needed grunt labor. She was happy all the way around—she'd held up well, the work had been horrible and the money under the table the best wages she'd ever earned.

The two women were at the table, the food spread between them. The wine unopened but Julie had helped herself to a beer. Jessica held her hands on the table. They both turned as Hewitt came in. The music was a woman singer-songwriter unfamiliar to Hewitt, just loud enough to be heard and nothing more.

"Hey Hewitt," Julie said, her eyes bright upon him. "I've been working down to Grafton a few days and thought I'd stop and eat supper with you. How're you doing?"

Hewitt thought This should be sort of interesting. He said, "Julie. It's good to see you." He walked over and leaned to hold her shoulders and kissed her on the mouth. "I see you got a beer. And you introduced yourself to Jessica here, isn't that right?" And looked to Jessica and back to Julie. Jessica was watching this with her neutral faintly interested face, the one that would slide into a pretense of boredom if she became unhappy with how things were going. Julie had resisted his kiss just slightly. Hewitt knew no Charlie expected her home tonight—if nothing else the wine was proof of that.

Julie said, "Jessica says you two are related someway."

Hewitt grinned. Maybe a bit larger then called for but he felt like it. "That's right," he said. "It's one of those just barely connect the dots sort of things." He glanced at Jessica and did not grin but smiled at her and hoped she saw the difference. He went on. "Yup, her family and mine go back, Christ over half a century now. To my dad. Yet we never laid eyes on each other or even knew about it all until a few weeks ago. Hey, Julie, it's good to see you. Life is full of surprises."

Jessica stood up. Hewitt knew she'd understood the subtext of this conversation, most likely before he even walked in the door. She said, "Might be I should leave you all alone."

Hewitt looked at her. "Why?" he asked, his timbre plain: he wanted her to stay. She was where she belonged. She studied him and sat again.

Julie drank some beer and looked at Hewitt. She said, "I've got some steel in the back of my truck I'm having a hard time working with. You want to walk out and take a look at it?"

"Why sure." He moved forward and prodded among the packages on the table. Then turned to Jessica and said, "Can you start a fire in the grill?" What they called a grill was a stonework firebox with a chimney that burned hardwood. It took at least an hour of feeding in the held-back apple sticks to get a bed of coals large and hot enough to cook over. Jessica said, "A course. It's the same wood in the shed you used the other night, right?"

"That's it."

She nodded and said, "Go on. I can make a fire."

As Hewitt suspected there was no steel in the back of Julie's truck. He walked on down the stairs of the forge. The big doors were open and light appeared to strike the sky and reverse and fill the room. Julie was right behind him. At the bottom of the stairs he turned and reached for her but she pushed him back and came down so they were both on the same level. She was in gray Carhartts, steel-tipped boots and an old T-shirt once maroon now washed to near pink. Her honey sun-streaked hair was pulled back into the long single braid she'd worn ever since he'd known her. Her face beginning to show lines along her jaw and bird tracks running from her eyes toward her temples. Those eyes green as waterglass. Stark upon him.

She said, "You want to fill me in here? Couple three weeks ago you nearly fucked up my life by calling me in the middle of the night. And Hewitt, you did not sound good."

"I wasn't good."

"Shut up. I worried over you and worked my schedule so without being too obvious I could get away for a few days down this way, earning enough money in the deal so Charlie knew it wasn't bullshit. It's very important to me that Charlie trust me. We fit just fine, Charlie and I do. Except on this one thing. A long time ago I knew I could never go through life loving only one person. But there's a cost Hewitt. The only way I can explain it is deceit's not a pretty thing but it's less ugly then the alternatives. But that phone call, that was downright stupid and sloppy. I expect better from you, Hewitt."

"You deserve better. It won't happen again."

"You want to tell me what brought on that brain fart of yours?"

"No." He held her gaze and then said, "Maybe sometime."

She eyed him, her mouth a tight screw. Then she nodded and said, "So are you fucking her or is her story true?"

He paused long enough so her eyes settled on his and held there, waiting. He said, "It's true."

"About your father?"

"And then some. Quite a bit. Oh, hell, Julie."

And he told her of Emily and where and why his phone call to her had come from. As best he knew. It was not a long telling but by the end he was sweating and had stepped back to sit on the big anvil, his feet planted apart and his hands on his knees, his elbows feeling like rusting joints. When he was done they stood looking at each other in long silence. After a bit Julie came to him and ran her hand over his head slowly in small gentle circles until he brought his hand up and lightly held her forearm. They remained that way. He could feel the muscles in her forearm and the improbably soft skin over those muscles and the fine hair of her arm.

Finally she said, "Let's go see if there's a cooking fire ready yet. And drink some of that wine."

IT WAS AN interesting evening. Julie and Jessica talked mostly to each other, the sort of small probing gentle talk that women undertake with each other and not once mentioning Hewitt who busied himself preparing the food. Then inside to eat with the second bottle of wine and Jessica announced suddenly, "I was a vegetarian until I met Hewitt."

Julie carefully maneuvered her grease-smudged wineglass down to the table and said, "He does that to people."

Hewitt sat and watched these two women laughing. Understanding as a great gulp of wine that they were not laughing at him but at all of life and the unpredictable slam one person brings to another and where that may lead and how no one ever knows until it happens. And he was filled with sadness. Within minutes he was not back all the way but returned enough to smile at the platter of ends of blackened food and faces and hands charred and slippery and the buoyant heat of the wine mixing evenly with the warm night and he made a note to himself that perhaps he should drink more wine and less beer.

Julie stood up. She said, "Jessica? Would you be happy to pile all this shit in the sink and then finish this bottle of wine?"

Jessica was steady, her eyes red splotches. She said, "I do believe I could manage that. Although I'm not sure I need the wine."

Julie said, "Of course you do. Because you're going to want to go sit on the screen porch or in the garden or wherever you want. But I'm going to take this man upstairs and he's not even going to have a chance to wash his hands."

Hewitt said, "Hey now."

Jessica said, "Do it."

★ ★ ★

TWENTY MINUTES LATER sleek in the goldenrod light of midsummer evening Julie said, "What's the matter?"

Entwined side by side, her leg brown as the rest of her lifted over him. Through clenched teeth he said, "Nothing," and thrust harder and turned his mouth to her breast and then slipped out of her. He lay still a moment and rolled on to his back, one hand resting on her breastbone, the other crooked at the elbow so his palm was under his head. They lay silent, Hewitt feeling the harsh rise and fall of her chest measured against his own even breathing. Then he stood from the bed and walked to the window and looked up the hillside, his penis slick and slack. Through the open window came evening birdsong: meadowlarks, orioles, different warblers from the woods or orchard. And through the house, seeping up through floors and walls, beams and joists, floorboards, plaster and lath came his old vinyl thump *Let It Bleed*.

From the bed Julie said, "Hey, baby, it's okay. We can slow down."

When he didn't respond she said, "Why don't you come back over here?"

He inhaled and his shoulders lifted, then fell as he let out the silent sigh. He wanted to get dressed but turned and went back to the bed and slipped down beside her, lying on his back with his ankles crossed. He reached to draw her close. She stiffened before she relented but wouldn't rest her head on his chest, instead propping up on one elbow to look him face to face.

"Is it because Jessica's downstairs?"

Hewitt waited, feeling the flush of a great unexpected peace come over him, buoyed by the glow and his own certainty but was in no hurry to speak, knowing once he did there was no reversal. So instead of answering her, he gently pushed her elbow away and pulled her down tight against him and held her a long moment, both breathing together, his arms around her familiar back and as he held her he felt something give way in her and she relaxed against him and they held each other.

Without letting go he said, "No. It has nothing to do with Jessica. Nothing at all."

"Well, if it's not little babycakes, what is it then?"

He said. "Julie, I care for you a lot. You know I do. But—"

She reared up away from him and said, "You sonofabitch you bastard," and began to pummel his chest, swatting also at his head. She had strong arms and the blows hit hard so he wrapped his head with one arm as he reached and felt and then his other hand rested against her chest and he pushed hard, not a blow but straight-arming her away long enough so he could scramble from the bed. She was up and after him and he danced backward as he grabbed his pants with one hand and an old cane-seated chair with the other, the wood light and easily lifted and held between them as he struggled into his pants, dancing, the chair bobbing and he almost laughed, the cruel absurdity combined with the ridiculous fear that she might splinter the ancient chair. Then he spun quickly away and settled the chair against the wall, snagged the button on his jeans and turned to face her, ready to bearhug her and tackle her back to the bed if that's what it took. But she was standing center of the room, upright, bold, naked and defiant, her sneer aimed at him. He thought a laugh might be hidden there but wasn't sure. He kept his ground and said, "Can we just settle down and talk like normal people?"

"Go ahead, normal person. Go ahead. I want to hear it straight from your mouth."

"Aw, Jules."

"Don't fucking *aw* me."

"It's hard for me too, you know."

"It didn't seem so hard."

"Do you have to be nasty about this?"

"It just came to you midpoke, is that what you're saying?"

"Julie. Shut the fuck up."

"I'll tell you what. You talk and I'll get dressed. I feel like an idiot standing here, hung out to dry."

He briefly wanted to stop—to go back to her and gather her and kiss all of her, to travel her body with his mouth and hands and feel her come to and then under him, to ride her sweet lusty generosity once more, or not only once more but to take it back, all the way back to the ground they'd gained and maintained for more years then he could count. But she was already pulling the ragged T-shirt on and he knew he'd taken it this far and had to go the rest of the way—that she already knew the pith if not the words of him.

He said, "I guess I already told you. Down in the forge. About Emily. You know it didn't go very well. But—"

"Hey, Hewitt, save it, okay, man? I got the picture. No more friendly pokes with Julie. Because if you're pure then maybe God will notice and give you marks for good behavior."

"Come on, Julie."

"I'll come on. I'll come right the fuck on. Hewitt, you're one serious head case." She lifted a hand to stop him. "A lot of people might disapprove of what I do but at least I'm fucking alive. But you, you might as well eat mothballs or something. I'm sorry, I'm genuinely sorry for you. Although you'll be fine. You've got your little foundling, your little pint of pain from the old days that will never come again but you can latch on to her and do the good Samaritan shit, however that works, and if you don't watch it you'll turn right into a fucking saint. Saint Hewitt of the Long Lost. But you know what, buddy? It doesn't mean diddly-shit to me. So just go fuck yourself Hewitt."

He was short of breath. Then, tone quiet but deadly he said, "Julie? Get out of here."

"Oh poor Hewitt. Snared like a rabbit by his one and only true love. What horseshit!"

"Get out."

"Fuck you! Oh shit this is so stupid I can't believe it. Listen Hewitt. If you ever, and I mean ever, call me again I'll drive down here and use your head as a fucking anvil. You got that? Dickhead." She turned and stalked out of the room and down the stairs.

He stood a long moment. It was silent below. No music, no voices. He heard the slap of the screen door and then her truck start up. She idled a moment and then backed around hard and ground gears and popped the clutch. He walked over to the window but by the time he got there she was already gone from sight. He watched out the window and then in a low voice said, "It wasn't like I had it planned."

HE HEARD THE popping of the needle on the turntable and went down and lifted the arm and replaced the album in its sleeve, knelt to slide it away and paused, then pulled free another record and put it on. Walked to the kitchen just as Hank yelped I'll never get out of the world alive. The sink was piled with dishes and he thought about going to look for Jessica but stopped—he had no desire to explain anything she'd overheard or Julie's departure. He turned back to the sink and washed the dishes, dried them and then scrubbed the countertops and range and scoured the sink. Murphy-soaped the kitchen table. When he was done it was near dusk and he walked out on to the porch. The Volkswagen was gone. He wondered if she'd left during or after the aborted passion from above, then recalled the stylus on the turntable and decided it was before. In her shoes he'd have done the same thing. She had plenty of places to go, people to visit. He wasn't certain but thought she'd made friends with one of the young guys who worked for Roger. He stood watching as fireflies came out dancing and winking in the flower beds and smiled into the night, hoping she was having a better time than he was. And then thought, I'm fine. I'm just fine. And walked out barefoot in the dark to the mailbox and collected several days' worth of mail and brought it back into the house, leafed through it on the kitchen table but there was nothing of interest or pressing need. He snagged a beer and went down the hall, wanting to hear the other side of the Hank Williams record.

AT MIDNIGHT HE was up among the apple trees. All he wanted was an immaculate Volkswagen chugging up the valley and into the yard. He was no longer certain why, except his chest hurt and he knew it would stop if she drove in. There was a sweep of loathing once more not for what had happened with Julie but how and that passed, because he'd treaded water enough times already to know there had been no malice, certainly no intention for the timing with Julie. His honesty with her was all it had been and nothing more. He'd worked hard already trying to determine if he could've done it differently but couldn't see how. Even if he'd considered deceit his body hadn't allowed it. After a time, suddenly tired all the way down to his toenails he rose and made his way down the hill. At the house he turned on the light over the stove for when Jessica did return and in the dark made his way upstairs and in the dark undressed and bent over his bed and in the starlight smoothed the sheets and climbed in, smelling the faint broth of sex and then pulled up the light blanket and lay for a bit with his head on the pillow. Way up on the hill, far along the ridgeline he heard a yelp and then an answer and a short trill of coyotes singing.

He was up early and didn't need to check her room to know she wasn't there but did anyway and at least the mounds and stacks of her clothing remained. He went to the forge and worked hard until late morning and when he came out he was soaked right through his jeans with sweat, his head a skullcap of wet hair and the Bug was in the yard. He stalked past the car, grouchy and glad she was back. He walked up the brook to the pool to swim and then had no choice but to pull back on his clammy jeans. The house was quiet as he made a sandwich of leftover lamb and eating it, walked through the lower house, finding her in one of the chairs in the red room, her feet curled under her, head fallen against one shoulder and a book tumbled in her lap. There was mustard and black grease on his hands. He leaned toward the book, a collection of poetry. It wasn't one from the library off the living room. He was curious where she'd found it, who'd given or loaned it to her and for what purpose.

Too much thinking, he thought. Leave yourself alone.

He climbed the stairs in sockfeet. It was the middle of the day and hot but the shroud of fatigue from the night before was fully upon him. In the bathroom he scrubbed down, again with cold water. He crawled into bed, pulling the top sheet to cover his hips and groin. A fly trapped against the screen came floating and found him and twice he snapped up to slap at it. The sharp brush of wings and greenback as it droned away. Then he slept.

THAT EVENING OVER canned clam chowder and salad they were both punchy and off-kilter. Hewitt thought perhaps there was some mild jealousy about but decided to downplay the mess with Julie.

He said, "You went to the bookstore?"

"Yup. I was feeling antsy and decided to get some books. I haven't read much the last couple of years. And just so you know, last night I wandered around Hanover and got talking to some guys and ended up at a party out in the country somewhere and had a real good time." She shot her eyes at him and back to her soup. "Don't worry, no strange boy's going to be mooning around here. I had fun and got what I needed. It's been a while."

"Sure."

They ate a little more and then she said, "I like your friend Julie."

Hewitt nodded. "It's doubtful we'll be seeing her again anytime real soon."

She looked at him. "What happened?"

He looked away, out the window above the sink, over her head. He said, "It's complicated."

Jessica waited and when it was clear he wasn't going to elaborate, stood and gathered her soup bowl on top of her salad plate, circling the table to not pass behind him. Hewitt sat and watched her small tight back as she washed her dishes and the pot used to heat the soup. He ate a crust of bread and drank from his beer. Then she turned from the sink and took up what was left of her beer, walked to the hall and stopped at the jamb and looked at him. She said, "I wonder if you ever stopped to count up the number of ways that woman Emily has fucked up your life." And went down the dark hall.

Hewitt watched her go. Then, riled at this puncture of his privacy he called in a soft voice, "You don't know anything about it."

He couldn't see her but her voice came floating back, soft and friendly to loving. "I know enough."

FIVE DAYS LATER ninety-two-year-old Emmett Kirby was found dead. It was George Contrell found him, going in to talk about the scant second cutting of hay the drought was sending up. But it was Rob Dutton who stopped by Hewitt's to break the news—Hewitt already alerted by the racing ambulance and then the county sheriff and state trooper cruisers running hard past his place, sirens off but lights flashing. But Emmett's place was far enough up the road so Hewitt had no idea what the tragedy was, the road going all the way to Bethel and then Randolph and on from there. It could've been anyone. Some kid on an ATV with a broken leg for Christ sake.

He was up out of the forge late morning when he heard the truck turn in and seeing it was Robbie knew right away it was much closer to home.

Rob Dutton was a cool man, sharp-eyed with a slow temper far back beneath his assessment of the range of catastrophe that came his way. He was fire chief and town constable both. He stepped from his truck red-faced with anger, wearing his shoulder pistol outside his shirt and Hewitt knew without looking there were at least two more in the cab of the truck, one under the seat and another in the glovebox and all loaded. Along with a deer rifle in the window rack.

Jessica had been puttering in the flowerbeds growing alongside the barn since the first ambulance siren blast alerted them, as if she did not want to get far from Hewitt. But when Robbie got out of his truck he looked at her once and said, "I need to talk to Hewitt, here. Could you go on to the house or something."

She frowned at Rob and Hewitt simply said her name. She looked at him and turned and walked up into the high flower gardens where she could see them but not possibly hear.

Robbie was direct. "It was the worst thing I ever saw, Hewitt. Whoever it was, tied him snug into that chair of his by his stove. There was cigarette burns on his arms and face and his hands were busted with a chunk of stovewood and we know it was stovewood because there was splinters stuck in the backs of his hands. Not to tell that we found the piece of wood on the floor dropped next to the chair. But not before that fucker battered his head in. His skull broke open two or three places. Shit." Robbie paused and swallowed several times.

"I thought I was gonna puke again just telling you. Nothing touched except one kitchen cabinet left open and the top shelf empty. I guess you know what was missing. Shit. It wasn't a secret old Emmett had a stock of painkillers. Heavy-duty stuff, I don't know what all. The state boys said they'd find out. There was an empty bottle dropped on the floor. They'll get some prints from that. But the way it looks whoever it was, once they hurt him so bad he told em where to find it, they swallowed some down and then finished him off. Goddamn motherfucker. I mean, he was all fucked-up and most likely it was a gift when that asshole raised up that stovewood and busted his head open. Most likely Emmett was already gone. What was done to him would stop the heart of a man half his age. Fuck all. It's outa my hands and I probably broke some kind of law coming here and telling you but you known him since you were a boy and, well, I thought you ought to know. The state boys'll be by to talk to you, see if you heard or saw anything out of the usual. And everybody knows you got a houseguest who's a stranger. Fuckin A, Hewitt."

"Jesus Christ," Hewitt breathed.

"Yeah, well. I guess He was otherwise occupied a couple mornings ago."

Hewitt nodded. "You know anything else yet?"

"Nope. But the ambulance had to take him to Hitchcock for a autopsy and then I guess Chris Maxham'll be taking care of things. Likely there'll be something in tomorrow's paper."

"You hear, let me know."

"I will. I will, Emmett. Holy shit I just called you Emmett, didn't I? Idn't that something."

The two men were quiet a bit. The day seemed to be seeping the news into itself and holding it. After a bit Hewitt said, "Hey Robbie?"

"What?"

"You got any pull with those state boys?"

"Not much. Why?"

"I know they've got to come down and talk to me. And I know they're going to want to talk to Jessica too. That's the girl. But . . . well, she doesn't work things through the same way you or I do. She's not crazy, not dangerous crazy at least. And she never even met Emmett. Had no idea of what he might've had stashed away in his house. You hearing me?"

Rob Dutton looked at Hewitt and said, "I'm not protecting anybody, Hewitt."

"Fuck you, Dutton. Those county and state boys have their ways and you know what I mean. It's the kind of shit could let me come out one morning and find her sucking the exhaust pipe of her car. You understand that?"

Rob looked at Hewitt a long time. He said, "Tell the truth Hewitt. You have any reason to even suspect the tiddliest she might have been involved in this business?"

Hewitt thought slowly over the past few days. There were gaps certainly but not even the faintest of flags. He said, "Not a cunt hair of a possibility."

Rob studied him and then said, "I'll do what I can. But no promises."

"Thanks, Robbie."

Dutton got back up into his truck. He looked out the rolled-down window and said, "If you're fucking with me I'll come and put a hole in your foot, you hear me?"

Hewitt nodded and said, "You're welcome to it, it comes to that. That's how sure I am."

HE WALKED UP in the garden and told Jessica as simply as he could what had happened and what they might expect. She sat through his telling but wrapped her arms around her ribs and rocked slightly back and forth. When he was done she kept rocking until he touched her shoulder and she stopped like a stone, looked at him and whispered, "Sonofabitch," and stood and walked toward the house.

He spent a long afternoon waiting for the police, state or county, to arrive. But they never did. Hewitt reckoned the cops had something else to sniff out. Late in the day he went back to the smithy to clean up from his suddenly disturbed work. He came out into dusk and saw her, waiting for him by the barns. She had her old sleeping bag under one arm and a paper sack gripped in her other hand.

"Well, now," he said. "Going camping?"

"I don't want to be in the house just now. It's too small. I'm going to walk up and sleep out in the woods."

"Woods can be spooky at night."

She pointed. "There's a fair bit of moon. And it's warm enough. If I find a cranny amongst those big trees I can sleep fine and be hidden and hear anything coming before it sees me."

He wanted to touch her face. He felt she was sliding and didn't even know it. He said, "I'd say you're right, at least as far as people. But the creatures, they'll smell you even if you lie still as the tree you're sleeping under. It's a nice night to sleep in the woods. You have some supper in that sack?"

"Extra clothes. I'm not hungry."

"Sure. Neither am I."

"I'm sorry about that old man."

"Me too. I knew him all my life."

"There isn't any safe place, is there, Hewitt?"

"I guess not."

She paused and then said, "Those police never did show up."

He nodded. "I think we're pretty much written off as suspects. You want me to grab my bag and come sleep in the woods with you?"

"No. You stay at the house. One of us has to not look crazy in case they come."

"Jessica."

Then a long pause. She hitched up her gear and turned to look up the hill toward the ridgetop and then back to Hewitt. She said, "There's been twice I really thought I was going to die. The once I ended up with a black eye and being raped. The other time I got the shit beat out of me by one of those boys I was talking about, one of those nighttime big-ass boys. That was the worst. They're real smart about beating a woman so she feels it all over except on her face. But I didn't know that—I just thought he was going to kill me. It scared the crazy right out of me. I just rolled up in a ball, cut my cheek on a piece of broken glass on the pavement. He just kept working me over, kicking the backs of my legs and my butt and my back. I felt like my insides were breaking apart. When he finally quit it was all I could do to walk. And I peed blood for two weeks. Every part of my body was black and blue. It was a bad time and I was near broke but I inched my way out of that town. I couldn't drive but a couple of hours before I was hurting too bad. I finally found a back road that ran along a river with a place to hole up for a few days. It was last summer so it was warm. I ate food out of cans so I didn't need a fire. I swam in the river and that helped. Mostly I slept. Some old fellas come along fishing and surprised me but they was kind, gave me some food and left me be. Although as soon as they left I headed out. It was enough of a break so I'd quit blaming myself for what had happened. Quit believing I deserved it. Goddamn Hewitt, the world's an ugly place."

He studied her a long moment. Then he said, "There's certainly enough ugly to go around. Go on up in those woods, see if they'll help. But just one thing, okay?"

"What?"

"You get cold or spooked or whatever come right back down quick—don't wait long enough to know if you're imagining things or not."

"You think whoever it was—"

"I don't think anything. Except a couple days or nights ago somebody tortured and killed an old man right up the road and nobody knows yet who it was or where they are. That's all I know."

She stood a bit. Then she said, "Maybe I should stay here. I just want out of the house. Space around me. I want to look at the stars."

Briefly, he was brilliant. "Sleep in the orchard. Go up above the barn and find a nice soft bed of clover and sleep amongst those old trees. That's a fine place. Peaceful and lovely as can be."

HEWITT WASN'T HUNGRY but he sat at the kitchen table and drank a beer. Here's to you Emmett. Half a century ago Emmett had been spreading manure when the apron chain on the spreader jammed and he'd whoa'd up his team and climbed back in the body to try and work it free and somehow got his foot caught under a spacer, crying out as he slipped on the slick boards, inadvertently signaling the team which simply stepped up to the job and went on to the end of the field, made their turn on the headland and headed back down while Emmett was pulled through the whirling rows of teeth and beaters and dumped on the ground like an empty sack—cut and bruised, with a broken leg and arm as well as a punctured lung and damaged kidney and large intestine and three vertebrae crushed in his back. His wife had found him when she saw the team standing in the dooryard when she went looking for him for noon dinner. She'd died before him and Emmett survived—a crooked gentle old man.

Hewitt moved to the living room, thinking he might play some music as part of this private memorial. But in all the years all the times he'd been in that old farmhouse he'd never once heard a radio on, never so much as glimpsed even the oldest of gramophones. Perhaps Emmett was one of the last where music meant singing the old songs and hymns learned at home. So he instead sat silent in the dark. As the old man must've so many nights, the long winter nights especially. With one or more of the dozen house cats up in his lap. The cats had moved from the barn to the house after his wife died.

He wondered why Emmett had not recognized the maniac intent of his attacker and given up the goods more easily. To not put himself through what so clearly was going to be a long and agonizing death, undoubtedly aware from the beginning there was no way free of this particular mess. And then Hewitt knew. That toughness, that holding-out had nothing to do with the attack, the pain, the ever more certain death. And this translated into scorn for the punk, the shit, who was trying to inform an old man his body was capable of sustaining great pain. Hewitt knew Emmett would spit at the thought of anyone trying to use the obvious against him.

He could see in his mind's eye the old man in his kitchen and his wormy hands gripping the frayed edges of his chair, and wondered what would become of the cats. And resolved to inquire and try to bring home at least one or maybe a pair. For Emmett. For himself. The barn cat was wobbling and ancient and there was a fair chance that a new cat on the place would be the end of him but perhaps not—cats were uncanny in determining territory. And Hewitt liked the idea of having a living extension of Emmett alongside him.

HE WENT TO bed a little after ten. He briefly stood at his window looking out over the farm in the pale moonlight. He could see the orchard, the faint illuminated lump of a girl in an old duck sleeping bag.

At two he woke and gazing out the window, was wondering what sort of night she might be having, how disturbed, how cold and wet with dew, how long she would lie awake studying the great dreaming limbs of the apples over her, her tent against the night sky.

At five o'clock he woke from a deep dreamless sleep to find her curled in her damp bag on the oval rug beside his bed. He lay studying her and then ever so quietly slipped out the other side of the bed and made his way downstairs.

THAT EVENING HE dressed and after a small argument she drove him into Bethel to Chris Maxham's for the calling hours. He tried his best to convince her to come in with him, arguing it could dispel any lingering doubts about her.

"I'll wait with the car," she said. "I don't know any of those people and I don't want em peering at me while they should be attending to the business at hand. Which is gathering for your friend, right?"

In the end she showered and changed into her dress and boots although she made a stop in Lympus on the way and bought a pack of cigarettes. So she could have something to do while she was waiting for him.

The next morning he was getting dressed once again, this time planning to catch a ride with Walter to the service at the Lympus Congregational Church. His face was red from shaving twice in twelve hours. Jessica was not coming. The night before had been fine but she felt each and every person who went into or out of the funeral home cast long eyes toward where she leaned against her car, smoking. Which Hewitt, while assuring her it had been her imagination, was certain was true.

So she was staying at the house. Hewitt was back in his suit, his jaw raw and his throat constricted by his tie, waiting for Walter. When she came into the kitchen in his old sweatpants and a couple of layers of shirts although barefoot, waving her cheap revolver at him. It made him jump and a swift mirth passed over her face. Then she said, "All right, asshole. Where's my goddamn shells?"

For a moment he didn't know what she was talking about.

"Hello? The clip? Where's the fucking clip goes in this gun?"

"What do you want that for?"

She looked at him and tilted her head and tapped the end of the pistol barrel against the side of her head as if to determine if her skull was hollow or held a brain. Then said, "Because I don't want to be stuck here alone without it."

Hewitt did his best to breathe deep without appearing to do so. He understood. A man-killer was still somewhere. On the other hand she knew, at best, maybe two dozen people she might recognize on sight. He didn't want to come back from the funeral and find a clueless client belly-up in his front yard. After what seemed a very long time he walked to the shelf above the stove and handed her the clip. He wanted to give her advice but it was too complicated and he wasn't sure where to begin. And then the Thunderbird rolled into the yard.

So he said, "There's my ride. It'll be two three hours, maybe a little more. And do me a favor. Stick that gun down in your pants under your shirt where you can get to it if you need to but don't shoot any police and also if anybody else does show up, you start by assuming they're just here to see me. Okay?"

"Hewitt. Don't ever fuck with my gun again, you hear? I've had it for years and if I need it I want it all there. So okay your own self."

THREE DAYS LATER a twenty-three-year-old boy and his sixteen-year-old girlfriend were found in a cheap motel in White River. The boy was dead, the girl unconscious. The motel owner grew uneasy because only one night had been paid for but the maid reported a DO NOT DISTURB sign dangling on the door. The room was strewn with empty prescription bottles. The dead boy had deep lacerations in his hands, some still embedded with wood splinters. The girl was taken to Dartmouth-Hitchcock where she remained in the intensive care unit. The boy had a police record dating back to junior high and was on probation at the time. The girl was clean, although no one had reported her missing. No family members of either were available for comment.

THE DROUGHT HELD, relieved by two afternoons with billowing clouds of empty promise that delivered short runoff downpours— enough to keep people mowing their lawns and that was about it. Then it was just too hot to work. "Too hot to fuck," is what Roger Bolton said when he stopped by with a pair of young males, a red tiger and a black tiger, the ones Hewitt had requested from Emmett's pride. Roger said the others had found homes the same way, word going out and people taking them on. The cats only knew Emmett and were terrified, backed into the wooden chicken crate and hissing as hands approached the lid. Hewitt knew he couldn't let them live in the barn —they were house cats and the old tom in the barn would fight them into leaving. He and Jessica closed off some of the downstairs so the cats had the kitchen and pantry and living room and that was all. For the time being. They'd get used to the people and the space and slowly be allowed more of the house.

Jessica said, "What're their names?"

"I don't have any idea. Hell, he had a dozen or fifteen. I never knew which he was talking to, most of the time."

"We need to name em then."

"How bout that's your job."

"That's easy. My grandmother always had tabby cats—"

"What's a tabby cat? These are tigers."

She frowned at him. "Whatever. The point is, during the time I knew her best she had a pair just about like this. Red and black. The red cat was named Rufus and the dark one Tom—original, I know, but that's what she called em. And they were her best company. So, if it's all right with you."

"Yup. That sounds fine. Are you taking em over or are we going to share?"

"You don't know much about cats, do you Hewitt?"

"I always thought I knew all I needed too."

"Well, you don't. We don't share. They're the ones do the picking."

THEY SPENT AN afternoon at the big swimming hole on the White River near Stockbridge but there were too many people. So they enlisted Walter and left his jeep in Sharon and rented tubes and floated one long afternoon of riverdream, their faces, shoulders and knees being burnt deep and painful except for Walter who wore sunscreen as a mask, his dark eyes and hair glistening within the thick layer. Jessica told him he looked like a woman at a spa but Walter just raised one smeared eyebrow and said, "I've been burned before."

Roger hired Jessica again, this time for a longer job, helping to tear down a nearly collapsed immense dairy barn up in Chelsea. He'd pick her up in the gray dawn and often it would be close to dusk when he dropped her off again. It wasn't as nasty as the first job but offered challenges she accepted as if she were going back to school. The third day on the job she arrived home outfitted with a first quality leather toolbelt, complete with a tape measure, a cat's paw pry bar and a solid Estwing hammer. And a decent pair of steel-shanked work boots. The barn was a wealth of material. Old long boards a foot and a half wide, planks in the same dimensions but three and some few four inches thick. And the structural beams. She sat over dinner one evening and described to Hewitt the ten-by-ten beams found, each cut from a single tree. Thirty-eight feet long. She liked the work. She found she was without fear and could scamper along a hayloft beam thirty feet above the ground to pry loose the three old spikes holding a much more recent support pole. She was awed by the fact that the entire frame was held together with wooden pegs, trunnels, and explained needlessly to a silent Hewitt that the word came from jamming together the old words tree nails. Which, she said, after all is what such a massive peg is.

Twice during this time she did not come home until very late. She'd gone out with the guys to the Switching Crew, a bar in Royalton that long ago had been a freight and passenger depot. This information volunteered in the early morning as she was making a sandwich for her lunch, ready for Roger. It was all she said but it was clear to Hewitt one of the young men who worked for Roger was involved. Well, he thought, watching her big-booted stride down the drive toward the road, lunch sack in hand, toolbelt low on her hips, pulled down on her right side by the weight of the hammer, that was probably a good thing.

He refused, even secretly, to take responsibility for how she was getting along. Partly because her accounts of her past, splintered as they were, suggested she'd coped well for lengthy periods before. And partly because he suspected that the sheer drive of the physical work might be slopping water over whatever snippets of fire nipped at her heels.

And so they went along.

THEY RETAMED THE two young cats quickly. Jessica knew to leave them be at first except for strategic tins of sardines and tuna—forbidding Hewitt to buy canned cat food, only dry mix, using the treats to draw them forth. Within days Rufus and Tom had begun to test their new home, the new people, darting from furniture, a rolling ball of tussle in the corner of the living room. Quickly enough they seemed to have forgotten what they had witnessed or more likely in the way of cats were content in the here and now. In any event, each would lie sprawled on a lap and bat with their paws at hands and, if ignored, would rise and slide up a torso to rub their fine delicate skulls against the sides of their person's face. And, as Jessica had known, as if through some hidden lottery Tom clearly preferred her company and Rufus liked both equally, often ending up on Hewitt's lap by default.

HE HAD WORK to do. A fireplace screen but the fireplace was a giant from the earliest, oldest house all the way to Plymouth, five feet tall and eight feet long. A rare survivor from when it was both furnace and cooking facility and all the house could boast. A pair of hitching posts for a horse farm in Strafford, with the exact height from bare ground scribbled on an index card, the rest of the design up to him—the sort of job he loved. All in all he was doing well and the winter was already as full as he usually wanted. But this year he was curious to see what he could actually produce. To be a full-time working smith. To see how it felt. He'd never done it. In the early years because he wasn't ready, then because he didn't care and finally because he gained the mastery to easily say no. But now he was after something new.

THE EVENINGS JESSICA got home early they would now sit up in the garden as the heat of the day drained and drink a beer before going down to the house for supper. The days were hot and dry but the sun was dropping earlier each evening. August was approaching. He received an invitation to Nort and Amber Snow's annual summer party, held in early August because too many people went away to their camps toward the end of the month for summer's last pause and also, although not everyone knew it, because Norton's birthday fell somewhere in there, the exact date never revealed. It was a party for the town and not for himself, an impulse Hewitt understood and respected. The invitation read *To Hewitt and Friend*. Which didn't surprise Hewitt, in fact pissed him off a little bit because if Amber didn't already know there were easily a half-dozen people she could've asked who knew Jessica as Jessica. Then he calmed, thinking this might be Amber's idea of tact, worrying that *Hewitt and Jessica* might suggest what she was unsure of. What in fact Hewitt guessed with the exception of Walter most everyone was wondering. He'd spread enough information so the tittle-tattle tongues had some information to work with. There would be at least a couple of women at the party who catching Jessica alone would be direct in their interrogation. And she was reluctant enough about going as it was.

"Shoot, girl. You already know half the people'll be there."

"You say. Maybe it's the other half I'm worried about. Or maybe it's the half know me I'm worried about."

"Now what the hell does that mean?"

"You know as well as I, Hewitt Pearce. There is nothing like a party for someone or another to let loose whatever little bit's been itching away at them."

He paused over that, taking a long swallow of beer. "Yup. But those types, most of em anyway, all you have to do is nod and smile. It'd be one of the older ones would presume on you so. People get to a certain age they think they can stick their nose in anywhere like it's a God given right, delivered to em in the mail. I don't think you have a thing to worry about."

She considered this. And then said, "I don't have any choice but to go, do I?"

"Yup. I'm happy to say you're sick in bed with the summer flu."

"And that won't fool even the fools."

He grinned at her. "We don't have any fools in Lympus. Just the righteous and the strange. And then the ones you think are most boring and normal until you find out about the man who prefers panty hose to longjohns or the woman who taught school for forty-five years and lived all that time with her female cousin except for the little snag that they weren't ever related." He paused and laughed. "Sort of like you and me, but also not. See what I mean?"

"Hold on," she said, leaning forward in her lawn chair. "Who's the man wears panty hose?"

"Not telling."

"Summer too? Does he go back to boxers or whatever or does he switch to panties?"

"Don't know."

"Come on, Hewitt."

He stood up. It was almost cool, the sun down, bats streaming from the barn. "Let's go dig up some supper. And no, I've got no idea what he does in the summer. I never asked him."

# Eight

He settled on the Strafford job, a pair of horse hitching posts. Anne Corning, the woman with the farm, was a casual social friend, told him what she wanted was something all his own and she didn't care when. Hewitt admired Anne. Of others importing studs from Germany or Holland and breeding them to imported mares to drop foals worth twenty thousand dollars when they hit the ground, she was stubbornly scornful. Anne kept three blooded Thoroughbred studs from Kentucky and near twenty big grade Belgian and Percheron brood mares and had a reputation for producing some of the finest hunters in New England. If one of her foals worked out as a dressage prospect that was fine with her but not a goal. Not one of her horses could be registered. But once ridden most of her customers couldn't care less. And for those that did she was happy to provide referrals to other stables. As she told Hewitt, "You can't ride paper although that doesn't stop jackasses from trying."

Hitching posts. There were a couple of basic designs for such things but both were cast and ugly besides, so other than being models for what he wouldn't do were worthless. He sketched floating ideas right off the front of his brain without pausing to consider them. It was an interesting exercise and was going to take a while to work out.

Midafternoon he heard the Volkswagen pull out. He kept working until he had a heap of scrap paper on the floor to burn off in the forge and nothing to show for the effort, except half a dozen ideas discarded, which meant he was that much closer to something that

275

would work. It was enough for the day. He left the forge and walked to the house, wondering vaguely about something to eat and if it was too early for a beer. In the kitchen he discovered it was past six, as well as a note on the table.

*Gone to see Roger about some work. I might go shoot some pool or something. Be back tonight sometime. Probably. Jess*

He smiled and wondered if she'd prefer to be called Jess, walking toward the fridge for a beer and to peer inside and think about dinner. Then with as little thought as changing his mind and deciding on water he turned and went to sit at the telephone table and called directory assistance, jotted down the number and dialed. The phone was already ringing when he considered the possibility one of her children might answer and almost hung up but for the idea she'd somehow know who the caller had been.

She said, "Hello?"

"Emily, it's Hewitt. I was just calling to see how you're doing."

A silence and then, "I'm well enough, thank you. I'm surprised you called."

She was neutral, nigh flat. He said, "If this is a bad time, if you're eating dinner or whatever, you can hang up. Okay? But honest to God I hadn't thought about this at all but I came in from working and simply walked over and called you. I only wanted to say hello and let you know I think about you and hope you're doing all right."

"Is that so?"

"Well, Emily, it pretty much is."

"What am I going to do about you, Hewitt?"

"Not a thing. Not anything at all. But I guess I wanted to let you know I'm here. Meaning if you ever need an ear, just someone to blow off steam to, you can call me. I'm not going to show up on your doorstep again. No need to worry about that. And I won't call again. But there's one thing I'd like to say, if you'd give me the chance."

A longer pause and then she said, "What?"

"I want to be exactly clear, here, Emily. I don't want or expect you to forgive me. Nothing I can say will change what I did. I know that. But every day of my life the fact that I hit you, that I struck you, has eaten at me something wicked. As it should. And I only want to say I'm sorry. Sorry for all the pain I caused you, sorry for not figuring things out sooner, sorry for what I did. Nothing can change it, but there you go. I wanted you to know."

She said, "It was a long time ago, Hewitt. I've got to go."

The line went dead.

He got a beer and then returned it to the fridge. He made a quick jog down cellar and pulled out a ten-year-old California cabernet—something he'd bought a case of and was ordinary at the time although he'd sensed promise. He had no idea if it was a good label or year but had enjoyed the couple of bottles sampled from the case years past. Upstairs he pulled the cork and carried the bottle and a glass out to the stone bench in the garden, poured a glass and let it rest. It was strange but he was exhilarated. He tried the wine and it was fine and would get better. If nothing else, forgetting the earlier episodes of the summer, her blasting phone call, even her abrupt hang-up this evening, he'd finally done what he'd wanted to do. And he'd done it well, as well as he could. He'd finally closed as much as could be the circular everlasting wound opened in himself all those years ago. He'd said what could be said.

At dusk he carried the half-finished wine down to the house. Jessica wasn't back and he hadn't expected her and somewhat to his surprise the house exuded a tranquility—some extension of his mood certainly but also the solitude was welcome. Enough evening air came through the windows so the house was comfortable, pleasant but not hot as it had been the past weeks. As he walked through turning on select lights the pools below the lamps enhanced the mood. Both cats trailed him, one or the other twining about a leg whenever he paused. In the living room he considered music but could think of nothing and let it go. Walking back to the kitchen and the wine he understood that part of the attraction of the quiet was its temporality; the house even in hush was suffused with the presence of Jessica.

He was pouring wine and jumped when the gong of the phone sounded, imploding his mind with all the distinction of a late evening phone call—too late to be a client or even the few friends who might call. He overfilled the glass as he turned and reached to sweep up the receiver, knowing it was trouble of some sort.

"Lo?"

"Jesus Christ I can't believe I'm doing this."

"Emily?"

"I didn't want to talk about it Hewitt. So I hung up. Sides I was already late for Dad's birthday party at the cottage, his seventy-fifth, a big deal and he's starting to look his age but Christ he had all the kids, all the grandkids out fishing or sailing and the girls have a slumber party and John's going home with his buddy Peter and I wasn't in the best mood anyway when I got there. Then Elsa swooped in and cranked up the blender and yeah we managed to make nice while avoiding each other in between passes at the margaritas and I'm wandering around thinking There's old Hewitt, bashing himself all around the barn for walloping me across the head twenty years ago and he doesn't know shit. Hey, how you doing, Hewitt?"

"Had some margaritas?"

"This is not a courage call, okay?" She laughed without humor. "How bout you?"

"I've got a glass of wine."

"Oh the drugs just aren't as much fun as they used to be, are they?"

"You sound fine to me. I quit the hard booze a while back. I still smoke a little now and then."

"Ah, Hewitt. Well, I have to take a pee test every couple of months. State law. I am not drunk but Hewitt the time has come to end your fantasy of me, of who you think I am. You don't have the first idea. So let me enlighten you to the true Emily, the girl you once thought you loved. You ready?"

"You alluded to my not knowing shit."

He heard her swallow. She said, "Sorry old pal. Some things die harder than others. Maybe I'm talking bout myself, maybe you. Sure I loved you Hewitt. But life goes on. And there we were that winter doing nothing living with a bunch of folks ten years older also doing nothing and it was time to change, time to grow up and you, you were happy as could be until you realized I wasn't but that's not how it works, Hewitt. I'd already gone ahead and contacted Cornell and they were happy to have me start in January and that's what I wanted. Not to freeze my ass off in the big old house smoking dope and waiting tables and not coming back to Vermont with you and sitting on my ass while you got your life in order. Hewitt, I was gone, already gone long before I told you."

"I figured that out."

"No, you did not have shit figured out. Because you still don't because you can't but you're going to now. Hewitt, you remember when you were sitting out in your car and I came and rescued you from freezing to death and I wanted for an hour or two not to let you go and then the next day you went on your way and six weeks later, two months later I'm a late freshman trying like crazy to catch up and there I am pregnant again."

"Emily——' The faintest edge of the bombshell going off.

"I was too young, too young was all I could think, maybe it's that age or maybe not thinking things through all the way, maybe the times, maybe I was fucking terrified, maybe I was just a selfish bitch but I wasn't going to let that stop me. And I didn't. So there you go Hewitt. But wait. It gets better. I closed that problem like a door, like nothing at all except not getting even further behind and went right straight along and I was golden, Hewitt, I was fucking golden. So golden the next year." She paused and he heard her drink, Hewitt now the central explosion: another child, another, two of them. She raced ahead. "The next year I was taking premed courses and flying. And I went straight through until my first year of medical school I fell in love with

Marty who was in his second year. I brought him home and we talked about a clinic together and he had the whole thing worked out in his head before I was done with my tour of the town. But then, you know, then Hewitt, at the beginning of my second year I forgot about my diaphragm one night—"

"You know what, Emily? I don't want to hear about this."

"You know what, Hewitt? Too bad. And there I was knocked up a third time and I sat down and it all rolled over me like a wave I never even saw coming. And Marty wanted me to abort. And God, it was hard, Hewitt. But you know what? I was done. I couldn't do it again. We were already in off-campus housing and we got married and I quit school. And held up a household while he finished and had another baby while he was in residency and then we came back here and I was raising two babies while Marty was doing alone what I'd thought we'd do together. Understand, Hewitt, I love my kids and can't imagine life without them. And so I held in there and when they were old enough I went back to school and got my master's in psych and set up shop, trying to help people make sense of their lives. Hey, maybe it was what I was meant to do . . ." She laughed that caustic laugh again. "What am I saying? It's what I do. But you see, you see Hewitt? You see how it started? It was accidents, Hewitt. It was accidents, and then, and then it wasn't."

She fell quiet. He could hear her breathing. Heard the rim of a glass hit the phone and then her swallowing. He stared at a knot whorl on the desktop, his own breathing measured, biting deep in his lungs. Finally as she took a deep breath, about to speak, he spoke, flatly level to contain himself, anger coiled tight.

"For years," he said, "I thought of that baby, that child we could have had. That would've come from the two of us. I gave up trying to imagine it, boy or girl, but I always thought somewhere out there was a child of ours, the one who could've been. And what it would've been like having that child, you and me. How different life would've been, what we would've made of it. That was your first baby, Emily. With me. And now you tell me it wasn't one but two. Two babies, Emily. Two children. Two accidents you say. Accidents? Fucking accidents, Emily? Those weren't accidents, not then and not now. Never. But hey, at least our children made you quit at two. I'm sorry about those accidents, Emily. I am. Oh Emily I certainly am. Who the fuck do you think you are? You want to know how it feels to me? Right now tonight?"

She was silent.

"As if for twenty-three years I was standing in a summer garden watching a certain firefly wink on and off and all that time instead it's not a firefly but a pair of fucking headlights screaming toward me. And I'm frozen there. I can't get out of the way. Run right over. That's how I feel."

She had to have her hand over the mouthpiece but he could hear her crying. He said, "Good night, Emily."

HE SAT FOR time uncountable gazing at nothing. Nothing seeped and seethed around him as the house settled from the heat toward night, nothing some bleak version of peaceful despair, of funereal quietude. Nothing dribbled through his hands like some form of water, heavy water, mercury, some invisible poison that pooled around his feet and upward through his heart and mind. Nothing in his soul. And then wondered what that phone call had cost Emily, if she'd won what she'd set out to or not and knew she hadn't, knew his anger however taut was nothing to match her own upon herself. That those two lost children lay heavy upon her as they did now him but in ways worse—all the years not only with those two lost children but the two living—not replacements or substitutes but surely in black moments grim reminders of those others. That she too lived with those holes and always had and always would.

SOMETIME LATER HE abruptly rose and emptied the wine down the sink and filled a quart jar with water and walked out into the night, crossing to the forge where he went down in the dark, shutting the door behind him. He flicked on the light over the bench and pulled close the chair to his drafting area. He tore the top sheet off the pad of graph paper and sharpened a pencil from the tin with his pocketknife, took a long swallow of water and then bent over the pad and in a top corner swiftly drew a rough rounded triangular shape, something not flat but of three dimensions, known to his eye and hinted by swift strokes of shading. Below that in the center of the page he sketched out the cage of iron bars that would begin far below the triangle, rooting them in the earth and then spreading and splitting apart at ground level as they rose to encase the triangle and joining again at the top to taper into a braided stream ended by a topknot of three thick iron strands, rounded and smooth as rope from which would rest a single three-inch ring that would swivel in every direction, swivel so that a tied horse might move about without wrapping itself around either the ring or the foundation below. There would be two of them.

Built around stones. And he knew exactly the stones he sought: white hard granite flecked with quartz and marbled with black veins and blots, softly rounded but with a base of sorts and three-sided to a smoothed round top—triangles, yet not, something older, worn, more forgiving of time's passage and the travails of ice and rain and wind, of tumbling water and grinding glaciations. Encased within iron, beautiful stones, beautiful hitching posts.

He drank from the water and opened the drawer under the bench vise and dug for the small stone pipe and tin canister, opened it and pinched off a bit of bud and struck a farmer's match on the face of the vise and drew in the smoke and held it, then slowly let it out. He was tasting last year, what the earth around him had thrown up to offer. He struck another match and finished the bit, even as the first lungful shimmied through his bloodstream and into his brain. He put pipe and canister back in the drawer and looked once more at the sketch and then tilted back to study the wall of tools. He had no need to consider the sketch further.

He'd find the stones up in his own woods. He had none especial
in mind but knew they were there and would reveal themselves. And
he would build and install the hitching posts and a job of work would
be done. Secret cenotaphs and it wouldn't matter if he never saw them
again or if time to time he decided to drop by to visit and pass them
on his way to the door. They would be there.

The stones of memory. Memorials hidden and plain as day. And as
such stones they held multiples, conjoined, intertwined, a small community related all ways, always. Two children never born, two children never grown, two children grown arrested by time, the bond of
two broken but never gone, two hearts, four hearts, two hearts, two,
two alone. A speck of time enshrined, a bolt of love defined forever
silent. And one day the iron would rust away or be torn up and discarded but the two stones would remain somewhere even as unimaginable time passed over and around them and they became smaller,
rounder, small slips of pebbles some child one day might pluck from a
road or streambed and hold a moment before tossing back toward where
they came from; those intentions and emotions and hearts of human
creatures only particle inhabitants of that grand journey.

He put out the lights and entered into the starry yard and saw
the car parked there and went on to the house which was dark but
for the same kitchen light he'd left on hours before. He turned it off
and sat in the dark to unlace his boots and quiet as a thief went up
the stairs and as he turned into his bedroom he heard her voice from
down the hall.

"You okay, Hewitt?" Sleep-drifting drowsy.

"Tops," he said. "Go back to sleep, sweetheart."

He waited a moment but she didn't respond.

HE WAS UP and out at first light, taking coffee with him in a
thermos and working on the sketch, roughing out measurements—
having to work from the top down so when he went looking for
the stones he would hunt an appropriate range of size. He went as

far as he could and then was daydreaming known sections of the woods, the brooksides and tumbling deep ravines, trying to let his mind's eye see the most likely spot to seek his stones when Jessica came in barefoot and quiet as the dawn. At the moment he was bent studying the long dead worm trails in the beech tabletop. When she placed a hand on his shoulder he came close to knocking over his coffee but swiped the mug up at the last moment. He twisted around to face her.

"Hey, Hewitt."

He swallowed some coffee, pointed at the thermos and said, "Coffee?"

"I've had mine."

"So, did you have fun last night?"

"I did." Her face solemn, attempting to give nothing away but he saw the flick of mischief in her eyes. She said, "Roger offered me a job. Full time. Or, as he said, until the snow or cold lock us out. Carpenter's helper."

"Are you going to do it?"

She scrutinized him and then slowly said, "I asked Roger could I study on it and he said Yup, long's I wanted although not to piss and moan if I took too long and he gave the job to someone else. He just wants to get me going—there isn't anybody else or he'd already a hired em. I don't care to fetch and tote for others much but that's how I'll learn. And I think I might like to learn. It'd be good to know how to make things. He runs a small enough crew so I'd be doing more right from the get-go. So, I'm tempted."

Hewitt poured more coffee from the thermos. Casual, he said, "You seemed happy enough working those other jobs with him. And you're right—it's good to know how to make things. And he does all sorts, small and large. You'd learn a range faster with him than most. Like he said, you'd have downtime too. You wouldn't feel . . . you know."

"Boxed in? Tied down?" She was serious and yet Hewitt felt there was something else going on. She said, "Also, I wouldn't feel like I was underfoot like a stray dog. More like I was pulling my own weight." She paused and then said, "I think, if you can take a minute, this might be a good time for us to sit down and sort of talk about what we're doing here, the two of us, and what you think it means and what I think it means, that sort of thing."

He said, "I guess. If you need to."

"It's more your business, Hewitt. The reason I think we need to talk is while I was having my cereal a pair of phone calls came in. I let the machine pick them up but there was no way to miss hearing them."

Hewitt said, "What's going on?"

She looked at him a moment. "I'm not sure. But Mary Margaret said she and Beth and Meredith spent the night in Brattleboro and should be in around early afternoon and not to worry they'll bring groceries."

"Holy shit!" Hewitt stood up, started for the stairs, turned back to Jessica and pretty much froze. He felt like the man in the movies trying to go eight directions at once.

"She also said for you to not run off, they're only coming for a couple days."

"Oh, cripes."

Jessica said, "So, ah, fill me in here. I mean, that's your mother right? And sister and I guess her daughter?"

"Jesus, Jesus," he said.

She walked over to him and took his upper arms in her hands. "Hewitt," she said. "Get a hold of yourself. Seems like the thing for me to do is just disappear for a few days. I could get a motel room. It's not a problem, okay? We'll get this figured out right. It's only nine o'clock. I could help get ready for them. You know, clean sheets, shit like that. Whatever."

He took a breath. "Right. No. You're not going anywhere."

"Hewitt. Let's get up into the air and you think this through. You don't need me here. I mean, how many years since you last saw them?"

"Oh boy," he said. "Just hold on. Slow down. Phew. Come on, let's get outside." And he turned and went up the stairs, the clump of his heavy boots shadowed by her flat footfalls behind him.

The sun was breaking through and the fog was lifting in long spirals and the sun was hot where it fell. They went to the front porch where he sat on the old pew bench running half the length of the porch. She pulled a metal yard chair around and faced him.

"Listen," she said. "I'm serious. I can help you clean up a little and it won't take me ten minutes to throw my shit in the car and be gone. Really, it's fine."

He shook his head. "I'll be damned. Mother, Mary Margaret's what she calls herself even if I refuse to, she was up for a week two summers ago. It was a little prickly here and there but mostly we get along and she understands my deal here. She wasn't married all those years to my father and not learn a thing or two about men like me. But my sister Beth? And you said Meredith too? Good God, the last I saw them was at least ten years ago and boy oh boy was that a disaster. The little girl, she was maybe six, yeah about six, seven. And I scared the shit out of her. Maybe I teased her too much. All dressed up like a teenager and frightened of every goddamn thing, like she'd never seen dirt. And I didn't know shit about little girls or how to be with her but I guess she saw the teasing as mean or maybe it was—that was still a pretty rough time for me. And Beth got tighter and tighter and it all ended fucked-up. Shit. What time is it?"

Jessica didn't smile but reached out and ran her hand into his hair and gently rubbed his scalp. As if to cool the boiling. And it helped.

He looked over at her and said, "Okay. Okay, Hewitt. Deep breath now. I'm a grown-up, right?"

She laughed.

He said, "First things first. You're going nowhere. Give me a few minutes and we can figure out what to tell them. Although, if there's time, I don't know, you said they're only coming for a couple days, but if there's time I'd like to tell Mother who you are. Okay we can't use the same story we've been using. Mother'd see through that in a minute. Let's just stick with what we've got—your car broke down out on the road and Walter has been helping you get it fixed and you've been working for Roger Bolton. That covers the basics and is true enough so we won't mess it up. That way you can still be Jessica Kress. You know?"

She studied him and then mildly said, "Boy. You're fired right up."

"Sorry, sorry. It's just a lot. Damn, Mother. She knew better than to give me more warning. She's a tough old bird."

"You sure it wouldn't be easier if I was to just go for a couple days? It sounds like maybe it's going to be enough of a handful as it is."

He felt suddenly calm, as if he'd expelled the worst of his anxiety by talking. Hewitt looked at her and grinned. "I can't make you stay. And I certainly understand if you want to go."

She frowned a moment and reached to touch his hand. She said, "Okay. I'll stay. I'm kind of curious. About them, you know, your family. And maybe also your mother but you talk to me before you tell her who I am, you hear? And, also, if I get feeling too weird I can always, you know, go visit a friend."

He stood and used her hand to draw her up also and swiftly he moved to embrace her. Then he said, "Let's go look at the bedrooms and figure out where they'll all sleep. At least there's a closet of clean linens."

She grinned and said, "So I'm a maid now?"

"Just like me, sister. Just like me."

Then her face darkened and she said, "Hewitt?"

"What is it?"

"There were two messages. The second one, she didn't say who she was. But I've got a pretty good idea."

He paused and looked at her, not sure if his tottering was visible or a thing wholly within. Then in a calm voice that came from some distance said, "I guess I better go listen."

He left her on the porch, knowing she would not follow, would most likely even go down off the porch and out into the yard, away from the house, away from him. At the door he turned and she was turning away as expected. He said, "Wait."

And drew his pocketknife out and said, "If you want, why don't you go through the garden and cut an armload of flowers. They'll help freshen up those rooms."

She reached for the knife. "That's a good idea."

"WHAT WAS THAT old line of yours? Nights make deals that dawn unseals? All I want right now is to run away to Argentina or someplace and disappear. But I can't. That's how we get old, isn't it? I'm feeling pretty damn old this morning. I was pretty pissed most of the night, feeling sorry for myself, you know, how can you treat me this way with all I've been through? That was a gut punch, Hewitt, and you know it. But it made me remember things. More than just those last few months when everything felt wrong with us. The rest of the time. God, Hewitt. I miss my husband. I don't *know* how long it really went on but I wouldn't have played the make up and live with it game. I would've booted his ass out the door. But he took that chance away from me. Which is pretty much what I did to you, what you were telling me last night. Fuck, I feel like life ran over me and backed up and did it again. What did I do to deserve this? Does innocence or best intentions excuse anything? I used to think so but don't anymore. You're right—those babies, yours and mine, they were scraped out of me like bumps in my road. But we can't go back there.

We can't change it. I can't change it. God, Hewitt. I so want to be a
bitch and say I didn't do anything to you, you did it all to yourself.
Wouldn't it be nice if I could say that? I'm sorry. I just wanted you to
know . . . What? I don't know . . . Oh, damn it. I've got to go, I'm
late. Am I late for everything? Is that what it is, finally? Don't answer
that. In fact, do not call me. Don't call, Hewitt. Maybe I'll call again
sometime but leave me be . . . Take care of yourself old friend."

He played it one more time and then midway through caught
himself and hit the erase button.

He could use a shower with a family of women about to arrive.
But doubted there was time and then rallied. He was just fine. You
bet. He could handle the women. At least, best he could tell, Beth's
husband was not along.

He washed his face with cold water and went out to find Jessica.


MEREDITH WAS A stunningly feminine version of her grandfather. Hewitt sat watching and listening to her, learning her acutely at
the same time he felt he was in the presence of his father. And the
only other person, there or anywhere, who knew this, was his mother.
Something within him softened toward his sister—Beth unable or
unwilling to see her father in her daughter.

They were sitting in the garden. The slab of granite bench had
been covered with a cloth and held what remained of a salad, the
gnawed cobs of new corn, a platter with the carcasses of a pair of roasted
chickens, plates stacked with dirty silverware and the remains of a roll
of paper towels, pressed into service as napkins. Beth and Mary Margaret were drinking gin and tonics whose consumption they seemed
to coordinate so both repaired together to the house to freshen their
drinks. Hewitt strongly suspected this was for Beth's sake, a chance to
regain her balance. He was touched by what he'd never seen before,
this fragility in his sister. Meredith and he were drinking red wine,
she only seventeen but not only handling it well but aware of what

she was drinking, prewar St. Julian. Selected intentionally when she asked for wine earlier.

"Red or white?" he'd asked, as if it didn't matter to him.

"Oh, red. Thanks."

Off he'd gone to the cellar.

Now out in the warm evening all of them together, Jessica quiet but not separate, sitting at one end of the slab in one of the chairs they'd gathered—Meredith at the other end with her mother and grandmother along one side, leaving Hewitt a side all to himself, which he liked because he could move his chair back and look easily from one to another. Although he was mostly engaged with Meredith and this not unseemly, since she was, at least ostensibly, the purpose of this trip.

Jessica was drinking a slow single gin and tonic. She had a jar of spring water on the table also. Her feet tucked up in her chair so she was sitting cross-legged.

And Meredith, in white shorts and a lemon T-shirt, was stretched, almost slouched in her chair, her long legs and arms draped, swept down, spread along the ground. Her feet also bare. She had thick auburn hair, parted on one side but high over her face and heavy on to her shoulders. She was almost six feet tall, not heavy but strongly muscled, the sort of girl who ran track or swam or played soccer. Another girl of that age and size might've been self-conscious but Meredith struck Hewitt as someone who never once had looked in a mirror and wished herself other than what she was. Her face was strong and keen, eyes large and bright.

She was radiant and Hewitt listened to her and watched his sister and understood Beth no longer quite comprehended her daughter, as if a stranger had grown out of the winsome but anxious little girl he remembered.

Meredith was a rising high school senior and she and her mother and grandmother were on a whirlwind driving tour of half a dozen colleges in the Northeast.

Meredith explained, holding her wineglass by the stem and resting the base on her thigh where a red semicircle formed on her brown
skin. "Daddy says it's crazy of me when I can go to Chapel Hill or
any of the UNC schools for in-state tuition and get as fine an education as anywhere at an nth of the cost but I've spent my entire life in
North Carolina. I want to live somewhere else for a while. To see
another part of the country."

Beth said, "Merry, honey, now that's not true. You went to Grand
Cayman last spring with your girlfriends and we all traveled through
France and Italy and spent that month in Ireland."

"I had fun in the Caribbean but Mother I was not exactly im-
mersed in the local culture. And France and Italy were great but Daddy
went after it like it was a job and to this day I can't tell you where we
went in what order. At least until I dropped his video camera on the
Spanish Steps which you two never did believe was an accident but at
least he slowed down a little bit. Except then all he could see were
those cute boys everywhere and he glued himself on to me like I was
about to be abducted." She turned to Hewitt and said, "At that point
I believe I would have enjoyed an abduction, you know, a short one.
What this is all about is I grew up in the South, around my daddy's
family—did you ever meet him?"

"Why, of course he did," Beth said.

"It's true." Hewitt nodded. "I danced at your parents' wedding."

"Don't start," said Beth.

Mary Margaret said, "Wasn't that girl a cousin of Evan's?"

Hewitt said, "What girl?"

Beth said, "See? Let's not start."

Hewitt said, "Yes, Meredith, of course I've met your father."

"That's a story I'd like to hear sometime." She glanced at her
mother and grandmother and back to Hewitt. "Mom never pretended
to miss Vermont but there's a big part of my history here. This place
right here." She waved one long arm in a languorous motion over
her head. "Right?" she said to Hewitt.

He said, "It's a fact. I can't say if it's cause for excitement or not but there's been Pearces on this big chunk of mountain for a couple hundred years. And before that I guess near another hundred and fifty years down there in Massachusetts or Rhode Island or both. Before it got too crowded."

When she just looked at him, he said, "That's kind of a joke. But I guess you'd have to live here to get it."

She nodded, as if she understood that. Leaned to the table and took up the bottle of wine and portioned it out to empty it. Hewitt saw she poured herself a bit more than himself and he liked her even more.

She said, "It's a lot of things, making me want to come to school up here." She leaned forward in her chair toward Hewitt, her wine-glass held out between them. She said, "I'd like to ski. I'd like to learn what winter's like. Not a few inches of slushy snow but real winter. I'd like to see that, live in it."

He wanted to ask what she planned for her life, what her dreams were. Because he knew the hard strong way, at her age nothing would ever be as true again in her life. But this was the sort of question idiot adults asked. So he kept quiet. Which was not a problem. She was happy to talk to him. He was thrilled, vibrant with her presence, attentive and feeling suddenly very adult as he knew his job was to let her roll and keep his own senses a step ahead of her as best he could. At the same time he was registering the three other women all watching this take place. Fuck them, he thought. I'm her uncle. If she did end up in New England for a few years it would be a grand thing and they would get to know each other.

"And I want to know about my grandfather." She came without effort upright in her chair and was leaning forward close to Hewi She said, "Did you know there's a painting of his in the North C lina Museum of Art?"

"I think I knew that," Hewitt lied. He'd let that sort of mation come and go—it had nothing to do with the man. I like he was going to drive around the country stalking his father's paintings.

"But you have the book?"

And he knew she was not talking about old exhibition catalogues. Something twinged, a memory of a letter requesting his recollections or any relevant papers. But it had been years ago, not the best of times for such a thing. He remembered getting a bound manuscript in the mail but had read only the title, something professorial and mildly ridiculous. *Thomas Pearce, the Folk Figure: Emotion and Abstraction in Midcentury Art.*

"You know, I don't," he said. "I sort of retreated from all that. I mean, I'm glad it's out there. And you should be proud, very proud of your grandfather," and did not allow his eyes to slip toward his sister but kept them focused on her daughter. Which was not that hard because she was so close he could smell the sour food and wine breath of her. He said, "Because he was an artist. A very good one. With the soul and spirit of greatness. He was a fine man and had terrible things happen in his life but he continued to open himself over and over. Which is one hell of a thing for a human being to do."

Beth said, "Hewitt, what're you talking about?"

Hewitt stood. He said, "Nothing. Nothing, Beth. It's heading toward dusk and dry's it's been the mosquitoes are finally out. So I say we pick up and move inside."

Mary Margaret and Jessica were quickly up. Jessica, rising, slapped the back of her neck. Hewitt loved her for that. Beth hesitated, her eyes hard on him and her lower lip clamped over her upper lip. Then she slowly came up. Standing she looked at her brother and then her daughter. Finally she said, "It's been a long day. Let's get cleaned up and start thinking about bed. We have a ten a.m. meeting at Middlebury tomorrow. It would be a very bad idea for you to be hung over for that." And took the stack of bowls and platters and stalked off through the dusk toward the house, her footing a little unsure, her gait rocking and each step forward gained as if to test the ground before she moved ahead. Then Mary Margaret caught up with her and passed her and so led the way, Jessica trailing with most of the rest of the supper debris.

Meredith stood. She was close to Hewitt. They were alone but knew they had to go on to the house. She said, "It freaks my mother out when I ask about Grandfather Pearce."

Hewitt raised his wineglass and drained it. He said, "He was always kind to her. In his way. I think she just wanted something else, some idea she had about normal life. Which did not include a father locked up most of the day and night making paintings that not many folks around here understood. She never got past that, I think. He was a good man but she's six years older than me—in ways she knew a man different than the one I did."

"Gram's told me some about him."

"It's tricky. She doesn't want to come between you and your mom."

"Gram's complicated."

"That's the truth."

There was a pause. The house was lighting up. Window by window. Then Meredith said, "Uncle Hewitt?"

"Please," he said. "No uncle. Hewitt's enough. The rest makes me feel like an old man."

"Okay." She cleared her throat. "Hewitt. That girl. Who is she really?"

"I told you. The daughter of an old friend—"

She cut him off. "Now you're lying to me."

He looked at her in the gathering dusk. Seventeen years old. He said, "You're right and I apologize but there's good reason for it. I'll tell you all about her when the time's right."

"She your girlfriend?"

"Hell, yes," Hewitt said. "She's my friend. And I'm hers. And I would say it's fair to pronounce we love one another. But that's it."

She touched his arm and said, "Do you think I'm stupid? I saw how she watched you."

He was quiet. Then he said, "Meredith. It's been a long day. And I'm glad you're here."

They were halfway through the dark windowlight-splotched gardens when she pulled up short and said, "I guess we'll see. Won't we?"

In the kitchen his mother was at the sink, washing dishes. She turned and hugged her granddaughter and told her good night. The small old woman like an alert chipmunk tugging hard once at the looming back of the younger woman. Tender words and cheek kisses and Meredith went down the hall and upstairs.

Hewitt watched his mother working in the house that had been hers for not only a long time but undoubtedly the peak of life. Where every day brought uncertainty nagging like a hen pecking at the snow on your boots—if a painting might sell, if the children were healthy, if she could keep them that way, all of them. Where—despite her protestations in favor of the retired golfing life and the friends like herself who had survived that storm of middle life—she had lived her life.

The Irish girl.

She turned from the sink, well aware he was there. Without hesitation she took her old seat at the table and Hewitt sat across from her.

"Hewitt, you look good."

"I'm all right. You seem well."

She waved her hand. "I'm getting to be an old woman. No, I don't complain but there it is."

"Still playing golf?"

"Of course. I still won't use those damn carts though. When that day comes I'll quit the game. I've had to give up the tennis."

"That's too bad."

She shrugged. "And just when I was getting good at it." She paused. "But Hewitt, I'm relieved. When I was up two years ago you seemed yourself again but there was still something lonesome about you. Although I'll tell you now—after that trip was the first time since you were a teenager that I started sleeping through the night without worrying about you."

"Oh Mother, I was fine."

"So you say. I don't believe it and neither do you but what's past is past. You seem better now. And that's what counts, isn't it?"

"You know," he said. "You do seem tired."

"Well, I'd hope. After more than a week in the car with those two."

He studied her. She had a faint smile but was serious in her own way, love without regret and honest assessment. The same woman as always. He said, "So why'd you come? The peacemaker?"

"I suppose. I wanted to see you. And I wanted to make this trip with Meredith, see it fresh again if you'll allow me a fancy."

"She's a humdinger. Reminds me of Dad."

"Yes. She does me too. I'm doing my best to keep my nose out of it but my heart hopes she comes to school up here."

"To learn the place, as she said?"

Mary Margaret Pearce sighed. Then she said, "Well, yes. And she's too young to understand but she's the only Pearce blood a generation down. And you know how your father felt about this place."

"Well. I plan to stay right here until I die. But if she did come north and fell in love with it here there's always room to build another house. Like you say, she's young. It could be ten or fifteen years before she sorts all that out. But, if it's assurance you want, even if the unlikely miracle strikes and there's a wife and half a dozen screaming monkeys running around here, a piece of this would always be hers."

They were quiet a bit. Enough just being across the table from one another. Then, in a quiet voice Hewitt said, 'You never told Beth about Dad, have you? I mean the history—"

"I know well enough what you mean."

He tipped his head. "Why not?"

Mary Margaret was gravely direct. "It's complicated, Hewitt. I know how such things are viewed today and certainly don't agree with all of it. But the history—the history of those two was always difficult —the hardest parts before she'd even recall. When I realized I was pregnant I was terrified. I'd no doubt of his love for me. But we'd been together three years and the man couldn't even bear to be in a room with babies.

"Hewitt, when I finally had to tell him, he took himself up the hill and stayed locked in the studio for three days I'd take meals up in a basket and hang them on the door. And I sat down here in this big empty house and cried, I'll tell you that. On the fourth day I screwed up my courage and marched up and rattled the door until he let me in and I told him I'd leave if he wanted but there would be no back alley abortions for me. And he looked at me with those terrible eyes and told me he'd never considered I might.

"I was home a week from hospital before he'd take her in his arms. He stood the longest time holding her and then without a word passed her back to me. Half an hour later I found him in the woodshed crying. And I left him alone with it. Even if he'd wanted to I doubt he could've explained how he felt.

"Now be careful what you think. And recall the times. I was the mother and he was the painter. But he was a father also. He took his turns with her and spent his time and if a wee child comprehends more than we think perhaps she also comprehended the great struggle within him. It was the year she was two, near two and a half that I saw the change occur in him. It was as if he'd been holding his shoulders rigid for years. Then one afternoon we were out on a blanket.

It was a fair early spring afternoon and she was crawling about him as a child does and he began to laugh at her, her knees and hands all mud and her face daubed with it like a wild Indian. Now I'm not saying there was a sea change after that—you remember the man yourself. Ah, Hewitt, the loss of a wife and child is a terrible thing and something none of us can understand truly unless we've been through it.

"And as there are two sides to every story, there are two personalities involved. You'll recall they were always at sixes and sevens. By the time she was eight or nine, she began to have a hard time. She thought he was odd, strange. She hurt him terribly several times. The quiet deadly ways a girl can hurt a father. One afternoon when she was thirteen she marched up to the sugarhouse and let herself in. She stood there with her arms across her chest and demanded to know why he couldn't be like other fathers. He told me later it was as if he'd been slapped. He lost his temper and demanded what she meant by that. She was crying and told him she just wanted him to be normal. He asked her, 'What would you have me do, get a job in a factory? Is that what you want girl?' Oh he was in great distress that night after the two of you were in bed and he told me. He tried for days to make it up to her. He had no shame for his work you know. But that she did, and he reacted that way, it was a horrible thing for him. Ever afterwards there was a distance between them. And when she left for school and took her major in hotel management he was devastated. An effing waitress was what he said. 'No matter how high she might rise in the business she'll never be anything more than an effing waitress.'"

"I never knew that. I just thought she wanted to get away from here. I thought she wanted to make her own way."

"Well, she has now sure. And I can't help but think, at least with her, that we made some mistakes. We never made a big deal out of his success. Or the money that helped him arrive there. After he died and she got her share of the estate she never said a word to me about it. Of course she was beginning to do well enough on her own, but still. As you know it was a gob of money and she never asked the questions you'd think she might. Not even if it was truly her fair share. She just took it and never spoke to me again about it until last year. When she told me right out of the blue the money had gone into a trust for Meredith. Which she doesn't know about and won't until her thirty-second birthday. That being the age your sister settled on. So you see my boy, it was like she never wanted it in the first place. Or could not accept when it came that her father had been deemed that worthy by the rest of the world. Oh I love Beth so dearly. However it happened, she was just born to be unhappy in this life. There are people like that, you know."

"Mother."

"Ah, here comes the pronouncement."

"Don't you think, honestly now, Beth would be better off knowing the entire story? That it might help her to understand him a bit more? Mother, she's almost fifty."

"She is," Mary Margaret said. "But I don't happen to agree with you. She's tough as steel but poke her the right way and she'd fall apart. She's one like that."

"Mother."

"I'm a modern woman, always have been. Otherwise I never would've considered a Protestant lump like your father."

"You just don't quit, do you?" Grinning at her.

"When I do you'll know it. Dropping a tear on my casket I hope."

"Ah, there's the Irish coming up in you now. I'll have you know when that day does come, I plan to throw myself into the grave atop your casket weeping."

"Don't be making sport of your mother."

"Oh, I'm not," he said. "I figure it'll be my best hope if it turns out you're right about God and I'm not."

"Hewitt."

He said, "So Meredith obviously doesn't know about her grandfather either. The whole story, I mean."

"No. One fine day it'll be me that tells her. But no time soon. She's a fine girl, considering everything, a very fine girl. But not ready for that yet. Now that's a bit of a fib. She would find it fascinating. But, things being what they are, for the next year or two at least, she'll have enough on her plate."

"What's that mean?"

"It means children will never leave an old woman in peace. It means that as soon as Meredith is settled into college, Beth intends to divorce Evan."

"Aw, no."

"I'm afraid so."

Hewitt said, "Do either of them . . ."

"No. It's all Beth. Beth trying once more to get control over every bit of her life."

"You've talked to her? Damn it Mother, she's not that stupid. You can't spend twenty years of your life with someone and then try to erase it and begin again."

Mary Margaret was calm. "I had my little say. To no avail of course. But it's part of why I came along on this trip. It's going to be hard on the girl, harder than her mother can imagine. But at least if Meredith is up here in a different land with different people doing different things, I can hope she takes to it enough so it eases some of the pain and shock. Because that's what it will be."

Hewitt said, "And then there's Uncle Hewitt close by."

"No. There is no such assumption. That part is up to you."

"Of course. But Mother I'm already wild about that girl. After just a few hours. You think I'd turn my back if I even suspect there's need there?"

"Don't be histrionic. She may choose to see you once or twice a year. Perhaps the worst imposition would be to want to spend Christmas with you instead of going home where there is no home anymore. Just calm down."

"I'm fine."

"They're off to Middlebury tomorrow. They can do without me for much of a day. So, this girl Jessica?"

He ignored this. He said, "You're going to stay here tomorrow while Beth takes Meredith to Middlebury?"

She said, "I was asking about this girl living with you, Hewitt."

"I know. But she's not what you're hoping. For Christ sake, Mother, she's near young enough to be my daughter."

"And so? There were ten years between your father and myself and it never made a bit of difference."

Hewitt paused. Then he said, "I'll tell you what Mother. Let's not talk about Jessica tonight. Let's leave that for tomorrow when it's just the three of us and the others are over to Middlebury for the day."

Mary Margaret screwed her face with interest. "Why?"

"Because it's not a subject for tonight."

She heard some edge in his voice and he could see she was about to press, the privilege of a mother. So he said, "I've been in touch with Emily."

Oh she was good. Her eyes widened all the way out and then her lids slammed down so she was peering between slits and her whole face was disapproval of the woman who, right or wrong, had harmed her son for so many years. She might well know much or most of this harm Hewitt had generated himself through his churning engine of passion but that made no difference to his mother. It was the girl, the woman responsible. For if her son loved her, and she rejected him, what sort of woman could she be? He was put in mind of the mothers of death row men—love unconditional. Her hackles were up. And he loved her very much.

Dryly she said, "And how is she?

Hewitt told her, more or less. He left out the part about his trip to Bluffport, saying only that he'd made a condolence call and that they'd spoken a couple times since, all of which, ground down to the finest of lenses, was technically true.

A woman whose life was transformed not once but twice by tragedy, she was not inured to it but empathetic and regardless of how
she might view the woman who stood like a figure at some far station
well down the line, at the back of her son's near madness and pro-
longed grief, when he told of the death of that woman's husband she
closed her eyes and her lips moved silently and briefly.

When he finished she sat a time silent. Then she said, "I'll not share
my thoughts because my advice is unwanted and would be unheeded."

"I know your thoughts Mother."

"Perhaps you do and perhaps you don't."

"Leave her be. That's what you think."

"It's not that simple, Hewitt. You see, I know you also. Now,
every adult child thinks they know themselves better than their parents do. It's the nature of things. What I'm saying is I can see you
from the outside, something hard for a person to do for themselves.
You have an entrenched life. She may feel hers is less so just now but
she's not someone who just fell into you, now, the way you are. And
there are the children. If they were younger, maybe. But teenagers.
They would drive you insane. And mean to do it and there would be
nothing you or she could do to stop that."

He was silent. She waited, watching him and then sighed. Finally
she said, "So what do you intend to do?"

"For the moment, nothing. She needs time. I have that. I've got
work to do. And Mother, I'm well aware the odds against her coming to me."

"But if she did . . ."

"I'd open the door."

MEREDITH, JESSICA AND Hewitt ate eggs and bacon and toast.
Mary Margaret and Beth had yogurt with fruit. Then out into the yard
to see mother and daughter off. Meredith was in a simple pale blue
and white dress and sturdy sport sandals. Beth in dark slacks and pink
blouse under a charcoal sweater, her hair with barrettes so slight wings

were over her ears. At the last minute Meredith turned to Mary Margaret. "Gram? Are you sure you don't want to come? This is the one
I'm most interested in, so far."

Mary Margaret said, "No, honey. I want to spend the day with
Hewitt. And you'll be fine."

"Oh, I will. It's just you see things Mom and I seem to miss."

"Well, Merry. Why don't you try to see what you think I would
be noticing?"

Meredith shook her head. "I can't," she said "I'll never see what
you do." And stepped down into the already running car, her mother
at the wheel and they went out of the yard.

Mary Margaret said, "Of course you will girl. You just need to
live long enough."


JESSICA STOOD AT the stove, pulling the coffee toward the
front to warm again. The fire was dying but the stovetop gave off
strong heat. Mary Margaret saw what she was doing and said, "Good.
I can't give up my coffee even if they say I should. I still need my
three cups."

Jessica said, "This'll be just a moment."

Mary Margaret nodded and said, "That's fine. My bladder's burst-
ing. Those two held the bathroom hostage, without a thought to an
old lady."

Hewitt said, "Go on and freshen up, Mother. There's no hurry to
start the day."

Jessica and Hewitt stood looking at each other, both listening to
her tread up the stairs, a slow one foot at a time climb.

Hewitt said, "So, are you ready?"

A pause. "Hewitt, I'm not sure I see the point. What's to be gained
by telling your mother that the niece of her husband's first wife is staying here with you? How can that possibly be a thing she'd be better
off knowing? If I was her all it would do was make me wonder what
it was I might be after. I don't want her mistrusting me, Hewitt."

He peered at her. "You holding up all right?"

"Okay. I'm a little jittery."

Hewitt poured coffee into his mug and hers. "For me it's simple. Mother needs to be told. For many reasons but mostly because if you and I continue to get along and you hang around here she's going to push to learn the truth. I told her, in a vague sort of way that I'm back in touch with Emily. But she's got radar like the government and she's already working on theories about what's going on."

"What are you talking about? What's going on?" Mary Margaret was back in the doorway, looking from one to the other.

Hewitt said, "Jesus Mother. Don't you flush?"

"I certainly do." She crossed the room and poured coffee, added milk from a carton in the fridge. "And haven't you heard about conserving water? Speaking of which you need to change the gaskets in the faucets of the tub and sink upstairs. At Broad Oaks they sent around a pamphlet about the unnecessary use of water. And not just because of the drought but because there's long-term stress on aquifers all over the U.S. and people still want green lawns in August. And the sprayers stay on all night at the golf courses. People are such damn fools. And you didn't answer my question. What's going on?"

Hewitt fooled with the front of his shirt, checking the buttons. Jessica turned and took the last strip of bacon and ate it. Hewitt said, "Why don't we all go sit down?"

Mary Margaret shot her eyes back and forth between them and then said to Jessica, "Don't you work? Don't you need to"—she worked one tiny brown spotted fist in a circle—"get ready to go to work? I can talk to my son here. He can tell me whatever is the big secret suddenly kept from me. Or is your whole story a lie?"

Jessica looked at the old woman and said, "I work but not full-time. And my story isn't a bit of lie. You just haven't heard it yet."

"Okeydoke," Hewitt said. "Let's all settle down. It's no conspiracy against you, Mother. Goddamn it I don't need prickly women right now."

"Prickly? I'm not prickly. Maybe I said people are damn fools but I was not including myself."

Jessica said, "Hewitt, maybe I should take a walk and let you and your mother talk."

"I don't think so, girlie," said Mary Margaret. "Whatever nonsense you're up to here I want to be able to watch your face when it comes out."

Jessica halted, a distinct sensation since she was standing still. She said, "Yes. I do believe you're right. And, to tell the truth, I want to watch you as well."

"Ah there now. The bee can sting, can she?'

Hewitt set his mug down on the chrome bar along the front of the range with enough force so the handle parted and was still clenched in his hand. "Calm down. The both of you. Let's get this done with." He tossed the broken handle into the sink where it clattered in the sudden silence of the room.

In the living room he commanded both to sit and they did, not touching but side by side on the couch. He wouldn't look at Jessica, not wanting to know if her face was calm or panic rising. He went to the mantel and took down the manila envelope and removed first the photograph of the painting and silently handed it to his mother.

She held it a moment, squinting, and then reached under her sweater and drew out glasses and put them on and studied the photograph. Then placed it on her lap and looking only at Hewitt said, "I've never seen this before. But I've seen one somewhat like it."

"The one you're thinking of Dad gave Grandmother when he visited up here around 1946. When the both of you moved into the house he crated it and left it in the basement. I found it a while ago. It's hanging in the red room and you must've seen it when you were up two years ago."

She tilted her head to one side, scrutinizing him.

He drew out the other photograph and handed it over.

His mother took her time with this, a deep concentrated study. Only once did she glance up and that time briefly at Jessica beside her and then back to the photo. Her hands held it from below as if it were both precious and alien. Finally she turned it over to see if there was writing across the back or a studio's mark. Or just to see the reverse side. Then she carefully did not offer the photograph to Hewitt but placed it on the couch faceup between herself and Jessica. She sat looking off a time at the wall to one side of where her son sat. The three shelves of vinyl recordings and above that the shelf running the length of the wall that held the old clock and a variety of found items from around the farm, as well as things her husband had collected here and there as he traveled and other things that were gifts. A shelf of curiosities, each with its own personal whisper of history and each also with a power and luminosity Thomas Pearce had either recognized and drawn forth or imposed upon them. Her eyes ran along that shelf and then up toward the bare wall with a single painting, not her husband's work but some ancient Pearce patriarch who had always held that place on the wall. Finally she flicked her eyes across Hewitt and back briefly down to the photograph and then up to Jessica. Who sat with her hands loose in her lap and her face turned, waiting.

Mary Margaret straightened her back so she was upright, gathered on the couch. She said, "Everything was destroyed in that fire. I never until this moment saw an image of her. But the resemblance is clear. Who are you?"

This said with all the bravery the world can bestow upon an old woman, which is a great deal. Nevertheless Hewitt heard the tremble in his mother and wanted to protect her. From the bristling tragedy that had found and bound his parents? It was too late for that, too late by at least a decade before he was even born. And so sat silent, leaned forward in an old ladderback rocker.

Jessica lifted both hands and worked fingertips in circles in the muscles below her cheekbones, above her jaw. Then dropped her hands into her lap and said, "My mother was Celeste Willoughby

Pearce's younger sister, Candace. Candace Willoughby Kress. I always knew about my aunt. My grandmother told me stories. When I was a little girl they found me more than once up at the cemetery before those stones, the ones for her and that little girl—"

"The hell." Mary Margaret stood. "What do you want? Why are you here? There's no money you know. He's been dead twenty-three years and there's nothing left but this crumbling farm and a little cash to help the Social Security see me through until I croak, and if there's a dribble left it goes—"

Hewitt was at an even tempo with the rocker, one leg crossed over the other knee and without pause he said, "Mother."

She stopped. Arrested. She looked about the room, not at the two people sharing it with her but at the room itself, the pine sideboard, the empty stuffed chairs, the cobwebs in the upper corners, the threadbare hooked rug, the great cold fireplace. Searching for something, near bewildered as if what she sought might be some younger self. Or another soul altogether. Someone to advise how best to proceed.

"I knew almost nothing of your aunt, their little girl. Has Hewitt told you how we met? Thomas Pearce and myself?"

The room was quiet except for the slow crunch of Hewitt's rocker moving back and forth from the edge of the rug on to the floorboards.

Softly Jessica said, "Yes." Mary Margaret looked now deeply at the girl, tilting her head to take her in. As if she were finally equipped for true appraisal.

Mary Margaret said, "By the time he came to me he'd buried all that as far inside as he could. It was a worry, a great fret to me for a time, wondering how he divided himself between past and present. Don't get me wrong. Plenty of times I would catch him with his eyes clouded to another world, another place altogether. I was brave enough to never doubt he'd return from those times to what was right before him. And he always did. Even on his truly bad days I knew it was all part of how he had to work, the stations of his mind."

She stopped and then looked at Hewitt. Who had stopped rocking but settled with his knee still crossed over the other. Serious and tender, he said, "Go on, Mother."

She concentrated on him, then looked sternly at Jessica. "I think," she said, "I've said enough for the moment. You must understand although I know enough to know most things are never truly finished, I did believe my husband's past was one of those small pockets that get lost forever. And I give nothing away, do I now, by saying I was frightened of unknown revelations those first years but slowly came to believe it truly was all gone, all but the torment of memory in his head. Only to learn this morning nothing's ever trusted to be done with. The past rears its head when we least expect it. Maybe when we least want it. Although there, you see, I can lie as easy as the next; there is no good time for the past to break down doors. And look at this. Sweet Mother of Mercy, you're just a girl yourself. Yet here you are. So you located Hewitt. It's easy enough to do these days. But why come? What did you think to find? What are you after, truly now?"

Jessica looked down at her hands. With her head tilted her hair fell raggedly forward, enough to obscure her face from the woman seated next to her, but not from Hewitt who watched intently and saw the familiar shades slide over her face and thought he knew what was coming but made no effort to intervene, guessing it would make it worse, at best not wanting to push things further with any wrong thing he might say.

Jessica stood, her hands still joined, now wringing each other before her. She looked at Hewitt's mother and said, "Mrs. Pearce." And then shot her eyes to Hewitt as if drowning. "I'm so sorry. But I can't do this right now. I have to go. Oh shit, Hewitt, I'm sorry but I have to go right now I—"

He was up out of the chair and took her elbow and walked from the room, casting one glance back at his mother and went with Jessica into the kitchen and out on to the porch. Once there she paused and looked at him, her eyes splintered wide upon him.

He said, "You're okay. You're okay, honey. You just do what you need. You want to walk up into the woods or what?"

"No. I'm going to drive. I'll just drive around. I don't know. Maybe I'll call later. Or just disappear for a while. A couple days. How long are they going to be here? I don't think I can handle this. I've got to get out of here and I don't know if I can come back because I know you have to walk in there and tell your mother what a fuck-up mess I am. So I don't—"

He put his fingers gently on her mouth, stroking down over her lips. He said, "Jessica?"

She looked but did not speak.

"Jessica."

"What?"

Hewitt silently took a deep breath. "Take a drive. A nice slow easy drive around. But make me a promise."

"Why?"

Hewitt pressed his teeth together over his inner lower lip and then said, "Because we are sworn to each other. Don't you remember that?"

She looked straight into his eyes and he was frightened by what he saw reflected there, not sure if it was himself he was seeing or her revealing the nadir of her despair. Finally she said, "Yes."

He said, "You better. It's only the second time in my life I've done that. Which means when I do I'm serious about it."

A silence. Then she said, "What's the promise you want?"

He wanted time but didn't have it so his mouth shot from his hip, shot from his heart. He said, "I want you back here this afternoon."

She reared. "I can't begin to promise that."

He said, "I want you back this afternoon. These people, strange or frightening as they might seem right now, are just people. So come back. I want you here. Because, after they're gone home, I want you to know them the best you can. Because it's like that old lady in there said, there's what you know and then there's all the layers beneath. So promise me you'll come back. Please."

Her face was still struck hard, those muscles not yet let go. But she was nodding, that small steady metronomic dipping of her head. Then she stepped forward and kissed his cheek. "If I can I'll be back. But, Hewitt?"

"Jessica."

"I have to take care of myself first."

Hewitt said, "Go on, get out of here. Go for a drive. Go visit Walter. And if you get lost try to do it someplace you can find a pay phone and call to describe where you are."

"You asshole. I will never. Not ever. Be rescued." And she turned and jogged down the steps in the morning sunlight and ran across the lawn toward the yard and her waiting VW.

HE FOUND HIS mother up in the garden on the granite slab near the sundial. A little hunched even in the warmth of the morning, the sun full upon her—not cold but worn down.

She'd sensed him and was waiting. He climbed up and sat beside her.

"You've kept the garden up."

"It's been a dry summer."

"You should divide the peonies this fall."

"I thought I did it last year. But maybe it was the year before. They're devils. So old they're almost royal the way they rear on up year after year."

"Ah, no. They're just good plain Catholic plants, multiplying the way God intended."

He considered this and said, "Do you regret not having more children, Mother?"

She bit the word off. "No."

After a time she said, "Are you going to tell me about her? This Jessica?"

Hewitt had come prepared to do this and so told almost everything. He chose not to relate the whole story of his father's trip to Mississippi for the funerals of Celeste and Susan, seeing nothing but hurt in telling of that final scorch upon his father's heart. But everything he did say was true. When he was done they sat some time more in silence. Mary Margaret had bent at one point during the telling and plucked up a small globe of white clover blossom and she held it close to her face, close enough so Hewitt could also see the hidden color beneath the white of the bloom, the faint pale pinks that were deep at the base of the small ball, before all joined together as a knot in the center.

"Poor child," Mary Margaret said. That out of the way she said, "You can't save her, you know."

This irritated him. He said, "What it is, is we get along. For a time I thought I was helping her. Until I realized she was helping me."

"So? What then? Are you going to marry her?"

"Goddamn it Mother. It really pisses me off when you don't listen to me."

"Oh. Listen to you, is that what you want? Believe whatever you say? It's not allowed that I have my own thoughts?"

"My marrying Jessica is not a thought. It's provocation. In a strange sort of way she and I are family, you have to remember that. It might seem a long reach to you but it's not to either of us. Mostly we're friends. It's good Mother. Good for both of us. I've told her this is her home for as long or whenever she needs or wants it. Whatever else may or may not happen in my life, she'll always be part of it. That's the only thing I know for sure. She's not taken the place of anybody else. She's just a place in me all of her own. One I never knew was missing until she showed up. For Christ sake, Mother, can't you understand that?"

He was sweating hard enough he could smell himself.

Mary Margaret sat beside him, not looking at him. Her eyes off over the garden, down over the road, the hills beyond. She was no longer slumped but upright and her eyes were bright as she looked out over this land of her life. Hewitt had no idea what she was thinking, what to expect.

She made him wait.

When she leaned toward him she said, "You're a good man, Hewitt. I believe your father would be proud."

Then she stood and walked down out of the garden and left him there.

BETH AND MEREDITH returned late afternoon.

Meredith fled her lips across his cheek and to his query about the morning she said only, "I liked it." Then excused herself and went upstairs to nap. He was in the kitchen with his sister and their mother; Beth drinking lemonade from a can and Mary Margaret fussing and arguing with the old range, working with the propane side although he knew she preferred the wood. But it was far too hot a day for wood and so she wrestled to produce the old-style pot roast and a pan of sweet and sour cabbage and small roasted potatoes.

Beth was advancing a litany of complaint over the day. The cost of the school, the long silent ride there and back, how Meredith more or less abandoned her for the campus tour, even what she perceived as the brusque tone of the "parent counselor" assigned to her. Hewitt did his best to murmur sympathetically without committing himself.

Seated across from his sister at the table, wondering if he might get up and snag a beer from the fridge. Slowly he became aware she was no longer looking at him but down at the table before him and he followed her gaze only to discover one renegade hand drumming fingertips on the table. He stopped this and was looking up with a skewed grin to meet his sister's eyes when their mother turned from the stove and spoke.

Mary Margaret said, "You two are driving me mad. Look," she paused and pointed at the clock. "It's after five. Why don't you get something to drink and go outside and leave me be. Do that, or I'll drive you out with a broom. And at the moment I'm inclined to a heavy hand."

Beth said, "I'd love a gin and tonic."

Hewitt stood. "Want me to make one for you? A beer's all I want for now."

Beth said, standing, "I'll make my own, if you don't mind."

Hewitt said, "We're leaving, Mother. There's nothing wrong with the cabbage except for the splash of sugar you've forgotten to add."

BROTHER AND SISTER were outside, down from the porch and stood side by side in the draining heat of the day.

He looked at Beth and said, "So. Is there somewhere on the old place you'd like to see again? We could go into the gardens or up the hill to the orchard."

Without pause she said, "I want to go to your studio."

He knew what she meant but still had to say "Where?"

"Your, I don't know Hewitt. Where you do your work."

"Okay," he said. "But why? I mean, you're welcome. You never expressed interest before."

She looked at him and said, "Should I apologize for that, Hewitt? That's where I'd like to sit and chat with you. It's private there, isn't it?"

Hewitt said, "Come on then."

He perched up on his usual spot on the bench by the big vise while she wandered around and peered into the hearth, picking up tools and putting them down again in not quite the right place and he said nothing. It was warm but not hot here and after a time she pulled out his small Windsor chair from his drawing table and sat. He then slid off the bench and opened one half of the big double doors so a little more air flowed through.

There was a silence. It drew out and lingered and then began to gain weight. Until it lay between them palpable as a cable.

She said, "By any chance, do you have any dope?"

It was the last thing he expected to hear from her. But her asking made clear the deep reach of her need, that she wanted something from him never before touched upon. He said, "Well, maybe so."

He slid off the bench and pulled open the drawer and without ceremony lifted the tin on to the bench, opened it and crunched a bud and rolled a joint. Still silent he lit it and smoked and handed it to his sister. She smoked and passed it back. They did this without speaking right down to the point where they were using his needle-nose pliers to pass the roach back and forth. When it was done he set the pliers, still clamping the tiny resin-soaked tip, on the bench. Then he hoisted himself again on to the bench and sipped his beer, watching Beth with her tall gin and tonic—he'd watched her make it and the splash of tonic was a mere gesture.

"This is where you work."

"Yup."

"There's something peaceful about it."

"Mostly it's the hard work. There are times when I forget about everything else except what I'm working on. That's pretty cool. But there's nothing mystical about it. It just means I'm doing the job the right way. Or have figured out what needs to be done and the work takes over."

"I've never once in my life known that feeling. I mean, I know when I'm doing a good job. But it never gets under my skin. That's what you're talking about, isn't it?"

Hewitt said, "It's true, I get pretty wrapped up in the work. Sometimes I can't tell where the work ends and my life begins. But when a job's done, it's done. And I have to start all over again. From scratch. That can be scary, sometimes."

Beth said, "I never thought about that part, the unknown, the starting over. I always assumed you just did it. I mean shit, Hewitt, my biggest pain in the ass is being called at three in the morning because the setup crew is short three tables for a morning banquet for four hundred people. Like, what? I'm supposed to have them in my closet? No. Because I'm

314

the person to call at three in the morning. I like my job, but it's just details. Otherwise it's the same thing over and over."

He sipped the beer, then took up the pliers and the matches and worked to get one more small hit from the roach.

He said, "Beth."

Beth said, "Jesus, Hewitt, I'm blasted. I'm stoned as a river. What was I thinking of? I haven't smoked pot in years. This is really strong. And I just spent a long day getting far too stressed out with my almost adult daughter whom I've lectured no end about the evils of drugs and now in what, half an hour, I'm supposed to walk up and sit down to supper and I know the first thing I'm going to do is look across at Merry and think she's got no idea her mother is wasted and right then I'm going to start laughing and fall off my chair. Jesus."

"Hey," he said. "You're okay. It's good but old, it'll wear off pretty quick. And I can always walk up and get another drink for you and that'll help and we can sit here as long as we need to. Nobody'll bother us."

"Wow," said Beth, looking out the windows at the slow summer evening. "I'd forgotten how pretty it can be here. The light, the air so clear, none of that humid haze I've gotten used to."

"Hey Beth?"

"Yeah?"

"I'm glad you're appreciating the evening. Just don't ask me if I've ever really looked at my hand, okay?"

She studied him a minute and then broke out laughing. Not stoned giggles but a good deep laugh and listening, he had to wonder how long it'd been since she'd laughed like that.

When she regained herself, her face had softened and it was only then Hewitt realized how old she looked. Worn in the small ways of a woman who worked out, exercised, watched what she ate, dressed carefully and used cosmetics artfully.

She said, "Do you know I've always been jealous of you?"

"Really? You didn't think I was some kind of fuckup? I thought I got lumped in there along with whatever else it was you were leaving behind. I mean, Beth, you made no secret you were going and not looking back."

"Well, Dad and I didn't get along very well once I hit my teens. I know he always thought that was his fault. You know Hewitt, you get to our ages and you start to understand what regret truly means."

"I know that pretty well."

"Once I got past my teenage pissy pants stage and well on into my twenties I realized it was my fault, that business with Dad and I."

"Me."

"What?"

"Dad and me, not Dad and I."

She grinned and said, "Will you stop?"

"You know how Mother is about grammar. Christ I'd like to tape her sometime so she could hear herself, all that Irish slipping in."

"She'd be mortified."

"No," Hewitt said. "She'd wave it off. Tell us English was her second language or something like that."

"God, Hewitt, when was the last time we sat and talked to each other like this."

He paused. Then he said, "Probably the spring you threw out my gallon jars of tadpoles."

She said, "You called me a fucking moron with no curiosity and I asked how many years in a row it would take for you to understand that tadpoles always turn into frogs."

"Is that what we said?"

"It is." He sipped for a pause and said, "Beth?"

"Hewitt?"

"Mother told me about you and Evan. Is that what you want to talk about? We can talk about anything. I just wanted that out in the air."

She was quiet a moment and then said, "It's not only Evan I'm trying to sort out. But he's a good part of it."

Hewitt said, "Okeydoke. Let's tackle it."

She leaned back in the chair, her long legs sprawled. She said, "If I tell you, you have to promise you won't tell anyone else."

He said, "Scout's honor."

She said, "Damn it, Hewitt, you were never a scout."

"I didn't mean it as a joke. On my honor then. Lips sealed until death and beyond if needed."

She said, "Evan's gay."

He was quiet a moment and then said, "Jesus, Bethy. I'm sorry."

"Sorry? It's nothing to be sorry for. Now, at least. I know what you mean but sorry was for all the years things seemed wrong without a reason. I wasn't even angry, Hewitt. I was relieved. It explained things that otherwise kept falling back on me. Years of that. Did you think it was my choice to have only one child? That I'm one of those dried-up women married to her work? Hell no. As far as I can tell I like sex as much as the next woman—in fact between us chickens sometimes I thought I wanted it too much. Still do, as far as that's concerned. Although I tried my damnedest to be good and mostly was. The funny thing is, once he broke down and told me, I stopped any of that, uh, extracurricular activity. For the time being. I guess because I didn't need it for the moment and also, there was enough else going on. And more than before, there was Merry to think of."

"Does she know?"

"Not yet."

"Does he, uh—"

"Have a boyfriend? Of course. I don't know how it works for other men but for Evan he always wondered, that's how he put it, but didn't know until he met the man he's in love with. Hewitt, he was crying when he told me. Even as I sat comforting him and holding his head in my lap and angry as hell I also knew it was one of the most difficult moments of his life. You can't live with and love another person without understanding them that deeply. And yes, I do love Evan. Among other things, we're always going to have Meredith. Whom, I might add, thinks her parents are candidates for disaster anyway, but that's another story."

"Umm," Hewitt said. "Is all this a little bit behind the idea of her going to school up here or was that fully her idea?"

"Evan and I've worked hard not to let on about any of this. Perhaps we were wrong—"

"Beth, she's pretty sharp and there's bound to be some seepage, if you know what I mean."

"It's been two years, Hewitt. I imagine there's been some, as you say, seepage. But here's the sweet part—it was Evan so determined to try and maintain things for her. I can't tell you if that was his only incentive. It's going to be a nightmare for him when the time comes and perhaps he wanted time to prepare himself. I do know he's been incredibly discreet. In fact, I haven't met the other man myself. Not because I wasn't willing, and not because Evan doesn't want me to, but simply because he's terrified he'll lose his daughter. The guy, and yes I know his name is, like Evan, from an old Carolina family and so understands just what a shitstorm it's going to be and I think's wise enough to stand back and let Evan pick and choose his time. Which brings me to the next part of the story.

"After we get home from this jaunt and hopefully Merry has her eyes wide on the future we're going to take a week at the condo on the Outer Banks, just the three of us, before school starts. And we're going to sit down and explain it to her. This was Evan's idea but I agree with him. He's not going anywhere, not yet. But he says it would be unfair to wait until she's all set to start college and dump it on her then, and at the same time break apart the home, the house she grew up in. So the idea's to explain things, rather in less detail, and then assure her how much we love not only her but also each other and go through another year, letting her get used to the idea without it being a stark reality. Knowing Merry, she's as likely to pipe up and ask why Dad took so long to tell her what she already knew, as to break down and get angry or whatever. She could do both. She could fly apart and force the issue —we know that. But that's the immediate big picture."

Beth took a big drink. Hewitt said, "Does Mother know any of this?"

"She thinks she does. But she thinks it's all about me. A nasty bit of me's waiting for the surprise to register on her face. Of course, I'll still catch hell, she'll be sure it was my fault somehow, but there's nothing I can do about that."

Hewitt shook his head. "Bethy?"

She sat, her silence the question.

He took a breath and said, "I just want to say I think you're crackerjack. You, you and Evan both, are handling this incredibly thoughtfully. And kind, it sounds like. I mean, as tough as this is, it could've been a real mess. I'm just, I'm just, well, proud of you."

She shot him a grin. "Thanks, Hewitt. Although, you know I have to consider the source."

He grinned back, then asked, "So, do you have . . . plans?"

She said, "I've been talking to people at work. I have to sort things out with Meredith and Evan and I want to see Meredith through her senior year and her first year at college. By then I'll be ready for a change. They own resorts all over but the two I'm interested in are in Arizona and Hawaii and, well, I'm pretty much guaranteed a job at either place when I'm ready."

Hewitt already knew what else she was speaking of. He said, "It sounds like a good idea to me."

"I don't know what Mother will do. How she'll take it."

"Don't worry about Mother. I can't see her chasing you around, especially once you get things tied up and done there in North Carolina. I get the sense she's pretty happy with her life. She was complaining about getting old but also made it clear she's in a place that feels right to her."

"That might change if I wasn't twenty minutes away."

"It might. But you can't worry about that."

"Perhaps you should. What if she moved back here?"

"I don't know, Beth. But I haven't heard the least thing makes me think she'd ever want to live up here again. And if she has other ideas, well, I'll just deal with that when the time comes."

"It might not be so simple. If her mind slips."

"Things are never so simple as we'd like to think. But I'll wait until that day and see what happens. Maybe I'll call you for advice." He smiled.

She shook her head, not a negative but like a horse shivering itself into waking. She said, "You were right—that was good pot but it didn't last."

"It's just getting old."

"That covers a lot of territory."

"What do you think, should we walk up to the house?"

"I guess so." She paused and then said, "Thanks, Hewitt." Standing from her chair. "It's something we should've done a long time ago.

He slipped down from the bench. "We just let it slide a few years, Beth. But don't you ever fuck with my tadpoles again." He started up the stairs. "Are you ready for them?"

"No. But let's go see what mischief Mother's cooked up."

And Hewitt hesitated, a shiver of prescience within him.


HE CAME INTO the living room just in time to see Meredith standing by her mother, leaning a little as she held before her a photograph, saying, "Isn't it the most amazing thing? How much Jessica looks like her? And Gram says you never even knew."

Hewitt stopped, inside the door. Only his mother was facing him, in the wingback chair across from the bookshelves. She was waiting for him, her face set, her mouth that tight little line, eyes cold and hard. As if daring him to condemn her for this breach. It was decades old and one she'd initiated but once Hewitt turned things around, when

Jessica arrived in Hewitt's life and he'd welcomed her, this, then, in Mary Margaret's view was the same as a betrayal. For what had been secret and therefore binding between mother and son was gone. Gone and not only that but she'd been displaced. The niece of her dead husband's long-dead first wife was living here under what had once been her roof. And not just welcomed but held a bond that didn't threaten as much as circumvent her own bond with her son.

At that moment Hewitt despised his mother. At the time his sister had finally come to him, she was being taken away. And Hewitt wondered to what extent his mother had been working quietly all those years to make clear to her daughter that she would never, could never, meet her father's expectations. Add to that, this, using the innocent enthused teenager as messenger.

But Beth was saying, "So this is her. Oh, and their little girl." She turned to Hewitt. "And God, Dad looks so young."

Hewitt stood silent, holding rage, waiting.

And Beth said, "It was never your idea to keep this secret, was it, Hewitt? No, of course not. That had to be Mother." And her moment of soft wonder gone, the muscles of her face locked and her eyes brittle as hoarfrost. She turned to Mary Margaret and said, "It wasn't difficult to learn about. A surprise, certainly, and one that cast him in a whole new light for me. But Mother, really. I let you have your little secret but the winter after he died I spent a bunch of time in the libraries at Duke and UNC. It was easy to find the old articles about him, even the ones that predated the fire. Did you think I was so lacking in interest or curiosity or love for my father that I wouldn't dig a little bit? Did you really think I wouldn't want to learn more about the grand old hermit painter stuck back in the hills with the little Irish goblin hissing at the gate? I mean, Mother, look at yourself."

She turned to Hewitt and said, "Where *is* Jessica? I've waited a long time to have this out with Mother but right now, she's the one I'd like to talk to."

Mary Margaret stood trembling and her face working. "There is nothing I did that was not in your best interests."

Beth swung back and said, "That's rich."

Hewitt looked at Meredith. She was pulled up, fascinated and stricken at once. Hewitt said, "Do you have your driver's license?"

The girl's face moved through questions but she sensed the swelling and tightening of the room and said, "Of course I do."

"Then you and I are going to take a ride. This business is pretty simple except it's been made more complicated than it needs to be and it's up to your mother and grandmother to work it out. But they need privacy. So, are you ready to go?"

She said, "Let me run get my purse."

He said, "I'll be by the car."

Beth said, "Wait a minute."

Hewitt said, "Meredith, go. Now."

She looked at her mother. When Beth was quiet she looked at her grandmother and back to Hewitt and then walked slowly from the room. The three listened to her hit the hall running, her feet flying up the stairs.

Hewitt did not look at his mother or his sister. Instead he looked out the window at the dying of a long day. He spoke to that day. "When I come back." He started over again without pause. "When we come back I want this all explained and settled. Every bit. I'm sorry, Beth. I have a share in the blame going back to the night Dad died. Goddamn it I wish I'd figured that out earlier."

He turned to his mother and said, "I don't know why you did any of this. Then or now. But it's out now so let's see what you're really made of. You tough old bird, you."

Mary Margaret looked at him. She said, "What should I say if your little friend returns while you're gone?"

"Tell her the truth. All of it. You're not the first person she's discovered that lied."

No sound in the room but some collective loss of oxygen. The walls grew closer.

Then they heard the toilet flush upstairs.

Hewitt said, "I'm going outside to wait for Meredith."

Beth said, "Where're you taking her?"

Hewitt paused at the door. He said, "For the moment, a better place than here."

HE WAS OUT by the Saab, his arms folded atop the passenger side, when the screen door slapped and his niece came down into the yard. In sandals and jeans faded just right and a man's white dress shirt with the collar and a couple buttons undone and the sleeves rolled up. Her face composed and set, her eyes hidden behind dark glasses. He knew she was all over the place and he thought briefly of driving but the Saab with its North Carolina plates was too strong a magnet. And he figured if she drove she might become more comfortable, the rush of anxiety releasing into the job of pushing that car out along the roads.

She said, "So, what's going on?"

He said, "I guess we go for a ride."

He slid into the passenger seat and watched her fold down into the driver's side and power the quiet engine to life. She glanced over at him. Hewitt said, "Out the drive and then right."

"Can I ask a question?"

"Just one." He grinned over at her.

She worried her bottom lip between her teeth. She said, "So that woman in the photograph was Grandfather Pearce's first wife and she also was Jessica's aunt which is where the picture came from, but Mom never knew anything about all that?"

"Clearly your mom did know. And that's all you need to know right now. Your mother will fill you in on the rest of it. But not tonight. Tonight is between the two of them."

"Wait though. If Gram knew about her, the first wife I mean, and it's clear you did too, why was it kept a secret from Mom?"

Hewitt took his time. Finally he said, "You know, Meredith, sometimes people make decisions that seem best at the time. But life is quirky, and things revolve around in a way you never expected and you come to realize the earlier decision wasn't such a good idea after all. And that's all I've got to say on the subject for now. There's big hash for your mother and grandmother to work out this evening so I thought maybe you'd rather be out riding around than sit and listen to them. Because my guess is once they get going, there's going to be a rumpus."

"You kidding? She's gonna be righteous pissed. And, you know, a part of me would like to hear what all they have to say."

Hewitt said, "What your grandmother and mother have to discuss goes well beyond who knew what and who didn't. And sometimes it's best if it's just the people involved trying to work a mess like that out."

"So what's the plan? You want some tunes?"

They were coming down into Lympus and before Hewitt could respond with the suggestion of going out to dinner which was the only thing he'd thought of so far, he saw the green Beetle parked before the store.

At the same time Meredith said, "Hey. Isn't that Jessica's car?"

MEREDITH WAITED IN the car without question, as if knowing Hewitt's long day had started well before she and her mother returned. So he was alone as he stepped on to the porch of the store and met Jessica coming out, a large paper sack clutched to her chest. She glanced at the car and back to Hewitt.

He said, "Hey, Jess."

"So how're things back at the ranch?"

He nodded. "Right at the moment, the ranch is sorta tense."

"So what are you and Meredith doing? Escaping?"

"Yup. What's in the bag? Supper?"

She grinned and said, "I got a twelve-pack of Bud and two bottles of goddamn-break-the-bank zinfandel in this sack here."

"So you could tie one on?"

"Hey, Hewitt? What's the date?"

"It's the tenth of Aug— Aw, shit. Nort and Amber's party. I forgot all about it." He paused. He'd had his mind set on treating his niece to a nice dinner but it was an easy guess she'd prefer a party. He looked at Jessica. "You mind if Meredith comes?"

Jessica grinned again. She said, "Think about it, you rascal. What a fucking entrance you'd make."

He paused and studied her. He said, "For a girl with a long difficult day, you seem pretty full of yourself."

She said, "After I got done pretending to run away it was still too early to come back to the house so I went and visited a friend. One of the guys I worked with for Roger. That smoothed me out a little bit."

Be damned but Hewitt felt his face flare. Jessica saw this and shook her head and said, "Oh, Hewitt, you love too much. You need to work on that."

"Hey, fuck off."

"Will you grab this sack? I'm about to lose the bottom off it. And all we did was cop a buzz and go swimming. So here's the thing, do we ask your niece—"

"Meredith."

"Right. Do we ask Meredith if she wants to go to a party or do we just kidnap her?"

"A party? Christ, Jessica, she's seventeen years old. She was ready to go anywhere. A party's just what she needs."

"Well then. Let's saddle up and ride."

They left the Volkswagen at the store. Parking would be hard enough at the party and then there was the question of how many vehicles they wanted to be responsible for come the end of the evening. Jessica piled into the backseat of the Saab and before they'd even backed out from the store had popped the tops on three beers and handed two up front. Suddenly Hewitt felt like the old man, the responsible one. Then told himself Fuck it, the party was an institution and the only cop around was Pete who'd already be there and as long as no one pissed him off would leave everyone be. It was a party, for Christ sake.

From the backseat Jessica said, "Nice car. Music?"

"What do you like?"

"I don't care. Something loud. Something nasty. Something that says The party has arrived."

So Hewitt rolled in as passenger, the cars parked along the road disregarded as they went straight up the drive and parked on the lawn, the two young women screaming back and forth to each other over the seat back, the car awash with sound that seemed impossible for a mere automobile. Bass notes rumbled through his body as if he was standing five feet in front of a stack of amplifiers one side of a stage. He had no idea what they were listening to. And didn't care. It's all rock and roll, he thought.

People peeled away from the careful array of grills and tables set out on the lawn spreading evenly on the graded hillside behind the house as the car came in but once it was stopped they came close to see who exactly had invaded. Hewitt was first out of the car, a vague notion of apology in his head but then the girls came out behind him and somebody yelled, "Goddamn, Hewitt Pearce finally found a better ride than that old Farmall, idn't that so, Hewitt?"

He introduced Meredith to a handful of friends and drank a couple of beers. Then Hewitt found a plastic cup and poured it mostly full of Jessica's wine and he wended slowly through the groups and clusters of people and made his way up where the lawn grew steep in a stand of mature paper birches. Here he found a nice place to sit where he could watch the group below him, his back against the smooth trunk of a birch. Unlike so many August evenings this one was still warm and Nort and Amber had flanked the lawn clearing with cit-

ronella torches and candles in buckets, the thin odor dispelled over
the people. Everyone he knew in Lympus was there, those he knew
by name and long association and those he knew by face and perhaps
name but always family affiliation. There was a cluster of younger
people he was less clear about, but guessed a good number were among
those who jeeped up through his pastures on to the network of old
roads that ran like the last relics of memory of a people over the land.
It was a good place to sit and observe. He wanted to sit alone with his
wine and watch the people of his life having fun. Sometime later he
might go down and join the group. But for now, aside from the peace
of the spot, he was where he wanted to be.

A couple of young men had settled around Jessica and he studied
them briefly trying to determine her secret lover and then gave that
up as a foul old man's sport. For her part Jessica was holding up well
and he watched her move through the gathering and was mildly surprised by how many people she stopped and talked with, not simple
exchanges of greeting but chunks of conversation. He felt not only
somewhat at ease but comfortable, even a pleasant tenderness with
the idea she was not holding close to him but reaching beyond, perhaps beginning to make something of a life here.

The fireflies of late summer were out and a few stars could be seen
over the valley. Someone had stuck speakers out on the deck and the
party tapes that Amber was famous for were playing—mostly rock and
roll and most of that from the sixties and seventies but a good sprinkle
of old country and new country and stuck in here and there strange
little things she'd dug up, television theme music or a single song from
a musical, *Mary Poppins* which went right into Talking Heads' "Burning
Down the House" into Pete Seeger singing "Kumbaya" into the
Stones' "Salt of the Earth." Amber made good tape.

For a time Jessica had stuck close to Meredith once Hewitt slipped
off. But Hewitt watched his niece making her way in and around the
group of strangers, wineglass in hand and cigarettes gotten somewhere,
Meredith working through the people as if it was what she'd been

raised to do. Which he guessed she had. He got a kick out of the way she'd approach an older man, mostly the farmers in their good jeans and western pearl-snap shirts and not wait for them but extend her hand to shake. Hewitt thinking Most of those old boys never dreamed they'd ever again hold a pretty girl's hand, even so short a time. Frank Sawtell, eighty at least and using an aluminum walker, managed to keep hold of her hand while he jerked the walker out ahead one-handed and made the rounds with her. Hewitt couldn't hear him but would bet a nickel Frank was presenting her as his fiancée. And Meredith not only seemed to put up with it but enjoyed herself best as Hewitt could tell—she was right there with Frank, never once a panicky glance around looking for Jessica or Hewitt to rescue her. And Hewitt could tell when Frank was tiring of the effort and she eased in close to him and kissed his cheek and went off, her empty wineglass raised as a standard. But when she came back through the crowd to pass Frank a bottle of beer and go on her way, Hewitt shook his head—she was a rare one.

Sometime later somebody shut down the stereo and Frank's son Buster had his fiddle out tuning and running scales. Listening, Hewitt thought We're about to get ancient here. And indeed those old tunes from French Canada and Ireland and Scotland and some through Nova Scotia and Cape Breton and others picked up here and there began to jab and poke and claw at the night and then settled down into an endless string of jigs and reels and laments—the single man with the single fiddle more vivid and more deeply amplified than anything wrung through the electronics moments before. A few couples, some old and others young, began to dance on the grass. Some of the steps formal and ancient as the music, and other couples just breaking loose with their bodies leading them as the music drove them. He saw Meredith out there jigging and bouncing in the soft grass of the lawn. No way to tell but he was certain she was barefoot. Part of him wanted to go down and dance with her. But the greater part was happy just to watch.

The wine was halfway down in his cup. Enough to mute the volcanic day. Enough to, finally, fall all the way back to that other early morning message. Emily. Emily had called again.

He couldn't call her back, but for the moment was content with that. He was a different man from that youngster. Thank God or time. Or the events of this summer. Or some magnificent rolling-up of his life to this point. He would wait. Like a quiet whisper behind a door she didn't even know was in her house. With the wine soothing and smoothing he wished she were there beside him.

And then there in the near dark she was sitting beside him, in the blue dress he'd last seen her in, her face tilted a little to one side but looking at him, silent. He observed her. As he did she flowed back and forth between the woman he'd glimpsed that summer and the girl forever etched in his memory. There had been, long ago mostly, so many evenings when she appeared before him. So many nights beyond counting he had talked to her. And she had been silent, listening—a phantom pulled by night and whisky and the aching pain of his soul to come before him and suffer audience. But tonight there was none of that. He had nothing to say. He no longer believed any power was in these visitations he conjured. But it was a pure pleasure to have her sitting, however briefly, beside him on the hill.

Broken without regret by the bobbing climbing white shirt suspended above near invisible jeans of his niece seeking him out. She settled into the space where Emily had been. She had a new beer and shook a cigarette loose and struck fire to it, fire that lit her face and blocked out for a moment everything else and when the lighter went out there was only the glowing end of the cigarette and the party below and beyond that the dense star-dancing summer night.

Hewitt said, "Having fun?"

"I am," Meredith said. "It's really cool coming here. To the party, I mean."

"I saw you got yourself a new boyfriend."

She looked at him in the dark and laughed, a quiet laugh far back down in her throat. She said, "Isn't that just the shits? He's such a sweetheart."

"You say that only because he had you in a crowd of people that all know him. If he'd caught you alone you'd be gasping about the dirty old man."

"Well, he's got quite a trick going with that walker. I mean he had me by one hand so I had to help with the walker and all the time his other hand floated around a good bit more than I cared for. How bout you, Hewitt? You okay setting up here by your lonesome?"

"Oh, I'm fine. You know there's always a geek who likes to sit in the corner and watch what's going on." He smiled and said, "So has all this crap with Mother and your mom scared you off the idea of school here?"

In the assured voice only a seventeen-year-old can have, she said, "They're not my problem. I liked Middlebury, I liked it a lot. And I kind of like the idea of being close by a relative. Because the next couple years are going to be pissant weird between my folks. The way I see it, the more miles between the two of them and me, the better off I'll be."

It was quiet. Hewitt wasn't sure how to respond and then thought, If she's going to trust you it has to start right now. So he said, "I expect you're right. All the way around. Most likely weirder than you think. Those things usually are. But if you're here, I'll leave you be except when you want to come see me. You know what I mean?"

After a moment, her voice floated, "It'd be nice to have a place to come to."

BUT FOR A single dim light from the living room, the house was dark as the two cars drifted into the yard. The three of them made their way to the house where Jessica slipped through the pantry and the connecting office to the hall, all in the dark, her footfalls muted by the stair runner except when she hit the eighth step with its giveaway creak. Hewitt turned on a light in the kitchen and drank water, Meredith standing behind him, waiting. He looked at her and she shrugged and together they went into the living room.

The museum light was on over the stereo shelves and Beth was wrapped in a dark robe, curled on the couch, somehow more substantial in the near dark than if the room were bright. There was a single LP jacket and sleeve propped against the shelves and Hewitt wondered what she'd been listening to, what this evening had prompted for translation into music. He said hello to his sister and she repeated the word back to him and then spoke to her daughter.

"Did you have fun this evening sweetie?"

"I did. I had a really good time."

"Good. Come give me a kiss and get along to bed. We've got a long day tomorrow. Your Gram and I decided we'd drive to Burlington for your interview at UVM and then get on the interstate and head home."

"You mean we're not coming back here tomorrow?"

"No. You've had ample occasion to get to know your uncle, and if you end up attending college up here you'll have more time. But meanwhile, both your grandmother and I want to get along home. Now, give me a kiss."

Meredith looked at Hewitt. He said, "I suspect your mother's right. If you go to college here, that'd be great but, you know, even if you stay in North Carolina doesn't mean you can't come for a visit. If you want, come for your winter break this year and I'll show you back-country skiing you can't even imagine. Think about it. And I'll see you in the morning. We'll have a big send-off breakfast."

Meredith went to her mother and bent for her cheek.

Beth said, "Oh, honey. Are you still smoking?"

"No. I mean, I bummed one. That's all."

"Oh ho," said Beth. "And I'm the Queen of Sheba. Get out of here. Go on to bed."

★   ★   ★

HEWITT TOOK HIS seat in the little rocker by the shelves.

"You know, Hewitt," Beth said. "All Mother had to do tonight was admit she'd done what she'd thought best but now knew was wrong. But she couldn't do it. All it would've taken was one small admission from her and she and I could have been different with each other. Which would've been a damned nice thing. I just don't get it. Does she hate me so much? Because I had a hard time with Dad for a few years and never had the chance to make it right? I mean, how many people does that happen to? You know? And why in the world did she attach her life so closely to mine? What the fuck's that all about? Jesus, Hewitt, I'm closing in on half a century. Is it just me, Hewitt? Or is there something a wee bit off-kilter with this whole thing?"

Hewitt rocked. "I'd say so." He paused and said, "You know, Beth? People always have secrets. And secrets make fear. Have you ever tried to get her to talk about her life and family in Ireland? That she left behind when she was barely into her twenties?"

"Not word one. Except for the ancient ancestors, the kings of Ireland."

Hewitt stood up. He said, "I don't think it's meanness, causes her to do what she does. Some skewed sense of self-preservation. I don't forgive her anything that shouldn't be. But I also suspect we all do something similar on some level."

Beth stood also. She said, "I know. I know I'm faced with a long road before Meredith will forgive and understand her father. And me too."

"I bet she'll get it quicker than you think."

Beth said, "You know, I've done the best job I could. I really did."

"She's a great kid, Beth."

She said, "I've got to go to bed, Hewitt. But, hard as this visit's been, I'm glad I came." And she stepped close to hug him.

AFTER SHE'D GONE upstairs he sat for a while in the quiet house, aware it might be as full of his family as it ever would be again.

# Nine

For several days Hewitt felt a precise exhaustion, particular in location and frustrating because something long waiting had been clarified—but only to a point. The morning of their departure Mary Margaret had been chipper as if nothing untoward had occurred during her visit, although she barely said a word to Jessica. Who later said, "I liked Meredith. And your sister. But it was fucking weird watching your mother trying to figure out what to do about me. She's a piece of work."

"She can be," Hewitt said. "Remember what a panic I was in when you walked into the forge and told me they were coming? But she's my mother."

He could only imagine the three long days of their journey home.

He kept his eye on Jessica, grateful she hadn't left as well. She certainly could have. But she remained and he was watchful in a casual way and went about his work as best he could because it was the only thing to do. She'd made no effort to contact Roger about the offered job and this troubled him but he remained silent. Give it a little time, he thought.

THERE CAME A day the heat did not abate but the sky was low and the air sodden. That night it began to rain, a broken series of showers and longer patches of quiet steady drizzle, then on throughout the day. Following that day of steady rain there was another of sporadic showers and short drenching storms. And the earth ate most of it, although the brooks roared on the hillsides and the river swelled muddy with foaming back-curled waves. The next dawn revealed a world of thin cleansed air and a few goldenrod in early bloom and the lone wild crab apple was bitten by leaves edged in yellow and red. Otherwise the replenished earth insisted summer was deeply intact, spurts of growth in the meadows darkly rich and the leaves of the trees had lost their drought droop.

He was gazing more or less blankly out the window over the sink and made a mental note to check the woodshed. If the weather remained cool and bright it would be a good time to take a few days and scour the woodlot for dead or dying trees to cut up and split for the winter. He was wondering, in an unworried way, if Pete Snow recalled his tall tale of looking for a small cart for woods work. An ancient but serviceable wooden manure spreader was in the barn. Years ago he'd removed the beaters and apron chain and replaced the rotted floorboards with sturdy two-inch hemlock planks. The tongue of the wagon had been cut down so horses would never again draw the spreader but the Farmall could handle it easily.

The first of the water was trickling through the grounds when a disembodied voice in the dark of the hall said, "Is that coffee?"

"Good morning." He poured coffee for both of them and said, "I've got to go out to the forge for three maybe four hours. Something about a job got figured out in my head. But after lunch, I was thinking of taking the tractor and tools up to the woods and cut some firewood for the winter. It's going to be a glorious day. I'd really like it if you came up to help me. It's not hard work. I like to go along at a comfortable pace. It's just such a fine time of year to be outside."

She took a long time looking him square eye to eye. Finally she said, "I need a decent breakfast. There's piles of linens mildewing in the baskets. I've got some reading I want to do but I can pitch in. And it sounds like it might could be nice working up there. And Hewitt?"

"Jessica?"

"I'm fine. I really am."

★  ★  ★

SOMEWHERE IN THE night Hewitt realized in order for his hitching posts to work, for them to hold the stones, the iron encasing them
had to be bowed in such a way as not to touch them or over the years
orange lines of rust would lie upon the rock. Yet at the same time the
posts must not endanger a horse—no gaps a nervous hoof could get
caught in for instance. So the iron must hold the stones neatly as a
cage and it was this design change he sat configuring and refiguring
throughout the morning. The exact dimensions could not be determined until he found the stones but the symmetry had to be in place
before he even laid eyes upon them—the idea had to be fully formed
so he'd not be tempted to compromise.

When he'd first come in he'd left the door open at the top of the
stairs and then opened the lower double doors. The air in the forge
breathed cold from chilled iron and steel and brick and at first the
outside air wasn't much warmer but fresh. By the time he was on the
third sketch the sun was up enough so the air flowing through was
warming and the row of windowlights over the upper door threw
down small broken rectangles of light. It was around that time the old
orange and white splotched barn cat trod silently down the stairs and
settled against his right boot. The cat usually only came to the forge
in the most bitter weather, standing in driving snow outside the upper
door and yowling righteously until Hewitt heard him over the sound
of his work and went up to let the old fellow down to spend the afternoon curled tight against the side of the hearth, the bricks warm and
the earthen floor warm and well out of the way of both Hewitt's heavy
boots and the sparks, the bits of hot metal that would fly from the
cherry metal beaten upon the anvil.

So Hewitt gave little thought to the cat. With the wet of the past
couple of days he was just an old cat looking for a warm spot. And
Hewitt was in that exquisite thrall when he was overtaken by design—
those moments when all the rest fell away and he was only working.
He made his way through the series of sketches and measurements,

never needing to move and only marginally aware of the small weight
of the cat on his boot.

The final plan he spent a great deal of time over, checking and
rechecking his measurements to the point where he could no longer
quite make sense of the numbers, which meant he'd taken it as far as
he could without the stones themselves. Slowly he emerged from
this state of concentration that was near narcotic. He had his hands
flat on that final sheet of graph paper as if it might fly away. He looked
out the open doors on to the day. Hours had passed. From the far
corner of the desk he lifted a cold chisel Timothy Farrell had made
many years ago and presented to Hewitt as a gift. Hewitt never had
used the chisel on iron, although there was no practical reason not
to—he had far older and less well-made tools he used regularly. But
the cold chisel was special and so stayed on his makeshift drafting
desk as a paperweight.

He thought then of lunch and the afternoon up in the woods. The
world at that moment held perfect symmetry.

It was only when he began to move that he felt the weight of the
barn cat against his boot. He looked down and saw the cat was not
against the side of his boot but over it, the cat stretched out as if wanting to quietly get as close to Hewitt as he could without disturbing
him. Stretched so, the cat's head was down on the floor one side of
the boot and his hind legs and tail sprawled from the other side, so his
chest, his ribcage under the tattered coat was so visible Hewitt didn't
need to bend to be able to count the ribs. Or to realize the cat was
dead.

Hewitt gazed down. Then bent and picked up the dead cat and
held it on his lap. The cat was ancient, so old Hewitt wasn't sure but
thought it had already been in the barn as a kitten when his father
died. The cat came in the way of country cats—appearing one day
and taking claim of the place. Hewitt held the wornout body and
knew it didn't matter when the cat had come—it just seemed he'd
always been there. Mostly shy and hidden but then showing up at the

oddest of human moments. And somewhere in the back of his mind Hewitt had always known he was not truly alone, that there was a witness. Not so much a companion but a quiet discreet soul tucked back in some corner of the barn.

Holding him, Hewitt felt he was holding primeval evidence of his own life but also a secret life now, as with all lives passed, lost to time. The cat didn't even have a name. He was the barn cat.

After a bit Hewitt went out the lower doors of the forge, cradling the body against his chest and mostly out of sight of the house went around to the back of the barn and let himself in. Avoiding the house because this business was between him and the cat and no one else. In the barn he found a burlap feed bag and stuffed a corner deep into his back pocket and got a spade. It was not a question of finding the right spot. The orchard was, for the cat, an extension of the barn—a good place to hunt mice and moles. Hewitt laid the cat on the burlap sacking and dug a good deep hole, the black dirt coming easy and then wrapped the cat and settled him down in the hole. "Catch a mouse, old fella," he said and with his hands pushed enough dirt back into the hole to cover him and then used the spade to finish the job. Last thing he set the chunk of sod back into place and lightly tamped it with his feet. Then wiped his hands on his jeans and carried the spade back to the barn.

Once back outside he looked around at the day. It was an exquisite day, a fine day to die, he decided. For an old cat a much better one than some frozen winter morning.

He went to the house and washed his hands. The house smelled of laundry soap and the triple lines above the flower gardens were billowing with sheets. The table was set with plates holding thick tuna sandwiches. Glasses of ice water and a bowl of bread and butter pickles.

She said, "I figured if we were going to buck wood we needed a big lunch."

He sat and ate a pickle. He said, "This is great."

She was in the heavy boots and work clothes she'd bought when she was working for Roger Bolton. Her gloves lay on the edge of the table.

She took a bite of her sandwich and still chewing said, "Good morning?"

He took his own bite and chewed slowly and swallowed. Then said, "I got something worked out I've been stewing over."

She ate a pickle and drank water and said, "What were you doing up in the apple trees?"

He told her.

She put down her sandwich and said, "Oh, Hewitt."

"He was an old cat. He'd a good life."

After a long moment she said, "And you feel like you ignored him most of the time."

Hewitt stood up, half his sandwich still on his plate. He said, "Don't be an idiot. He was a barn cat. And he and I watched out for each other. In our own ways. I'm not wanting lectures from you. But in an hour or so, if you want to hike up, I'll put you to work." And picked up the remains of his sandwich and stalked from the house.

By the time he saw her walking through the woodlot with a thermos jug, he was feeling pretty good. He'd cut up an ash brought down by an ice and wind storm the winter past, and a rock maple collapsed from the same storm. The ash was solid, its death a result of the tree forking some twenty feet up and once half of the crown went the stress was too great for the rest of the tree. The maple was another matter—standing dead so most of its smaller limbs had long since given way, leaving the huge rough bole topped with thick stubs of limbs. Probably only half the wood was salvageable, the rest punked or rotten. Still and all he had a pretty good-sized pile to split and was ready for the water he'd forgotten in his pique.

He'd saved a thick round of the ash to use as a chopping block and sat on that with his feet and knees spread, his jeans littered with sawdust and oil stains from the chainsaw and watched her approach.

She was dressed for work and silently handed him the thermos and stood watching while he tipped it back and drank, the water so cold he couldn't drink as quickly as he wanted, the cold almost paralyzing his throat. He capped the jug and said, "Just what I needed. Thanks. Time I get this split up, we'll have us a load. You can start stacking the small stuff in the spreader, just keep an eye on me and don't get too close. Some of these buggers, when they split, can send a piece far and fast enough to break an arm or take out an eye. And I've got to watch for myself. Okay?"

"Sorry about the cat," she said.

"Yeah, well. Let's work a while. It's taken the piss out of me."

SPLITTING WOOD'S A CURIOUS enterprise. Each round has slightly different properties, so each reacts differently to the axe, and the axeman, after splitting two or three thousand chunks has a pretty good idea of what to expect. Still there are surprises—the greatest danger for himself as well as Jessica being that wild hurtling piece that refused to simply fall into the growing pile around the block. Twice his shins took a sharp rap from such pieces. But mostly the pile grew and from time to time he'd pause to push away the split wood building around his legs and roll close more of the big rounds.

When the splitting was done, they both took a wordless water break. Jessica's face was red from the work and the golden light fell around them in the woods and mixed with the smell of the freshly opened wood so the silence between them was easy. The beauty of the day needed no comment. With both stacking, the split wood began to fill the spreader fast. They'd almost finished the first load when the incessant beeping of a car horn came up to them. They couldn't see the farmyard from this spot but the sound clearly came from there.

"What's that about?" Jessica asked.

"Trouble." Hewitt was setting the chainsaw and gas can, jug of bar oil and the axe atop the load. Last thing he grabbed up the thermos. Climbing on to the Farmall he said, "Come on, hop up on the bar behind the seat. Hold on tight."

She looked up, still on the ground. "I'll run down. Nobody knows we're up here."

"Whoever it is will hear the tractor, you'd let me start it."

She looked away through the trees toward the sound of the horn, then back at Hewitt. And took off at a serious lope, a good pace for the woods.

Hewitt started the tractor and cursed, "Fucking girl." The tractor lurched forward and he could only get up into second until he was clear of the woods. He had no idea who would be sounding so persistent an alarm or what for. He'd already scanned the sky and it was free of smoke.

In the upper reach of the pasture the lane improved and he tried third gear but the load was rocking even after he idled down so he dropped into second again. Then cleared the rise of land and could see the farmyard and recognized Priscilla Warren's red Wagoneer. Pea, as everyone called her after her size, was the rural mail carrier and although it had only occurred a few times over the years he guessed she had a piece of registered mail, something she needed his signature upon. She was trying to save him the slow tractor ride to the post office.

Jessica was bounding through the lower reach of the hayfield and into the yard. She slowed, stopped and walked on. Pea was out of her truck, kneeling over something on the ground. And once again he didn't know what had come upon them this afternoon but knew it was not good. He saw Jessica suddenly spurt the last fifty feet and also go down on to her knees.

There was no way for him to travel faster. He could've shut the tractor down and locked the foot brakes hard and chocked the wheels of the loaded spreader and run himself but it would save little time. So he drove along and pulled around on to level ground near the barn before he shut down the tractor.

Tom lay dead cradled in Jessica's arms. Jessica bent over the cat, her body a question mark that had lost interest in its answer, a low croon coming from her that was not a cry and not meant to soothe the passing but from some deep pit, a low humming keen. It was not a good day for cats.

Hewitt went down on one knee and placed a hand lightly on Jessica's shoulder. He looked over at Pea and saw a smear of blood on one hand, blood from Tom's mouth most likely when she'd picked him up from the road. Hewitt already knew the story. But he patted Jessica's shoulder twice, his eyes on Pea as he tilted his head and then rose. Together they went around to the other side of her truck.

Hewitt liked Pea. Ten years his senior, the mother of three children whose husband some years ago had left to join a Buddhist monastery in the Catskills. The story was he'd told Pea to hold on, he'd return a better man for all of them. To which Pea responded she'd empty her deer rifle into him next time she saw him and his Masters at the monastery better be prepared to assist him in his vow of poverty with child support, or she'd sue them to the last inch of their tidy nonprofit status.

She said, "I'm sorry as can be about the cat. I was just slowing up toward your mailbox when he broke out the brush and streaked cross right in front of the truck. I didn't see him but a second but I heard the thump. He was dead before he even knew it."

"It's all right, Pea. It happens. Thanks for blowing the horn. It would've been harder if we'd just found the cat on the road."

"I know. She all right?"

"She will be. Thanks, Pea. You already got yourself at least a half hour behind."

She said, "I never made it to the box. You want your mail?"

He said, "Naw. Just stick it in the box tomorrow."

She stepped up into the truck and leaned out the window. "Hewitt. Tell her I'm sorry for me."

★ ★ ★

HE BURIED THE second cat of the day a few feet away from the first. Jessica silently refused to come, retreating to the house. This time when the hole was dug and the wrapped cat rested, he paused thinking of the short life of the cat, rescued from Emmett's and teased back to his playful dominating self. A cat to be reckoned with. A lovely cat.

When he came back around the barn from the orchard the dooryard was empty. As he stood the front screen door popped open and Jessica was outside, running. Coming toward him. Her face a clamor of anxiety and terror spilling up and across it. She ran past him out the driveway on to the road. He followed and stood watching as she fell to hands and knees working up one side of the road and down the other. She was pushing deep into the brush and brambles along the roadside and down to the brook on the farm side of the road. Then she'd climb back and go up the road fifteen feet and start all over again.

She was searching for Rufus. He went toward her, pushing his way into a black raspberry thicket, ducked low toward her agitated stream of kittykittykittykittykitty the rapid chanting a lament.

They worked together both sides of the road a quarter mile up from the driveway and then walked down and did the same the other side of the drive. When they abandoned the roadside search and walked back up the road in the fast drooping afternoon, he said, "We'll drive up to Emmett's. Could be they were trying to go back there."

Jessica was silent. In the driveway Hewitt got behind the wheel of the VW and she slid into the passenger side. Backing around, Hewitt told himself fuck the law, he was the one in shape to drive.

There was not much to be found or seen at the Kirby place. The house was wrapped with yellow police tape and someone had covered all the ground floor doors and windows with plywood sheeting. Together they made a slow circuit of the house calling quietly for the cat. But there was nothing. Except the abyss of Emmett Kirby.

He drove them home. She asked nothing and he said nothing. He only prayed Rufus would return from wherever he was hiding.

He pulled into the driveway and parked by the barn. Jessica sat looking out the window on her side, drifting deep within. And he thought I'll follow until I hear the crack and then do my best to jump down and be there to catch her, to break her fall.

Jessica trailing, they went through the dusk to the house, darker inside than out. Hewitt turned on lights in the kitchen and continued through the pantry and office and up the stairs and through all the upper rooms, even the spare bedrooms, lighting them up, leaving the doors open. He was heading toward the top of the stairs when he heard a small choked-off scream from below and went at dangerous speed down the stairs into the living room, dark still until as he passed it his hand hit the overhead switch. Jessica was on the couch, Rufus held tight to her chest.

Hewitt stood not moving. Christ, what a relief. Rufus was here, alive and tight against her, his fine sleek skull pressing against the side of her face. She was rocking from the waist up, holding the cat. Then he realized what he was seeing—the cat was fighting her; pulling his head away and squirming and as she grasped tighter the hind legs digging and reaching, finding purchase in her thigh and clamping hard into her flesh to push himself loose and Hewitt was moving across the room when Rufus got a front leg free and clawed the side of her face. She screamed and the cat struck again, on to the same ripped cheek. She hurled the cat away in a blurred pinwheel. He struck the floor yowling and darted from the room.

Hewitt had one of those stand-alone moments when he realized things had just gone from bad to deeply worse.

She was bleeding, one hand pressed against her cheek, the sobs held back broken free now, a spitting erratic moaning cry as if words were trying to force through. Hewitt was over her, leaning down, his hands on her elbows, gently lifting her, his own voice a sweet lowdown croon. "Honey he didn't mean to hurt you he was just scared come on now we've got to wash this out you've got to let me see it," and she let him lift her and came against him, the hand still pressed tight, streaked with blood and he circled her belly just below her ribs with one arm and felt the shaking there as he guided her up the stairs to the bathroom where he let go of her and ran the tap until the water was warm, still talking as he found a clean washcloth, alcohol, gauze and adhesive tape, lining them along the rim of the sink, bringing order, trying to allow calm with his own even motions as he said, "You're okay, you're all right, it's just scratches, we'll just clean it up," and had the washcloth wet and warm folded into a square and he reached and took away her hand and held it down under the stream of water as he brought the cloth up and gently damped it against the long slashes starting high near her temple and running down close to her ear and out on to her rounded cheek. When he touched her with the cloth she moaned and pulled back, her eyes not meeting his but skittering like a trapped animal and he raised his other hand and easily cupped the back of her head, brought down the washcloth and rinsed it one-handed, squeezing it out and she looked down at the bloody flow of water in the slow draining sink, and he brought the cloth back up and tamped again, this time holding it in place as he tried to determine the next few steps. He took her free hand limp at her side and brought it up and pressed it on to the washcloth and said, "Hold this right here," and then quickly unrolled gauze and folded a flat pad and laid it on the sink and tore four strips of the tape and tagged them next to the gauze and reached up to the shelves and got a clean dry washcloth. All the while Jessica standing rigid, her fingers trembling where they held the wet cloth against the wounds and her lips sputtering unmade words.

Hewitt reached and took the cloth away and rinsed it again and dabbed again. The blood was slowing but not much. As he did this he also stretched for a handtowel and draped it over a shoulder and still holding the wet cloth in place, opened the alcohol and poured a wide circle into the clean folded washcloth and he felt her flinch and took away the wet cloth, dropping it into the sink as he dabbed with the towel, pressing gently to dry her face and he said, "I'm going to put some alcohol on there and then bandage it and you'll be fine," even as he swept away the towel and brought the alcohol up and pressed it hard into her flesh and her voice caught and yowled the thrown cat's cry and he had the gauze up and was taping it in place when she caught her breath and sucker punched him in the solar plexus. There was water on the floor and when he stepped back doubling over he slipped and managed to catch the sink with his hands as he went down, saving himself from smashing headfirst into the porcelain.

Then he was upright, recovering, alone. He kept his grip and stared for a moment at the wadded washcloths and bloodstains in the sink. Well he'd fucked that up. The water was still running and he cupped his hands and several times splashed warm water over his face, breathing deeply, letting the cramped muscles around his lungs relax. Then he took up the thrown-down towel and dried off and went looking for her.

SHE WAS WRAPPED in a ball in one corner of the couch, her feet under her, turned so her back was bowed toward him, her T-shirt pulled up to cover the wound on her face, the march of her spine rising from her exposed lower back. No longer crying but breathing in deep ragged sweeps of her ribcage and back. The gauze pack was on the floor near where he stood.

A screen of the world slipped. Before he moved, his mind was stepping to bend and lift her, to cradle her against him but then as if it was his only plan picked up the light ancient armless rocker and rounded the couch, setting the chair down and himself into it so he was face to face with her.

Her eyes two wide black grindstones, stark, inert, a gaze into some distance not only beyond but through Hewitt. He held tight a shiver and leaned close, his forearms along the couch back, hands overlapping and he brought his chin down and rested it on his hands—as close as he could get and not reach to touch her, let his fingers sift down on to her hair.

He said, "Jess, honey? I didn't mean to hurt you."

"What do you think it was like, Hewitt?"

"I was only trying to get it over with."

"Nothing he probably even saw just some unimaginable thing coming over him so sudden and furious to drive his life out of his ears and mouth and nose. What if it was you or me, what would be the thing that could do that, just bolt out of the sky this roaring power then all you are is pressed right out of this world? What would that thing be? And why then? It would be a terrible angel of the Lord to be able to do such a thing. Wouldn't it?"

"Something like that, I suppose."

"Maybe it just is. Maybe it's what it always has been and always will and everything else is nothing but a stupid trick, a bad joke we play on ourselves to pretend it makes sense. But there is no sense and you know it and don't you pretend you don't. This is the night of the dead soul, the night of the dead cat, just a cat like any other cat, just like that old man Emmett was just a man rolled over by the black that hides always behind the light we think we see, the light we all pray is there."

Hewitt said, "Maybe we're only breaking down that light into colors we can see. How do you explain the dark? The whatever it is when there's no light. That light you pray for."

"I don't pray, Hewitt."

"Not ever? When that guy was beating you up and you were balled up on the ground?"

"I'll tell you what. If someone gave us God they were just cowards and if God was the one gave us God then He's plug ugly meanness is all I can see. If this is all only some sort of test He can shove it up His ass because just how long, how long a test does He require? People talk about His plan. There's no plan, people!"

"Well now, I've felt that way plenty but then something happens, and I look back and see how one thing led to another and how it couldn't have turned out anyway but the way it did, although it was never what I thought or hoped for. So how would you explain that? Isn't that some sort of plan? Some hidden map to life?" Struggling to ride with her, to do what he'd promised himself—to be there when the bough snapped. To cushion her falling.

"It's not hidden. You connect it backwards, Hewitt. I grew up with God as frightening and spooky as Boo Radley. But you know what? God is either a long-ago fragment of history's fucked-up imagination or plain sick of us and taken up with new, more interesting projects. He's sidelined us for good but I have to wonder Hewitt if we all stopped doing things the way we do and started doing it some other way altogether then maybe way off in the far beyond place of the universe He'd stop what He's up to now and lift up His head and shake it thinking something's missing—there's an old old sound I don't hear anymore and after a while maybe remember us and come a bit closer than He seems to be now and see we've stopped doing all those things we do over and over to each other and maybe then there would be a God."

"I don't know," he said. "Maybe it doesn't matter if we invented Him or He invented us. Maybe we're barking up the wrong tree. I don't try to understand it but decided a long time ago, the only things in this life worth much to me are things most people pass right by. Everybody loves a pretty sunset but how many walk through a snowstorm that turns to sleet and watch the ice form on every smallest twig and branch and dead leaf on the ground or sit on a raining spring evening and see the hundreds of shades of green on the hill across with its little smokes of mist rising or one long slant of light that comes through a break in the clouds for half a minute and then is gone? And maybe it's just a random ball of rock and mud and water but for better or worse the old earth is all we really have for sure and even if it's an illusion, a fracture between what's truly out there and what our eyes see and our brains believe—

well, there's nothing I can do about that but I do know one day I'll go back into the earth and whatever was me, the me that thinks and feels and cries and hurts and smiles, well that me will either find out what else there is or will become some part of the earth again and either way it's all right. It's all right with me."

Her eyebrows pulled tight. She said, "How do you ever get your brain to slow down enough to see all that?"

"Listen, Jessica. You remember the fella played the fiddle at the party? Well, his dad used to be about the best around and most every Friday night a whole bunch of people would get together at one house or another and clear out the kitchen and sing and dance and play fiddle and guitar or piano all night long, the women cooking up big meals at midnight and going on right until dawn was breaking and they'd load up their old cars or buggies and go home and start right into a full day's work without a snatch of rest but they didn't *need* rest because how they spent the night did the job. It'd be nice to think that those were better times, maybe something we've lost for good but you know what? You know what, Jessica?"

She said. "Tell me."

"There was also always some old hermits tucked back who didn't go to those kitchen junkets, those ones who would show up at the store a couple times a year to buy salt and sugar and coffee, whatever they couldn't grow or hunt or get one way or another, who might appear at haying time to earn some cash money or at butchering time in the fall because they knew how to do it best but otherwise they kept to themselves and there were some thought they were simple or not right in the head but you know what I'm thinking—"

"What?"

Soft, questing, he said, "You tell me."

Slowly she ventured, "They were the ones like me?"

"No, Jess. Like us. They were the ones like us."

"You're not quite so fucked-up as me."

"You're not as fucked-up as you think you are."

She lifted her head a little, her eyes curious, quizzical. "So, what, Hewitt? You think I just spit myself out my own window ten years ago? You think I just was in the wrong place all those years? You think I just need to shed my skin, like putting on a new set of clothes? You think it wasn't only everybody else but me also, that was all wrong about me? Come on, Hewitt."

He said, "What about your grandmother? Was she wrong, too?"

She looked away. Then back at him and nodded. "Maybe she was. Maybe she was strong enough to walk with it and let it hold her up rather than press her down. Maybe that's what she saw in Celeste, too. And wanted for me. She did what she could—hell she gave me the keys out. But she was up against a brick wall with my mother and father. And she died before I was old enough to understand why she was telling me all those stories, what she was really trying to give me, to show me." She paused, chewed her lip and then grinned quick at him and said, "See? It still comes round to being fucked-up if I couldn't figure that out until now."

He grinned and said, "You're just a late bloomer."

"A slow learner."

"Nope. That's me. That's my cart to haul."

"You pulling hard?"

"Hard enough, girl. Hard enough."

"What would happen if you quit? Let go of it?"

"How'd this get turned around from talking about you to talking about me?"

"Hell, Hewitt. I thought we were hashing out the universe and everything else under the sun."

He was quiet a moment and then said, "It's like years ago I got happily up on the horse and started to ride. It was rough riding too. But after a while, you realize your legs have grown into the side of the horse. There's no longer any horse, any you. It's all one big motion forward."

"Is that the life you were talking about?"

He only looked at her.

She said, "Maybe you should just shoot that fucker in the head. And see what happens."

He said, "Remind me again. Who was it said you were crazy?"

"I did. That was me."

"I see." And he rose a bit out of the chair toward her across the couch and she came up as he reached and held her, their faces side by side, her T-shirt falling back down and she whispered into his ear, "Hey, Hewitt."

"Hey, yourself."

She leaned back, her arms still around him, up around his neck now and said, "So how's my face?"

"Stunning," he said. "Except for those long stripes that look, well, they look like you got in a cat fight. But they'll heal."

"You think so?"

"They will. They'll heal fine."

"What I'll do," she said. "Tomorrow I'll go out and buy some vitamin E capsules. And split them open and spread that stuff on. That works real good."

They were quiet a short while. Hewitt's mouth was dry and he was trying to figure out what to do next.

And Jessica lifted her chin, looking at him.

When the telephone rang.

They both heard the click halfway through the second ring as the machine picked it up and he could hear his own heart as he held his breath.

Muffled, urgent. "Hewitt?"

He was looking at Jessica and her eyes were floating blank, all the way back to their dark tight glazed legion, and he wanted to say It was all right when Emily disembodied and tremulous came through the machine again. "Hewitt, it's Emily. If you're there please pick up. Elsa." She paused and gathered herself. "Elsa tried to kill herself. Hewitt please be there, please pick up, God where are you?"

His eyes ripped, torn as he pushed up, his legs asleep from the knees down, Jessica pushing away, head turned, and then he was stumbling running to the kitchen where he caught up the phone.

"I'm here." Craning his neck trying to see down the hall, the empty end of the couch.

"Oh thank God."

"What's going on?"

"You were the only person I could call. God, isn't that strange? But you're the only one that knew everything or at least that I knew did. There're plenty who suspect and I'd guess even more after today. And Hewitt, it's been one hell of a day and the kids are freaked and half an hour ago I gave them each a Xanax so they're finally sleeping now. And no, I'm not doping my kids but Elsa pulling this three months after their father—"

"Don't explain yourself to me. Now, what happened?"

"She's all right, she's in the hospital, they pumped her stomach, she's on IVs, the monitors look good although she's still out and it could be a while before they know if she has any damage, liver, kidneys, nervous system, brain—the works. But it was a miracle, I guess. This was not one of those cry for help deals—she was serious. She had empty bottles lined up like soldiers, plenty of them swiped from other people, those were painkillers, most of them, including some from Dad. I guess she figured she needed them more than he did and he could always get more, right? The way Elsa thinks. Plus she had a good supply of her own. Little Miss Organic had scripts from a shrink in Fairport for about every possible medication for depression you could come up with. God the stories she must've spun. She'd been refilling them right on time but not taking them. She was hoarding them all summer. Ever since, ever since Marty died."

"Was there a note?"

"Is the cat out of the bag? I don't think so. But I won't know for sure for a few days because driving back from the hospital I thought wouldn't it be just like her, as a final proof of how seriously she took it, if instead of a note she'd sat down and written and mailed a letter. Or letters. Well, we'll see. At least if she did it wasn't today, or at least from her own mailbox because that's what saved her life."

"Em?"

"Hewitt? God, you haven't called me that in years."

"I'm right here but could you hold a sec? I really need a glass of water."

"Go ahead. I'll wait."

He set the phone down and went to the sink, ran water into a tall glass. He could hear movement upstairs. It sounded like she was pacing around her room. He wanted to run down the hall and call up to make sure she was all right but didn't have the time. And wasn't sure it was the best idea. For any of them. He went back to the phone.

"Back."

"Where was I?"

"Uh, mailing letters."

"Right. Like a lot of people the guy who runs the rural mail route out there in Guyanoga has a soft spot for Elsa. And she gets stuff in the mail all the time but only has a dinky regular box, not one of those big farm mailboxes. But instead of leaving her a slip like he's supposed to telling her to pick up a parcel at the post office he'll bring it along and pull on up the drive and honk his horn. If her car's not there he leaves it inside the porch. Short story, car's there, no Elsa swinging out to meet him and do her Elsa thing. So he has a bad feeling and checks the door. I don't know what it's like in Vermont but we still don't lock our doors here—"

"Just summer people."

"And there she was in the kitchen. She's got one of those old-fashioned daybeds she likes to keep by her woodstove but she was mostly down on the floor when the mailman poked his head in. She'd vomited but it was backed up in her throat. The mail guy knew enough to reach in and clean it out with his fingers and then dial 911 before he went back and started giving her CPR."

"So they got her to the hospital. What's next?"

"As far as what happens when she comes around, well, Hewitt, I don't know. Unless the doc and the cops scare the shit out of her, which might happen given the shape she's in but would be pretty much a first for her, she'll have some story to tell is my guess. Or she may just let it roll. The survivor crap, you know? A fresh start, a clean plate."

"What about you?"

There was a pause. Then Emily laughed and despite or because of the circumstances it was the first time he'd heard that particular laugh in decades and his heart lurched. She said, "What about me, what *about* me? I'll tell you what about me. When this whole thing washes clear, if there're no letters and she has a story that holds up and if she hasn't fried her brain or her organs, I'm going to drive out one fine afternoon and have a talk with her. And the shit is going to get scraped right off the spoon. The deal will be simple—I'll keep it a secret but she has to come and tell Nora and John what she was doing and what happened."

"Oh, Jesus, Emily. I know you're pissed, righteous pissed. And I'm sure you want to push her face in it and that would do the trick but what about the other side of it? You talked to me about that. I mean, that's their father you're talking about."

"I wasn't the one screwing his brother. And like I think I told you, if I'd found out before he died it all would've come out anyway. Look, Hewitt. Sooner or later they're going to learn the truth. If it's sooner they'll be angry at him and I can be the voice of reason, trying to explain that these things happen and blah, blah, blah. But if it's later then the only one they'll have a real right to be pissed at will be me for keeping it secret so long. Didn't you tell me that? And, Hewitt?"

"Emily?"

"I don't want to get into this right now but you know what it's like to learn years later that things were much different than what you thought at the time. You following me?"

He took a drink of the water and quietly said, "I see your point." Then still quiet but stronger he said, "As a matter of fact I've been through quite a bit of that sort of thing myself recently. More than you know. And so except for one thing I'd say I strongly agree with you."

She sighed and said, "Of course they're too young. But Hewitt, think. What if it'd happened five years from now? If they were both off at college and the same thing happened? Would they be old enough then?"

"Okay."

"That's it. The horns of the dilemma. All I have, all I can do, is deal with what's here and now."

They were quiet again. An easy quiet, not so much waiting for the other to speak but a natural pause as if they were in the same room.

So Hewitt said, "You know, Em, I really am terribly sorry you're going through all this."

She waited and then said, "Thanks, Hewitt. I'm taking that exactly as you intended. And Hewitt?"

"What's that?"

"You always were a gentle man. Even when you didn't know any better."

He smiled and said, "I believe I'll accept that exactly as you intended." Then he said, "So, today and Elsa aside, how're you doing?"

Oh shit thin ice again he thought as soon as he said it.

She let him wait. Or was collecting. Finally she said, "I really don't know. Some days almost good. Mostly. Other days are more difficult. I'm absolutely lousy at my job but what in the world would I do if I quit but sit around the house and get morose and probably start sipping wine at noon? I try to keep things up for the kids but I have to be careful there, it's a delicate dance with both of them coming and going emotionally at different times and my trying to gauge when they need their solitude and their own time to grieve and be angry and all that and when they need Mommy, which pretty much describes the wide arc of their swings. Nora's gotten too quiet and John's pushing me, staying out later than he's supposed to and I know he's smoking pot with some of his skateboarding buddies but I figure to hold off on the riot act right now, at least until this business with Elsa resolves itself and maybe the combination of what happened to his father and almost to his aunt will scare the bejesus out of him and if that doesn't work then all I can do is sit down and talk to him. Who knows, maybe I'll take the big jump and sit down and get stoned with him, tell him stories about the old days, see if any of that sinks in. Except my regrets from the old days don't have much to do with drugs and rock and roll. Oh God, Hewitt. I was with my mother at the hospital today and she's still strong and tall as ever, not a stoop to her although her hair's pure white now and she looks great. I mean she's looked great and it's been Dad I've been worried about the past few years and all the sudden I looked at her, she was on the other side of the bed holding Elsa's hand and gazing at her face as if her presence would wake Elsa or maybe just beaming all that mother-love toward her daughter hoping it would be felt, and I could see the sag in her, the muscles of her face slowly giving way, pulling downward and I thought My mother has gotten old and I didn't even notice and how the hell did that happen? Especially when I look in the mirror every morning and see myself."

"Hey, Emily?"

"Hewitt, if you're going to say something stupid about how I haven't changed I'm going to hang up right now."

"Uh, well. I think I sort of badly covered that early this summer but right now I was going to ask if you could hold on a minute?"

"Do you need to go?"

"No. No, no. I'll be right back. Okay?" And didn't wait but set the phone down. While she'd been talking he'd heard muffled steps coming down the stairs but it was only when he heard the front screen door snap back that he realized those steps were muffled because they were trying to sneak.

He didn't bother with the living room but went out the kitchen door on to the porch where it was full dark and he reached back inside to snap on the yardlight just in time to see Jessica rising from where she was stuffing something into the backseat of the Bug and under the bright yellow light she turned and glanced toward the house, the invisible Hewitt up on the porch and she turned swiftly and slid in and cranked the engine, the headlights coming on and lighting the side of the forge. He dropped down the steps in a swift trot and as she backed around he called out her name. She popped a little gravel as she went over the bridge and then was on the road heading south toward Lympus and he stood the brief moment it took for the headlights to be swallowed by the roadside trees and the sound of the engine to drown in distance.

Aloud he said, "She's gone for a drive. That's all." Then turned not believing himself and walked back to the house and climbed the steps, the full day falling over him so his feet and legs and back and head drained at once away from him and he was empty as could be.

"Are you all right? I heard the door."

"No. I'm fine. It's just—I'm back now."

"No. I think I should let you go." She was contained, retreated, cautious. She said, "It's been so good of you to talk with me. I'm better. I think I can sleep now. All the sudden I'm sagging."

"Em, I'm really okay."

"No, you're not. But I love you for lying. And I really am going to say good night."

"All right. Emily?"

"Yes?"

"I do hope Elsa's all right."

There was a pause and then she said, "Thanks, Hewitt. I do too. And not just so I can give her hot holy hell."

"I know."

"Good night, old friend."

"Good night, Em."

★   ★   ★

AFTER A WHILE he got a beer from the fridge and went into the living room. He stood a bit and drank some of the beer which didn't taste very good. Finally he set it down and walked around the couch and picked up the rocker and brought it back to its usual place. Then went slowly up the stairs. All the lights were on above, as they had been. He paused at her door and saw what he expected, went on to the bathroom and it too was stripped of her things. He went back to her bedroom and sat on the unmade crumpled bed. Two drawers were open and empty and the top of the bureau bare of her usual stacks of clean clothes. In the corner behind the bed he saw her work boots and crumpled toolbelt, still with her tools. And on the bedside table a single book was left. The toolbelt and boots rang of disdainful discard. He picked up the book, a slender volume of poems with a stark black cover bolted with a white slash. *The Great Fires*.

He carried it to the bathroom and began to fill the tub, water straight from the hot tap. He went downstairs and retraced his route, turning lights off along the way. Back upstairs he paused at her door and reached in and twisted the knob switch and the room went dark also. In the bathroom he stripped and felt the water and turned on the cold tap, then laid out a fresh towel by the tub. Before he stepped in he picked up the book, intending to read at least the first poem to see what she'd left him and a scrap of paper fell free, planed and floated down toward the water surface. He snatched it up after it landed and read the smearing message:

*I love you but so what*

FOR A COUPLE of days he moped about. He received a postcard from Meredith informing she'd settled on Middlebury and looked forward to seeing him next fall, adding a postscript saying hello to Jessica. He found several tins of sardines in the pantry and slowly bribed Rufus back into the meager society of himself. He finished bringing down the cut and split wood and stacked it in the woodshed and judged he had enough for the winter and a good bit besides. So he got a few things done. His brain was largely other places. Rufus following him. The sardines had convinced him Hewitt was the big fellow to stick tight to.

The third evening he went straight from his supper and called Emily. It seemed a reasonable amount of time.

"Hello?" The voice sweet, curling up toward a tentative question.

"Emily?"

"It's Nora. D'you want Mum?"

It threw him a bit. He wondered if face to face hearing the girl speak he'd still hear her mother. He said, "Yes, thanks." Waiting, he heard the distinct clink and rattle of a supper table.

"Lo."

"Hi, Em."

A pause and then cheery, "Hi, how are you?"

"Okeydoke, bad time to call. Sorry. Is everything all right?"

"Oh, thank you. Yes, she's just fine. Went home today. What a scare she gave us all."

"No letters?"

"There don't appear to be any, although the doctors say wait and see."

"Which means you still plan to talk to her with your kids."

"Oh, absolutely, I'll tell her you called. It's so thoughtful of you to check in."

"I'm almost always around later in the evening. At least until eleven or so. If you want to talk sometime."

She laughed, again that low lovely Emily laugh. "Well, you know I will. Listen, I have to run. But thanks again. Oh, and before I forget, Mother sends her best. Bye now."

He stood with the dial tone in his ear until he realized he couldn't make sense of any of it. Except Elsa seemed to be all right. After a bit he realized that was enough. If Emily had spoken to her mother about him that meant something but it could all be part of the camouflage.

He sat up that evening with an ordinary bottle of wine, just what the occasion called for. Around ten a light drizzle began, so quiet at first he didn't understand what he was hearing. At eleven thirty he went on up to bed, passing the shut door to Jessica's room. He supposed he should strip the bed and wash the linens. In the morning perhaps. Vaguely recalling waking sometime indeterminable the night before and going down the hall to lie facedown on her bed, his head deep in her pillow, the scent of her almond soap clinging as he breathed it in.

NEXT MORNING WAS an ideal day to work in the forge, the sort of day he loved to be down there moving around the hearth, the heat just enough, maybe the doors open, the dim light, the steady drip of rain on the roof, the water glazed windows, the bright color of the worked metal precise and easily readable. Then another idea came to mind. Because the same way such weather heightened perception in the forge, it did the same in the woods. And he was a man after stones.

An hour later, with his denim barn coat and a billed cap with the Agway logo pushed back as far as it could go and still keep the rain from his eyes, he was up in the sugarbush with the tractor and manure spreader turned wagon. Still littered with chunks of bark from the firewood but now holding a heavy crowbar, a couple of light chains, a come-along and one of the three Flexible Flyer sleds that hung on the interior shed wall where he parked the tractor—sleds that predated his childhood and his father had recalled using on winter days as a boy. It was a lot of equipment for a simple job but Hewitt knew that given the random array of woodland, the two stones he sought would be found down in a steep draw or tucked away uphill with no easy way to get them to the tractor and wagon. Thus the tools.

The woods were perfect. After the night and day of steady easy rain everything growing was a bit pressed down and back, opened. And all things, trees, lichen, brush, berry canes and stones, especially stones, were sharpened in outline, brighter in their color, more distinct. Revealed. It might take the entire afternoon but he felt confident he'd find those he needed for the hitching posts. It would be more of a trick than a job. Because he needed two stones near identical which was like saying he needed two clouds or two women identical.

In his jacket pocket he had a scrap of paper with the rough measurements he'd concluded could be utilized and a small eight-foot tape measure. But those were last resorts. He was confident he'd find the stones by sight, recognition.

In the way of such things he found the first within half an hour. And uphill as well. He didn't even need the measuring tape—it was the right stone. All it took was a short rocking with the bar to free it and then wearing heavy gloves he rolled it slowly down to the flat where he paused and considered getting the sled to haul it to the spreader but it had worked so well underneath his lift-and-roll hands that he abandoned the idea and spent the better part of an hour bent over moving the smooth-cornered triangular stone along the woods-floor. There was no hope of getting it rolling because of the shape but still it went along and, as importantly, he was growing deeply intimate with the surfaces of the stone—information that would be invaluable once he was turning it into the base of a hitching post.

Once he got the first stone loaded it was no more than another half an hour of tramping when he located the second. The rain had picked up but he was soaked through already so it made no difference. He was exultant. He'd fully expected to spend days intermittently searching for these near matching stones. And here they were. He was tempted, once more, to think the day was providential. But decided it was just luck and the sense to get out in the revealing rain.

Two hours later not only had that sense of luck changed but he was close to serious trouble. True, right away on finding that second stone he knew it would be more of a job, but seemed doable. It was about thirty feet down the slope of a small draw. So he'd need to wrap it in chain and then use the come-along to get it up to level ground. But the bank was soaked and soft from the rain and although he wrapped the chain around the stone all he had to do was tip it gently with the bar and it lifted and tumbled all the way down to the bottom of the draw. Where a small brook was now flooding. He spent an hour fussing with the other chain and the come-along stretched as far as the cable would allow and the stone was only ten feet out of the brook up the slope. And his chains and cable were stretched to their limit to hold it. The come-along barely reached to the top of the draw, fully extended and no matter how many times he threw himself against the handle the come-along wouldn't budge, the slope and angle and length adding to the wet ground and the weight of the stone.

A smarter man would've left it there. But at the moment Hewitt was determined, not smart. It was only after he'd unhooked the tractor from the spreader and backed the tractor slowly to the lip of the draw and found himself heaving up and down as the tractor ground and worked itself over the remains of a stone wall now spread along the lip of the draw that he began to doubt the plan. But all he had to do was transfer the upper hook of the come-along to the tractor drawbar and edge forward and all would be fine.

Except the tractor was at the edge of the draw with its rear tires tilted in nervous angle up on the old wall rocks. And then, even with the engine shut off, the tractor in gear and the brakes set, he'd had the bowel-loosening experience of being down in the draw after slowly, carefully moving the hook of the come-along to the tractor drawbar, then going down to remove the deeply driven crowbar from behind the desired rock but no sooner did he pull the bar free when the rock tipped backward, toward him, unbelievably toward him, and as he jumped free he looked up and saw the back end of the tractor edging down over the lip of the draw toward him, those hind tires slipping easily off the rocks they had seemed to rest so securely upon. He stood back and watched as the tractor slid partway down and then those small front tires somehow caught at the top and the whole thing came to a halt. Hewitt was so frightened he didn't even know he was. He stood staring at the tractor, waiting for it to continue. Only after an undefined period of time did he think to look at the source of all this, the fucking stone he was trying to extract. And saw it was lodged against a tree, going no further downhill.

He moved away fifteen feet or maybe more and sat down on the ground. Looking at the whole thing. His first thought was he was well and fucked. His second was but for a handy tree he could right now, this very moment, be crushed by his own tractor. Dead. Very nearly the stupid accident.

"WELP, HEWITT, WHAT you got here," Bill Potwin paused to spit, savoring the line, "is a tractor on the rocks."

Late afternoon, still raining, they were up in the woods with Bill's old pickup, one side panel replaced bright yellow against the burnt brick dull red of the rest of the truck, the lace and filigree of rust running around the lower edges. But the truck had a heavy V-8, near waist-high mud-grabber tires and, most important, an electric winch with heavy cable mounted on the front end. Bill used the truck around the farm but also admitted he liked to get off in the woods roads and see how much a mess he could get himself into and back out of again. Hewitt, like a good many others, knew Bill especially liked to do this in October, in the weeks before deer season started, traveling at night and for the sake of wisdom carrying along a heavy electric flashlight, more truly a spotlight, and naturally his deer rifle. Because the light could come in handy if Bill did get hung up bad and needed to see where the headlights wouldn't allow and the rifle just because. Bill always hunted the first week of the season and always managed to get his deer, which, at least in his mind made the two or three others already cut up, wrapped and in his freezer, legal. As far as Hewitt was concerned it was Bill's business; he was certainly not the only farmer to feed his family most of the winter on venison. They might get sick of it but it was meat on

the table. And with more of the old marginal farms growing back
up to woods there were plenty of deer for men like Bill, as well as
the usual hunters. Deer died of starvation. More deer, Hewitt guessed
were killed by running dogs each winter than by men like Bill
Potwin.

Bill went on, "Climb up on there and let it out of gear and
let off the brakes and then get the hell off in case the cable don't
hold."

"I thought you said that cable could hang an elephant."

Bill looked at him and said, "Did I say how big a elephant?"

Hewitt grinned. He was soaked through all over again and a little
chilled. He said, "Okay, let's do her."

He started toward the tractor that had the winch cable strung and
hooked tight around the front axle. The snub nose of the little tractor
pointing mostly toward the treetops, as if studying something up there,
taking in a view it'd never seen before. Hewitt slid a little down the
bank, reached up and got a purchase on the steering wheel and began
to hoist himself up.

"Hold on! Hold on a friggin minute!"

Hewitt jumped back off the tractor, landing on the slippery bank
and went down on one knee. He pulled himself up away from the
tractor and clawed his way to the top of the bank. The cable seemed
all right and the tractor hadn't moved. He looked at Bill.

"What's the problem?"

Bill grinned. "You got the rock, that stone, whatever twas you
was after up here? You got that still hitched up to the ass end a the
tractor?"

"Jesus Bill, I bout crapped my pants."

"Welp, Mister. You got that rock fastened on or not?"

"It came loose when the tractor gave on me. It's not right the front
of my mind at the moment, if you see what I mean."

"You know, Hewitt. Right this minute you got the safest most
capable rig you could get to keep your little tractor from rusting away

its last years down that gully, and you're balking over adding on an-other piddly couple hundred pounds? Of a stone you got to get some-how anyway?"

Hewitt just looked at him.

Bill grinned and said, "There's one, two lengths of log chain the back of the truck you need it. A course I'm happy to scramble down, help you get it hooked up tight, you want."

Hewitt said, "Why don't you set up in your cab, get out the rain. I can handle that bastard myself. Though an extra piece of chain might come in handy."

Bill nodded. "Help yourself."

FORTY MINUTES LATER Bill drove down the hill with a twenty-dollar bill folded in his shirt pocket, in time to help his wife and chil-dren with the evening milking. After towing the tractor and hitching post stone not only up but out to the clearing where the old manure spreader waited with the first stone, Bill had wordlessly stepped down from his truck to help Hewitt get the chains and come-along free of the stone and then the two of them hoisted the stone to rest in the spreader bed along its near twin. Bill then leaned his elbows on the side of the spreader and from all appearances was ready to settle in for a chat.

"Getting some jeezly rain at last. If it'll last. Goddamn what a dry summer, bout to burn everything up it was."

Hewitt was still separating chains, his from Bill's. He said, "Couple days of rain, a week of sun, couple days of rain, then sun again—why if it kept right on like that till freeze-up we'd be set wouldn't we?"

Bill darkened a little bit. "Sometimes I think we'd be better off without all the predictions. Wrong half the time anyway. And the old folks, my granddad, they could read the weather better than any of those slick shits on the TV. Probably better off that way. We don't even know what we don't know anymore, seems like."

Hewitt paused.

Then he said, "That's the God's truth."

Bill said, "Whatever happened to that cute little piece a ass was around most a the summer?"

Hewitt jimmied the iron bar in across the back of the spreader. Not as if the two stones would roll out going downhill or as if the bar would keep them from doing so but for the pure pleasure of mashing the bar in place instead of backhanding Bill. With that done, he straightened and shot his ragged coat cuff to look at his watch.

He said, "The truth is I don't care much for that sorta talk Bill. You understand. It'd be like if I was to talk like that about one of your girls. Good Lord, Bill, I appreciate the hell out of this but don't you got cows with full udders right about now? And I got to get this load down the hill, myself."

Bill nodded. "Mother and the boy'll already be to the barn. I best get going, if you're set, Hewitt."

Hewitt grinned then and said, "Hell yes. I'm good to go. Thanks again Bill."

The Farmall was hitched again to the spreader and so for the shortest of times through the woods Hewitt followed Bill. Then the big tires on the truck ahead seemed to stop and clutch and dig and press deep and Bill went on through the sugarbush around the ridge and out of sight down the hill along the lane through the pasture and hayfield, most likely making a mess of the summer-baked smoothness of the track but that was okay. Hewitt putted along behind. In the end, all things said and done, Bill Potwin had enjoyed a break from his regular routine, twenty bucks he'd probably not disclose to his wife and had a pretty good story to tell around—Hewitt Pearce got hisself in a world of shit the other day and Bill bailed him out.

On the other hand Hewitt had his two stones, the tractor wasn't lost or damaged, he'd spent a pleasant damp afternoon in the woods and he'd given Bill Potwin something to talk about. On the whole a pretty good score. There wasn't a farmer or logger up and down the valley who at one time or another hadn't gotten into a bad pinch and had to call for help. The worst would be some jokes about his antique tractor, calling Bill Potwin for help, or both.

He pulled both tractor and spreader into the big open-floored hay-loft on the backside of the barn. He wanted the stones in the forge but that meant creeping down the bank and around to the big doors of the forge and it was too wet for that. At least today. He shut off the tractor, walked by the spreader and ran his hand over first one stone then the other. They were right. They were right for now. The truth would be revealed tomorrow when he had them both upright side by side on the floor of the smithy. He'd had enough adventure for this day.

A LITTLE AFTER dusk he was sitting on the front porch, listen-ing to the rain on the roof, a pale yellow rectangle from the window lighting the other end of the porch, a citronella candle burning on the railing against the last of the mosquitoes. It was cool with the rain and he wore a flannel shirt open over his T-shirt, nursing a glass of wine. He wanted whisky. He was thinking about that, and why. If the old sealed bottle had been in the cabinet he knew it would still be sitting there; if the bottle he'd emptied down the sink was there instead he considered and decided it too would be untouched. So it was the wanting, not the whisky. Over the years he'd had plenty of times like this but like most everything else no event was an actual repetition of any other. Which was also a part of quitting it. His little return earlier in the summer he chalked up to the events, and perhaps a final desire to test himself. He didn't rule out a further test in the future but then the future was something Hewitt had come to view as no more dis-cernible than dreams.

Several hundred fireflies winked and danced in the lilac thicket. Rufus had followed him out and lay on the pew bench alongside Hewitt. They were comfortable together. But the cat reminded him of Jessica as did the daunting emptiness of the house behind him. How many years he'd lived alone there and how short a time with another person under the roof to reveal the loneliness all over again. He toyed with the glass, turning it in his hand, and admitted that it wasn't another person, it was Jessica who revealed the emptiness. Despite her moments she'd fitted in and around him about as well as anyone ever had. Perhaps it was the simple nature of their relations—the lack of demands upon the other, the deeply personal cohabitation whose peculiar closeness invited no greater commitment. Despite that final night and her flight. Despite that final note.

He was grateful for the book of poems she'd left behind. That first night, after his bath he'd opened the book in bed and read the first poem. Then read it again. And once more. He'd placed the book down, open on his chest and studied the ceiling cracks and faint stains of age and wondered if he was selfish, selfish as the man in the poem, the man living alone. And perhaps he was but it had taken an uncommon mind to formulate solitude to selfishness and then allow solitude to carry the day. He'd decided then to savor the book. A poem a night. To finish the day, to allow the day and night to crawl down and spread around him diffused by the words of a poem as deliberate and contemplative as a lover. Better than the drenched sleep of whisky anyway.

He stood and walked to the top step and stopped at the edge and peed down into the grass and the telephone rang inside, in full stream and he smiled again, reasonably sure who it was. Perhaps after all it was the right time to once again be alone.

Emily was speaking through the machine. "Oh, I was hoping you'd be around—"

"I am. I was just peeing off the porch. Sorry about calling last night at suppertime."

"I thought it was kind of funny. And the kids didn't blink. Not that they were listening. And they're certainly not listening now. Jesus, Hewitt, it has been a day."

"I was about to ask how you are."

"Thank you. How're you doing, Hewitt?"

"I didn't mean it as a hint. You want to tell me about your day?"

"Umm. I guess that's why I called. Is that all right?"

"Emily."

"Hey, the ground's still shaking under this girl's feet. I've had all afternoon and evening alone and still can't believe it. Nora went out to the farm and John's wherever John is, doing whatever he needs to do and I've got no idea when I'll see him again and frankly don't blame him except maybe I wish I could trade places with him. Sort of. Not really. Oh you know what I mean. God, I'm a mess, aren't I?"

Hewitt said, "Let me guess."

"Oh you know. But not the way I'd planned although I've pretty much given up on planning anything Hewitt. Elsa came rolling in first thing this morning. I was ready to go to work, my second day back after I had to take a couple of days off and Nora and I were eating breakfast and John was still asleep when I heard the car come up the drive and knew who it was. Christ, she looked like shit, like she'd been up all night. She was dressed pretty normal, I mean for her, just jeans and a summer blouse not her usual—well, you haven't seen her but she dresses like a goddamn gypsy or an old hippie, mostly like we all, I mean the girls, remember the chicks, the ladies, how we used to wear all that velvet and lace and Indian print flimsy skirts—"

"I always sorta liked that look."

"Didn't we all? But that was then, you know, Hewitt? Jesus, peeing off the porch. Every now and then I still squat in the grass if there's too many people inside or if I just don't care. It kills my kids. And the old jiggle doesn't work as well as it used to."

"Hey, Em?"

"Right here."

"Are you stoned?"

"I'd kill for a joint right now and could probably find one if I trashed either of my kids' rooms but no, Hewitt. I looked a long time at a bottle of wine but between you and me I've had a good share of those alone at night bottles this summer and decided to call you instead. So it's just where my brain is. Can you deal with that?"

"Let it roll, girl."

"Thank you sir. So I went to the door and she wanted to talk and I almost took pity on her and said wait until another day but frankly I didn't care and on top of that she'd driven over without even calling which was chickenshit of her so I stood there with my Mama Bear arms folded and told her damn right it was time to talk and then told her how it was going to be. She started to cry when I said the kids but then stopped. Hewitt I was blazing and told her what the fuck sister, there was nothing new she was going to tell me, it was the children, my children, Martin's children, that needed to hear it from her. She got that kicked puppy look and I just leaned down and told her it was not my idea for her to fuck my husband and since he wasn't around to do it then it was her job to tell them the truth. She tried the line about wishing she wasn't alive and I reminded her she'd already screwed that up as well so fucking grow up and get her ass inside and wait until I got John up. It was one of the weirdest moments of my life, Hewitt. Right up there with, well, with about anything you could imagine. Because there I was tromping through the house feeling like at last something *real* was about to happen. Because this whole summer's been a fucking haze. At the same time knowing I was about to change my kids' lives forever and I hated that, hated that so bad I got angry all over again, not just at Elsa but at Marty too and so by the time I dragged John downstairs it felt like it was all laid out. That it was not only what had to happen but that it was happening the way it was supposed to. I can't explain that."

"Sure, you can. Things swirl in chaos but there's always some form within it waiting to be revealed."

"Hey, that was good. You old hippie. So we all sat around the kitchen table and I didn't say a word. She looked at me like I was supposed to help her somehow but that wasn't my job and the kids already knew it was something big and bad about to roll over them. They're teenagers for God's sake and teenagers smell bad shit a mile away and they'd already been asking me what happened to her and why and I held up okay with that, telling them she was clearly very upset about something that must have been bothering her terribly to try to kill herself and in the meanwhile be grateful she hadn't succeeded. Well, of course I gave them the talk about no matter how bad things seem, and sometimes life does seem pretty bad, suicide's never a solution because it doesn't ever change what was so bad to start with. You know, the standard mother's prayer sort of talk. So they knew she was there for a big reason that somehow included them."

"What did she say?"

"She glossed it at first, which didn't surprise me. Then told them the night he died their father had been at her house and they'd been drinking and it never should have happened and John was slumped way down in his chair with his arms across his chest and said, 'Just drinking? Or what?' and she looked at him and he said, 'You cunt, you fucking cunt,' and Nora looked at me and Elsa started to cry again and John said, 'What the fuck're you saying?' and suddenly Nora jumped up and threw a sugar bowl that missed and started to shriek and I almost moved to stop Nora, and then stopped myself because it had to happen and she was brilliant and ferocious. Jesus, Hewitt, it's frightening when you see your child spill over and become an adult all at once, although that's not fair, she'd spent the summer trying to figure out what it meant that her father was dead but this was the moment, you know, the blinders are gone, all the childhood stripped naked and the adult all the way out. And I was proud of her too. Proud and a little shocked because she was doing the numbers faster than her brother which made me wonder if I'd been worrying about what the wrong kid was up to, thinking she was one of those slow quiet burns but she had it pegged. The first thing out of her mouth was 'How long? How long was this going on? This *fucking*,' and she spat that out as the nasty thing it was and Elsa turned Ice Maiden saying they couldn't understand and she was looking at me like it was my fucking fault when John stood up and put his hands on the table and leaned across to her and said, 'What? I don't understand fucking someone you're not supposed to? Dad was an asshole and you're a slut but it's not something I can understand, is that right?' and walked around the table and stood looking down at her and told her he was sorry and she looked up blinking and said, 'What?' and he told her he was sorry she was still alive. Then he walked out of the house. Or tried to because I ran down the hall after him and caught hold of him and tried to tell him not that it was all right but something stupid like it takes a long time to forgive anybody and he turned and held me like the man that he is and told me he'd never forgive him for what he'd done and he was crying but he told me he loved me and then was gone."

"Holy shit," Hewitt breathed. "He's a brave kid."

"Well, that was today, Hewitt. There's plenty of time for him to change his mind. I'm prepared for that. I'd be worried if he didn't, to tell the truth."

"So what happened then?"

"It was wild. I don't even want to think what the neighbors heard. When I got back to the kitchen Nora had Elsa by the hair and was screaming at her, I mean shrieking. How everybody knew she'd fuck anything with pants and I just held on to the door with both hands and let her rip. Because if I stopped it then I'd be stopping Nora from what she had to do. Elsa was hunched over and crying and Nora was jerking her hair and saying about everything one woman can say to another but shrieking it, screaming it, and sobbing and I thought Well there you are Marty. That's how you helped your children grow up. And all the sudden Nora quit, let go and backed up and bumped against the fridge and stood there huffing her tears and pounding her fists into her legs trying to make herself stop crying and then she did and looked at me and said, 'Mom? I'm getting in the car and don't even think about trying to stop me because I am all right to drive. I'm going to Gram and Gramp's to tell them what a *skank* their daughter is and I don't give a shit what anybody thinks but they're going to know the truth.' And I thought You can't let her drive like this she's only got her permit and then I realized I didn't really have a choice, Hewitt. I had to trust her and I had to let her finish what was started. So I told her the keys were in it and please have Mom call me later. Oh, Hewitt, she was grand. She stepped into her sandals and took her purse off the back of her chair and slung it just so over her shoulder, pushed her hair back and picked up her sunglasses from the table and put them on, all the time never so much as glancing at Elsa and then walked out of the room."

They were both quiet a bit and then Hewitt finally spoke. "So, then what? You and Elsa alone."

"I kicked her out. She was blubbering sorry left and right so without knowing I was going to I grabbed the front of her blouse and twisted it up in a knot and told her I didn't care if she went home and OD'd again but if she had an ounce of courage she'd tough it out, if nothing else not to fuck my kids up even more. I couldn't care less what she did with her life as long as she kept it away from mine. And that was that. I walked back into the house and shut the door. Although I did stand there waiting until I heard her drive away. Because I wanted to know for sure she was gone before I went upstairs and fell apart."

After a bit Hewitt said, "Soooo . . . Have you heard from your kids?"

She said, "Well, I know where Nora is and like I said I just have to trust John right now. But there's more. Dad pulled in at noon."

"Uh-oh."

"You know, it wasn't so much what he had to say that hit me as the look on his face. We sat out on the porch and he had his cap on his knee, telling me Nora was okay and putting up the last of the peaches with her grandmother and he sat there fiddling with his fingers and looking off at his pickup like he wished more than anything he could drive off and get back out in the fields. So I reached over and covered one of his hands with mine, Oh Hewitt, those great big mitts of a farmer's hands, all nicked and scarred and spotted with age and I told him whatever you've got to tell me, it's going to be easiest if you just go ahead, it can't be worse than what I've already gone through and he looked at me and said, 'Maybe, maybe not. But hard for me,' and I knew then what he was going to say. So I patted his hand and sat back and crossed my legs and waited. And he squinted at me and told me if I'd been young and only married a few years and didn't have children or just little ones perhaps they would've acted differently but he and Mom simply couldn't tell me what they'd suspected. Because I was a grown-up, you see. But for a while they'd known there was something with Elsa and Martin, how anytime the whole family was together, holidays, birthdays, times at the cottage, it was clear there was something going on. He looked off and said some things are as old as the world and the one time he and Mother spoke directly about it Mother wanted to go talk to Elsa and he talked her out of it. And when he said that he looked back at me, as close to crying as I've ever seen him. He told me perhaps he was wrong, most likely he was wrong, that if he'd let her, or encouraged her because she wasn't sure what to do either, then maybe things would've turned out different. He reminded me how when I was growing up us kids knew there was distance between himself and his own father. All because he and Granddad got into a terrible argument about something, and things were never the same and he'd vowed to never interfere with his own grown children. Then he squinched up his mouth the way he does and said but this was something different and he hoped I'd forgive him. I turned toward him and said there was nothing to forgive, that he'd done the right thing and wasn't a bit responsible for how things turned out. And then, Hewitt, all the sudden I was bawling like a baby and he got down on his knees in front of me and held me, held me like I was a little girl and Daddy was all I needed. No one else ever could comfort me by holding me the way he can."

He heard her crying so he waited. Then she said, "He asked if I wanted to ride out with him and get my car and I said I'd rather not and he said he and Mother would drop it off that evening after chores in case I needed it but unless I felt otherwise Nora wanted to spend the night. I told him if that's what she wanted then it was probably the best thing. Then I went upstairs and slept, just all given out. I came down a while ago and the car was here and on the kitchen table was a fresh peach pie. And guess what, Hewitt?"

"You sat down and ate the whole thing."

"With ice cream." She laughed. "God, I can't explain it. Maybe I really am going nuts. I mean here I was at the end of this totally bizarre fucked-up day at the end of a totally bizarre fucked-up summer and I sat there and ate a whole pie. But you know what? It was great."

"Sure it was. It's good to be reminded there are good things. Like pie."

"Do you eat pie, Hewitt?"

"There's a woman in town bakes and now and then I get a pie."

They fell silent. Then, her voice suddenly shy, Emily said, "Hey, Hewitt. Tell me about your life. How you live."

He considered briefly and immediately decided to skip almost all of the last twenty years, at least all the parts that touched upon her, or the absence of her.

So he talked about his forge, his work, the satisfaction it gave him, wanting her to know he had moved far beyond the simple reproductions she might recall but at the same time being matter of fact, as if his mastery and control over his work was nothing more than an obvious progression and truth was it was not that hard to do because he'd always felt the difficult image he projected of himself was truly not only self-preservation but a real and lasting inability to comprehend or cope with the world's rush of demands. Her own responses were simple as well and so he knew she was hearing exactly what he intended, which was far more than what he put into words.

When he was done she said, "So you did it. You made the life."

He chuckled honestly and said, "Or the life made me. But you know, Em, all that aside, it's been a strange summer for me also."

She was silent then and he'd expected that. So he told her what she didn't know; of his father's first marriage and the loss of that first wife and daughter and then went on and told her about Jessica. Here he was more forthright, thinking rise or fall, whatever happens or doesn't with Emily, if Jessica returned or not, he owed it to both to be clear as he could be. He told how she'd arrived, the strange difficult first days, the ways he opened to her and how Jessica slowly responded, how she'd finally come to tell him who she was, the episode with his mother, sister and niece, and only here fudging a bit, how she'd departed and how he had no idea if that was to be a short or long time but as far as he was concerned, and he believed Jessica knew this also, there always was, and always would be a place for her with him.

When he was done Emily said, "I've seen people like that. Not too many because Bluffport's off the path for most but they've ended up here. Some come from right here. They're hard to work with—they seem to want help but once it's offered they pull away. I don't know what it is, Hewitt. You said she had meds but wouldn't take them?"

"I never saw any. But they were in her past, at least."

"That's frustrating. Because they could really help her."

Hewitt was quiet and then said, "So is it really all about drugs then? Or has the world narrowed up so tight it just squeezes the bejesus out of some of us?"

"It's not drugs, Hewitt. And the world has always squeezed."

"I know that pretty well, Emily. But I'm not rambling around the country not trusting a living soul."

She said, "Yes, it sounds like you're doing just dandy. Like I said, living the life."

"I still believe most of what I knew was true when I was nineteen, if that's what you mean."

"But who do you trust, Hewitt?"

"Well, Em. I trust myself. And a couple of good friends. Not much beyond that."

"I see."

"Well, you asked. I still trust you. I mean the spirit, the essence of the woman I once knew. I'm trying real hard not to fool myself but Emily, I have to tell you, tucked in around the edges, is the same woman I placed my trust in a long time ago."

A drawn out silence and he guessed again he'd blown it but also again felt he had no choice but to tell her how he saw things. It was so quiet he could hear the soft rain. He waited and was about to give up and admit it, apologize because he had to and let it go. Or let it go and see what happened. He'd learned something over the summer although at the moment wasn't sure what it was.

Then Emily said, "What about Jessica?"

"What do you mean? Do I trust her? Do I trust what I know about her?"

"Do you trust what you feel about her?"

He paused and said, "I trust what I feel about you. But I know how I feel about her."

She said, "I hope you do. I hope so, Hewitt."

Then there was only the rain.

# Ten

A splendid late summer or early autumn morning with Hewitt deep in the defile of Crawford Notch heading east, the roadside thick with purple asters and here and there on the lower reaches of the gorge slashes of red among the trees below the cliff faces stretching above, the single hawk too high to be identified drifting effortless the thermals of what would be a pleasantly warm, near hot isinglass day. Walter's jeep with its hardshell top and sturdy road-eating tires, nothing beyond what it was intended to be, a small hardy engine, not a workhorse but more akin to a donkey; plain, functional, able to grind on long after fancier beasts had fallen in the harness. And to the point of the day—a vehicle designed to blend into its surroundings. As Walter pointed out when Hewitt called at break of day, requesting nothing but merely laying out the situation.

He got caught behind a log truck and so eased back and tooled along, relaxed and enjoying the ride, contemplative but not over-thinking anything. Nothing at all. A part of this peaceful vitality was the day before he'd installed the completed hitching posts, after calling two days before that and telling Anne what needed to be done to prepare. So his twin monuments, his stones encased in their elegant refined cages were now in place and looking exactly as he envisioned, wonderfully unique but immensely practical. Placed either side of her main stable entrance, anchored deeply so the hardest frost would never budge them, surrounded by mums, the oiled rubbed ironwork complementing the white walls of her barn and the black-painted cast bars within the open stall windows. Once they were in, Hewitt was patiently agreeable as one of the long-legged Thoroughbred studs was led out and tied for a bit to see how a horse would react and he behaved as all expected and hoped—he nickered for his mares and stablemates, peered around at the clustered humans and then began to crop the lawn bordering the beds and took a trial nip at the mums. After he was led back inside Hewitt and Anne conferred briefly and he undercharged her, making a joke about selling rocks and adding they came with a lifetime guarantee. He asked if he could have a couple of minutes alone before one of the guys gave him a lift home and Anne glanced at him and nodded, disappearing into the cool depths of the barn.

The only thing he'd done to the stones was use an old buffing head to gently polish their surfaces, so the black spots and veins and the golden flecks of pyrite sharpened in appearance, not enough so even a thoughtful observer would discern his effort but the effect was what he wanted—the stones would appear always as he'd found them, glowing wetly in the lustrous subdued light of a rainy day. He'd squatted about five feet back midway between the posts and studied them. Sometime during the finishing work it came to him that the stones were for more than Emily and himself and their unborn children but comprised a vast circle of his past, back into his father's life, his father's lost wife and child and then as something breaking open in him; to all of the gone, the long lost, however close or remote within the broad net of his life.

HE'D GOTTEN UP at his usual time and it was dark outside. The summer was indeed shrinking toward what Hewitt thought of as the long lovely dark time—not forgetting the pleasures of autumn and Indian summer or the usual brown drab of November but thinking ahead to those short days where the forge was a haven and the world periodically refreshed itself, the deep shoveled paths between house and forge and out to the mailbox, the dark oily glisten of the hemlocks and spruce in the low afternoon light, the mighty gliding strides on snowshoes up through the pasture and woods along the old road or as the snow deepened anywhere at all he wanted to go, the dead-falls and cumbersome boulders of summer as good as gone, coming again to stand on the hill above the place and spy out his neighbors' lights up and down the valley, the small glow from the single streetlight in Lympus, and along the hills to the south and east a smear of light from Sharon. Or the nights few and rare when the streams of green-ish or more rare red, yellow and green aurora borealis pulsed against the sky, never forecast, never expected but only immediately and wondrously there—the lights always a gift beyond the reach or ex-pectation of humans. Although when they were out the telephone network buzzed, one of the few times he loved the phone, the ex-cited voice on the other end and he'd do his part, make a call even as he was strapping on his snowshoes in the kitchen before clattering down the porch steps and off into the snow.

Now as the coffee made he was still aglow from the hitching posts and headed toward the forge to sit and sip as the fire caught and burned toward the furnace of ancient gods, the smiters and alchemists of iron, bronze and brass. And go again through his stack of notes not only to see what caught his eye but with a strategic edge—midwinter he didn't care to be caught with a project so large he might need the big doors which could be wedged by snowfall and the impacted slides off the roof until whatever thaw, January or March or even April would once again open those doors. So he was thinking all this when the phone rang and even as he'd thought he was getting used to these unusual calling times, knowing who it was.

"Hey there."

There was a pause and then, tentative, "Hewitt?"

"Jessica? Jeezum! Where are you? What's going on?"

She made him wait. Then said, "Portland."

"Oregon?" Praying she heard the tease.

"You sound kind of out of it," she said. "Have you had your cof-fee yet?"

"I've got it right here."

"Portland Maine."

"What's happening there?"

"Oh. Not much. What's up with you?"

He sipped the coffee, scalding his tongue but trying to slow it down to whatever level she was calling from. He said, "Not so much either. Well. I finished those hitching posts and got em in the ground yesterday."

"How do they look?"

"They look good." All he needed to say. "Roger called. Wanted to know about you. I told him you were off on a toot. He said if you showed up he still had plenty of work."

She was quiet and he wondered if mentioning Roger was a mistake. Then realized she was sniffling, crying and trying to hide it. She said, "My car. It's all smashed up."

"Jesus, are you hurt? Jessica?"

He heard the snap of a lighter and pull of a cigarette and she told him the car had been parked but the brakes or whatever gave out and it rolled backward down the sidestreet hill she'd left it on and rear-ended fast and hard into a light pole, an old wooden one and the car was trashed and then she began to cry again, not trying to hide it this time.

He said, "Oh, goddamn, honey. I'm sorry. But you're okay, right? What about the cops?"

"They were nice about it. I mean, I wandered back and found three cruisers parked around it and a tow truck already there and they established it was my car and all the papers were up to date. The light pole didn't even budge. Although it was a job getting the Bug pulled off it. Aw, damn, Hewitt. It's gone. It's really gone."

"Was that this morning?"

"It was yesterday afternoon."

"Where are you now? Where're you calling from?"

"A hotel. Right up the top of the hill from where it happened. But I couldn't sleep and figured you were up—"

"Hey Jessica?"

"Hey, Hewitt."

"What do you want to do?"

She made him wait. Later he realized it wasn't that. Finally in a small voice she said his name again.

"I'm right here."

"Can I come back?"

DESPITE THE OFF-SEASON it was a slow push through North Conway and he idled along, his elbow out the window. It was almost lunchtime but he wasn't hungry and even if he had been wouldn't have stopped. There would be time enough for food in Portland. But years ago, the spring before he'd gone to work with Timothy and met Emily, he'd made a trip over here to spend a day with a smith, a long tall man with a beard halfway down his chest who had a small shop in town with the usual array of fireplace tools and kitchen utensils, latches and hooks and racks for pots or hanging outdoor clothing. The shop was all burlap and bright paint with Dylan on the stereo and the man whose name Hewitt could no longer recall had taken him out of town to his handbuilt cabin in the woods where his forge was and in a short afternoon taught Hewitt how to true-weld, using two pieces of flat stock straight from the forge. Over and over until he got it right. Two little boys ran naked through a vegetable garden with a high tight plank fence against deer and a woman worked out there without a blouse on, at one point bringing iced chamomile tea to the forge for them, her sloped breasts heavy, as lovely as anyone Hewitt had ever seen. The man told Hewitt they'd been at Woodstock and this at a time when no one would consider making that up. The man had dark brown eyes and the other thing learned that day came from those eyes—gently deep and patient but with an edge, a wariness to them. And Hewitt wondered what cost the man had paid for living a life according to a wheel of his own design. In some ways not so different than his own father, or Hewitt later realized, himself. They'd smoked

381

some bad homegrown together and Hewitt had gone on his way, carrying the precious three pieces of welded stock with him. It was an afternoon forever etched and yet he'd never gone back, being too preoccupied with his own life for so many years that when it occurred to him to try and find the fellow again there seemed no point. It had been what it was—a moment. One brother to another.

Stalled in traffic, hikers in shorts and fancy boots flocking across the street, Hewitt recalled Timothy's initial riddle about the strongest part of a chain. Then the road opened up and the traffic thinned, somewhere he'd lost the log truck, and he passed a sign welcoming him to Maine.

He'd forgotten the riddle until the spring after everything had fallen apart with Emily and he was finishing building his own forge and had gone to see Timothy's uncle Albert in Bethel, to visit and gently learn if the offer of the tools was still in place. They'd sat most of an afternoon and drank a bottle of hard cider when Albert had leaned forward in his padded chair and asked Hewitt the very same question his nephew had and Hewitt paused—Timothy had never answered. Albert smiled and said, "Ya damned young fool, ya'd better learn it once and not forget. The strongest part of a chain is the weakest link. Now, hand me that cane and let's hobble out and see if the rust's ate all that stuff up or if there's any good to it yet."

The landscape was changing again, leveling out, rolling, scrub pines and some nut trees, oaks and hickories back from the roadside, houses coming closer together, the shoulders now not only sandy white but glimmering with sunlight reflected from bits of crystal; quartz sand.

He'd talked to Emily several days ago. Calling intentionally late in the evening and wanting to be the one to do it—to give her time after the episode with Elsa but not so much she'd feel awkward calling him. She'd clearly been happy to hear from him, only asking him to wait a moment and then coming back on and saying, "You can hang up now, Nora. Nora? Hang up. I mean it." There came a mewl of a sigh and the faint click.

"So everybody's returned safe and sound?"

"I'm not sure how sound but yes. To my surprise John tried to tiptoe in about two hours after I talked with you. He and I sat up talking much of the night. Far from any resolution but a step along the way. Nora still hasn't talked to me about it, brushing me off with her stone face but I know she and Mom talked or maybe Nora just listened but they had a serious discussion. She'll talk to me when she's ready. I think she's figured out it wasn't my fault. I'm not so sure about John yet."

"Elsa?"

"Oh, she's still alive, as far as I know. Maybe it'll change and I do hope it'll be years and years but right now I don't want to hear a word about her."

"What about you, Em?"

"Well, I did sneak off to Rochester a few times to talk with a therapist. He asked the usual questions about our personal life and how we balanced the kids and work and all that stuff that I'd already done myself and I was as honest as I could be. I'm not a perfect person Hewitt but I was a pretty good partner. Anyway, the third time I was talking with him, he told me everybody's got a stone jar deep inside them only they know the contents of. Some people just leave it be. Others have to peek now and then. Some get snared by it. I sat back and thought about it a bit and stood up and thanked him and told him I didn't need another appointment and came on home. Because I'd realized my stone jar's not very important to me but obviously Martin's was to him; if you poke around down in there too much you find ways to justify it and the ways only have to make sense to you, not to anyone else."

"I like that idea."

"Well, yeah. I'm moving forward, which is stupid because of course I am—it's either that or be crushed by it all and—"

"That's not the way you've ever been."

"Thanks. I try."

"You sound good, Emily."

"Actually there's some big news."

"What's that?"

"I've got a buyer for the clinic. Well, two buyers. A husband and wife team about five years out of medical school who've been working in Buffalo and saw the place was on the market. I like them and they're crazy about the idea. I guess a few years in Buffalo took most of the idealism out of them, trying to balance between patients who resent being patients and dealing with all the paperwork for the state and the government. Little old Bluffport looks pretty good to them. They've rented a house and we're supposed to sign papers this week, although it'll be a couple of months before we can close."

"What about you?"

"Professionally? They were sweet about it. I think they really hoped I'd keep my office there for some continuity and to make their transition easier but that's what the receptionists and the two nurses are for. I'll keep my practice but find a new office. A clean slate. I think it'd be best for me and my patients as well. It's tough to unburden yourself when you're sitting there wondering if your therapist is listening to you or thinking about her husband who used to be down the hall. But what about you, Hewitt? What're you up to?"

"Not much. Well, I'm finishing up a pair of hitching posts. Real ones. I mean for real horses, not something to stick in a yard. And I had fun with the design. It was a bit of a challenge. Well, something more than that—there was a bunch of personal horseshit symbolism wrapped up in the whole thing. It felt good. They go in tomorrow and that's the real test but at the moment I'm tickled with them."

"Horseshit symbolism for hitching posts. That's kind of funny. Do I want to ask what that was?"

He was thoughtful. "I don't think I could tell you. It's a little like those stone jars you were talking about. Not weird shit just a lot of things entangled and interwoven that even if I could lay em all out would sound silly but kept inside make all the sense in the world."

She was quiet a bit. Then said, "You sound good."

"Yup. Mostly."

She hesitated also and then said, "Despite being a damn fool, you've been a good friend, Hewitt. A good friend through all of this."

He said, "Well, thanks. I hoped to. I might've learned a couple things myself."

They were suddenly in a tight squeeze.

"It's funny, isn't it Hewitt? You get older and time wails on by but it's also lost the urgency it had when you were young. The path's not endless anymore and maybe that's it—if you're going to step forward you want to make sure where you're stepping. Cause there isn't a second chance."

Then they were both quiet.

She said, "I meant—"

"I know what you meant, Em. I feel the same way."

"Good," she said and then her voice pitched down a little. "Of course you do." There came another pause. She said, "Hey, Hewitt?"

"What's that, Emily?" He was feeling gentle, tender, uplifted precisely.

"You heard from that girl? The one who was staying with you?"

"Jessica," he said. "No." And added, "Not yet."

MIDAFTERNOON HE was sweating lightly, merging with traffic and following signs, both agitated and amused that the small urbanity of Portland would so throw him off but in fact it'd been years since he'd driven in any traffic to speak of, even his lightning trip to Bluffport and back had all been on roads he knew well, mostly interstates and thus hard to screw up. And it was not warm but hot, the heavy ocean air smelling of possibilities and he realized he hadn't seen the ocean in years either and doubted he would this time beyond a possible glimpse. Then he was off and moving uphill into the Old Port section of town, the streets here just streets and manageable, at least until he very nearly pulled into what he thought was a street but was cobbled and blocked

off with metal posts—ordinary slightly ornamental cast objects he noted
as he reversed in a three point turn, not letting the horns get to him,
guessing, hoping if a cop was around they'd see his plates and realize
the misunderstanding. Somehow this process calmed him and oriented
him as well and he began to drive around the old downtown, swanked-
up but nicely as far as those things went. He circled around and around,
extending his range and going up and down hill streets before returning to the central plateau of downtown. Guessing there was a fair
chance he'd passed up or down the fatal Volkswagen hill. He was
looking for her hotel and when he finally saw it realized he'd passed it
once already but drove by again. He'd expected a cheap rooming house
sort of deal and only at the last second registered the name on the
maroon canopy awning out above the sidewalk, the brass and plate
revolving doors, the two cabs and a town car pulled along the curb
and the liveried doorman. And drove by the hotel parking garage next
to it, and went on to circle the block again and look for a place to
park—he wasn't about to pay five bucks an hour just to park Walter's
jeep.

Now that he knew where it was he parked a few blocks away. So
he would have time to stretch and get used to the flow of people on
the sidewalks. And when he walked into the lobby of the Eastman
Park Hotel he'd simply be arriving at a destination. His jeans and
T-shirt were clean enough and he left his sunglasses on—wanting the
crucial sense of distance they provided. He walked along, taking in
the shop windows but moving with a slowed deliberation, smacked a
bit by the realization that the whole drive over he'd simply been coming to rescue Jessica because she'd asked but was now a little nervous
about seeing her. And wondering what she'd been up to and how long
she'd been staying at a fancy hotel and then stopped dead center in
the sidewalk. He thought It's not my business where she stays or what
she does. And then just wanted to see her.

He walked on, easier now. He came to the intersection where
the side street led down to the Eastman Park Hotel. He crossed over

and stopped again, now a little jittery. The hotel was downhill to the north and between it and the intersection where he stood was a small park. What he guessed was a park. The size of a city lot and all concrete except for a few young trees with tapered drooping leaves he couldn't identify, the slender trunks rising from a circle of chipped mulch. He didn't give the trees much hope. There was a bus stop of fogged Plexiglas out on the sidewalk and the rest of the space was on several levels, almost as if making a small amphitheater. People sat or stretched in the sun, reading newspapers or eating, small groups chatting. The far end of the park was the old brick side of the hotel, rising six or seven stories, fading paint with the name as a block-letter banner across the upper side between ranks of windows. He looked back at the park, mostly kids, some women in a cluster, a few men in ties with their sleeves rolled up. A woman sitting with her knees together, head down, reading.

He looked again. Red tennis shoes, black jeans, white T-shirt, black choppy hair. As he watched she lifted her head and looked about. Not toward him and not as if she were expecting or inviting anyone but a measured reconnaissance for close or approaching danger. Then turned back to her book. And that instant stunned him. The recognition was immediate and absolute: it was Jessica but not Jessica—a stranger no stranger at all but someone who knew him in ways no one else ever could or would, someone who'd allowed him in, who'd cracked the door and sat back watching and waiting and now was entering fully into him as his ribcage split and spread and broke apart and his body flushed hot then cold and hot again and he wondered if he was having a heart attack. He rocked gently in his boots. Here she was. She reached up to push that lock of hair from her eyes and turned a page. Her head bent down, he saw the oval of skin at the top of her back, her neck rising out of it, the tendons taut. And he'd thought her fragile. And then knew she was fragile but only truly to him, a delicate precious vessel of life that perhaps he might lift and encircle and in doing so crack open his own fragile vessel. All this and he thought

How could I have missed that, and at once wondered if he had. And now was fully Hewitt standing at the edge of a concrete gully with no choice but to walk the new old Hewitt over and see what happened.

He came up enough from the side so she didn't see him until his shadow fell over her and as she looked up he said, "Whatcha reading?"

She blinked without smiling and closed the book so he could see the cover and it was the same book she'd left for him and for a moment he wondered if this was witchcraft or something greater and she grinned then and said, "Hey Hewitt," and stood. She was a level up from him so they were face to face.

His mouth stretched around an irrepressible rubbery smile as he said, "Hey, yourself, you."

She held up the book and said, "I got to missing it so I got myself a new copy. Damn, it's good to see you."

"It's a great book," he said and then reached for her and she came into his hug. Then she felt his hands moving deeply into the muscles of her back and his lips working her name into the skin of her neck and she pulled her head back and looked at him and he met those eyes with everything he had and said her name as benediction, plaint and prayer and she came back fully into him and now her hands worked his back and shoulders and her lips and teeth making their own chassé over his neck and face, and as if ten thousand years had led them their mouths came together and his hands dropped to the small of her back and hers came up tugging hard his hair, their tongues and mouths some fruit never tasted waiting hanging for them.

Somebody whistled and he heard but didn't care but slowly as if taking flesh away with her she extracted just enough to look at him again.

"Be damn," she said, face flushed. Near invisible freckles over her nose. Somehow, he'd missed those.

"Jessica." His voice not quite right.

"Right here." Her shaky smile.

"The question, the question . . ."

She cocked her head, a teased nervous smile.

"The question is do you want to spend the night in Portland?"

Her smile was gone but she was glowing and he realized her hands hadn't stopped working on him. "No, baby," she said.

"What do you want? Can you tell me what you want?"

"I want to go home."

IT WAS LATE afternoon before they got out of town. After retrieving her duffel from behind the desk of the hotel they got directions and drove far up along the waterfront and found the yard where the Bug had been towed. Loaning the jeep, Walter suggested Hewitt check the VW carefully but with the engine pushed through into the backseat, the rear axle and transmission ripped free, there was no mistaking it was beyond resurrection. Jessica got her paperwork from the glovebox and then together they worked to liberate what was left of her stuff, clothing mostly, some books, a little box retrieved after great effort from the battery compartment beneath the rear floorboards—dope too good to be left behind. They found a clam shack and ate lobster rolls and she told him other than the oversized bath, the room service lobster had been the best thing about the hotel, also admitting if she hadn't consumed platters of crayfish in her childhood she not only would've been stymied by the lobster but wouldn't have known how to suck and squeeze to find the sweet morsels in the legs and along the belly. As they went along with all this one or the other would reach and they'd sweetly ferociously entangle again.

Then driving in the jeep with the windows down they were mostly quiet, certainly comfortable. She had her shoes off and her feet up on the dash and one hand rested atop his on the steering wheel. What shyness there was rested in words and just then they didn't need words.

At one point he said, "I guess we might need to think about getting a new car."

"And give up your tractor?"

"Well, I'm sorta serious. I should go legit, I'm thinking. Seems about time."

"Or bikes. We could get bikes. They'd work."

"They don't do so hot in winter. What about a truck? A small one. Not one of those tricked-up monsters. It'd come in handy now and then for my work."

After a bit, as if she'd been testing it out in her mind before speaking she offered, "Maybe I could drive it if I went back to working for Roger."

"A course you could."

"I'd be one of the regular guys then."

He glanced over and grinned and she grinned back.

AFTER NORTH CONWAY they were in the shadow of the mountains and the sun was losing on the far side and Jessica crawled into the backseat and spent a few minutes punching down a nest that she curled into and went to sleep. Leaving Hewitt with his thoughts, driving now with the headlights on, few other cars on the road. The windows still down for the bracing air although he turned the heater on so some warmth would find her. When she'd announced her intention to sleep he'd known he now had no choice but to attempt some reconciliation of the day against the weight of the summer passed as well as his adult life. It was inevitable and better now than later, was what he thought. But it didn't happen. He came up out of Crawford Notch and the western sky was glowing green and the land was darkly green and he felt washed in some peculiar matchless grace, where for the first time in years, outside of the forge, likely since childhood, he was simply and exactly where he was, doing what he was doing. An ordinary pleasure. Perhaps. Driving home with a woman he loved sleeping behind him.

She was still asleep when he pulled into the farm in the dark. The kitchen light was on, left from this morning. Several lifetimes ago. He slid the driver seat forward and bent and lifted her and she

didn't fully wake but wrapped her arms around his neck and he carried her easily up into the house, only a small strategic silent battle
with the screen door. She was a wonder in his arms, neither light
nor weight but a solid form he felt he could carry endlessly over the
face of the earth.

She came awake when he snapped on the overhead light in his
bedroom.

NOW AND THEN life cracks open like a giant stone to reveal
the delicate wisps and webbings that patch together time, sweet fi-
brous tendrils of the heart's songs and time itself bends and warps to
become unrecognizable as even time but is rendered in snatches and
fragments that aren't to be resolved by clocks or wheels or phases of
the moon. Where meadows meet hedgerows and meld into woods
and the ancient earth is laughing and heaving in consort once again.
This a door not out of the world but deep into it, where humanity
and life itself gain or regain the unknowable spectrum within a newborn's cry or a dying breath.

BUT FIRST.

THEY STRUCK A wobbling cumbersome dance about the room
kissing, hands run wild until she knelt and like a child with presents
stripped the laces though the eyelets of his boots and then she was on
the bed, on her back, her T-shirt gone, her hips up as she tried to
push her jeans down and he gripped the bottom cuffs and shucked
them off her legs and she lay all the way back and stretched her arms
above her head—never seen, never naked before him dressed or
undressed—her ribcage lifted and her breasts arching dark exploded
nipples and the muscles of her arms and legs running quivering hard
upon the bed and then he was naked and she reached for him as he
tore the purple underwear from her and she gasped a wet round sound
and then he was down above her as she lifted her knees to cradle him

and he pressed gently and paused as eyes both locked and held and agreed and then she was flooding him and he was all the way inside her, all of him within her as they rocked and she was kicking his butt and thighs with her heels as he wrapped his arms around her head and arched up, her hands wild across his back, her nails carving unknown glyphs, markings, brands, into him and then her legs fell out and she began to gasp something close to his name as her hands slid down and pulled him deeper into her, and he went heavily against her chest, forcing the air out of both of them as his hands slid down to the round spread of her, the taut heaving curves of her hips opening to the slick, the primordial swamp locked and held forever throughout all beginnings until this moment and then he felt her clench and his semen streaked out of him, and light spangled behind his eyes as he lifted his weight, her breath a breathless suck back into her, and then sinking again upon her.

ROLLED OFF, SIDE by side, adjoining legs twined, her face wet against his neck and cheek as she wept.

SITTING CROSS-LEGGED face to face, touching, leaning mouths, minds soft and wondrous—stilled.

LYING WITH HIS head on her inner thigh, looking up at her face above looking down talking then words small forgotten of great consequence. Only needing to turn his head to run his tongue through the damp curls and then open her only reaching up to grasp her hands when she tried to move and this way slowly without wanting to end, the taste of no other woman, her breath gaining and then hitching as she locked her thighs.

DOWNSTAIRS STILL DARK he made an omelet and carried it back up with a fork and a bottle of Vouvray and one glass.

★   ★   ★

THEY SLEPT AND loved again. A long bath and there was sunlight speckling the large tub never meant for two and they slept again. Flies in the warmth slow drowsy waking and lying under only a cooling breeze from the open window. Because she asked he pulled on jeans and walked out blinking into a day to the jeep. He brought her bags of clothes in and she pulled on a thin sleeveless top with narrow straps over her shoulders and new underwear and together they went down to forage the fridge and then Hewitt went back up while she put music on.

ALONE IN THE room, his room, their room, the sounds of "Whipping Post" a shock and then absolutely right and he stood waiting her, his pants off again when he saw the frame upright on the table and he took it and as easily as shelving a book tossed it out the window.

AGAIN IN DARK but with a candle brought up from below, sitting through a long steady shower, an old thin quilt around them sharing wine again, cheddar and a tin of smoked baby oysters and the rain stopped, and he wondered aloud if they were the only ones awake to hear the rain from start to end and she replied No there must've been other creatures in the woods and fields having a wet night, stroking him as she spoke and then again love.

THEY SAT IN bed reading poems aloud. By daylight, by candlelight. *The Great Fires* was the only book in the room and the only one they wanted or needed. She wept when the dead wife was reincarnated as a dog and both man and dog recognized each other and the man knelt and told the dog stories of old friends.

THEY LAY IN a cold morning fog under heavy covers and talked of strange dreams and the shortness of life and she put her hands around his neck and told him she could kill him and he told her he knew that.

He told her of the two hitching posts and everything they meant to him, of everything they held silent forever within them. After a bit she asked if they should talk about birth control and he said he didn't think so. She looked him in the eye, nodded and curled back into him.

He slowly tickled her awake once in daylight and they wrestled off the bed on to the floor and loved there. Moving across the floor until they were headfirst in the closet, her head knocking lightly against the plaster. She woke him in darkness with her mouth around him and when he woke again later he asked her if it had been a dream and she told him it better not have been. They sat in the kitchen naked and ate the last of the eggs and she looked thoughtful a long moment and he knew what she was thinking and so picked her up and carried her back upstairs. Not ready to stop this yet, thinking he would starve for love. A package of venison stew meat was thawing in the pantry.

They took another long bath and went back to sleep. Hewitt thinking they were both catching up on all the sleep lost as well as everything else in life thus far. Later he slipped out of bed to the kitchen where he worked up the stew for a long simmer and baked drop biscuits, then carried up the basket of biscuits and butter and black currant preserve with a bottle of wine.

They were set for days.

He was drowsing in after-love stupor, hot with the afternoon when suddenly he sat up. She was standing by the bed in her underwear and the top with thin straps. She leaned to his raised head and kissed him, her breasts against his shoulder. Then she stepped back.

"What?" he asked.

"I think you better get up."

He was wet with sleep-sweat and slowed. He pushed up and looked at her. All but her eyes were calm.

"What is it?" he asked, rolling to sit up, his feet on the floor as he reached for his crumpled jeans. When she didn't respond he stood, hauling the jeans up. He ran a hand over his face. Her eyes direct and defiant, waiting.

"There's a woman on the porch. I think you better go talk to her."

She was precluding further discussion or information but he didn't need either one. He walked over and kissed her.

"I'll be right back," he said and went just as he was down the stairs and through the house.

She wasn't on the porch anymore but out in the sun, leaning against her car. He opened the screen door and went out, stopping on the top step. Emily saw him and raised a hand in small greeting.

A scattering of blown early leaves rattled across the porch behind him. He ran a hand through his hair, took a deep breath and let it out.

Then went down toward her.